Eyes

IMANIA MARGRIA

A Rose Book

Lilyan Margaret Publishing

Covers designed by Carl from Extended Imagery
Interior Design by Imania Margria

Imania Margria
Visit my website at www.imaniamargria.com

First Printed in the United States of America

First Completion: February 2014
Final Revision: January 2023
First Printing: February 14, 2023

A Rose Book
Lilyan Margaret Publishing
www.lilyanmargaret.com

ISBN-13: 978-1-7352755-0-5

Dedicated to: Those with persistent hearts. Never give up on your dreams they will come true, eventually. Also, I want to thank all my friends from 2009- now, my karateka, Hanshi Hermann, and my family. Without these people in my life, I would not have had the strength or inspiration to write this book. Thank you all. I love you so much.

Dear Reader,

Thank you for choosing to read Eyes. This book was the first novel I ever completed but took forever to finally publish. Just like every book I write, it has a special place in my heart. Just like a flower in a garden, each bloom may look similar; but if you take a closer look, you will notice their differences and the small intricate details that make them unique.

I have mentioned before that the inspiration for this story came from my love for the legendary books by Mario Puzo, the Godfather series. I was first introduced to his books through the movies. But because of the graphic content, I could not watch it until I was much older. When I was a junior in high school, I became obsessed with the Godfather game: Don edition, and that is how the concept for this book developed. My main character for the game is the primary love interest in this book, Darian Mancini.

I hope you enjoy this tale. It is not a mushy, clean romance. It is a dark, romantic suspense. So, if that is not your cup of tea, then I thank you for purchasing my book anyway and hope you will read it with an open and unbiased mind.

I hope you continue to read my books and enjoy their individual charms. I spend many long, caffeine-filled days and nights creating unique worlds and characters, driven by different passions, to share with you in the hopes you will enjoy and cherish these tales as much as I do. My goal for 2023 and on is to create wonderful stories and content for you, my reader, to enjoy. Thank you very much for your support. I hope you enjoy Amadora's journey and continue to follow her through many more to come. Blessed Be.

Sincerely,
Imania Margria

CONTENTS

Part 1: Transformation & Infiltration   1

1: The Morelli Family   2
2: The Plan Begins   36
3: The Switch   58
4: Johnnie Barbone   73
5: The Tearing of Hearts   89

Part 2: Escalation & Revealation   100

6: The Worst Enemy – Fear   101
7: The Truth Revealed   114
8: The Annual Autumn Ball   130
9: The Aftermath   158
10: The True Enemy   179

Part 3: Reflection & Obsession   194

11: Memories of a Lost Love   195
12: A Promise of Forever   218
13: Love of a Fallen Angel   235
14: A Sister's Scorn   252
15: Lana's Desire   265

Part 4: Confrontation & Realization   273

16: Torn Between Love and Lies   274
17: The Rules of the Game Change   285
18: Beware the Viper's Lair   295
19: The Rose's Thorns   305
20: The Rosilli's Heir   317
21: The Tears of True Love   326
22: The Ultimate Goal   329
23: The Heart's True Desire   340
Author's Thoughts   348
About the Author   351

This world is not for the weak. If you're not strong enough to endure the darkness and blood that awaits, you will crumble bit by bit. You must decide if this world is worth sacrificing everything for.

—LANA ROSILLI

Transformation & Infiltration

The Morelli Family

*'If my family won't accept me, then I will prove to them the extent
of my potential and the folly of their underestimations,' Thoughts of
Amadora Morelli.*

The sun illuminated the Morelli complex's burgundy stone walls as a
black vehicle drove up the gray cobblestone driveway and parked in
front of the main manor. Men dressed in dark suits stood on the lush
lawns surrounding the manor. They stopped what they were doing to focus their attention on the driver of the vehicle while he opened the car door.

A tall man emerged from the car, adorned in a navy vest and matching suit pants,
stepping onto the cobblestone. He closed the door and walked around the car to the
lawn on the opposite side. Once both his feet stepped upon the freshly trimmed grass,
he adjusted his hat over his eyes shielding them from the piercing pursuit of the summer sun while he scanned the house in which he grew up, reminiscing of the many
years that had passed since he last called it residence. Seeing his childhood home
again filled him with joy. His small, heart-shaped lips parted, revealing his perfect
white teeth as they created an endearing expression. His hazel eyes sparkled as they
followed in suit with his charming smile.

At the immediate sight of him, the men, in front of the manor, gathered around
him with welcoming expressions; they greeted him, hugging, and kissing his cheek
with respect while speaking in their native tongue. His smile broke into hearty laughter as he responded and greeted his brethren before returning to his vehicle.

He walked to the rear door closest to the curb and opened it, scooping up the little girl seated there. She reached her chubby little arms towards him once the door
opened. He embraced the small child warmly, placing her on his hip, as he turned
towards the path leading to the manor. He paid little attention to the goings-on as he
traversed down the white stone path leading to the manor while affectionately cuddling and caressing the girl while carrying her to the mansion door. He shifted his at-

tention only once to see the source of his daughter's gaze; she watched in amazement as the servants ran past them toward the car, retrieving their luggage.

The moment they reached the door, an aged man greeted them. His tall, slender form towered over him and his daughter; With the many lines and crevices embedded into his face, his appearance looked worn and grim; his thin, pale lips curved when he caught sight of the man approaching the door.

A month passed since the man last returned to this place; but the butler, Barry, seemed to have aged in that time. The butler's hair, which was once a rich, chestnut hue, had several silver strands decorating it. The way he slicked back his silver-washed locks thinned out his face even more and added to his sullen disposition. His emerald eyes, which once sparkled like the jewel itself, were now dull and tired. He seemed like a shell of his former self as age and time slowly transformed him.

"You've finally come. We have been anxious about your arrival," Barry greeted. The depth of his plain monotone voice contradicted the smile he wore. Barry waved for them to follow him while ushering them into the foyer at the base of the grand stairway. "I'll fetch your mother and sisters. Wait here, Sir."

Word spread rapidly of his arrival; because as soon as Barry left, he heard quickening footsteps coming from the second floor. Within moments, a beautiful young woman wearing an ivory and pink rose-imprinted dress dashed down the second-floor halls and down the marble stairs towards where he stood. Her long dark-brown hair floated in bouncy curls, framing her soft bronze face; entangled in their delicate tendrils was a small white flower. Her dark eyes sparkled with joy when she recognized the man standing in the foyer cuddling a young girl.

While he placed his daughter gently upon the tiled floor, he saw from the corner of his eye a young woman approaching with great speed. A pleased smile crossed his face while he stretched his arms out to embrace her.

"Gunny! Gunny!" Joyful exuberance radiated from her young face as she thrusted herself into his arms. She kissed him gently on the lips, squeezing her arms tight around his neck. He swung her around, letting out a robust laugh while he did.

"Dora, what a pleasant surprise? You're lively as ever."

Gugliehno glanced towards the archway leading into the living room where his mother stood observing quietly with content and smiling lovingly. Returning his gaze back to Amadora, his little sister, who was still firm in his embrace, propped on his hip as if she were a child, he observed her closer; he noticed her sun-flushed face and her beautiful dress, which was lightly dusted with dirt, and the white flower in her hair; and instantly he understood the reason for her current state, causing his smile to grow in amusement.

"It looks like you were in mama's garden again."

"Yes, of course. It's my favorite place on the entire property," Amadora smiled, brushing her hand against the white rose nestled in her hair. "I love tending to the roses, especially the white ones. They are my favorites."

"You haven't changed at all," Gunny's infectious smile grew as he kissed his sister lovingly on the forehead. Innocence emanated from her as she gloated about her love for the enormous garden encasing the entire mall. Her eyes sparkled when she told him about the new bulbs she planted and hoped would bloom in the coming spring. Hearing his little sister's stories and watching her recant them with such pride and excitement, made Gugliehno even more glad to be back in his childhood home.

"So, have you only been gardening this month, Dora? Is that how you spent the end of your summer? What about school?" Gunny asked playfully, hugging his sister.

"I asked Papa if I could take the year off. He said it was fine if I returned next fall. But I haven't spent all my time solely in the garden. I went with mama and papa to Italy."

"Italy? I didn't know you were going there," Gunny looked surprised by the news his sister revealed to him.

"Papa decided it was a good idea. He and Casimiro had some business up north to handle; so, mama and I went to Sicily to visit Zia Marta and our cousins until they met us there," Amadora explained, smiling warmly.

"It was a lot of fun, Gunny. Cugino Mau and his wife just had their baby; and we got to see him for the first time. Then, they showed us around their new estate. They asked about everyone. We should visit them together next time."

"Yeah... maybe next time, Dora," Gugliehno's smiled faded slightly as his mind processed the information he just learned from his sister. He petted her head and turned around to where his wife, Susan, stood surrounded by her their two oldest children. She was slowly rocking their youngest daughter, who wriggled in her arms and becoming irritable from the long trip. His mother helped her daughter-in-law by attending to the two older girls tugging on their mother's dress.

"Gunny, now that you're here. Let's have lunch together," Amadora cooed in excitement.

Gugliehno faced his sister, who was looking at him with eyes large with expectation. He met her warm smile with one of his own, cupped her face in his hands, and lovingly cleaned the bits of dirt from her face with his thumbs.

"Me and my girls need to settle in, and pops is going to want me to see him soon," He saw the joy fade from his sister's face in response to his words. "Don't worry. I'll be here all weekend. We can get together tomorrow or Sunday if there's time. Then I can tell you everything I did this month."

Amadora's enchanting smile returned to light her delicate face. He released his hold of her and flashed her a reassuring smile.

"Gugliehno is right, Amadora. You know how busy your siblings are when they return home every month. Leave him be for today and help me bring them to their rooms," Fiorella Morelli, Amadora's mother, instructed. She reached to her side and grasped the hand of Gunny's middle child, Little Aniela, and guided her to the stairs. "Since Polo volunteered to sleep in the house on the northwest side of the mall, we will put you in two of the bedrooms down the hall from our room. We would move you into one of the other houses on the complex, but your father refuses to have his grandchildren so far from him."

Gugliehno followed behind her and started up the large chestnut stairway for the second floor. Susan fixed the cranky babe on her hip while grabbing her purse she set to the side. She tried to soothe the baby, Roselia, by whispering soft reassuring words into her ear as she followed behind Gunny and her mother. Amadora was going to follow them when she felt something grab her hand. She looked down to her side and saw the eldest of Gugliehno's children, Loretta, cuddling up to her.

Loretta resembled her mother almost precisely. From her long, blondish brown hair, which was tied into two curly ponytails with lavender ribbons, to the gigantic pair of jade eyes embedded in her chubby heart-shaped face, she was a tiny version of her mother. The child dressed in a similar, elegant fashion like her mother. She wore a long lavender dress with a large silk ribbon tied back into a bow around her tiny waist and a pair of ivory shoes.

When their eyes met, the little girl beamed at her aunt. Amadora picked up the child and rest her on her hip. Loretta wrapped her little chubby arms around Amadora's neck in an affectionate embrace. She kissed the little girl's cheek, embracing her before following the child's mother, father, and grandmother up the grand stairway.

They turned down the west corridor of the manor and walked down its long narrow spans until they reached two doors at the end of the hall. By the time Amadora reached the room, Gugliehno was already unpacking their things, Susan tended to their baby, Roselia, while Gunny's middle daughter, Aniela, bounced on the couch beside her mother babbling on about what she wanted to do while they're here. Amadora set her niece down, so she could play with her sister; then she returned to her mother's side by the door.

Fiorella Morelli, the matriarch of the Morelli Family, laughed as she watched her granddaughters skip around the room; Amadora noticed the warmth in her mother's eyes. Her mood differed from how it normally was during the month. Her mother was always warm and kind, but her disposition was more routine than genuine. Even though she tried to hide her genuine feelings behind her smile, Amadora knew the absence of her children caused her mother's influx of emotions. Since most of her children were grown adults, they had their own lives to focus on, such as their businesses, family, or school. Most of her children moved to different parts of the country with their own families to run different parts of the family business. Fiorella understood why her children had to live far away from her; but she missed the days her home was packed with her kids. That's why her father arranged for everyone to come together at the end of the month.

He wanted to rid the loneliness his wife felt from the distance between their family. Soon after her youngest son moved away, this tradition began; and for almost two years, this small reunion became a necessity. No matter what their children were doing, they dropped everything to meet at the end of each month.

"Gunny, hurry. You don't want to keep your father waiting," His mother informed. "You know how unpleasant he becomes if he's the last to know of your arrival, so please don't forget about him. Make it your top priority to see him as soon as you're done. Understand?"

"Okay. Tell Pops I'll be there in a minute," Gunny answered, smiling, and placing a few articles of clothing in the drawer next to the bed.

Fiorella stepped back into the hall with Amadora and motioned her to follow. They walked back down the hall towards the opposite wing to her father's study. The sweet smell of her father's cigars filled the air of the east wing as they drew near. Amadora smelled the tangy citrus scent of the lemons her father favored and kept on his desk. Besides his cigars and scotch, lemons were one of her father's necessities. He loved to peel and devour the sour fruits slice by slice as easily as if eating oranges. Her mother always joked about her father's strange habit: "He needs to eat the lemons so their bitter taste can counteract his sour moods. Without them, he would stay grumpy all the time."

Regardless of his reasons, Amadora appreciated their fragrance. Their scent was fresh and invigorating. Keeping fruit with such a potent scent was a brilliant habit, especially somewhere where he did most of his work. After many long nights working late in his office, their scent did what coffee could not. The energetic high from coffee wore off after a few hours, but the fresh tangy scent of the lemons lasted longer, keeping one roused and focused.

Their smell was as pungent as those of the cigars. The two scents battled between one another as they neared the cedar door of her father's office. Her mother quietly turned the knob and opened the door, entering with Amadora close behind her.

Inside the study, Amadora immediately saw Bruno, her father's dog, laying in front of the fireplace on top of an antique cerulean rug. It was his favorite spot in the entire room because he could monitor his master and anyone coming into the study. Bruno popped up his head when they entered the room. As Amadora passed by Bruno, he nudged her leg with his colossal head urging her to show him affection. Amadora bent over and rubbed his head. She grabbed him by his thick furry neck and embraced the large dog lovingly.

"Hi, boy. How are you today?" Amadora whispered softly while rubbing his belly.

The large black and white husky wagged his tail happily at her soft touch. Bruno, one of her father's most treasured creatures, went everywhere with her father. Bruno was a very important part of her father's life as her father's personal bodyguard. Bruno saved her father's life a few years ago. The scar embroidered on his right leg was a reminder of his courageous act.

Bruno took a bullet for her father after a business deal went south. Ten years ago, her father tried to expand his businesses in Atlantic City. But several of the properties were owned by some rival families and real estate moguls. At the time, the rival families tried to muscle in on the few businesses her father owned in the area to try to run him out of town. But her father didn't cave. He made deals with some business executives to buy their properties or become partners in the businesses he opened.

One businessman her father relied on was a real estate tycoon, Elijah Kroger. Kroger was known for his hostile takeovers of several high-profile businesses across Manhattan. Ever since he started his conquest in Atlantic City, he found it difficult to get patrons for his properties as long as the rival families were intimidating their patrons and workers by sending men to rob and physically persuade them to hand over their businesses.

As their intimidation tactics grew, Kroger realized he needed some muscle of his own to counteract the damage they did. Since most of the cops and local government officials were already in her father's pockets, Kroger reached out to him. Kroger saw an answer to his troubles and eagerly agreed to a partnership with him. They agreed the Morellis would become partners in his waterfront properties if they provided security from the rival gangs and government officials.

The deal was finalized, and her father gained half of Kroger's waterfront properties. The businesses flourished for some time after they formed the new alliance. However, their newfound success and the Morellis' growing control of the city became a threat to the rival gangs. They plotted for a way to drive the Morellis out and back upstate. Their plan was to take out Don Morelli.

Five years after the partnership began, Kroger acted strange and demanded changes to their agreement. Her father granted him a meeting at his office in their South Jersey home. There they sat with Gunny, Casimiro and Elda present going over Kroger's new demands.

What happened next shocked everyone in the room, Amadora was not sure if the precious pooch sensed something bad would happen. But when Kroger stood to leave, he tried to secretly withdraw a pistol from his coat pocket, while pretending to put it on, and shoot her father. Before he could aim the weapon, Bruno lunged at Kroger. Kroger struggled to free himself from the dog's fierce grasp, but Bruno sunk his teeth deep into his leg.

During their vicious scuffle, his gun went off and shot Bruno in the leg, releasing

Kroger from the dog's grasp; but he did not enjoy his freedom for long, because her siblings, father and their men surrounded him with guns trained on him, ready to open fire. Kroger dropped his gun and was led away to be dealt with for his betrayal.

Once the issue was resolved, Bruno was immediately attended to. They removed the bullet and stitched his wound without a problem. Within no time, his wound healed, and Bruno returned to his playful self.

Ever since that incident, Amadora's father went nowhere without his faithful companion. Wherever he went, there was a place for Bruno at his side.

The sound of Amadora cooing over Bruno alerted her father, who was reviewing some paperwork.

"My precious Dorina, what a wonderful blessing to see your smile this morning," He set his papers on his desk, rose from his dark, leather armchair, walked over to Amadora's side and kissed her firm on the lips. "My gorgeous Fiorella, what brings the two of you to my study this morning?"

Amadora jumped to her feet glowing with excitement and blurted out, "Papa, Gunny is here!"

Her father shot a glance from his wife to his bubbling daughter and smiled. "Is that so? Send him in. There's a lot we must discuss," He kissed Amadora's cheek as he addressed her. "When Elda and Zanipolo arrive, you'll tell me. Won't you?"

She nodded. "Yes, Papa. I will. What about Giacinta? What about when she arrives? Do you want me to tell you?"

"Yes, of course. You have such a good heart," Her father replied as his smile faded. His deep voice, which was clear and audible, trailed off as he continued. "I wouldn't have remembered her, since she barely comes to see me when she's here."

With a motion of his hand, he dismissed Amadora. Amadora kissed her parents and left. At least, that was what they believed. Unknown to her parents, Amadora snuck into the giant library next to her father's study.

Bookshelves covered in dust and cobwebs surrounded Amadora, making it difficult to breathe; but she was used to the dense air. The library was left neglected because her father put a huge lock on the door, keeping everyone out even the servants. Only Amadora and her father had a key to unlock it. Amadora "borrowed" her copy from her father's office and never returned it.

Her father sealed off the library after Amadora graduated high school under the pretense that no one used it anymore, but Amadora knew the real reason behind her father's actions. His true reason for concealing it hid in its depths.

After retrieving a copy of the key, Amadora snuck into the library often to listen to her father's business meetings with her siblings. Her intrigue for her family's business drove her to do these covert expeditions. Even though her brothers, Gugliehno

8

and Zanipolo, told her bits and pieces about their work during the month. They left out the specifics because they knew about Amadora's desire to join the business and her father's unwavering position to keep her far from it.

Amadora knew some details about how her father started his lucrative business from what she learned from her brothers or what her father told them.

Her father owned various businesses in the tristate area and in California. Most of his businesses were one hundred percent legitimate except for a small portion of his clubs and shops that double as fronts. He also made money by offering protection to small business owners who were in his or her siblings' territories. Because of her family's vast connections with government officials and police officers, all their extracurricular activities that tread the less than legal line were ignored or covered up.

Amadora learned more about different aspects of her family's business empire from utilizing the secret of the library than from any other source. She walked past the rows of bookcases into a deep crevice of the library along the farthest wall. When she reached the area, a small wooden bookshelf full of trivial novels stood against the wall. She pushed it aside, revealing a small ornate iron vent. She replaced the cover and climbed inside. She crawled deep into the broken vent until she came upon another grate.

Amadora sat in front of it, remaining as quiet as she could; and within moments, she heard everything that was said in her father's office.

"I don't understand, Fiorella. I can't tell if Amadora has the heart of a saint or doesn't realize how much her sister despises her?" Basilio turned to his wife, placed his finger under her chin and kissed her lips to calm the rising anger he suspected grew inside her because of his words. Fiorella disliked when her husband complained about their children, especially Giacinta, because she felt he criticized her more than the others. Basilio understood his wife's concerns, but that didn't stop him from getting his point across. "I don't understand how anyone can hate a girl like our Amadora. She's a wonderful girl with a big heart. She'll make any man lucky to have her as his bride one day. When it comes to Giacinta, I have my doubts."

"Leo, stop. You're too hard on Giacinta. She might be more difficult to handle than Amadora or Elda, but she will change. You must give her a chance. Please," Fiorella pleaded when she realized her husband lost all hope for his middle daughter.

"Give her a chance! She's already twenty-one, has dropped out of college and spent tons of my money to lead a lude life of partying and God knows what else with no thoughts of her future. She gave up any chance of a decent union because her perverse actions harmed her reputation."

Basilio turned from his wife, took a cigar out of the golden box on his desk and popped it into his mouth. He cut the tip, lit it, and then took several long pulls before finishing. "Face it, Fiora. Giacinta is a lost cause and will never change. It's better for us to cut her off before we spend the rest of our lives bailing her out of her gambling and drinking habits. If we don't, she'd probably end up prostituting herself out for drugs. I'd rather wipe my hands of it before I see the downfall of one of my kids."

"You're cold-hearted, Leo. You need to get rid of your stubborn pride and believe in all your children. It wasn't long ago when Polo had similar problems. Now, look at him. He's doing well for you in California. If Polo could change, then so can Giacinta. You must have faith."

With those words, Fiorella headed towards the door. She paused when she reached it and gathered herself, mustering enough strength to hide her disappointment and annoyance through a respectful tone as she spoke once more to her husband. "I'm going to make lunch. It should be ready in an hour. I'll have it brought to you."

With the tension still heavy in the room, Basilio did not respond. He only returned to his desk and puffed on his cigar. From the silence that followed, Amadora knew her father was probably thinking about what her mother said. Her father, who rarely lost his temper, never hid what he thought from her mother. She was the only one who could get underneath his skin and push his buttons without him feeling any ill way towards her. Fiorella Morelli was the only one he allowed to witness his true feelings.

Silence washed over the room after her mother left. Amadora, who still lurked quietly in the broken vent, turned to crawl back out; but as she moved, she heard the door to the study open and someone enter the room. Amadora turned back to the iron vent and pressed her face against it, hoping for a glimpse of who it was. Amadora couldn't see the person's features, but she recognized the gold ring on their left pinky with a cyclamen flower engraving. There was only one person she knew who wore that ring, Gugliehno.

"Pops, you wanted to see me?" Gunny asked, strolling over to his father's desk.

"Gunny, come and sit down. I'm glad you're here," Basilio welcomed his eldest son and motioned for him to sit in the chair across from him. "How was your trip?"

"It was fine. Susan and the girls fell asleep during most of the ride, so it was quiet," Gugliehno responded, leaning back in his chair.

"How are my grandchildren?" The don smiled softly.

"They're as lively and independent as ever. They're the smartest kids I've ever seen. Loretta started school and can read and write better than kids five years older than her. She's also taking piano lessons now."

"Piano? She is truly a Morelli woman, intelligent and talented," Basilio smiled with pride. He continued to puff on his cigar while he ruffled through a folder on his desk and pulled out a small stack of papers.

"Yes, she is. She's just like her mother," The mood shifted in Gugliehno as his voice turned cold. His mind was less focused on the current subject, but on something else.

10

"You seem off, my son. What's bothering you?" Basilio asked, noticing Gugliehno's odd behavior.

Gugliehno shook his head and snapped out of his awkward mood and forced carefree expression.

"Nothing, pops. I heard from Amadora that you all went to Italy. You never informed me you were planning to go there for business. I know how much you dislike going there unless for urgent business or necessity. So, did anything happen that I should know about?"

"No. My sister had some trouble with her daughter-in-law's family. I just went to mediate with Casimiro. While I handled the situation, Amadora and your mother visited your uncle Marion and your cousins in Sicilia. I didn't want to bother them with this foolishness."

"I hope it wasn't anything serious. What happened?" Gunny watched his father as he leaned back and trained his eye on him.

"Just a minor dispute with some locals and her son, Nero. That boy has a temper that makes him do stupid things, and his actions cause lots of problems for my sister since her husband died. I don't know if she can handle him on her own," The don explained, remembering the difficult situation he had to deal with a few weeks prior.

"That must run in the family. Weren't we dealing with a similar situation with Polo not too long ago?" Gugliehno joked.

His words caused the don's thin lips to curl in amusement.

"I don't know about that. You were always very even-tempered even as a child. And Zanipolo wasn't that bad. He was a saint compared to Nero. Dealing with drinking and gambling is an effortless task; but dealing with someone who starts fights with just about anyone for any ridiculous reasons, that's a problem."

"What did you do to resolve the matter?" Gugliehno asked, curious about the fate of his short-tempered cousin.

"I talked to him," The don responded, taking the last few pulls on his cigar before putting it out in a crystal tray on his desk.

"Talked, huh?" Gugliehno scanned his father in disbelief.

Gugliehno spent years working by his father's side and observed his tactics when dealing with professional and personal matters. His father remained neutral when dealing with business matters; but when dealing with matters of respects and family, he could be as menacing as a shark. Disrespect from anyone regardless of relation could bring out the worst in his father.

"Yes. That's all he needed. He's not a bad kid, just misguided," the don continued.

"Are you planning to bring him here to work on his temper?"

"Yes. I am. I have Casimiro dealing with getting his papers together. I just don't know where I should put him. I can't keep him with me because I don't have the time or patience to babysit hotheads. And God forbid he disrespects your mother or anyone in my household. I won't be able to restrain my actions then. I can't send him to Los Angeles with Zanipolo because it would seem like I'm rewarding his bad behavior; also, Polo would pity him instead of guiding him. That would be counterproductive. I could send him to Atlantic City with Elda, but she would be too difficult on him. Additionally, I can't take the chance he might say or do the wrong thing to her, because we both know Elda wouldn't hesitate to fix the problem..." Basilio rubbed his brow and his mouth twitched in distaste at the mental thought entering his mind at that moment. "*Permanently...* I love my eldest daughter. She can be the sharpest and coolest head during most situations, but that's only because she internalizes her feelings. When she finally blows, her temper's worse than a category four hurricane."

"He can work under me. I can have Lorenzo find a place for him, and my men aren't known for giving new recruits an easy time no matter who they are," Gugliehno volunteered.

"That sounds good. I'm glad that petty matter is settled. We can talk more about arrangements when Casimiro comes back," the don took the papers he was reading prior to Amadora's and his wife's arrival earlier. The room fell silent as he searched through them and underlined certain sections. When he finished, he returned his attention to his son. His expression was serious, and the surrounding air shifted completely, making Gunny feel uncomfortable.

"Casimiro gave me your reports about our businesses in New York. Everything seems under control; but I see you're having trouble with collecting from the Mancinis. Tell me what's going on. We've never had trouble with Domenico before," Basilio replaced the papers on the desk and studied his son for answers.

"That's true. But it's not Domenico we have trouble with. It's his son, Darian."

"Why is his son creating problems?"

"Domenico is getting old, and his health isn't what it used to be. So, his son returned home and took over his father's store. He's a veteran with a strong distaste for people in our line of work. He refuses to continue giving into 'thugs who extort from the weak to exert a false sense of security and control.' His words exactly."

"Extortion, huh? I guess Darian doesn't know why Domenico was paying us to protect him and his store."

"No. I don't think so. But if he knows, then he doesn't care."

"Well, we can't lose Mancini. Try to convince his son once more. If he still refuses, then you'll need to persuade him in a less direct way. You must show him why he needs our protection."

"How should I do that?"

"Simple. Have someone outside the family rough him up. Make sure he can't connect them to us or that we had anything to do with it. Show him what kind of thugs will come after him without our protection."

Gugliehno nodded in comprehension of his father's orders. With the core of their business matters taken care of, the mood lightened along with Basilio's expression. He told Gugliehno more details about their trip.

Amadora could tell by the shift in their conversation that they would no longer discuss anything about business until Polo and Elda arrived. She quietly crawled out of the vent and sealed it tight. She replaced the small bookshelf and escaped the room. Amadora walked over to the golden engraved mirror by her father's study and took a gander at herself. She was entirely covered in dust and dirt from taking refuge inside the vent, so she ran to her room to clean up and change before any of her other siblings arrived.

Amadora ran to the west wing, following the winding hall and down the narrow stairwell to the southwest side of the manor where her room was located. As she dashed past the servants, she accidentally bumped into someone standing in the center of the corridor by her bedroom. The impact caused Amadora to fall backwards onto the cool wooden floor. Amadora apologized and looked to see who it was; the color drained from her face in fear when she saw the woman standing in front of her.

The woman wore a long, form-fitting turquoise dress. Her light brown hair was tucked beneath her large broad-brimmed turquoise hat; pearl lace gloves encased her small hands. At first glance, Amadora did not recognize who she was until the woman turned to look at her. When she recognized the woman, it was by her soft blue eyes, which glared at Amadora with a rapidly growing anger. It was her older sister, Giacinta.

Out of the women in their family, Giacinta was the most beautiful amongst them. Her skin was smooth, fair and flawless like a porcelain doll with only a touch of color accenting her cheeks. However, her elegant appearance masked her true nature. As Giacinta scowled at Amadora, she noticed her perfect mask crack as her actual feelings shone through.

"Watch out, idiot!" Giacinta growled, examining Amadora. She looked over at Amadora before scoffing in disgust. "Why are you so filthy! Did you roll around in mother's garden! What are you, a pig! I'm surprised anyone tolerates you! You act like a child! You'd better not have gotten your filth on me!"

Amadora lowered her head in shame as she responded softly, "I'm sorry, Giacinta. I didn't see you." It took all her strength to restrain her threatening tears and continue speaking. "You seem fine. I didn't get you dirty."

To reassure herself, Giacinta reviewed herself in the mirror and hurried into her room, slamming the door shut behind her. Amadora looked after her sister, her strength wavering by the exchange she had with Giacinta, forming tears she desperately wanted to hide. She did not understand why her sister treated her like this. She didn't want her father to be right, but he was. Her sister despised her, and her foolish heart was too hopeful to see it. Anyone else would've fought back if Giacinta treated them like that, but Amadora could not.

In her mind, she replayed the times when she and Giacinta were close as children. Her heart reflected on those memories, causing her to always rationalize the way her sister treated her. But could her heart use those precious memories to excuse her sister's horrid actions forever? Or would Amadora have to harden her heart so she could finally realize the truth about her sister?

Amadora escaped into the solitude of her room, allowing the captured tears to fall as she closed the door behind her. She leaned against the wooden frame, glancing up to the ceiling; her tears, she could only see the white blur of sunlight reflecting off the engraved ceiling; her soft sobs prevented her from questioning the heavens. She slid down the door, collapsing to the floor. Amadora gathered her knees into her arms, cradling them as she freed her captive tears. She never knew hatred before in her life, especially from someone who was family. Amadora did not know what she did to make Giacinta despise her so much; because once in a distant past, they were the best of friends.

Amadora wiped her face with the back of her hand as she tried to regain her composure. She used what little strength she had to force herself to her feet. She crossed her bedroom, heading towards the bathroom to do what she had planned to do initially. As she neared the bathroom door, a rustling sound came from her closet. Knowing that all the servants were busy with preparations for everyone's arrival, Amadora knew it was unlikely a maid would rummage in her closet, especially with the door shut behind them. She grabbed her desk lamp, taking caution not to make a noise; she stealthily tiptoed to the closet; and with one swift gesture, she pulled the door open and raised the lamp over her head to threaten the intruder. The sound of the door yanking open caused a girl to shriek in terror, which resounded through the entire room.

"No, Amadora! It's me!" The girl pleaded, huddling on the floor in terror.

Hearing the girl's cry, Amadora lowered her hand; her brow arched in question of her unexpected visitor. This visitor she knew well. It was her best friend, Samantha Johnson.

Amadora and Samantha have been friends since they were five years old. They did everything together, from going to the same schools or traveling. They spent most of their lives together and rarely stayed apart for too long. Samantha was the only genuine friend Amadora had. She was the only person who Amadora felt comfortable opening up to.

Their close relationship started reflecting on their physical appearance. They dressed in similar fashions, applied their makeup, and did their hair in similar ways. They were almost identical from afar. People frequently confused them to be twins and were shocked when they found out they weren't even related to one another.

However, their similarities only fooled strangers; while those who knew them well saw their differences easily. Samantha was smaller than Amadora in height. Her skin was also fairer than Amadora's and extremely sensitive to the sun during cloudless summer days. While Amadora easily received a deep bronze tan, Samantha turned red like a lobster when she stayed in the sun too long. Amadora was also more defined and voluptuous than her friend, which made Samantha somewhat jealous of her perfect figure compared to her skinny, flat-chested frame.

"Sammy, why the heck are you hiding in my closet?" Amadora scolded. "I wasn't expecting you today and thought you were a burglar or a perve. I could've killed you." She placed the lamp aside and helped her friend to her feet.

"I'm sorry. It was a spur-of-the-moment decision. Forgive me," Samantha smiled sheepishly as she fixed her dress once she regained her footing. "Barry said I could wait in your room until your return. You took so long I grew bored from waiting; so, to pass time, I decided to rummage through your clothes."

Samantha's explanation caused Amadora to burst into laughter. "So, you wanted to risk your life to wander through my ugly wardrobe? I don't understand your fascination with it. I have purchased nothing new since your last visit."

"Your clothes aren't ugly. They are charming," Samantha turned towards her closet and thumbed through the clothes. She pulled out a pink spring dress trimmed with white lace and showed it to her, smiling. "For example, this one is adorable. I love it. It's an outfit you bought in Italy, isn't it?"

Amadora's laughter faded. Her words reminded her of the haunting ones from her prior encounter. She walked towards her bed weighed with taunting remarks and conflicting feelings.

"Adorable! I don't want to be adorable!" Amadora covered her face while wrestling with her mind as it plagued her with every reason why someone as plain as her could never be anything more. Her voice calmed, but a slight tremble remained as she continued. "Adorable is something you use to describe a small child. I want people to see me as a woman, not a little girl. I want people to describe me as gorgeous or breathtaking, like they do when they see Giacinta."

Samantha realized at once the reason behind Amadora's strange behavior. She must have encountered Giacinta on her way here; her sister infected her with her venomous words and made Amadora feel miserable. Samantha did not understand how someone, who used to be so kind and warm growing up, could turn out so cruel and cold. The sisters were close when they were little. Samantha did not understand why Giacinta severed their bond.

After Giacinta banished all feelings for her sister, Amadora continued to cherish and respect her older sister. She helped Giacinta in whatever way she could, whether it was inadvertently resolving her gambling debts or taking care of her when she returned home in a drunken tirade. Amadora always reasoned why her sister treated her like dirt and with so much hatred; she looked away from the truth in the vain hope that one day her sister would break from the hateful spell she was under, and they would regain the bond they had when they were young.

Amadora's forgiving heart was something Samantha envied. If Samantha was in her friend's place, she would not be as open-hearted or kind, regardless, if Giacinta was family. Samantha held no respect for anyone who could be so ungrateful without reason to someone who constantly helped them. She did not understand how someone so poised and beautiful on the outside could be so heartless and grotesque on the inside. But as Samantha watched her friend wallow in her sullen disposition because of her encounter with that devil, she was only concerned about the state of her friend's heart.

Samantha placed a hand on her friend's shoulder to console her. "You're wrong. Your sister is no more a woman than you are. You are all those things. Your sister is a jealous tramp with a damned mission to make you miserable. Never make yourself feel any less than her. There is a reason you are so highly respected. It's not because you are Basilio Morelli's daughter, but because you have a uniquely captivating heart that accentuates your outer beauty. In fact, you are better than her, for that's something Giacinta could never possess."

Amadora wiped the tears from her red eyes; she turned toward her friend and encased her in a tight embrace. "Thank you, Sam. You're right. I don't understand why I allow her to influence me."

Amadora forced a small smile before releasing her friend, grabbing her towel from the back of her desk chair, and walking towards the bathroom. She paused only for a moment, turning her head slightly towards her friend as she spoke once more. "I am going to take a bath. I'll be right back. Make yourself comfortable. But please restrain yourself from messing up my closet."

Amadora disappeared behind the white wooden bathroom door, leaving Samantha alone in her bedroom to do as she pleased. Samantha traversed the scarlet carpet, circling around its vast spans observing everything she passed. She ran her fingers along every knick-knack upon her dressers and desk until settling them on the carved posts of Amadora's bed. She traced the carvings delicately in admiration, outlining every curve and crevice of the engraved roses. Slight ecstasy overcame her as she dropped herself upon Amadora's bed while her mind wandered to the land of conscious dreams. But her dreams were interrupted when her head hit something hard hidden beneath the pillows; she slipped her hand underneath the pillow to discover the cause of her new ailment. A flat wooden box sealed by a metal heart-shaped lock was the culprit. Samantha picked up the small box and inspected it. It was ornately carved with gold trim in the form of Venus, the roman goddess of love.

Her ethereal form traversed through a garden of white flowers adorned in long flowing garments. Samantha wanted to open the box, longing to discover the secrets the breathtaking goddess hid. She shook the box by her ear in an attempt of finding a clue to its secrets. Her curiosity and desire took possession of her, driving her to search for the key; but as soon as she placed the box aside to search, the bedroom door opened, and a man's voice called out from behind it.

"Dora, you busy?" Hearing his voice, Samantha stuffed the box under the pillows into its original spot. When she faced the door, she was caught in the unnerving possession of the enchanting dark eyes of Amadora's brother, Zanipolo. He smiled warmly when their eyes met. "Sam, I didn't realize you were here. How are you?" He searched around the room for a moment before returning his attention to Samantha. "Where's Dora?"

Samantha slid to the edge of the bed, nearing Zanipolo's position by the door.

"You say that as if you are surprised by my presence. That's silly of you. When am I not here?"

Zanipolo agreed through a powerful fit of laughter. She watched as he crossed the room over to the desk chair and sat upon it. "Amadora is taking a bath. If you want to come back when she's done, I'll let her know you were here."

Zanipolo's laughter ended, and a small smirk crossed his lips. "Are you trying to get rid of me, Sammy? You don't enjoy my company?"

Samantha averted her gaze to hide her flushed cheeks. The sound of his deep voice was velvety smooth in her ears. His playful personality and charming manner made Samantha feel unsettled. Along with his handsome features, they drew her into a spell that intensified the attraction she felt towards him. These strange feelings were not unfamiliar. They happened only when she was around Zanipolo. It was a reaction she had not yet found a cure for.

"I'm not trying to get rid of you, Polo," Samantha answered meekly, trying to conceal her flustered face. "I don't mind if you stay and keep me company until Amadora finishes."

Samantha gathered all her strength to rein in her emotions and hide them behind a friendly smile.

"I haven't seen you around lately. Are you still working with Elda?" Samantha leaned against the bedpost, nervously playing with the charm on her necklace.

"No. I'm taking over our businesses in California. That's why you haven't seen me for a while. It makes it more difficult returning home at the end of each month than when I lived in South Jersey with Elda," Zanipolo answered.

"I understand. That's far away and takes some time to go back and forth. Where in Cali are you based?"

"In Los Angeles."

"Los Angeles! That must be fun! Have you met any big stars yet?" Samantha asked, intrigued.

"What makes you think I would meet any big celebs? It's a huge city. The chances I would meet a Hollywood starlet is pretty slim," Zanipolo looked at Samantha with an eyebrow raised.

"You're Zanipolo Morelli, son of Basilio Morelli, one of the most influential and wealthiest business moguls on the east coast. I'm pretty sure you've got connections that can get you into the hottest spots where all the LA elite go," Samantha met his gaze with a soft interrogating one of her own. The serious expression on her face while she questioned him was softer than menacing, and her attempt to harden it made him bust out in laughter once more.

"I guess you got me," Zanipolo laughed. "I have been to a few of those 'big' Hollywood parties and met a bunch of stars and socialites. I also work with some to promote our businesses."

Zanipolo continued to explain his experiences in Los Angeles. She looked at him, her eyes full of intrigue and excitement, while he described his exploits. The details of each aspect of his glamorous life and his handsome expressions entranced her.

Captivated by the brilliance of his boyish features and charming smile that flashed whenever he recalled an interesting memory, strengthened the invisible hold he had on Samantha. She scanned every inch of his impressive features and tried to admire it without seeming obvious. Zanipolo's bronze skin amplified his flawless features; His rigid face, framing his walnut-colored eyes, seemed menacing but softened when he looked at her. His defined nose, full sensuous lips, and the dimple on the right side of his mouth that formed every time he smirked diluted his intimidating features, making him alluringly charming.

Even though he wore a brown suit vest, cream dress shirt and matching pants, the outline of Zanipolo's muscular form showed; its fierce structure sent shivers down Samantha's body at just the sight; Even though he sat on the opposite side of the room, his broad frame drew her in. Each part of his features was so remarkable, it seized Samantha in their unbreakable grasp, forcing her to give him all her attention. The warmth of his captivating smile only helped tighten the hold he possessed over her.

"Sammy... Sammy... Are you listening?" Zanipolo waved his hand in front of her sight to regain her attention. Samantha broke from her dazed state and became embarrassed when she realized what happened.

"I'm listening. Sorry I was just daydreaming about how amazing California sounds. I wish I could go there one day," Samantha replied, concealing her true thoughts.

"Maybe one day you can come over with Amadora. When you do, I'll give you a tour around the city. I'll show you all my favorite spots," Zanipolo smiled warmly.

"Really?" Samantha asked.

"Sure. It would be a pleasant change from my normal schedule. Talk to Amadora about it, and I'll make the arrangements."

"Thank you. I'll ask her about it later," Samantha returned his kindness with a subtle friendly grin.

"Ask me what?" Zanipolo and Samantha turned towards the bathroom door on the far end of the room. Amadora stood in its threshold wearing a different dress, but there was evidence she took a bath because her long, dark hair was damp. She pressed her towel against the curly wet ringlets framing her face, drying the excess water while observing the exchange between her older brother and best friend.

"I told Sammy that you girls should visit me in Cali. She's never been there; and since I have little to do on my free time, it would be a welcomed change to have you there," Zanipolo explained, his expression becoming more playful when he addressed his sister.

"I overheard that papa has you managing things out there. That would be a wonderful idea and perfect timing since I'm free until next fall," Amadora replied, placing her towel to the side and crossing the room to greet her brother.

"Talk it over, and let me know," Zanipolo smiled, kissing Amadora on the cheek.

"I will. But you better not use this as an excuse to slack off, Polo," Amadora teased playfully, jabbing him in the side. Zanipolo blocked her with his arm and lightly tugged at her cheek.

"No. You know me better than that. I'm a responsible man."

"Then why are you here? You know you're supposed to see papa immediately after you arrive," Amadora scolded, her voice slightly distorted by her brother messing around with her face.

"I know... I know... But I wanted to see my baby sister first since I haven't seen you in months."

Amadora swatted her brother's hands from her face, grabbed his hand and pulled him towards the door.

"That's very sweet of you, Polo. But I know you're just procrastinating, and I will not be held responsible if papa goes ballistic later, because you didn't report to him. Let's go."

Zanipolo's roaring laughter echoed as he followed helplessly behind Amadora. Samantha jumped from the bed and ran after them, trying to conceal her own amusement as she followed only a few steps behind the only man who made her senses go into a frenzy.

Giacinta ascended the stairs, heading towards the east side of the manor. She was going to her father's office so she could inform him of her arrival. Giacinta also had another agenda. One that created fear inside of her at the thought of even uttering it to him. She had to ask her father for more money because she was low on funds, and it was a long time off before she would receive her monthly allowance. She paused in front of the golden mirror across from her father's office and primped herself, checking to see if she was presentable enough for enduring this arduous task. As she fixated on her appearance, she barely noticed her father's advisor, Casimiro, pass behind her and head towards the stairs. He stopped when he saw Giacinta and watched her actions, slightly amused.

"Giacinta, it's been a while since I've seen you in this part of the house. You must be here to see your father?" Casimiro smiled cordially.

"Yes, I am. Is he still in his office?" Giacinta replied, turning toward Casimiro with a small polite smirk, which she used to mask her genuine feelings. Nervousness seized her entire being. It took all her strength to retain this expression.

"I believe he is in there with your brother, Gugliehno. They are waiting for Zanipolo and Elda to arrive. If you want to see him, now is the perfect time," answered Casimiro.

"I will," said Giacinta softly, maintaining her composure. "It seems father has you busy as usual. What does he have you doing now?"

"I'm supposed to find Polo and Elda and inform them that their father wants to see them after they settle into their rooms. How was your ride from the city? Was it comfortable?"

"It was adequate. I slept most of the ride over here, so I can't say much about it," In the middle of their conversation, Giacinta noticed Gugliehno leaving her father's office. He noticed them and smiled with a glass clutched in his hand.

"Giacinta, Long time no see. How are you feeling today?" greeted Gugliehno warmly as he crossed to her side and kissed her on the cheek.

"Gugliehno... I'm fine. How are you? How are Susan and your kids?" replied Giacinta in slight surprise by her brother's greeting. The last time she saw her brother was when he kicked her out of his home for acting inappropriately around his kids while intoxicated. His warm demeanor toward her seemed unusual, especially after their last encounter.

"I'm okay. Susan and the girls are good too," responded Gugliehno in his usual kind tone, his warm smile unwavering when he noticed her expression of surprise. "I better check on my wife and my precious angels. They are probably dying of boredom without me."

Casimiro smirked and nodded to Gugliehno's departure. "I better head off too. Nice talking to you, Giacinta."

"Same here," Giacinta replied plainly as she watched Casimiro and Gugliehno go about their way.

Alone once more in the hall, Giacinta inhaled deeply and closed the distance between her and the door to her father's office. She paused when her hand brushed against the knob; a chill crept down her spine at the icy touch of the brass under her fingertips; the cool sensation foreshadowed the result of her endeavor; it foreshadowed that it might not end in her favor. She deeply inhaled and exhaled once more before striking the wooden door with the back of her other hand. Her nerves raced in the prolonged silence that followed as she waited for a response.

"Who is it?" She heard the profound call of her father's voice from the opposite side of the door.

"Papa, It's... It's me, Giacinta. May I come in?" Giacinta stammered nervously.

"Giacinta... Of course, come in."

Giacinta entered her father's study with caution; she strode across the sunlit room towards her father's desk. Bruno interrupted her path when she walked past. The wretched mutt growled at her, causing her to jump in fear. He always growled at her whenever she was near him. Giacinta despised her dad's dog for the way he treated her and the fact he never treated that stupid little girl, Amadora, like that which made her feel as if the dog had it out for her.

Her father smiled warmly at the sight of his middle daughter's unexpected arrival. "Giacinta, I haven't seen you in a while. Come so I can have a better look at you," Basilio outstretched his arms and wrapped them around his daughter, ensnaring her in his embrace affectionately sealing his greeting. "My... My... My... You grow more beautiful each time I lay my eyes upon you. What do I owe for this unexpected visit?"

Once released from her father's embrace, she took a place in the chair across from her father, so she could have enough space between them when she made her query. "Well, Papa, can't a girl just visit her father without possessing an ulterior motive?"

From the strained smile on her face, Basilio knew that she wanted something more than a polite chat with him. His smile faded at the realization of her having a hidden agenda and reclaimed his seat as he uttered a response. "If you were Amadora possessing her whimsical reasoning, then I would believe you, but you aren't. You have a reputation for coming here only when you want something. So, tell me... what is your dire situation?"

His comparison of her to Amadora made her blood boil and pulse race. Anger tremored throughout her body, but Giacinta desperately maintained her composure and the smile on her elegant visage.

"Well, Papa, I need some money," Giacinta informed softly, her voice fading as her nerves took control.

"How much is some?" Her father's eyebrow arched as his fierce dark eyes observed her behavior.

"About one thousand dollars..." Giacinta answered with caution when she realized her father's interrogating eyes were upon her. She quickly averted her gaze; her throat was barren and dry, making speech difficult as her nerves seized her.

"A thousand dollars!" Her father's voice boomed with anger, making her quiver in fear. "What the hell do you need a thousand dollars for!"

"Well, Papa, I've had problems at a casino where I lost all of last month's allowance. Now, I need money to live on," Giacinta explained in a soft quivering voice.

It was hard to tell if he was disregarding her current disposition or his anger caused him not to recognize it, but he continued his scrutinizing rant. "But one thousand! That's too much for just living on! You are here most of the time! What do you need money to live on!"

"Papa, please! I need the money!" Giacinta begged; her voice broke as she pleaded to the heart of the man, but it came to no avail. She could tell by his brooding stature that his decision was definite. Her pleas were all in vain.

"Why do you need that much money? Are you doing drugs?" Her father's booming tone made Giacinta shrink away in fear. "You don't pay rent! You live in my penthouse and in my house for free! So, there's no other reason you'd need that kind of money!"

"Papa, no! That's not it. I'm not doing drugs! I need the money for debts!"

"What kind of debts? Gambling debts?"

"Well... Yes..." Her voice faltered when she responded.

Her father remained silent. He rose from his chair and crossed over to the liquor cabinet. Basilio grabbed a bottle of tequila and poured some into a glass. He consumed it all in one gulp and then peered out the window, hidden by the glare of the sun, making it impossible for Giacinta to read his countenance.

"Father, will you?" Her voice faltered along with her expression as she attempted to sway her father. "Please..."

He refused to look at her as he responded without emotion. "Get out."

Amadora, Samantha, and Zanipolo had just arrived in the east corridor of the second floor when they saw Giacinta running towards them drenched in tears. From the direction she came, it was clear she ran from her father's office. Her broad-brimmed hat covered her eyes, secluding herself from their presence. She was entirely unaware when Zanipolo intercepted her path and captured her in his arms. She buried her head into his broad chest when she recognized her captor, allowing her heavy tears to fall upon him.

Among all her siblings, Giacinta felt closest to Zanipolo. He was the only person in her life who understood her. He had always been there for her when she needed someone the most whether to talk to, console, help, or advise her, or just listen to her grievances. Zanipolo related to her the most because he was in her situation before. He went through the addictions of gambling and hidden pleasures; He went through the disgraceful task of begging his father for money to pay off his bookies, so he understood about the difficulties of breaking away from such addictions and the isolation of being the troubled child of Basilio Morelli.

She whispered his name weakly glancing at him with tearful eyes. He kissed her forehead; then he whispered in her ear some words of consolation and a promise he would meet her in her room once he reported to their father. She winced at the mention of their father before nodding in response. With one last hug, he let her go on her way, then watched after her as she ran down the stairs.

When he returned his attention back to the girls, a tall slender woman ascended the staircase, shaking her head in disgust. Her pale body was encased in a long ebony dress, which hid the true features of her frame as she towered over the girls. She was only a couple inches taller than Amadora, who stood at nine inches and five feet, but slightly shorter than Zanipolo. She turned towards Zanipolo and the girls when she noticed their presence; a smirk crossed her pale, thin lips as she peered over at Zanipolo.

"Well, it seems like little Miss Princess didn't get her way again," Zanipolo shot a harsh glare of annoyance at the woman for her remark. Her expression widened at his reaction, causing her to expose her pearly whites as she responded. "What, Polo, can you blame me for not showing sympathy? She's very spoiled. She probably deserved whatever happened to her."

"Elda, I thought I felt a cold chill coming from an open window a moment ago, but it seems I was wrong. It was just a warning of your arrival," Zanipolo sneered.

His eyes narrowed at his elder sister, glaring at her with irritation and annoyance. Her scrutiny of Giacinta irked him. She was not fond of Giacinta, taking any circumstance that occurred to criticize her. Zanipolo hated the way Elda treated Giacinta as if she was a stranger instead of a sibling.

"I missed you too, little brother," replied Elda, ignoring his sneer and intense expressions towards her. In contrast to the dark grin she wore, her eyes pierced with anything less than amusement. Her intense gray eyes were unflinching as they battled with his dark gaze. "I don't understand why you defend her. She wouldn't defend you if the roles were reversed. She doesn't own a loyal bone in her entire body. I don't understand. Why don't you see her for who she really is?"

"I defend her because she's family! You don't turn your back on family no matter what! I believe in that, and you should too!" Zanipolo retorted angrily.

"In this business, you can't trust anyone. Even siblings will turn on you when money is involved," informed Elda; her voice remained cold and indifferent, increasing her brother's anger. She ignored his reaction and waltz past him, heading toward her father's office. She called over her shoulder without turning to face him as she continued, "I suggest you come on, Polo. Papa will want to see you too."

Zanipolo did not respond; he reluctantly followed Elda into the office, abandoning Samantha and Amadora in the hallway. The two girls glanced at one another with awe and confusion frozen on their faces about the scene that just occurred before them.

"Dora, what just happened here? Giacinta crying and throwing herself in Zanipolo's arms? I never believed I'd say this, but she almost seemed human. I almost pitied her. I thought she was void of all emotions except anger and jealousy. I guess I was wrong."

"I agree with Elda; those weren't tears of sorrow. Those were tears of a spoiled child who didn't get what they wanted," Amadora responded coolly with dislike and anger hidden beneath her words.

Even though Elda could be perceived as a bitch for the way she handled certain situations, Amadora could not find any fault in her means; she was only perceived that way because she always spoke the truth, no matter how harsh it may be. Elda's words were true. Giacinta's tears were her version of a tantrum because their father denied her of something. She could not sympathize with her. She would not for the sake of her own heart.

"This is too much drama for me. Let's go to the garden for fresh air," Samantha suggested. Amadora nodded and followed her friend as they fled down the stairway and went outside to the garden.

Passing through the ivy-covered gate of the garden, the girls strolled into its lush, serene Eden-like environment. The warmth of the late summer air lingered heavily around them, adding to the peaceful ambiance. The tall rose bushes outlining the iron archway captivated Amadora's attention; their lush branches weaved between the iron carvings of the arch expanding above them. They welcomed them to the scarlet brick path, which ran through the entire garden; fully grown late summer blooms embroidered the earth along the path, their beauty illuminating the simple bricks. Amadora reached into the towering foliage wrapped around the arches and plucked an ivory rose from it; she removed the thorns before appreciating the true essence of the flower; she brought the small flower to her nose and inhaled the sweet, enticing aroma. The delicate scent caused her to become reminiscent of memories long passed, joyous times of her grandmother's garden at her villa in Sicily.

As a child, she spent many summers with her grandmother; she used to take her all around the lush countryside of the isle; they traversed through the island picking their favorite blooms, uprooting them, and replanting them in her garden. She spent many merry hours shadowing her grandmother as she tended to her garden. Her grandmother cherished her garden as much as she did Amadora; it was her greatest possession; she referred to it as "il mio mondo separato", or "my separate world". She used to tell her, "Una volta entri nei cancelli di un giardino, sei trasportado al mondo dove il cattivo non può entrare. Un mondo perfetto." (Once you enter the gates of a garden, you are transported to a world where evil can't enter. A perfect world.)

These words lurked in her heart, living in the recesses as a soft whisper and resounding only when her heart faltered. At first, she was ignorant of her meaning; but in time, she discovered its truth and wisdom. As she grew, she understood the true worth of the secret world surrounding her. She learned the true benefits of tending the earth and the blooms, which sprang from it, the beauty of creating new life. She learned their secrets as she catered to their every whim with her small hands shielding them from any ailment and pleasuring them with song and friendship.

In return for her tender care and nurture, they grew vast and large with luscious leaves and exotic blossoms, assuring her that by her hand they thrived and forever she possessed their gratitude. She basked in their serene majesty appreciatively as she reflected on the meaning of her grandmother's words. Being in a garden, tending the earth and exploring the simple pleasures it beheld stirred emotions, which could cure any ailment of the heart or mind. Doing something so pure and being in a place so serene eased all negative emotions; and because of its natural state, evil could not corrupt it. Even if disaster caused it to become barren, within weeks, life would flourish once more; though wild it may be, life would never cease to return.

Her grandmother was a wise woman with mysterious tendencies. She always told Amadora she was special. Her grandmother believed she was blessed like herself with a gift which prevented her from becoming victim to grave danger. Amadora scarcely understood her meaning. She asked her grandmother what she meant many times, but she only responded in riddles. Her grandmother told her she would discover in time her meaning. Maybe that was a blessing? Did she really want to chance danger to uncover her grandmother's meaning? She was not sure, but a feeling inside her hinted that she might discover it sooner than later.

While Amadora reminisced, Samantha walked ahead to the gray stone gazebo in the heart of the east garden. She took refuge inside sitting upon the little marble bench while waiting for her friend. She watched her quietly as Amadora weaved the little white flower into her dark curly tresses. The expression on Amadora's face sent worry through Samantha because she knew that expression too well; it was one which preceded a plot she concocted involving the two of them. Knowing Amadora like she did, Samantha knew whatever it was she had planned was probably huge.

Amadora noticed her friend's worried expression as Samantha watched with caution.

"Don't worry. I am not cooking up any schemes. I was just reminiscing about the past. That's all. You can calm down," Amadora assured gently.

Her intuitive response did not calm Samantha's worries, however; for she knew even if her words were true, it would not be long until she was scheming of a new endeavor for them to embark on.

Amadora glided joyfully over to the bench and wrapped her arm lovingly around her friend. "My dearest friend, you know I won't be angry if you marry my brother. I will be the happiest person at the wedding aside from you and him, of course. My best friend and my brother, how wondrous!" Amadora beamed.

Amadora's words caused the heat within Samantha's body to escalate, making her fair skin turn a soft crimson. Annoyance and embarrassment battled inside of her while she tried to figure out if her friend's words were of sincerity or mockery. Her blood pulsated violently in her veins as her emotions fought for control of her being.

"Stop teasing me! I have told you many times I am not into him in that way. He's more like a brother," Samantha snapped vigorously, releasing herself from her friend's embrace as her annoyance took control.

For a moment, Amadora was taken aback by Samantha's response, but her enormous grin swiftly returned when she noticed the state of her friend's visage. Samantha's face was as red as a rose; her large dark eyes were engraved with annoyance; her words, though they were strong, seemed to tremble clumsily from her mouth; also, by the tense nature of her body at that moment, it was obvious they were a foolish charade to mask how she truly felt.

"I'm not teasing you. I meant every word I said unlike you. You cannot fool me, Sammy. I've known you for too long. You can't even fool yourself. Even though your words say one thing, your body tells a very different tale. You say you think of him only as a brother; but if that was true, then why do you become flustered and nervous every time you're around him? And why does your body tense at a mere mention of him?" Amadora remarked; her grin faded to a small confident smirk when she observed her friend's reaction to her words.

Embarrassment washed over Samantha's countenance, causing her to avert her gaze from her friend to hide her flustered state. Her long dark hair shielded her well enough to give her the strength to respond strongly in her defense.

"You're mistaken. I don't become flustered by the mention of him," Samantha responded defiantly, standing her ground.

"I'm not mistaken, although, you clearly are. Can you not feel your body's response to your lies? You are flustered now, aren't you?" Amadora exploded into laughter, amused by her friend's obvious denial.

"No. I'm not!" Samantha snapped stubbornly, raising her small nose in the air. Aggravation became her. She refused to speak of the feelings she did not possess for Zanipolo any longer. "Let's change the subject. This one is annoying."

"Alright, fine. What do you want to talk about?" Amadora shrugged obeisant to her friend's request. She leaned on the back of the bench, stretching her arms behind her head and cradling it while observing the family of robins perched on top of the beams of the gazebo's roof.

"Tell me what you are planning to do to convince your father to let you join your family's business?" Samantha asked seriously. Samantha's words made Amadora's smile fade, and a frown replace it.

"I don't know yet," Amadora sighed. A sullen expression cast over her features as she continued. "He's too stubborn. He still thinks I can't handle it like my siblings can."

"I'm not sure that's his real reason. He might want to protect you," Samantha replied softly, casting her glance downward.

Samantha lacked any visible expression, and her color drained after uttering a few silent words. Amadora could not make out the words she mouthed, but she could tell it was about a sad event hidden in the depths of her heart. She saw Samantha act this way only a few times before. Amadora wanted to inquire on those troubled thoughts of hers, but she withdrew from asking her about it, since it seemed to be something Samantha did not want to share. She had faith that in time her friend would enlighten her on what was troubling her; but until then, she would wait patiently. Amadora tucked away her concerns deep inside and continued with their initial conversation.

"I don't know. He is being too overprotective. I can fend for myself and am not the weak, defenseless girl he thinks I am. I wish I could prove that to him somehow."

Samantha's eyebrow arched at Amadora's words in wonder of her meaning. But, before she could respond, Barry entered the garden and walked over to where the two girls were. When he stood at the entrance of the gazebo, he bowed respectfully and acknowledged the two young women with a plain expression.

"Miss Amadora, dinner is ready. I will escort you and Miss Samantha to the dining room."

The girls looked at one another in surprise because they did not realize how late it really was. They nodded in response and followed Barry inside the manor.

In the dining room, Gugliehno's daughters sat beside Fiorella conversing with Elda's husband, Antonio, and her son, Angelo, who sat across from them. Amadora and Samantha sat on the farthest end of the table away from her father's chair, which stood vacant at the head of the table. There were a few vacant seats near their seats. One was on the right side of Samantha, which was Zanipolo's usual seat; three seats across from them, next to Susan, were also absent their occupants; they were the seats reserved for Gunny, Casimiro, and Giacinta; there was also the empty seat to the right of her father's place, which was Elda's seat.

It did not take long for the vacant seats' occupants to arrive; Amadora's father, Elda, Gunny, and Casimiro were the first to arrive and take their usual seats, leaving only Zanipolo's and Giacinta's seats still vacant; they waited patiently for a few minutes until they arrived. Basilio waited until each took their seats before rising to his feet and beginning his prayer.

"It warms my heart to have all my family gathered around my table in such good health and happiness this month. The heavenly father has kept each one of you safe under his protective wings. As I look around the room, I'm blessed to see a bit of my mother's spirit in each of my children, living, protecting, and guiding you while you travel on your separate paths. I pray this meal will nourish our bodies and protect us from the sting of famine. May we cherish this moment together and the life we possess. In your name we pray, Amen."

A soft echo of amen fell over the table in response to the conclusion of his prayer. The sound of the plates being passed around the table filled the air. Soft conversations crossed the table along with laughter and gaiety drowning the silence in the room. The only one who would not join the joyful mood of the room was Giacinta.

She sipped her wine in silence as she watched Zanipolo converse with Samantha and Amadora. Rage and jealousy burned through her chest as she watched her brother smiling in amusement while focusing all his attention on Amadora and her friend. She swirled the crimson liquid in her glass, holding it nervously as her gaze focused intently on him; Casimiro, who occasionally glanced in her direction, noticed her peculiar behavior, and diverted his attention away from Antonio and Gugliehno.

"You know, scowling isn't good for a young lady like you. You should try smiling," Casimiro said, smiling politely at the solemn young woman beside him.

Shock overcame her in response of his words, causing her to redirect her attention towards him. "What are you talking about?" Giacinta questioned, slightly confused.

"I am talking about that frown you had on your face a second ago. It's not good to wear an expression like that on such a pretty face," Casimiro elaborated; his generous smile refused to fade as he continued to observe her beautiful countenance.

Giacinta's fair cheeks flushed a rosy hue in response to Casimiro's flattering compliment. She took another sip of her wine, hoping the large crystal glass would shield her current reaction from her attentive spectator. "I wasn't frowning, was I? If I was, then I'm sorry," Giacinta replied.

"No need to apologize. Is there something troubling you?"

Giacinta took another sip of her wine before responding; as if by doing so, it would prevent her from revealing too much. As if the actual reasons about her troubles would flow down her throat along with the wine.

"A lot of things are troubling me," Giacinta answered, frankly.

Casimiro's light green eyes smiled along with his lips. He could tell by her tone and actions that she would not reveal her troubles to him yet, especially here. He held back any other words that would press the matter further.

"Well. If I can help you in any way possible, just tell me. You know where to find me."

Casimiro observed her closer. Her behavior seemed as clear to him as the glass of water in his hand. He saw the confusion painted in the depths of her cerulean eyes. It emanated more vigorously than any of her other emotions. The cause of her confusion had nothing to do with anything in this room. He brought the glass of water to his lips and drank from it patiently awaiting her answer.

"If you can, I'll let you know. How was your month?" Puzzled by Casimiro's kindness, Giacinta indulged him with polite conversation. She also tried to scan his features for a hint to the reason he acted so nice to her. What did he want from her?

"It was fine. Thanks for asking. I did the usual. I accompanied your father, mother, and sister to Italy for business. Even though it was beautiful there, I had no time for leisure. How was yours?"

"Mine was fine. I guess... I spent time with friends. I stayed with one of them for most of the month. Nothing new."

"You know we are complete opposites."

"What do you mean?" Giacinta questioned, wide-eyed and confused.

"I'm all work and no play, but you're the complete opposite."

Giacinta's eyes pierced a threatening glare of anger at him as she took another bite of her food. His laughter faded when he noticed her expression; he tried to explain himself at once before invoking any misunderstanding. "I didn't mean it with disrespect, Giacinta. Please understand that."

She nodded frigidly, taking another bite of her food. She waited until he finished before responding dryly. "Don't worry. I understand. We're completely different."

Dinner continued for an hour or two until everyone had their fill. At the end of the meal, Basilio called Casimiro, Elda, Zanipolo, and Gugliehno to his office for a smoke and drink before they retired for the night. Samantha and Amadora exchanged glances when they saw her siblings exiting the dining room. They both knew now was the best time for Amadora to talk to her father. The girls excused themselves and headed into the foyer; Amadora turned to Samantha and hugged her for good luck. Once she released Samantha from her embrace, Samantha watched Amadora as she ascended the stairs. When she reached the top, Samantha turned away from the stairs and headed in the opposite direction.

Basilio poured whiskey into some glasses then handed them out. When everyone had a glass, he took his cigar box from inside his desk and placed it on top where anyone could take one. He lounged back in his chair, cut the tip of his cigar, and lit it while clenching it between his teeth. His dark gaze traversed the room over to Elda as he questioned her about Angelo and school. When she answered him, a knock sounded on the office door.

"Yes, who is it?" Basilio called out, taking a pull of his cigar.

"Papa, it's me. Amadora," Amadora responded from the other side of the door.

"Come in."

Everyone in the room greeted Amadora with smiles as she entered the room. She smiled respectfully in response while trying to rid the nervous rumbles in her gut as she stood before Elda, Zanipolo, Casimiro, Gugliehno, and her father. She walked to each, gave them a kiss, and then she asked.

"Papa, May I talk to you in private?"

A strong, hearty laugh escaped Basilio's lips in response to her words. "About what?"

The tone of her voice faltered when she uttered her reply. Her gaze fell to the floor as she averted it from her father's interrogating stare. "I want to speak with you about the issue I've always asked about, Papa. About me joining the family business."

Elda watched her sister with an eyebrow arched in disbelief. "You're still stuck on that? I thought you gave up on that idea by now," Elda questioned wryly.

Elda took a sip of her drink, thoroughly scanning Amadora for a hint of her response, and then she turned her attention to her father to witness his reaction to her sister's bold request. Elda, like everyone else in the room, knew where her father stood about Amadora being a part of the business. They knew he refused to allow her anywhere near their business, for reasons he never explained. Elda was probably one of the few in the room who did not mind Amadora joining because she was about her age when she joined. However, her feelings did not matter on this subject; it was her father's decision that mattered; his word was law, and he forbade her from joining.

Observing Amadora's behavior in that moment, Elda wondered if her father's decision was justified. She was not sure if Amadora was strong enough to handle the darkness guaranteed within their world. Amadora was pure and fragile, like a child. Elda doubted she had the stomach or maturity for this business. She wondered if her little sister understood what it took to succeed in their world.

Hearing Amadora's words caused everyone's smiles to fade; their gazes went back and forth between Amadora and Basilio; Basilio did not respond right away; he only scanned his daughter's face when her gaze met his once more.

"You're determined about this. Aren't you, Dora?" Gunny questioned gently, making Amadora face him so he could see the truth behind her words.

Amadora nodded her head yes in response to his inquiry; she did not remove her gaze from him when their eyes met; she did not even move his hand when he held her chin, preventing her from moving her head. Gugliehno saw the determination emanating from her eyes. There was a ferocious fire burning inside them that did not seem as if it would fade. The way she was at that moment reminded him of Elda when she first demanded to join. She had the same passion and persistence. Gunny released her chin and sat back down in his chair, returning his attention to his father. He wondered if his father noticed the same fire and determination as he did. He wondered if his father recognized what he had seen. Or was his father too blind with his own reasons to see the truth?

"Amadora, you know where I stand on that matter," Basilio responded dismissively, smoking his cigar.

She looked over at him; her soft brown eyes pleading along with her words as she spoke. "I know, Papa. But isn't there any chance you could change your mind? I am eighteen and know just as much about the business as any of you. I won't get hurt because I can take care of myself."

"You may know as much as we do, but it doesn't change that I want you nowhere near this life," Basilio responded plainly. He took a sip of his drink and turned towards the window behind him.

"But why, Papa? Is it because I am a girl? Or is it because I'm the youngest?" Her anger consumed her, but she tried desperately to conceal it; his rude behavior made it almost impossible for her to maintain her composure. Basilio's back was turned towards her, and he ignored her pleas. His arrogance had overcome his entire being. She did not understand his behavior towards her at that moment.

"You're too young to understand my position and reasoning. I think it's best for you to leave it alone and go to bed," When she heard his words, she understood they meant he would say nothing more about the subject.

"But why, Papa?" She pleaded weakly, but the words were too faint to be heard. Amadora retreated to the door without another word. She maintained her respectful composure when she reached the door; it took all the strength she could muster to turn back towards them and wish them good night. The only one who noticed her tears as she fled the room was Zanipolo, who stood near the door.

Amadora closed the office door behind her and dashed down the hall into the back stairs to her room. Samantha sat at the foot of Amadora's bed waiting for her when she entered her bedroom. She could tell by her friend's tear-stained eyes what the result was from her confrontation with her father. Samantha embraced her friend, guiding her to the bed so she could sit and relax.

"He didn't... He wouldn't even listen. He turned his back to me," Amadora cried frustrated into Samantha's chest.

"It's okay," Samantha rubbed her back in a consoling manner. "He said nothing at all? He revealed nothing new about why he doesn't want you to join?" Amadora shook her head as she continued to cry.

"What are you going to do? There's nothing more you can do now to convince him, right?"

Amadora pondered for a moment before responding. "There might be one thing I could do. It's risky; but if done right, I could attain all I desire. I overheard my father and Gunny talking inside his office earlier. Gunny needs someone to do a job for him. He needs someone, who's outside of the family, an associate, for this job."

"So, what does that have to do with you?" Sam asked confused.

"If I masqueraded as a guy, I could enter Gunny's circuit as an associate and work my way up. If I can prove to my father that I can survive on my own as a 'footman', he might reconsider his 'reasons'."

"But how will you convince your father to allow you to go to New York by yourself unsupervised?"

Amadora looked at Samantha, and then her eyes wandered over to her closet. "He won't know I'm there."

"How are you going to pull that off?" Samantha laughed nervously.

"You are about the same size as me, and you look like me almost exactly from a distance."

Samantha shook her head and waved her hands ferociously. "No! What about my father? How am I going to get his permission to go anywhere on my own?"

"You could tell him you're going to California with me. He'll let you go if you say that," Amadora smiled sweetly. "You'll impersonate me and travel to California in my place while I sneak off to New York. You can keep any clothes you buy while you're there."

"But how are you going to do this before Gunny returns to New York?"

"Gunny visits my aunt in South Jersey for two days after our family weekend. I have a friend, Anna, who lives in New York and is acquainted with some of our soldiers. She could introduce me as her 'cousin' who needs work. They should let me in by her word, and then I'll be set," explained Amadora, freeing herself from her friend's embrace and wiping the drying tears from her cheeks.

Samantha had her doubts about Amadora's plan; the risk was substantial and extremely dangerous. She rose to her feet and paced back and forth nervously. "But how will you get clothes for your disguise? You can't borrow your brothers' clothing because someone might recognize their previous owner."

"Anna has some of her husband's old clothes I could use. I'll be fine. So, will you help me?"

"I don't know. What do you want me to do if Zanipolo comes over to visit his sister? He'll notice I'm not you."

"Whenever he tries to come over to the house, try to seem busy or not be at the house. However, I doubt you'll have a problem with him, Zanipolo rarely visits the vacation home, where you'll be staying, so, you should be fine. He'll give you your space when instructed to do so by my father. Don't worry."

Samantha wanted to continue her inquiry but refrained from doing so instead nodded in agreement. She gave way to defeat as her friend embraced her once again in gratitude. Her concerns continued to wash over her, drowning her in her fears of Amadora's dangerous plan. They treaded in dangerous waters because they were trying to do the impossible, deceiving Basilio Morelli. It was a feat which had rarely

been attempted while resulting in success, but they would try regardless. They must accomplish this difficult feat if Amadora was to attain her greatest desire.

Giacinta pulled up to the alley next to Gino's Cabaret. She got out of her car and walked over to the side entrance, told the bouncer who she was and entered through the iron door. Giacinta's blood grew cold as she walked through the dark, narrow halls and followed the crescent moon-like curve until coming to the base of some rickety looking steps. She pulled out a slip of paper tucked away in her pocket and looked it over. Her hands grew clammy and cold as they shook uncontrollably while reading the piece of paper. Giacinta took a deep breath, tucked the paper back into her pocket, grabbed hold of the splintery wooden banister and ascended the stairs.

When Giacinta reached the top landing, a thick smoke surrounded her while half-dressed, inebriated women and men lined the hall, kissing and groping one another. She stepped over the high bodies sluggishly laying every which way and made her way to the haze covered archway on the far end of the hall.

Stepping across the threshold, the smoke intensified, making it difficult for Giacinta to breathe. She covered her mouth with her handkerchief and searched the crowded room for her target. Giacinta tapped on the shoulder of a drunk, topless woman and asked.

"Where's Marco?"

A large, sloppy grin crossed her smudged lips. The woman's watery green eyes curved as she grabbed Giacinta's arm and started dancing seductively. "Loosen up, doll. Don't worry about Marco and have fun with us instead."

The woman motioned to a greasy-looking man who had his tongue down another woman's throat while she ran her hand underneath his shirt and touching parts that Giacinta rather not envision. Giacinta withheld her urge to throw up and shook her head, rejecting the woman's invitation.

"I'll pass. Just tell me where Marco is. I have business to discuss with him."

The woman shrugged and pointed to a room in the apartment's corner. "He's over there, but he's busy at the moment."

Giacinta didn't respond to the woman. She just headed over to the room.

When Giacinta opened the door, she found herself in a massive suite not as swamped with smoke because the windows were open. Clothes scattered across the floor and the sound of moans of pleasure echoed through the air. Giacinta let her knuckles remain idle in the air in front of the door before rapping softly on its wooden surface.

The sound of her hitting the door roused the commotion under the sheets, causing a man to throw back the comforter and stop what he was doing. He was in the middle of ramming a rough, ginger-haired woman. He tossed his thick, dark hair out of his face as he latched onto the woman's thick body with his left arm and turned to see who interrupted.

"Go away! Can't you see I'm busy fucking this broad!" Marco's deep, raspy voice sent chills down Giacinta's body as it resonated through the room.

His fat, ruddy face looked annoyed until his eyes fell upon Giacinta.

"Giacinta, it's you," Marco smiled. He quickly withdrew from the woman and patted her on the rear. "Get lost. I need to talk to the Morelli princess about business."

The woman crawled out of bed, picked up her clothes and ran out the room. When she left, Marco motioned for Giacinta to close the door and come closer. Giacinta cautiously obliged and walked over to him. Marco sat naked on the corner of the bed with only a thin white sheet covering his man part. A cheeky grin crossed his face when he noticed Giacinta's timid behavior.

"What's wrong, Gia? You know I won't bite. Come closer."

"I'm not here for that. I'm here to talk about my debt. I need an extension on my deadline. It will take a bit longer than I initially hoped," Giacinta responded, trying to steady the tone of her voice to hide the fear embedded there.

Marco's face fell and a dark air surrounded him. His dark eyes glared at Giacinta, piercing her with dread and intensifying her worries.

"Gia... Gia... Gia... You know I can't do that," Marco shook his head in disappointment. "If I lent you my money, then I wouldn't care; but it was Lucio's, and you know how boss gets if he doesn't get his money."

"I know, but can't you ask him to extend the deadline for a week or two? This is a onetime thing," Giacinta begged.

Marco wrapped the sheet across his lap around his body and stood. He walked over to a quivering Giacinta, grabbed her chin, pressed his large body against hers pinning her against the dresser behind her. A devilish smirk crossed his thin lips as he moved closer to her ear and whispered harshly.

"Why don't you get someone from that rich family of yours to open their fat pockets and help you out?"

Giacinta squirmed, trying to break free, but Marco just pressed tighter against her body.

"I tried, but they won't help," Giacinta answered in between pained gasps as the pressure of his body restricted her breathing.

"That's too bad. Well, there is one way you can work off your debt," Marco slid his free hand up her leg, but Giacinta clenched her legs shut so he couldn't go any further and screamed.

"No!" Giacinta used all her strength to push him back. But as she tried running for the door, Marco grabbed her hair and punched her across her cheek. Marco was too strong for Giacinta to fight back; so, as she fell to the floor, she curled up to protect her as Marco savagely beat her.

Giacinta screamed, but Marco's swears drowned out her cries. Each blow was so excruciating that their pain along with the psychological damage made her linger on the verge of consciousness and unconsciousness. She couldn't feel her body anymore once Marco stopped punching her, pressed his large hand against her throat and choked her as he laid on top of her. Faint cries barely escaped her lips as she saw through a puffy eye Marco's fat, greedy face grin as he moved vigorously on top of her. Giacinta tried to push him off, but she was too weak. Tears fell down her face as she tried to scream, but the pressure of his hand against her throat prevented any sound from escaping. As he pressed his hand against his windpipe, she felt her mind drift farther away as the surrounding shadows engulfed her, dragging her farther into this inescapable nightmare.

The Plan Begins

'An unbreakable mask and cunning are the keys for executing a plan flawlessly.' Thoughts of Amadora Morelli.

After witnessing Amadora's tears last night, Zanipolo could barely sleep. He worried about his sister's state of mind. She was such a strong-willed girl but was delicate at times. It took all her strength to conceal her disappointment from the others. Amadora waited until she turned her back before letting a few tears escape. Only Zanipolo saw her heartache and the first tears fall down her cheek.

Sadness and shock stained her face, but that was not concerning him. No. There was something else taking hold of his senses and filling him with worry. He discovered something hidden behind those emotions in the dark recesses of her eyes. Something that amplified her strength tenfold. A fiery passion burning vigorously in the profound corners of her heart and hidden by her tears and transitory emotions. The fire was too strong to fade away. It fed off her failure and continued its relentless growth. That seized him with concern. For deep inside, he knew that last night would not be the final time she attempted to enter their world. Amadora would try again and again until she finally claimed what she desired. But how far was she willing to go to attain it?

Amadora might seem helpless and naïve, but that was a complete charade. She was far from helpless. Amadora was cunning, brilliant, strong, and resourceful. She had many skills that even he was unaware of. Zanipolo was the most familiar with her skills because he helped train her. He blamed himself for her relentless determination in becoming a part of their business; he should have never confided in her about his past missions; he should have never taught her how to shoot a gun; and teaching her to fight was his greatest folly, for it fueled the burning fire of her curious desire.

Zanipolo preferred his privacy even during their family weekends at the end of every month; because of this, he stayed in the west manor of the complex. It was not as grand as the main house, but it was big enough in its own right. Harboring five large bedrooms, a spacious salon, library, dining room, and kitchen, it was more than enough for Zanipolo. Since all the servants frequented the main manor to tend to the rest of his family, this manor was mostly vacant during the day, which left him in perfect solitude.

From his room, Zanipolo saw everything that went on in the westside of the main house. He trekked over to a window and checked the activities of the house in the early morning. Zanipolo brushed his messy hair from his face while focusing on Amadora's room. Darkness bathed her room, but that didn't surprise Zanipolo. Amadora had a habit of sleeping later than everyone else so she could eat breakfast with the cook before escaping into the garden.

Nothing changed with that girl. Ever since they were young, she adored gardens. She inherited her fascination from their grandmother. If she was not in her room reading, then she was in the garden tending to every shrub, tree, and flower. She spent every moment of her free time in that garden. When she was not tending to its occupants, she spent her time lounging by the creek which ran through the south side of the garden, contemplating its slow-flowing waters. Zanipolo could not understand her obsession with it. Her patience and dedication astonished him; he could not suffice the needs of such a quaint hobby but admired her passion for it.

Zanipolo crossed over to the fireplace on the opposite side of the room; he stared at the pictures on the mantle from his high school days, but his mind did not focus on them. Instead, he debated whether he should go to breakfast when everyone gathered or wait until Amadora went. These questions weighed on his mind. He had to understand the purpose of last night's scene so he could discover exactly where her desires lie.

At ten thirty in the morning, Samantha and Amadora entered the kitchen. For someone who normally woke well after noon, this was an unusual time for her to rise. As they crossed the tiled floor toward the kitchen table, the cook, Millie, walked out of the pantry smiling warmly when she noticed their presence. Her round eyes confirmed her surprise to see Amadora up at this hour.

"Miss Amadora, ain't it a lil' too early for you to be awake? Normally, I don't expect you til' around lunch. This is a pleasant surprise."

Millie possessed a jolly demeanor. She was a petite, portly woman, who was born and raised in Louisiana before moving to New Jersey. Her Louisianan accent was as thick as the blonde curly hair on top of her head. Her emerald eyes sparkled exquisitely as she invited the girls to sit at the table by the window. Millie's striking features along with her warm disposition lured in many people, especially the milkman who wandered around more times than his deliveries accounted for, which made her loved by many.

As the girls sat in their seats, Millie walked over to the stove, removed the glass cover off the yellow baking dish on top, scooped its contents onto two plates, then brought them to the girls. Amadora looked down at the lukewarm dish before her with adoration after recognizing the meal before her. It was one of her favorite dishes, baked egg casserole, comprising freshly picked green peppers, red peppers, tomato, and sausage baked in a fluffy sea of egg whites and yolks. She waited anxiously for Millie to place her utensils down beside her plate so she could devour the contents. Millie reached into the pockets of her apron fastened around her waist, pulled out a pair of utensils for each girl and placed them on the table beside their plates.

"Millie's famous egg casserole, my favorite! Thanks, Aunt Millie!" Amadora exclaimed cooing in happiness embracing Millie graciously when she reached her side.

"You're welcome, Dora," Millie replied joyfully, hugging Amadora in return. "Did you sleep well last night?"

"I did," Amadora responded, releasing Millie so she could sit down and chat. As soon as she freed her hands, she grabbed her fork and took a bite of her casserole. "How did you sleep?"

"Like a baby..." Millie started before being interrupted by Samantha, who rose her hand to gain her attention.

"Sorry to interrupt you, but do you have any orange juice?" Samantha asked politely while swallowing some of her food.

"Pardon me. I almost forgot. Let me get it for ya, honey," Millie smiled and rose from her seat to fetch the orange juice.

Millie was not related to Amadora by blood, but she was family, nonetheless. Millie met Amadora's parents at Ellis Island when she worked there as the head nurse for the women. She became fast friends with Amadora's mother, because her mother's vast intelligence and her flawless comprehension of the English language even though she was an immigrant.

Amadora's mother came from a family of scholars and learned various subjects and languages, which she later taught to Amadora, from her parents. She perfected her French and English skills with Millie, who helped them find a home and work when her parents moved to Jersey; Amadora's mother became a tutor while her father worked with Millie's husband at his grocery store.

Her father worked at their store for a few years; until one fateful night, after Gugliehno was born, Millie's husband died in a fire at his shop while closing up; Some of Lucio Rosilli's men burned it down after he refused to pledge allegiance to them. They also torched Millie's house while she prepared dinner for her husband when he returned. She fainted during the attack and could not escape. Amadora's father noticed the smoke coming from their house and rushed inside to save her before the growing flames reached her.

The news of Millie's husband's death hit them hard. Her father swore vengeance against Lucio Rosilli after learning he was responsible for his friend's death. He did petty jobs for a local gangster until he had the means of his own to build his own empire.

Following her husband's death and her rescue from a similar fate by Amadora's father, Millie felt indebted to her parents. Despite their protests, she swore her allegiance and unwavering loyalty. Even after their fortunes rose, she refused to allow them to buy her a new house and insisted on taking the position of their cook. She refused any special treatment and chose to live in the servants' quarters in the southeast corner of the complex. Unable to deny her wishes, her parents allowed Millie to live there.

Amadora visited Millie many times while exploring the garden. She could tell the burden of losing her husband still weighed heavily on her heart even after all these years. She told Amadora that he was her soulmate; and his absence left a vacancy in her heart that could never be filled, so she would live forever with only half a heart. Sometimes, when Amadora strolled past Millie's room, she heard her mumbling something in French. Her muffled words, distorted by the thick walls, made it difficult for Amadora to decipher their meaning; but by the sorrow deeply embedded in the tone of her voice, she could tell it was a heartfelt prayer for her husband. It was almost as if she was continuously apologizing for not being there to rescue him from his ill fate.

While the girls enjoyed their food and talked to Millie, Zanipolo entered the kitchen. Millie looked at Zanipolo confused; because out of all the Morelli children, Zanipolo was the first one to wake and dine in the morning. He possessed the same habit as his father and rarely strayed from it.

"Polo, did you just wake up?" Millie asked.

Zanipolo smiled sheepishly as he crossed over to the table and sat down beside Millie. "I guess I did. Well, after all the excitement last night, I didn't sleep until late."

"Excitement...?" Samantha queried.

A sharp pain in her side interrupted her after Amadora jabbed her discreetly with her elbow. Samantha clenched her teeth as the pain surged through her side, trying desperately to maintain her composure. She looked at Amadora, surprised by her actions, and was met by an intense look of warning from her friend. Immediately, she understood her meaning. The incident he referred to was Amadora's encounter with her father.

Samantha redirected her gaze back to her half-eaten food and continued eating as if nothing happened; but unfortunately for her, Zanipolo noticed her peculiar reaction and studied her closely.

"Are you okay, Sam?"

Samantha tilted her head, so her hair shrouded her face, preventing him from assessing her expression. She nodded she was fine and then continued eating her food.

"You don't seem okay, dearie. Is something wrong with the food?" Millie questioned, concerned. She reached across the table and placed her hand on Samantha's forehead to check her temperature. When she was positive Samantha was alright, she withdrew her hand and retook her seat. "That's good. You don't have a fever."

Sam looked at Millie and smiled softly. "No. It's not the food. The food is great. I choked on a little piece of sausage. That's all. Sorry to worry you."

"Be careful, darling," Millie warned.

During Samantha's exchange with Millie, Amadora noticed her brother watched her every movement without faltering.

"Polo, is there a reason you're staring at me?" Amadora questioned with slight annoyance in her voice as she countered his attentive stare.

"Can't a brother stare at his beautiful little sister without having a reason?" Zanipolo responded, surprised by his sister's words and tone.

"No. You can't. It's weird. Stop it," Amadora responded plainly, while drinking down the last of the orange juice in her glass and pushing her plate to the side. "Besides, you've never stared at me that much without wanting something. What is it?"

"You got me. All I want is to talk after breakfast. That's it," Zanipolo answered, bringing a glass of orange juice Millie poured for him to his lips and drinking its contents. He did not redirect his gaze from Amadora as Millie placed his food before him.

"That's it? You just want to talk? I wonder why," Amadora said faintly under her breath, casting her gaze to the empty table before her so she could not witness Zanipolo's unwavering stare.

After finishing their food, the girls tried escaping to the garden before Zanipolo finished; but he caught up to them as they passed the gazebo. Zanipolo maneuvered himself between them, extending his arm out for Amadora to hold as they walked. He flashed a charming smile to Samantha as he asked politely.

"Sam, you won't mind if I borrow my sister for a second?"

Sam smiled hesitantly as she nodded in agreement. Zanipolo and Amadora continued along the path, leaving Samantha alone by the gazebo. They passed the fountain in the heart of the garden; they crossed over the bridge and a creek which entered the southern part of the garden; there they paused in front of a mahogany bench alongside the southern path; Amadora sat down, watching Zanipolo carefully as he claimed the position beside her.

"You know exactly why I want to talk to you, don't you?" Zanipolo asked, smirking. His dark eyes pierced her very essence as they scanned her features.

"I don't have a clue," replied Amadora with a mask of innocent ignorance.

Amadora had to appear ignorant of his intentions, so Zanipolo would not realize her genuine desires and grow suspicious. She had a good idea of what he wanted to speak to her about, but he could not know she suspected his reasons to prevent future complications. She only prayed her charade could deceive him long enough for her to get her plan into action.

"Come on. Don't try playing innocent. You know very well what I want to talk to you about," Zanipolo's sweet demeanor quickly faded, becoming cold and emotionless. The cool atmosphere surrounding him replaced his previous warmth and caused Amadora's nerves to race. "Last night wasn't a good night for you. You can't hide that fact. But I understand more than you might realize. You have to understand. The reason Pops denies you is that it's too dangerous; and he wants nothing to happen to you."

Amadora glared at him, annoyed; she could not contain her frustration any longer; she was sick of people telling her what was too dangerous for her; she was sick of people misjudging and underestimating her.

"But I can take care of myself. I was taught by one of the best. Wasn't I?" Amadora's frustration hid behind the gentle grin she wore and her cool tone. "You haven't been harmed; and you've been doing this for years. What makes you so sure if you gave me the same opportunity I wouldn't fair as well as you have?"

"I know you think you're ready; but you don't understand how tough it really is out there. You need more than physical strength or knowledge of how to shoot to conquer the dangers of the business. You need to possess mental strength and courage. You must banish all your fears, even the fear of death. Do you understand?" Zanipolo watched Amadora, who stared at him expressionlessly. That fire still burned ferociously in her eyes. Nothing he said changed her mind. "Even though I trained you, I could never prepare you for that. I don't believe you're ready, Amadora."

Her body tensed at his words; her hands briefly clenched into fists before regaining her composure. She turned away from him, so she could hide her body's reaction to his words. She used all her strength to keep her emotions at bay.

Amadora knew if she fought her brother now, then he would grow suspicious when her father informed him of her plans to go to California. She could not risk him secretly investigating her because he becomes worried, she might try something while she's there. She could not risk Zanipolo discovering Sam disguised as her. Amadora had to relinquish the one thing she did not want to lose... Her Pride.

"Alright, Polo. I understand. I won't try again," Amadora cast her gaze down to the ground beneath her feet. Zanipolo looked at her reaction surprised; he could not believe he got through to her. He did it. Somehow, he convinced her to throw away her dangerous desire. Zanipolo had accomplished something many attempted to do but failed. With a victorious expression seizing his strong features, he embraced her

41

graciously.

"Thank you, Dora."

Amadora looked up at him with doleful eyes. "Can I return to Sam now? Please?" Amadora asked softly. Her mouth curved slightly, giving her a polite countenance. Zanipolo kissed her cheek and shook his head in response, granting her permission to return to her friend.

Once the girls were reunited, they waited until Zanipolo left before traipsing down the path toward the opposite side of the garden.

"What did you and Polo talk about?" Samantha queried in curiosity walking steadily beside her friend.

"He did most of the talking," Amadora corrected coolly. "He's against my determination to join the business. Zanipolo doesn't believe I'm ready."

Concern filled Samantha in response to Amadora's words. If what she said was true, then he might become an issue for her while she paraded around as Amadora.

"What did you say to him?"

"I promised him I would quit trying to enter the family business," Amadora replied plainly with a small grin.

Samantha's eyebrow arched in surprise. Amadora's expression betrayed her words, for it radiated with a confident humor. She realized Amadora was not backing down that easily. If it was that easy to convince her, then Samantha would have called Zanipolo to talk to her long ago. No. With the amount of passion and determination hidden in Amadora's heart, it would be impossible to persuade her from her dark desire now.

"He won't suspect anything when you get permission from your father to go to California?" Samantha questioned warily.

"No. Zanipolo isn't like that," Amadora nodded. "When my father informs him about my plans, he'll hide his suspicions-if he possesses any-but he shouldn't suspect anything. He should understand why I would desire my solitude. I doubt he'll question it; but we still need to be very cautious and careful, especially you, for the smallest thing could rile his suspicions. You must be wary and observant."

Amadora's warning was as much for herself as it was for Samantha. She knew she could not fool her brother for too long. He was extremely sharp and cunning. The slightest thing could set off his concerns, which would fuel his suspicious mind. If that happened, then she could not protect Samantha from his next actions. She was not sure how long he would remain ignorant of any suspicions toward her reason for escaping to California; and that fact worried Amadora the most.

"We'll continue as planned?"

"Yes. We will," Amadora and Samantha exchanged looks of dire seriousness. They both understood how dangerous the game they were about to play was; and they both understood the consequences. If it were to go wrong, for one girl it would mean dis-grace; for the other, it would mean death.

Concealed in the gray shadows of his office, Basilio hunched over his desk, wearily clutching onto his coffee mug as he struggled to bring it to his lips. His eyes were heavy from lack of sleep, but he kept them strong and focused on their purpose. Questions and wonders consumed his mind, for which he could not conceive any answers. He flipped through Gugliehno's report as if the answers he searched for were within its pages. Basilio hoped somewhere inside his report Gunny left a hidden message for him explaining Amadora's reasoning.

He kept the thick crimson velvet curtains drawn shut, banning the sun from penetrating the windows in the fear it would disturb his thoughts. Instead, he contemplated in the shadows unhindered by any disturbance. He was unaware of the hour, for his clock was hidden underneath his armchair's throw. The only sign of the time of day was his wife's arrival with his breakfast and morning coffee; and by the cool temperature of his bitter coffee, her appearance had long passed. He had not touched the meal because his consuming thoughts sustained him well enough. He was determined to figure out why his youngest daughter was so driven to be a part of this dark world.

He relied on Gugliehno to help him understand Amadora, but even he was riddled by her actions. The only advice he could offer was that: "The answer's in her eyes." His son's cryptic words had Basilio at a loss. He could not comprehend his meaning. He rationalized his eccentric response to being influenced by his consumption of too much bourbon.

Basilio could clearly recall every word spoken the previous night. Every word exchanged by Amadora, Elda, Gunny, and himself replayed in his mind. He relived the whole encounter all over again. The scent of alcohol, which had been in his glass during that moment, still lingered heavily in his mind. He still recalled the reflection of Amadora off his glass. Her faint-hearted expression continued to haunt him. Was his judgment correct? Was he not seeing the entire picture? Did he handle the situation well? Or was he too irrational?

A quick rapping sounded on his office door, causing him to bolt from his thoughts and back into reality.

"Yes," Basilio called to his visitor.

"Papa, it's me, Amadora. May I come in?"

"Yes. Of course."

Amadora entered and crossed the room swiftly to her father's side and kissed him respectfully on the cheek. Her loving gesture shocked Basilio; he expected her to greet him with yelling or a tearful plea for him to reconsider his decision; but she was content and warm, similar to her normal demeanor. She kept her pleasant expression as she walked around the desk and took the chair across from him.

"How are you today, Papa?" Amadora asked. Her gentle smile confused him. The way she treated him made it seem as if the encounter from the previous night did not occur.

"I'm fine. How are you?" Basilio replied observing Amadora's behavior for a hint to her reason for this sudden visit; but he could discover nothing because she did not seem to be out of the norm. She kept her normal cheery disposition with no hidden agenda from what he could gather.

"Fine, Papa. I'm just fine. I'm here to apologize for how I acted last night," Amadora smiled sincerely. "Now, I understand why you do not want me to be a part of the business, so I will stop pestering you about it."

Amadora's performance was flawless. She had to convince her father her words were sincere for her plan to work. She could not risk him growing suspicious. If he did, then he would make her plan impossible to execute.

Her words surprised him. His constant worrying could finally end, one with a satisfying ending. An enormous grin fought for control of his visage as her words echoed through his mind, but he fended it off when Amadora's gaze focused on him once more, causing them to vanish immediately.

"It's alright. I just want you to know I have my reasons. I only want what's best for you. And this life wouldn't be it," Basilio rose from his chair, walked to her side, and embraced her in his powerful hold as a cool relief washed over him. The embrace lasted only a few moments before he released her and grasped lightly to her shoulders, looking at her warmly. "You are my daughter, my youngest child. I love you more than life itself. I would die if I lost you."

"I love you too, Papa," Amadora replied, kissing her father on his cheek.

Amadora's cordial, respectful manner intrigued her father as she reasoned with him. He wanted to do something for her to make amends for being the reason behind her current dissatisfaction.

"Amadora, I realize you wanted to be a part of this world. I know you'll probably be disappointed for some time. So, please tell me if there's anything I could do to make you feel better?"

Amadora did not hesitate to voice her demands. "Papa, you do so much for me already; but I desire to get away from home for some time to clear my head."

"Get away? To where? To Italy?" Basilio asked, confused. He could not understand her desire to get away. She possessed everything she could ever want here. Why would she need to escape?

"No, not Italy. Zanipolo told me about his stay in California. It sounds like an interesting place. I want to explore the city by myself. Doing that will occupy my mind," The edges of her mouth curved, feigning genuine interest.

"You want to stay in Los Angeles with Zanipolo?"

"No. I want to stay at the beach house there by myself," She noticed her father's expression when he comprehended her words. He was tempted to say no but withdrew his immediate response after looking into her pleading eyes.

"I don't know. You'll be by yourself..." The sight of her soft brown eyes looking at him in that way made all thoughts of rejection fade away. "Maybe it would be alright if you promise me you will be careful."

Amadora exclaimed in joy and embraced her father in gratitude. "When are you considering leaving?"

"I was hoping to leave tomorrow. Since I hate goodbyes, I would like to leave before everyone else does," Amadora answered.

"Tomorrow...?" Basilio questioned, scratching his head. Her urgency made his confusion grow, but he concealed it; for it was her wish, and it was the least he could do considering the circumstances.

"Thank you... Thank you, Papa," Amadora repeatedly expressed her gratitude, tightening her embrace and kissing him gratefully on his cheeks.

"You're welcome. Now, be off. I have a lot of work to do," Basilio kissed her in return then signaled her to leave.

After leaving her father's study, Amadora went to the library. There Samantha waited patiently for her. She sat by the enormous grandfather clock, which stood tall by the window, looking over the eastside of the garden. Distracted by the book, she did not recognize Amadora's presence when she drew near. When Samantha finally noticed her, she immediately knew how Amadora's meeting with her father went. Her humongous grin of satisfaction proved Samantha's presumption. She could tell Amadora was excited because her plan was coming together.

Samantha knew it was her turn to get her parent's permission. Her mother would not be much of a challenge, but her father was a different story. Malcolm Johnson was a very stern man, who cared only about the law. Even as a retired veteran, the safety and law of the country were his top priorities. His family was second. He was not very fond of Amadora's father because he knew about his infamous reputation and dark world. He did not like his daughter being around Basilio or Amadora's siblings; but because of her friendship with Amadora and their mothers' fondness for one another, he concealed his resentment.

Carol Johnson, Samantha's mother, was more open-minded than her father. Her greatest concern was Samantha's health and happiness. If Samantha remained safe, she did not mind who she befriended. If they concealed the true reason for her trip to California, her mother would have no protests. She would be much easier to convince than her father because of her gentle, trusting nature.

"I'm guessing your father said yes," Samantha's lips curved slightly as she feigned satisfaction.

Samantha knew Amadora for years and was willing to do anything for her, no matter the dangers it entailed. She would not allow her friend to go through this plan on her own. It was too dangerous. Samantha would risk her life if it helped keep Amadora safe.

"Yes. He complied with my request, as I knew he would. That was the simple part. Now, it's time for the hard task of convincing your father, Malcolm Johnson," Amadora's smile quickly turned sour at the mention of Samantha's father. She knew very well how difficult her friend's father could be; but she needed to convince him for her plan to work. She had to gather all her charms so she could face her next enormous challenge.

No matter how much Giacinta scrubbed, Marco's presence wouldn't wash away. It lingered, leaving her feeling dirty and sick. Even when she caked her face with make-up, she still felt the pain from the bruises Marco left on her face. Looking at herself in the mirror above her sink was torture. She did not recognize herself. Anxiety, fear, despair, and disgust slowly transformed her into a monster.

Meeting with Marco extended her deadline, but she did not want to get rid of it in that way. She needed to rid herself of his hold once and for all, but how?

Since her father refused to help her, she needed to find someone willing to help her. Marco might have extended her deadline, but he was not someone to mess with.

Marco was a manager of one of Lucio Rosilli's exclusive casinos. Nothing mattered more to Marco in the entire world than his business, money, and control. His greed was his pleasure. He was extremely strict with the time he allowed for repayment of debts. If Giacinta missed this extension, Marco would not hesitate to claim the payment with her life.

Giacinta trembled at the thought of becoming one of his victims. She wrapped her robe tightly around her body to reduce the shivers rushing through her as she rushed into her room and sat by her vanity table; she looked blankly into its mirror as she reached for her brush. She brushed her hair in long even strokes as she looked over her pale expressionless face. She did not even wince when the soft bristles became entangled in her auburn locks because of her profusely trembling hand. Giacinta's fear about Marco was too great. Even though she was the daughter of New Jersey's most notorious Mafia boss, she felt there was nothing more her father or siblings could do for her. She had to find someone else to help her. She was so desperate and willing to do anything to get the money. But who would help her?

Gunny... He would not do it, especially after the incident at his home. He would pity her, and that was all. She did not need or desire his pity since it would not help her. Elda... Ha! The thought of her older sister helping her was a humorous one. Elda would rather see her suffer than help her, so she was out of the picture. Zanipolo... Giacinta could not bring herself to ask him, because she already owed him three hundred from a previous loan. The only one left. The last sibling she could ask was Amadora... She could not... She would not... She refused to ask her. Giacinta would rather accept her fate instead of asking her for help.

Amadora was the perfect child! She was the adored child! She could not do any wrong in ANYONE's eyes! Giacinta's body grew tense. Her teeth ground against one another behind her sealed lips as her anger raced through her veins. Her fingers clenched into a fist as her intense feelings took control. She hated that stupid little girl! Her father loved Amadora no matter what she did!

In a fit of frustration, Giacinta swung her arm ferociously across her vanity table, throwing everything on it to the floor. Glass, metal, and crystal breaking and clinking against the hardwood floor deafened her eardrums. She grabbed her left arm in pain as blood poured out of it and trickled down her hand. She swung her body, staggered to her bed, catching herself on her bedpost as the pain seized her body, paralyzing her.

Walking down the west corridor of the ground floor of the main house, shattering glass echoed through the halls. Casimiro sprinted towards the sound and busted into the room on the far end of the hall. Once he opened the door, his eyes drew to a figure draped over the wooden bedpost. At a distance, the figure was intelligible among the gray shadows, but as he drew near, the true form of the hunched figure became clear. It was Giacinta.

Casimiro ran to her side and wrapped his arm around her waist to help her to her feet. He looked closer at the weakened form slumped in his arms. Her skin was pale from her current condition. The blood stained the sleeve of her white robe red.

"Are you alright? You're bleeding... What happened?" Concern was prominent in his voice as Casimiro questioned her. Firm in his embrace, he cushioned her arm and examined it. He rolled up her sleeve so he could clearly see what her wound looked like and where it was.

Giacinta's blood loss made her feel faint and impaired her senses. But she felt someone holding her and opened her eyes to see who it was, but her vision blurred at first. But, after a few moments passed, her vision cleared, and she saw Casimiro looming over her.

Was she hallucinating? His touch felt real; but his figure was so extravagant that it seemed surreal. His enchanting light green eyes glowed as they traveled the length of her body, searching for something.

A few strands of light brown hair fell from their place and over his forehead as he drew her in closer. His firm grip around her body created an intense sensation inside her chest. She enjoyed his touch and embrace. She felt safe.

"Casimiro... What are you doing here?"

"I heard the commotion and came to investigate. Tell me what happened. Are you alright?" Casimiro wiped the stream of blood running down Giacinta's arm to find its source. He hid his concern behind his calm voice while he continued his observation.

"I... I fell... I fell back and my arm scraped against the glass bottles on my vanity table," Giacinta stammered as he concentrated on her injury.

Casimiro could tell Giacinta would be alright but would be light-headed from the blood loss. He secured his grip around her as he guided her to the bathroom. He brought her over to the sink and helped her grasp its edge for support while he went to retrieve a chair. When he returned with the chair and Giacinta settled in it, he grabbed a washcloth, turned on the water and soaked it. Once it was wet, Casimiro gently cleaned her arm.

While Casimiro cleaned her arm, he observed her wound closer. He could tell by the shape and depth of her wound that it was not caused by an accidental fall.

"This might sting," Casimiro warned before pouring hydrogen peroxide on her wound. He eased his grip when he noticed Giacinta flinch.

Giacinta could not understand why Casimiro was being nice to her. No one would have cared if something like this happened to her while they were around, even though no one, aside from Amadora, Samantha, and the house staff, came to this part of the manor. The thought of those obnoxious girls made her blood boil. She could not stand them. They were pathetic and annoying. She could not understand why Zanipolo spent most of his time with them.

She broke her growing anger and returned her attention towards her shining knight. Casimiro... his kindness intrigued her. She did not and could not understand him. What did he want from her? What was the real reason behind his kindness?

He was not family, at least not by blood. He had no obligations to her. So why did he care so much? It made no sense to her at all.

"Why are you doing this?" Giacinta questioned weakly.

"Doing what?" Casimiro wrapped her arm before meeting her gaze. His eyes softened as he smiled and pat her hand softly, signaling that he was finished. "There you go. Done."

"This..." Giacinta took her arm into her other hand, looked down at it, and then looked back at Casimiro. "Why are you being kind to me?"

"Why are you surprised? People can be kind. It's a normal reaction when you see someone's hurt. Anyone would've done the same thing," Casimiro flashed a reassuring smile, and Giacinta's heart fluttered.

The strange occurrence stirring within her caused confusion to seize her mind. His mesmerizing smile paralyzed her. The light streaming through the curtains enhanced his smile's warmth.

"It isn't a normal reaction, at least, not in this house. Being kind is a choice that one does only when they want something in return. It doesn't come naturally," Giacinta answered, averting her gaze to avoid the power of his eyes and their warmth.

"I don't fully agree with you about that. Kindness can be a choice, but it can also be a reasonless reaction. Just like the story of the Good Samaritan, people can do kind things just because."

"I'm not sure that's true. No one's ever helped me like you've done. You didn't have to do this for me, but you helped me with your own hands... You car..." Giacinta's words faltered when she realized her thoughts intermingled with her words. She covered her mouth with her good hand to prevent any more words from escaping her lips.

Casimiro noticed her hesitation. He did not want her to suppress her words. He wanted to know what she felt. He pulled her hand away from her mouth to free her captured words.

"Please don't stop. I want to know what you're thinking. What's wrong? How did you really get this injury?"

"What do you mean? Nothing's wrong," Giacinta turned her head, hiding her slightly flustered face with her long wavy hair. "I've already told you how this happened to me."

"That type of cut can't be caused by accident. The shape and depth of the cut indicate force was applied."

She returned her gaze to him. With that brief glance, she realized he would not leave until he knew the truth. His determination emanated from his eyes, gently hypnotizing her. His unflinching stare ensnared her, controlling her every move and preventing her from turning away. It seized her will and morphed it into its own, making her want to tell him the truth about what bothered her. From that moment on, she had to tell him the truth, because she wanted to tell him.

"I guess I should," Giacinta responded, closing her eyes to regain control over her senses. She gently removed her arm from his grasp and took a soft breath.

"You don't have to, but you'll feel better if you have someone to talk to. Trust me," Casimiro's caress was as gentle as his words. He cupped her delicate chin in his fingers and guided her gently to meet his gaze once more.

Heat rushed to Giacinta's cheeks when his fingers touched her. She felt her delicate porcelain skin become hot and flustered by the rising temperature, but she couldn't do anything to hide it from Casimiro. She was trapped once again in his grasp; and she was once again too weak to escape.

Casimiro could not hide his amazement when he noticed her reaction. She seemed innocent and sweet. This brief glimpse at her vulnerable side accentuated her beauty in his eyes, increasing his longing for her.

His touch... His words... His kindness stirred strange feelings inside her chest. She did not know why they made her feel like this. She wasn't sure if they were good. All she knew was that they made her completely vulnerable and safe at the same time.

Even though the protective air was a comfort, the vulnerability was something she could not afford to possess.

'Trust him... Easier said than done.' Giacinta conjured all the strength in her body to grab his hand and place it to the side. She held it to prevent him from interrupting her explanation. "Father probably already told you about the favor I asked him yesterday, so I probably don't need to tell you about that part."

"Yes. He did. I just don't understand why you need that much money? Don't you receive 900 dollars each month, anyway?"

"Yes, I do, but I have the same problem Zanipolo had a few years ago. Except mine isn't with a casino we own, but one run by Marco."

"Marco... Marco Pescalini! He's dangerous! You owe him money? When's your deadline?"

"I got an extension for a week after the original deadline in a few days. But I still must find some way to get the money by then. Since father cut me off, I don't know what else to do or who to turn to for help," Giacinta's throat burned as her trapped cries forced themselves to the outside world. She bit down on her lip to muffle her cries, but it was too late. Casimiro already heard them.

Casimiro recognized her fear. He felt his own heart falter as he watched a few tears fall down her cheek. Witnessing her pain, compelled a desire to scoop her into his embrace to help quell her ailments. But he refrained himself from doing so, because he wanted to help her in a more productive way instead.

"Don't worry about Marco. I'll take care of it. But I still don't understand how that led to your injury?" Casimiro stroked her hand while still in its possession and wiped a stray tear from her cheek with his other one.

"Why are you doing this? What do you want in return?" Surprise seized Giacinta along with a new type of fear, one caused by Casimiro and his actions instead of Marco. He scared her because she could not read him.

She snatched away her hand and stared at him, frozen in surprise. She could not understand this man. There was not a man alive who would do something like this without expecting something in return. So, what did he want from her?

"I'm doing this to protect you. I want nothing in return, but...." Casimiro answered.

"I knew it!" Giacinta's expression changed to one of anger. "You want something more of me! What do you want! You want me to be your sex slave and be submissive to all your desires! You want to control me and boss me around until I pay you back! What is it!"

Casimiro immediately shook his head no to all Giacinta's absurd accusations. His eyes gazed at her, surprised, and hurt, but his voice never wavered from his gentle tone. It took all his strength to contain how he truly felt at that moment, but he could tell he was not the true target for her anger and paranoia.

"No! What I was going to say, if I could finish, was stay out of casinos from now-on."

Embarrassment immediately masked over Giacinta, returning the rosy hues to her pale complexion. She covered her mouth with her hand as if by doing so would take away all the crazy assumptions she just said.

"Oh... I'm sorry. I just thought..." Giacinta paused as she reflected on the situation. "It's just hard to believe a man would do this for me out of the kindness of their heart. But I can do that."

Giacinta's expression softened while she looked into his eyes. "Please tell me... Is there anything else you want me to do?"

Casimiro's smile returned to his face once more by her words. He grabbed hold of her hand once more. "Only one more thing..." Giacinta's eyes grew wide, and her heart pounded in her chest at his touch. "Meet me in the garden tomorrow."

Giacinta blushed redder than before. Was he real? He was so generous and kind. She must be trapped in a delusion because she knew no guy who acted like him. He seemed perfect. He had to have some flaw.

Confusion seized Giacinta in response to Casimiro's sudden invitation. She feared his calm generosity and random kindness. His smile and soft gestures would trap and fool others, but Giacinta could not be so easily fooled. She could tell his actions were not as innocent as he wanted her to believe, but she was not sure how she could prove she was right.

He was genuinely perfect with no flaws. From his handsome features to his charming personality, everything about him seemed genuine, but she could tell the moment their eyes met that there was something else he wanted. She saw a small fire of desire burning in the deep corners of his emerald eyes. He wanted something else from her but was hesitant to tell her.

Anxiety grew like a wildfire inside Giacinta for the revelation of Casimiro's hidden desire. She wanted to uncover the truth so she could pull down the veil of his kind facade. She wanted him to show her his true colors, so he could prove the fact that never failed being true. That there was not a man alive on this earth who would do something without wanting something in return. She would not stop until she discovered his true intentions.

"Yes, of course. When should I meet you?" Giacinta answered, accepting his peculiar request warily.

"I will leave a note under your door an hour before the appointed time. Just make sure you check your room frequently if you leave," Casimiro brought her hand to his lips and kissed it softly before leaving. Flustered and confused, Giacinta could not utter a word in response. She only nodded when his eyes fell upon her one last time. Slight amusement returned to his lips in response to her answer.

Giacinta's body became paralyzed once more when his emerald eyes fell upon her one last time and his lips parted to voice his last words. "Until tomorrow."

When the car pulled up to Samantha's block, Amadora's eyes were drawn to her best friend's home because of its cheerful appearance. The small two floor colonial was painted in summery yellows and greens with bold ivory rectangular windows scattered lightly around its perimeter. The gray cement walkway leading to its small chestnut door was lined with colorful late summer blooms of reds and magentas. Everything seemed very inviting as they traversed down the walk, but the cheerful facade faded when they crossed the threshold of the ivory archway in front of the door.

Before Samantha even touched the doorknob, a shiver shot down Amadora's spine, and her friend was just as wary. This was not the first time Amadora noticed her friend's hesitation about returning home. Every time her friend neared the vicinity of her neighborhood, a dark shadow swallowed up her warm demeanor. The cause for her friend's strange reaction was a mystery to Amadora.

She was unaware of the identities of the shadows looming over the Johnson household, but she sensed their presence the moment she crossed the threshold. As she entered the dark hallway, she recognized the actual forms of the dark specters haunting the Johnsons' home. Loneliness, fear and pain were the culprits plaguing the house. By just taking one breath inside the shadow-filled home, she suffocated from the intense, lingering emotions.

Their presence affected her emotions, sending them and her reactions into a frenzy. She fought hard to prevent the spontaneous tears from flowing freely, which formed for unknown reasons regarding the dark secrets trapped within these walls, a dark secret filled with a great sorrow.

Amadora wanted to know the source of the sorrow, but its frightening hold pressed intensely on her friend's lips and heart. It kept them firmly sealed from revealing the truth to any outsiders. Realizing this, Amadora could do nothing but keep her own worries hidden and hope that one day her friend would find the strength and trust to confide in her.

Amadora walked cautiously behind Samantha as they entered the shadows of the living room. While they crossed the light carpet, they noticed a broad shadow lurking in the room's corner. When their footsteps hit the carpet, the dark figure turned its attention towards them. At the sight of them, the figure crossed the room towards where the two girls stood paralyzed.

The few rays of sunlight streaming through the blinds revealed a vague silhouette of a man. His figure was impressive, towering over the girls as he drew near. His build was fierce, just like his facial features. Piercing ice-blue eyes cut through the shadows as they focused on the girls.

Samantha immediately switched on the lights as he stopped in front of her. In the light, she saw his features better. They were rigid and strong; and his eyes emanated with intensity even though he looked at her in a soft nature. His golden hair was slicked neatly back, revealing his handsome features. She did not know who this man was, but there was something about him that seemed familiar to her. But she did not know what fueled this feeling.

"Excuse me. Who are you? And why are you lurking around my home?"

The man smiled crookedly as he took her hand in his, and gently brought it to his lips, kissing it softly. Samantha was too captivated by his handsome features and hypnotized by his intense eyes to take away her hand. "You must be Samantha. Your parents told me many things about you."

His charming behavior astonished Samantha. His voice was deep and brooding, but he had a strange foreign accent. It was not very thick, so it was very hard for her to detect at first; but when he said certain words, it was noticeable.

"Good things. I hope," Samantha answered partially to herself, observing him while she tried to decipher where her mystery visitor was from.

"Oh yes. They say only good things. They are very proud of you," His crooked smile widened as he responded. He spoke a few foreign words before introducing himself in English. "I'm Baldemar Diederich. I'm a friend of your father. I'm waiting for him to return from the garage, then I'm leaving. I'm sorry if I scared you, ladies."

"It's okay, Mr. Diederich. You only surprised us. You say you are a friend of my father? Why have I never met you before?" Samantha answered respectfully.

Baldemar noticed her suspicions towards him. He was about to respond to lessen them but hesitated when someone walked into the room behind the girls. Samantha noticed his hesitation and followed the path of his eyes to discover the cause of it. When she turned around, she saw the colossal figure of her father, Malcolm Johnson.

His broad stature loomed over the girls as he blocked the entrance. His eyes directed a sharp glare at Baldemar. The tension in the room intensified as he focused all his attention towards his guest. His green eyes emanated with annoyance and warning toward Baldemar. Samantha was unaware of the reason for her father's reaction, but she could tell Mr. Diederich's visit had ended; and she would not get the answers to her many questions.

"Diederich, here's the money I owe you," Samantha's father stretched out his hand and handed a large rectangular envelope to Mr. Diederich. "I expect I won't see you again until next month."

Mr. Diederich shook his head in response, picked up his hat, then took his leave. Her father walked his visitor to his car, following swiftly behind him as he walked out of the house. As soon as they left the room, the girls ran across to the windows and peeked out to the front yard.

They noticed the irritation and anger radiating from Samantha's father as he followed briskly behind Mr. Diederich. His deep voice boomed with harsh foreign words. Surprise seized the girls as they watched the two men exchange venomous words in a foreign tongue. Amadora listened carefully to their heated exchange; and after a few brief moments, she recognized the dialect and origin of their mysterious language.

"It's German," Amadora announced in a soft tone filled with surprise. "They are speaking German. I've only heard it a few times while in Europe, but I remember the pronunciation of the words and the dialect."

She turned her gaze towards her friend as she continued. "Sam, I did not know your dad spoke German."

Samantha met her gaze and instantly Amadora could tell by the emotion imbedded in her eyes that her friend was just as surprised as she was.

"I didn't know either."

It was not a secret that Malcolm Johnson was a patriot to the very core. There were many times he expressed his extreme dislike for anyone of German descent or immigrants from the country. He served in both the first and second world wars. His experience in the wars left a bitterness in his heart for Germans. He expressed his dislike often and publicly, so this new discovery about her father shocked Samantha.

It made her wonder how much she knew about her father. They did not have a close relationship like Amadora and her father. Theirs was one of cordial respect. They communicated more like acquaintances than family, so she knew little about her father or any of the secrets he might be hiding.

The way her father treated Mr. Diederich only confirmed Samantha's beliefs about her father's stand with Germans, but there was something about their exchange that made doubts stir inside her. The way they argued with one another seemed more familiar than Mr. Diederich made it appear.

She wondered about the truth behind their relationship as Mr. Diederich left in a huff, slammed his car door, and tore out of the driveway and down the street. Her wondering thoughts halted when she saw her father returning to the house. She drew the blinds shut, grabbed Amadora's arm, and dragged her to the couch opposite the window.

Samantha slowed her breathing when she heard the front door open and close. The girls sat firmly erect while his heavy footsteps strode into the living room. His stern features broke for a moment to produce a small imitation of a smile after he focused his attention on Amadora and Samantha.

"Amadora, it's been a while since I've seen you here. How have you been?"

"It has been a while. I've been fine. How have you and Carol been?" Amadora matched his smile with a warm one of her own.

"I've been good. I work at a construction site in Jersey City to help keep myself busy and support my family. Other than that, I've been alright," Malcolm walked to a dusty dark-green armchair in the room's corner and sat down before continuing.

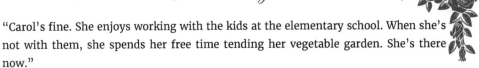

"Carol's fine. She enjoys working with the kids at the elementary school. When she's not with them, she spends her free time tending her vegetable garden. She's there now."

"That's great to know you are doing well," Amadora's smile grew as she responded.

"May I ask why you're visiting us today? Not that I don't enjoy your company, but I can tell by the look on Sammy's face that you aren't here for a social call," Malcolm took his big wooden pipe from off the side table and lit it, while he spoke.

Amadora glanced over at her friend to see the meaning of his words. Amadora noticed Samantha's transparency immediately by her downcast expression. Her behavior screamed that she wanted something but was too afraid to ask. Amadora wanted to nudge her friend to signal her to regain her composure; but she had to restrain herself because she felt Malcolm watching her every move.

"Well, Malcolm, I had a minor disagreement with my father and want to get away for a while I'm going to our vacation home in California. I would like your and Carol's permission to allow Sam to join me," Amadora returned her gaze toward Samantha's father. Her charming smile returning to diffuse his suspicions.

"California, huh? Who's going with you?" Malcolm pried, taking a big puff on his pipe and scanning Amadora with unwavering intent.

An ice-cold sensation ran up the lining of her spine as he examined her. It was clear he was searching for a weakness in her and her intentions. She relaxed her resolve, staying mindful of every action and reaction so not to expose her true intentions. She feared that if she even breathed wrong, it would reveal her true intentions.

"Samantha and Giacinta."

"Giacinta. That's the middle daughter, right?" Amadora nodded in response, confirming his inquiry. She examined him with care, trying to find any clue of which answer he leaned towards, but there was nothing. He was expressionless and unreadable. "I don't mind her. She's charming."

Small grins of mockery and amusement crossed Amadora's and Samantha's faces in response to his words. They knew the real reason Malcolm favored Giacinta, and it had nothing to do with her charms. He liked her solely because she had nothing to do with the family "business" like Amadora's other siblings.

"Daddy, can I go?" Samantha pressed. Her expression lightened into one of hopeful enthusiasm. She did not know how her father would answer, but she prayed for Amadora's sake it would be in her favor.

Malcolm's intense green eyes fell upon his daughter, scanning her thoroughly while he puffed on his pipe. His gaze did not last long before closing them to ponder on their request. A few minutes passed in silence with no answer. After ten minutes, he took one last puff, replaced his pipe upon the table, and then shook his head in approval.

"I'd normally say no but having you out of the house would benefit me. I want to make a few renovations, so with you gone should help it run more smoothly. You can go."

The girls exchanged brief expressions of shock and disbelief, before they transformed into gleaming smiles of gratitude. Samantha leaped out of her seat, crossed the room, and kissed her father on his cheek. She expressed her gratitude along with Amadora. The two girls rushed towards the door, returning to the car, but a booming call from the living room stopped them.

"Wait... Don't forget to tell your mother," The girls stopped, flashed sheepish smiles towards Malcolm and dashed in the opposite direction towards the backyard.

As soon as dinner ended, Basilio invited all his children, except Amadora and Giacinta, to his office for an important announcement. Elda, Gugliehno, Casimiro, and Zanipolo arrived at his office one after the other; however, instead of being greeted by their father's presence, they were greeted by an empty study painted by the yellow light of the tall clam shell lamps in the corners of the room. Confusion plagued the group as they claimed their desired places.

"Casimiro, do you know what my father wants to tell us?" Gugliehno asked, turning in his chair to his friend, who was standing behind him next to the fireplace, eyeing his watch.

Casimiro shrugged his shoulders. "No. I don't. He only told me to gather everyone here."

"In other words, you know as much as we do. Absolutely nothing," Zanipolo retorted grimly, sipping the rest of the bourbon in his glass while he reclined in the armchair. He swirled the contents of his glass, when he finished his drink, in the hopes it would calm his wondering thoughts.

While their focuses were elsewhere, the study door swung open, and their father glided into the room, holding a bottle of Dom Perignon and four glasses. He beamed with excitement, so much that he almost danced across the room to his desk. The don's strange behavior took aback everyone. They watched him in surprise as he placed the glasses on the desk.

"I have splendid news, my children! All our worries about Amadora are over!" He popped off the cork and poured the bottle's contents into the glasses.

Shock seized the entire room causing silence to fall upon the group. Gugliehno stared at his father; his eyes frozen wide as his father's words translated inside Gugliehno's mind. He could not believe what he was hearing. Amadora gave up. No. Impossible. There was no way the fire he saw in her eyes last night subsided so soon. Was there more to this sudden change? Or did he just overestimate her?

"Why is that? What's changed, Papa?" Elda questioned, breaking the silence while handing a glass to Zanipolo and Casimiro.

"She came to me this morning to apologize and declare she'd give up on her foolish quest," Basilio turned to Zanipolo, gleaming with triumph and pride raising his glass in salutation. "Whatever you said to her must've worked. Thank you."

Confusion took over Zanipolo while he acknowledged his father with the same gesture. Zanipolo said nothing out of the ordinary. He only asked his sister to give up on her suicidal desire, and, apparently, she listened to him. He could not whole-heartedly accept his father's gratitude, because he harbored a lingering doubt. The solution came too easily. Amadora gave-in too easily. Amadora never gave up, at least, not without a fight. But what was her next move? What was her plan?

"Zanipolo, whatever you said also convinced her to visit our beach house in California for a while," Zanipolo felt all eyes in the room fall upon him as his father continued his joyful announcement. He wanted to shrink further into his chair, but it paralyzed him. It was only when Elda interrupted their father's announcement did the attention shift.

"Why would she want to go there?" Elda sipped on her drink, observing her father for some sign of what was really going on.

Elda sensed something else was going on, but she did not know what it was. Her father said these arrangements were at Amadora's request; but were they really? She could not help suspecting her father was behind it. He would do anything to keep Amadora far from their world, even if it meant shipping her clear across the country. But if his words were true, then Elda suspected there might be more to her little sister's request than she let on.

"I don't know and could not care less as long as it keeps her mind off our business. I want you, Zanipolo, to keep your distance," Basilio pulled out a cigar, cut the tip, lit it and then placed the box on the desk to share with the others. When he was settled, he leaned against his desk and focused his attention on his oldest son. "And you, Gunny, I want you to arrange the flight. She'll leave tomorrow at noon."

The room fell into silence again. Everyone was too shocked to respond or protest. They suspected there was more to Amadora's immediate departure than how it appeared; but no one could figure out what. They were helpless. They could only sit back, follow orders, and pray their suspicions were wrong.

3

The Switch

'My fear is a thick darkness shrouding my heart with hopelessness and paranoia. But with him, a light I've never known dispels my fear, allowing me to find hope and peace. Is it possible for a man to create a feeling like this? Or is this feeling just a hallucination of my desires?' Thoughts of Giacinta Morelli.

C asimiro parked his black sedan in front of a small brownstone by Journal Square. He got out of his car, walked to the blue door, and rang the bell next to it. Ten minutes passed before a man in a black suit opened the door, looked over Casimiro's business card and showed him inside. The man guided Casimiro through the narrow hall and into a kitchen in the back of the house. When Casimiro entered, he saw three men sitting around a table eating breakfast and speaking in Italian. They stopped momentarily when they saw him, then the largest of the men smiled and waved Casimiro over. Casimiro nodded and smiled as he walked over to the table. He withheld the urge to take a deep breath as he clutched onto the large white envelope in his hand.

"Casimiro, I was surprised to get a call to meet from the Morellis' consigliere. I thought I was in trouble and did something wrong," Then man said, looking at the envelope in his hand.

"Marco, we've might have our problems before, but today I come in peace. I'm not here to settle a matter for my don, but for his daughter," Casimiro replied.

"Basilio Morelli's daughter? Which one could you mean? His merciless older one, Elda? His beautiful middle one, Giacinta? Or his pure youngest daughter, Amadora?" Marco looked around, feigning to recall which daughter he had business with. The flippant way he discussed the girls irritated Casimiro. He wanted to punch him but refrained from doing so for the sake of the family. Marco was an important asset to the Rosilli family. Going after him would spark an unnecessary war and needless bloodshed. Casimiro forced a cordial smile across his lips and held out the envelope.

"This should cover *Giacinta's* debt. Refrain from having any more contact with her from now-on," Casimiro stressed.

Marco took the envelope, opened it, and quickly flipped through the contents. A large ogre-like grin painted his face.

"Sure. I'm done with her, anyway."

Casimiro did not listen to the second part of Marco's response. He already tore out the house and headed back to his car. He accomplished his goal and saved Giacinta from Marco's grasp. Now, he was worried if he could make sure she kept her part of the bargain, so she did not wind up in this predicament again.

The morning of Amadora's departure arrived faster than she expected. Her father made haste preparations. He handed her the plane tickets at breakfast and informed her he arranged for her to have an escort, Gugliehno.

When her father informed her of this new condition to her spontaneous getaway, Amadora felt her entire world crack around her. With her brother bringing her to the airport and babysitting her until her plane boarded, her entire plan would be impossible to execute. She understood why her father took these precautions, since kidnapping her would be a marvelous prize for any of his rivals; but these conditions hindered her entire operation. Gunny was keen, especially when it dealt with protecting his sister. She could not risk going forward with her plan while he shadowed her. She needed to lose her protective shadow, but how?

Losing her brother or asking him to restrict his escort was going to be an arduous task. Gunny would never disobey a direct order from their father, especially one concerning her safety. Coming up with a way to make him reconsider his code of conduct would be the greatest challenge of her day. Finding a solution for this challenge would be difficult; but she had confidence she could resolve it when the time came.

Amadora went over her plan once again in her mind. She made sure Samantha made all the preparations for their switch at the airport. Samantha asked her father for money to buy a bus ticket to New York when she arrived at the airport. Samantha would also bring an empty suitcase for Amadora to use while she was in the city. It would help to store any clothes she bought for her charade.

Amadora coordinated everything from their actions to their clothes. Even though she had little time to plan, Amadora spent most of the night meticulously combing through every detail and step that needed to be accomplished before she reached her goal. She reviewed every probable outcome that could spawn from their actions and devised multiple solutions to diffuse them. She refused to let anything, or anyone get in her way and stop her from reaching her heart's greatest desire, not even her family.

Her older brother, Zanipolo, would be Amadora's greatest risk. She kept him at bay with her father's orders, but she had a lingering doubt that he would not obey them for long. Unlike Gunny, Zanipolo followed their father's orders to a certain point. He would find and use some loophole in them to do what he wanted. He would probably give Samantha her privacy but monitor her from afar. Suspecting this, Amadora packed outfits that required broad-brimmed hats. The hats would help to obscure his vision of Samantha's details, fooling him from a distance. There was someone else she needed to fool, Gugliehno.

If she could convince her eldest brother to watch her from a distance, then she needed an outfit that could capture his attention and obscure it at the same time. For this purpose, she picked out a long flowing lime-green summer dress and a large straw hat with a green ribbon tied around it. Amadora knew this outfit would keep her brother's attention even after the switch. To assure her brother wouldn't notice her after they switched, she told Samantha to wear her old catholic school uniform. It was a plain navy and plaid dress with a large navy hat with a white ribbon. Once the switch was done, Amadora would leave as Samantha; and Samantha would board the plane to California.

The first part of Amadora's plan was ready to be put into action. She hoped she could convince her brother to change his watch. Succeeding to do so or not was crucial. It would determine the early success of her plan. She refused to let anyone spoil her plans this early, especially her brother.

The drive to the airport seemed longer than it actually was because of the lingering silence. Amadora's mind raced with various thoughts, mainly on how to convince Gunny to relieve her of his overbearing shadow. Many possibilities floated around her head, but only one seemed plausible for this moment. She needed to use her charms to convince her brother.

When their car pulled in front of Newark Liberty Airport, one of her father's men opened her door. She stepped out of the car with the swiftest of ease and circled the rear, attempting to retrieve her bags before her brother did. Unfortunately, her brother was quicker than her. He already had her suitcases in his possession. She extended her hands to retrieve her bags from him, but Gunny pulled them away from her, grinning in amusement of her actions.

"Che cosa è il problema, Dorina?" Gunny questioned playfully. (What is the problem, Dora?) "Perché hai in fretta? Hai molto tempo." (Why are you in a hurry? You have much time.

"I'm not in a hurry, big brother. I just wanted to carry my own bags and don't want you to carry them for me," Amadora answered through a polite smile, attempting to mask her lies.

"Bugie (Lies). You know I don't mind carrying them for you. There's another reason behind your actions," His eyes were warm and gentle, but she sensed a prying intensity hidden deep inside them.

Amadora realized it would be impossible lying to her brother. She needed to tell him the truth, at least, close enough to it to persuade him. She matched his warm expression with a delicate one of her own.

"I feel uneasy having you and your entourage babysitting me until my flight boards."

"Babysitting? You know very well we're only monitoring you for your own safety. What's the matter with you? You've never minded my company before."

Amadora felt her brother's growing suspicions in response to her request. His gaze inspected her while trying to find the truth behind her actions. Amadora turned her head slightly, letting her hat conceal her eyes. She kept her air of dignity and pride, masking her frantic nerves as she gathered all her strength to continue with her charade.

"I normally don't mind it when we are in a more intimate setting. Here is different. Having all of you surrounding me like this, will draw too much attention," Amadora began returning her gaze to her brother. Her eyes pleading as she continued with a hint of exhaustion.

"I asked father for this trip to relax and keep my mind away from this world. No offense, Gunny; but I can't do that with you and your men shadowing me."

Gunny recognized the emotions emanating from his sister. It was clear she was more affected by the other night than their father made it appear. He remained silent for a moment while handing her the suitcases. Guilt made it impossible for him to deny her.

"Fine. We'll keep our distance; but I won't leave until you're safe on your plane. Your safety is my top priority, but I guess I can adjust my orders to make you more comfortable," Gunny kissed Amadora's forehead and waited at the foot of the stairs before following behind her.

Arriving on the second floor, where passengers waited to board their flights, Amadora scanned the vast terminal. Her sharp eyes glided over the multiple forms crowding around until they finally fell upon a plain but familiar silhouette sitting on the far end of the room. It was the woman's navy plaid uniform and matching beret that caught her eye. The style, although simple to the common eye, was unique among the variety of American apparel worn by the other passengers.

To someone familiar to the fashion, it was an obvious Parisian-style uniform. It was rare, especially considering where they were. Also, the coat of arms, growing clearer as she crossed the room, was unforgettable. It had the insignia of one of Paris's most prestigious and exclusive girl's high school.

One that many applied to, but they only accepted a select few girls. She highly doubted any other girls attended the school in the area, but one, Samantha. Samantha's top grades impressed *La Colombe Academy* the summer before her junior year of highschool. She passed the entrance exam with flying colors and accepted immediately. The only problem she had was paying tuition.

Her family had only enough to pay half of what they required for her tuition. Her father refused to get any loans from the bank and Amadora's father's help when he offered to pay off the rest free of charge.

It was only with the cunning actions of Mrs. Johnson that they could finance the rest of Samantha's tuition. By lying to her husband and convincing him the money came from a grant Samantha earned, Mrs. Johnson accepted Amadora's parents' generous gift, allowing her daughter to study there for two years.

The uniqueness of her uniform was the exact reason she told Samantha to wear it. It would be plain to anyone who saw it and would attract minimal attention, except for Amadora. Its unique style and insignia were immediately recognizable to her.

Amadora moved with grace while crossing the final distance between her and Samantha. Her friend's intense focus on the charms dangling from her wrist shrouded her from Amadora's presence. Amadora set her luggage beside her and sat in the chair next to Samantha.

Someone's arm brushing against Samantha's roused her from her daydream. She looked over at her neighbor and instant relief washed over her. She recognized the person right away but adjusted herself in a way, so, no one watching her could notice her lips moving.

"I've been waiting for a half an hour. What took you so long?"

Amadora took a brief glance around to map out where Gunny and his men were positioned. She lowered her head and fixed her broad brim hat, hiding her mouth from her distant guards.

"My father ordered Gunny to be my escort. I had to wait while they went over their regular safety precautions before leaving," She sighed as she recalled how difficult the morning had been waiting on her brother and his men. "It took me a while to get him to agree to give me some distance. We lost a lot of time already. If we're going to act, we must do it now. You head into the restroom, and I'll join you in five minutes."

Samantha grabbed her suitcase and rushed off to the ladies' room. Amadora followed her friend's movements with her peripheral until she disappeared behind a tall gray door. She scanned the room to see if her brother reacted to Samantha's movements. To her good fortune, he was too busy engulfed in conversation with one of his men to notice. She used this brief distraction to sneak into the bathroom.

Amadora walked into the restroom with a large grin plastered on her face. She embraced and kissed her friend as her excitement grew. "It's really happening, Sammy. I can't believe it."

Samantha hugged her back and forced a small smile in compliance to Amadora's joy, but her own feelings were far from the same. Doubt plagued her, but she suppressed it for her friend's sake.

"I don't know why you're excited. From this moment forward, things will be ridiculously hard for you, Dora. You'd better become serious. What you're doing is perilous. Someone might get hurt or worse."

Amadora released Samantha from her hold, and her smile melted away. "I know, Sam. Don't you think I understand all the risks involved? I'm excited not because I'm underestimating them, but because the reward for overcoming those obstacles will be worth any trouble and pain I face."

Samantha forced another false guise of understanding after hearing her friend's explanation. But Amadora's words could not quell the concern and doubt raging in her. She feared her friend did not understand the dangers awaiting them. The visions of her foolish desire blinded her.

Samantha did not tell her friend her concerns, because she promised to help her friend in her dangerous quest and refused to go back on her word. Amadora motioned towards the bathroom stalls, so they could switch clothes. Amadora walked into one stall, and Samantha chose a stall beside hers.

Five minutes passed, and Samantha walked out dressed in Amadora's dress and hat. She grabbed her bags, left the room, and headed towards her plane, which had boarded. Before she left the waiting area, Samantha turned around towards Gunny and waved goodbye.

Samantha's nerves did not settle as she boarded the airplane. She was afraid they would discover Amadora while she waited for her bus to New York since her bus would not arrive for another 20 minutes. Anything could happen while she waited for that amount of time. She prayed Amadora would manage in that time.

Amadora left the bathroom ten minutes after Samantha left. She looked around the terminal for her brother and his men, but they already left. Amadora felt relief wash over her. Her ruse worked, and the first phase of her plan was complete with no complications.

Giacinta woke up early because she was filled with anxiety and caution. She was excited to receive Casimiro's note telling her where and when they will meet. However, she was wary about his true intentions for helping her.

She did not believe he helped her solely out of the goodness of his heart. He was a man. Men were selfish creatures by nature. They only did things according to their own benefit. It was a rarity when they did selfless acts as if they were capable. She was not entirely convinced he was capable of such acts.

Giacinta grew up with Casimiro. She saw his closeness to her older siblings, Elda, and Gunny; even before her parents took him in when he was in high school. Everyone trusted and loved him as family; even so, Giacinta knew little about who he was or his actual personality outside the formal persona he always had towards her. Who was this person who her parents called son and her older siblings treated like a brother? Could she really trust his word that he would resolve her problem while wanting nothing in return?

No. That could not be true. No one who was involved in that dark world could be trusted, especially no one who continuously put on false airs when interacting with others. He had to be as crooked and disloyal as everyone else involved in her father's profession. He was a lawyer, for god's sake. Their entire purpose was to lie, to win their cases. It was impossible for someone in his line of work not to do something quid pro quo.

Her doubts about him multiplied and controlled her mind. A part of her was reluctant to accept his request to meet because of these doubts, but she was desperate. If he helped her get rid of Marco, she had no choice but to meet with him.

Giacinta looked over at herself in the mirror. She looked plain compared to how she normally dressed. She wore minimal makeup, had her long hair pulled into a loose bun with a few free strands framing her face and wore her favorite fuchsia dress, hoping its flattering hug on her figure would distract her plain appearance. She fixed the belt around her waist while fighting to maintain her thoughts.

Her concerns about Casimiro would not give her a moment's rest. Could he really be as generous and selfless as he seemed? She was not sure how genuine he was and was determined to find out his true intentions no matter what.

After Samantha's flight landed, she retrieved her baggage and headed to the new arrival's area. Amadora told her Zanipolo would send someone to take her to the beach house. This made her nervous because she was not sure if Zanipolo's men would see through her disguise. Amadora assured her that she had not met any of his men, but her reassurance could not qualm Samantha's worries.

When she reached the new arrival's area, she saw a tall, skinny man in cork-bottle glasses waving a sign with Amadora written on it. He was plain. His facial structure was youthful, making it impossible for her to determine his age. His short, light brown hair stressed his prepubescent appearance. He was dressed casually in black pants and a green shirt with prints of tropical leaves. He did not recognize her when she walked over to him. This helped quell her fears.

She waved at him, and he came running over to her side and picked up her luggage. "You must be Miss Amadora Morelli," he greeted her with a warm smile. His voice complimented his appearance with its high-pitched, nasally tone. "I'm Arnold. Mr. Zanipolo sent me to drive you to the beach house."

"Nice to meet you, Arnold. Are you new?"

"Correct, miss. It's my second week working for your brother," Arnold responded, turning from her and guiding her to his car parked in front of the airport.

Samantha waited beside the car while he struggled to put her suitcases in the trunk. Samantha fought back the urge to laugh. Arnold seemed too innocent, young, and weak to be in Zanipolo's employ. Zanipolo had little patience for his work and those he worked with. Samantha doubted he had the patience to work with someone like Arnold. Imagining him carrying out jobs for Zanipolo was a comedic thought.

"I heard he can be a strict boss. How do you like working with my brother?" Samantha questioned, opening the back door of the car and entering.

"I'm only his errand boy," Arnold answered, entering and starting the vehicle.

"You don't work with Zanipolo yet?" Samantha admired the palm-lined streets they drove down. The tranquil vision of the ocean captivated her. Californians seemed more carefree than Jerseyans as they went about their daily lives. Samantha envied the locals somewhat because she wanted to experience that type of peace.

"No. I haven't worked with him directly. I take orders from his right-hand man. I only have contact with Zanipolo when I drive him somewhere. And even then, he doesn't talk. He keeps to himself."

After a log bus ride, Amadora finally arrived at her destination. New Yorkers and tourists packed Herald Square station. Amadora ignored the hustle and bustle as she navigated the crowds towards the exit. She found herself absorbed in thought while she raced for the exit.

It relieved her to be on stationary ground once more. Being cramped in a bus for nearly an hour was uncomfortable on its own; but Amadora was stuck assisting a woman lull her baby to sleep while she tended to her other three children. Her charitable act left no time for Amadora to relax or contemplate on the next phase of her plan. She had a broad idea of what was to be done next; but as her feet touch the Manhattan sidewalk, her ideas faded.

Anxiety captured her as she scanned the crowd of taxis for her ride. Her eyes rested upon a blonde woman, who appeared to be in her thirties, standing beside a tall teenage boy. The woman held up a small white sign with the words "Rosa Bianca" written on it. Immediately, Amadora recognized her. It was Amadora's friend, Anna Bernini.

The unique sign Anna held was a part of their arrangement to hide Amadora's identity from on lookers. Even the plain gray dress, black sunglasses and hat Anna wore were all parts of Amadora's plan. Just because Samantha went to California dressed as Amadora did not mean she could not be recognized by one of her father's men in New York. Unlike with Gunny's or Elda's men, Amadora's face was well known by her father's men. New York City was the center of her father's business empire.

Most of his men were stationed in Manhattan, while some worked with Gugliehno's men in the boroughs. It was a risk for her to walk about the city undisguised when any of her father's men could recognize her at any moment. That's why Gunny's circuit was easier to penetrate and assured she could rise quicker amongst its ranks.

Gugliehno ran his circuit on merit and skill. The more skilled one was the higher chance they had of becoming an asset and promoted to important jobs. If someone completed some of those more difficult and important jobs, they gained favor among the top ranks of Gunny's circuit and a chance to gain respect from Gunny himself.

Amadora planned each step she needed to take to rise higher in the ranks. She also prepared for any hiccups that might come her way. So, even though she was annoyed when she saw Anna's son, Ricky, with her at the station, she did not express her emotions and remained cordial.

Anna looked like a model in her form-fitting gray dress, her short, curly golden blonde bob, tilted large-brimmed sun hat, and her captivating beauty stunned anyone who passed her. Her oval face, narrow chin, sharp almond-shaped gray eyes, golden brown skin and full red lips intensified the mesmerizing air around her. Even though she had a teenage son, she had a youthful appearance that made her look ten years younger than she was.

"Amadora, it's been a long time since I've seen you. We've much to talk about." Anna motioned her to the car where Ricky stood.

Ricky was very tall for his age. He was only thirteen and like his mother had silver eyes. He was extremely shy when meeting new people, especially girls. So, when Amadora stood next to him while his mother unlocked the door, Ricky tried to hide his face with his hat.

"Hi, Ricky, how are you?" Amadora smiled at Ricky when he opened her door.

"Fine," Ricky quickly opened the backdoor and went inside. Amadora shot a concerned look at Anna. Anna knew right away what was on her mind, just smiled, and then started the engine.

"Don't worry about Ricky, Dora. He's a good boy. He won't tell a soul. Your secret is safe," Anna tried to say as few things as possible in case anyone around here worked for Gunny.

Anna knew everything she needed to know about Amadora's plan. She knew she was supposed to get Amadora a job with a soldier as an associate. She also knew she was supposed to provide a house and meal for her. Anna normally would charge but owed her life to Amadora; and because of her loyalty, she would do whatever she could to help Amadora on her mission, even if it went against everything she stood for.

When Giacinta returned from lunch, there was a note on the floor in her room just as he promised. Giacinta shut the door behind her and picked up the note. She trembled while holding the note. 'I can't believe it. He actually kept his word.' She looked down at her quivering hands. 'Why am I shaking? He's no different from any typical guy. Why am I acting like this?'

Giacinta walked to her desk chair and opened the note. His scent lingered on folds of the envelope. The smell made it feel like he stood next to her as she read the thin paper.

"Giacinta, you promised me you'd meet me in the garden, and I'll wait there for you. Come quickly. I'll only wait two hours after I've delivered this message."

Giacinta pressed the note to her chest and took a deep breath, then put it into her pocket and left for the garden.

When Giacinta reached the garden, she did not see him at first; but as she walked deeper into the garden, she noticed a man standing in front of the orchids. He wore a gray suit and hat. She could barely see his light brown hair under his hat.

Casimiro turned around towards the sound of approaching footsteps. When he noticed Giacinta, he could not help but smile. She was so breathtaking.

Giacinta looked like a goddess with her long brown hair flowing over the long fuchsia dress she wore. Her body's soft curves showed with great definition through the delicate embrace of her dress. Her eyes were made from the sky itself. They were an ocean of blue. Their hypnotizing stare drew him in.

He walked over to her and reached for her hand to kiss it. "Giacinta, you came. I was worried you wouldn't."

Giacinta tried not to blush when he kissed her hand. She smiled and looked away. "Of course, I came. I promised you I would, and I wouldn't break it since you helped me yesterday."

Casimiro let go of her hand and smiled his enchanting smile. Then he held out his arm so he could escort her through the garden. Giacinta never really took the time to sit and admire the garden before; so, when she was with him, she noticed its beauty for the very first time.

When she walked with him in the garden, it felt like a new world. The flowers grew a centimeter more with every heartbeat. With every step they took, a new flower bloomed. Giacinta could not understand the new feeling racing through her veins. Was it the feeling her grandmother used to tell her about in her stories?

Casimiro stopped in front of a bench, and they sat down, surrounded by the serenity and silence of the sweet September air. He put his hand on top of hers and smiled softly. "I have good news."

"What?" Giacinta asked anxiously.

"I took care of your problem with Marco. You are no longer in his debt."

Giacinta could not believe Casimiro's words. He did it. He took care of her problem. She did not know whether to be happy or suspicious. It was too good to be true. There had to be something he was hiding. Something had to be wrong with him. One minor fault. Anything. What was it he wanted?

"You 'took care of it'?" Giacinta emphasized, looking at him suspiciously.

"Yes. I paid it off. You won't have to worry about it again as long as you keep your promise," Casimiro laughed softly. He noticed her expression and stopped laughing. "Why are you looking at me like that?"

"I'm sorry... I'm very grateful, but I can't believe you kept your word," Casimiro's smile changed when she said that. She ignored his expression and continued. "You are too good to be true. What is it you want from me?"

"I already told you why I'm doing this and what I want," Casimiro dropped his arm to his side, and she let go of his hand.

"There must be something else you want. What is it?"

"You're right. There is something else. But it's not what you probably hope it is. It's something different," Casimiro grimaced. His eyes lost their shine as they gazed at her.

"What is it?"

"You're not ready for me to tell you. When you are, I'll tell you," With that said Casimiro stood up and smiled wryly at her. "Well, I have to go see what your father wants done for today. I've spent enough time away. He might get worried."

Before he turned away, Giacinta stood and grabbed his arm. She held him for a moment, then gave him a kiss on the cheek. "Thank you. I'm truly grateful. I'm in your debt," Casimiro patted her hand softly, smiled then walked away.

When Sam arrived at the beach house, she could not believe how exquisite the house was. It towered over all the other houses nearby. It was the most enchanting place on the block. A black iron gate that was the base for grape vines that curled in between its bars protected it. She walked through the gates to be greeted by the smell of fresh oranges and other fruits. White flowers greeted her as they lined their way to the humongous bronze door at the end of the jade stone path.

As Sam looked at the carvings on the door, Arnold pulled a string on the side of the door, causing a loud bell to ring. Moments later, Sam was face to face to a tall man with slicked back hair and a mustache that curled at the ends. His smile was less than inviting. It was very intimidating and ridiculing. Sam knew right away that the man was probably a cunning man and that things might go wrong with him around.

"Miss. Amadora, nice to meet you," The man said in a soft British accent as he extended his hand. Samantha took his hand and shook it lightly as he introduced himself. "I'm your brother's business partner, Edward Lane. How was your flight?"

"My flight was comfortable," Sam tried to think how Amadora would act towards him. "I've had better flights. Since this flight was a last moment arrangement, it was adequate."

Sam walked past him, trying to act as snobby as Amadora acted with her father's men. She looked around and could not believe how extravagant it looked inside. "Sorry to hear that, Miss. Morelli. Hopefully, your living arrangements here are a lot more to your liking. I'll be at the office with your brother. Feel free to ask any of the servants to call me if you need help."

Sam looked around a second time and smiled. It was going to be like a well-deserved vacation. She could go to the beach, sit and relax, or she could stay in the garden that wrapped around the house. Her only problem was that she had to keep Zanipolo at a distance, which would be the hardest part; because whenever Zanipolo was near, she could not help but want to be close to him.

The weekend was over, which meant Gugliehno, Elda and Zanipolo would return to their homes within the day or so. Casimiro cared little about Zanipolo since they did not have a close relationship, but Elda and Gunny were the closest friends he had. With them away during the month, he had no one to talk to about his concerns other than Basilio. And even though he saw him as his own father, there were still some things that he could not discuss with him.

Casimiro's meeting with Marco bothered him. He was not sure if he should tell the others about it, so they could take precautions to protect Giacinta or not. He paid her debt in full, so he was sure a money hungry beast like Marco would be satisfied and leave well enough alone. But Marco had the daughter of a rival don under his thumb for God knows how long. Having that type of power and control must have been intoxicating. He might target her and try to lure her in again. The only solution was to get rid of Marco, but that would cause more problems than it solves.

Marco was cozy with Lucio and Lana Rosilli. His ruthless tactics helped expand their dealing in the world of narcotics and gambling. He was an important asset, even though his strange methods caused cataclysmic damage that almost drove their family into war with their rivals many times. If Casimiro came after him, it would mean a declaration of war. Currently, the Morellis and Rosillis had an understanding that even though they had a difficult past, they swore a ceasefire. The Rosillis promised to leave the Morellis alone if they did the same. So far, their pact has lasted for over twenty years. No matter how much Casimiro wants to protect Giacinta, he had a duty to keep the peace for the safety of the family.

When Casimiro entered the observatory, he saw Gunny talking to Elda about something she clearly did not like by the annoyed expression engraved on her face. Her face lightened when she saw Casimiro, and she leaped from her chair, ran to her side, and wrapped her arm around his and pulled him over to the couch to sit between Gunny and her.

"Finally, you're here. Gunny's boring me with his constant nagging about how I should make siblings for Angelo. Please tell him his pestering won't change my mind," Elda said playfully.

Casimiro laughed. "Gunny's not wrong. Being an only child can be lonely. Take it from an expert."

"But you're not an only child. You have us," Gunny smiled.

"Yes. You're my reasonable older brother, blood or not," Elda hugged his arm and smiled.

Elda's true self was more loving and playful. Many people never saw this side of Elda, because she had to maintain a tough facade to be in their business since women were rarely taken seriously if they showed any kind of weakness. But when she was around her older brothers, who knew her true personality since childhood, her mask never worked.

"So, why did you ask us to come here, Gunny?" Casimiro asked.

"I need to ask one of you to do me a favor," Gunny started. Both Elda and Casimiro signaled for him to continue. "You both know that Nero is coming to New York to be under my supervision. Well, I just learned from pops that the whole Nero situation was planned weeks prior. He already knew he was going to place him with me."

"That sounds like papa," Elda smirked.

"That wouldn't be a problem if Nero wasn't arriving tomorrow at my place. That's a problem since I must go visit our aunt. I told Lorenzo about some situation, but I would feel better if one of you could be there when he arrives and get him settled," Gunny said.

"I would love to help you, but I have a ton of things I have to do this week," Casimiro answered reluctantly.

"I'll do it," Elda responded plainly.

Relief washed over Gunny. He knew his father had his doubts about Elda dealing with Nero, but she should be fine with him for a few days.

"Thanks. It's only for a week. Will that be okay on your end?"

"No problem. Antonio can handle my businesses back home, so I can sacrifice a few days babysitting that brat," Elda replied dryly.

Casimiro and Gunny exchanged worried glances when they noticed her bitter tone talking about Nero.

"Please don't be too tough on him. Dad wants to rehabilitate him not..." Gunny swiped his hand across his neck. "You know."

Elda glared at them and looked away, disappointed. "Of course, I won't do that. I'm not some bloodthirsty she-demon. I can control myself."

"I don't know. Your track record suggests otherwise," Gunny joked.

"You're an ass," Elda narrowed her eyes at him until they broke into laughter. No matter what Elda's reputation was like, she always listened to her brothers and father. She would never strike unless ordered to, because she only wanted to do right by those who did right by her.

The moon hung high in the dark smoke-filled sky as a fierce fire burned down the center of Olivia's Imports, a vast warehouse and shopping district run by the Morellis. The crackling and sizzling of the flames as they consumed anything in sight drowned out the screams of the people trapped inside.

Sirens echoed in the distance, but help would not arrive in time to save anyone. Someone lurking in the shadows pressed on a button and a cascade of explosions ricocheted through the building. The force of the explosions sent debris flying everywhere and broke glass windows within a block radius. The gigantic frame of Olivia's Imports swayed until it collapsed.

The person took the switch and placed it in a nearby trash can and ran down a few alleyways until they were far from the catastrophe. They walked over to a dark van and opened the back.

Inside were three other masked people.

"Let's go," The masked person said, closing the doors behind them.

"Boss, how did it go?" said one of the masked people as he removed his mask and placed it to the side.

"Perfect..." The man removed his mask and grinned. "Another Morelli holding destroyed. The don will be pleased."

"I'm surprised the don wants us to do this. Wasn't the treaty his idea?" The masked man driving said.

"I don't care about the specifics as long as I get paid at the end of the day," Their boss said. "Did you get some souvenirs for me?"

The men looked at one another and nodded. "Yes. We left them in the usual spot."

"Good. Since I can't make those Morelli scum suffer, then I'll have to take my frustrations out on their men," The boss smirked devilishly.

In Anna's apartment, Amadora unpacked her things and was ready to talk to Anna about the arrangements for the days ahead. Amadora walked into the kitchen where Anna poured lemonade for the two of them at the table. She sat in a chair across from Anna. Anna placed a glass in front of Amadora and placed the pitcher down.

"It seems like you've finally cracked, haven't you, Dora? You want to try working your way into Gunny's circuit. How the hell are you going to do that?" Anna asked while putting some cookies on the table in front of them.

"By posing as your struggling cousin who needs some extra money."

"Still, how are you going to get rid of the fact that you're a girl? They will never let you into the actual business even if they believe we are related."

"If you'd let me finish, I was going to say... I will disguise myself as a man to convince them."

Anna placed a cigarette in her mouth, holding it between her teeth as she tried to get the match to light. After many tries, she finally lit it. She held the match in front of the end of the cigarette until the orange glow grew bright. After taking a few pulls of the cigarette, she took it between her perfect fingers and held it.

"I get it. But still, how are you going to hide those?" Anna pointed her cigarette at Amadora's breasts. "You know. If they notice those, then you're done in more ways than one."

Amadora looked down at her chest and looked away, blushing. "True, they aren't small enough to just hide under men's clothes," Amadora looked at Anna and stared at the cigarette holder for a few seconds. Then she looked up at Anna wide eyed. "Anna, do you have any bandages? The long ones you use to wrap your legs or arms?"

Anna shook her head yes, looking at Amadora curiously. Amadora noticed how she looked at her, so she continued. "Well, we've solved that problem. I can use those bandages and some fabric to tie my breast down, so they look flatter."

Anna tapped her cigarette on the side of the ash tray and took a sip of her lemonade. "I guess you could use some of my husband's clothes until you can get your own made up. They should fit you."

"Good. What about the soldier connection? It must be someone who won't recognize me," Amadora took a sip of her lemonade then stared at the pitcher as she tried to think of who among Gunny's soldiers she knew.

"Larry the Moose."

"Who?"

"Exactly. He's perfect. You don't know him. He just became a soldier recently and will do anything for me. He's perfect. His name is Larry Musilli."

Amadora held up her glass to the light and smiled devilishly. "Larry Musilli."

4

Johnnie Barbone

*"If Amadora Morelli is as pure and harmless as a white rose,
then Johnnie Barbone is as dark and dangerous as a monkshood
bloom," Thoughts of Amadora Morelli.*

Johnnie Barbone waited by the car while Anna sat inside a restaurant talking to Larry Musilli. He watched as Anna used her charms to convince him to take Johnnie under his wing. Johnnie tried his best to listen to what they said.

"Larry, give the boy a try... He's a fast learner and very... He's got a lot of skills..." Johnnie heard pieces of what Anna said to Larry.

"What skills? Does he know how to... and does he know how to... and does he know how to drive?" Larry's words drowned in and out because of its raspy tone and the thick window dividing Johnnie and them. Just the sound of his voice made Johnnie want to give him a throat lozenge or some mint tea for his throat. He was also a very short man from what Johnnie saw of him earlier. He wondered why they called him "Moose".

"Come check him out for yourself," With that said, Johnnie heard the footsteps of Anna and Larry coming closer to the door. He did not budge when Larry crossed the parking lot to look at him. He leaned on the car with his arms crossed and his eyes glued on his surveyor.

"Stand up, kid. I want to see how much work Annie here is givin' me to do," Larry said, looking Johnnie over. Johnnie stood and looked at Anna, who was standing behind Larry, with an eyebrow raised. Anna shrugged and watched as Larry continued observing Johnnie.

"Tsk... Tsk. You're a scrawny kid, aren't you? What happened boy you didn't hit puberty yet?" Larry grabbed Johnnie's chin and looked at his face, but Johnnie did not fight back. "Not a hair on your face. You're a pretty boy with skin as soft as a baby's bottom. Sure, you looking for the right job? How old are you, kid?"

"I'm eighteen, and I'm positive I want to do this," Johnnie said shortly. His voice was not deep or too soft. His voice was smooth like Zanipolo's.

"And what's a pretty boy like you want with a business like this, huh?" Johnnie's face became expressionless, and his eyes focused on Larry. He tried not showing any emotions since Larry's gaze focused on Johnnie.

"I guess Anna didn't tell you my reason," Johnnie looked at Anna then back at Larry. Johnnie shrugged. "Do I need one? Why did you choose this life, Larry?"

"You a smart ass, huh? My reason is my business," Larry snapped laughing loudly then glaring at Johnnie.

"Well. I guess you know my answer. Our reasons are our own. Why we enter this business, whether it's for a new life, to provide for a loved one, a family tradition, greed, a thrill, or to get revenge, whatever the reason, what does it matter?" Johnnie leaned back against the car and crossed his arms as he spoke those words. His icy gaze contradicted the grin he wore.

"You a cold-hearted son of a bitch. I can see it in your eyes. I like ya, kid. Meet me at this address at 8pm, and we'll see how good you really are," Larry smirked and handed Johnnie a piece of paper then turned back around to Anna smiling from ear to ear. "This one might be a keeper, Annie."

Anna smiled at Larry, then walked over to Johnnie and entered the car. Johnnie waited until Larry was back in the restaurant before starting the car to leave.

The sun's bright rays glaring through the windows roused Samantha from her sleep. She yawned and looked outside, stretching her tired bones. In the gorgeous angelic light, she glimpsed from the corner of her eye a note on the nightstand. She picked up the note, opened and read it silently to herself.

Dear Ms. Morelli,

I was notified early this morning that your brother, Zanipolo, will arrive this afternoon and requested to have dinner with you. Please send a response concerning your availability as soon as you can.

Sincerely,
Edward Lane

Samantha's blood ran cold, and the color drained from her face. How would she deal with Zanipolo? She had to figure out an excuse because he would surely notice Sam if he saw her. He was not a fool. He would figure it out right away. If that happened, the lord only knew what would happen.

Sam reached into the nightstand drawer, took out a piece of paper and pen, then wrote a brief note accepting the dinner proposal. However, she made sure she warned him that there would probably be a possibility she might not make it. She walked over to one maid in the hall and gave her the note.

The girl accepted the note and left to deliver it to Arnold so he could give it to Edward. Sam did not enjoy lying to Zanipolo. It was not good at all. If he saw through her lies, he would become suspicious and investigate why his 'sister' acted strange. Sam would be no match for Zanipolo if he became like that. Samantha heard tales about how Zanipolo gathered information for his father. He was discreet, and his targets rarely knew he was looking into them until it was too late.

Sam did not want to lie to Zanipolo. She knew lying to him would end up hurting them both, but mostly him. She did not want to hurt him and would die if she hurt him.

Anna walked through the door, threw her jacket on the cushion, then headed towards the living room. "'Johnnie Barbone' huh? What made you come up with a name like that?"

Amadora took off her jacket and hat, laid them on top of Anna's and followed her. Anna sat by the window so she could monitor the people passing by. "What's wrong with 'Johnnie'?"

"Nothing. You were just very convincing that it scared me. Are you sure about doing this, Amadora? Is there no other way to convince your pops?" Anna walked over to the liquor cabinet, took out a bottle of whisky and poured it into a glass. She took a big swig and looked at Amadora, who was taking her hair out of a bun.

"No. There isn't any other way. I've tried everything possible. If I do this, at least he'll know I'm serious," Amadora sat beside Anna. Amadora was expressionless when she answered Anna. Anna shrugged and took another sip of her whisky.

"Let me see the paper he gave you," Amadora handed Anna the paper. "I know this place my father used to work there when I was a babe... It's an abandoned warehouse now. Well, at least it's supposed to be since the fire that broke out there in '44. Gunny and his men must have bought and fixed it up to train newbies like you."

"Do you think any cops are going to be around there?" Amadora asked, looking at Anna.

"No, I doubt it. Your brother probably has every cop paid off from here to Pennsylvania," Anna pocketed the paper and turned back to Amadora. "I'll take you. That way I'll be nearby to watch in case something goes wrong."

"No. I'll go by myself, just tell me how to get there. I'll be fine. I'm no longer Amadora when I leave here to see him. I'll be Johnnie Barbone."

'When you're ready, I'll tell you.' Those words rang through Giacinta's mind. What did Casimiro mean by she was not ready? What was so important that he could not tell her until she was 'ready'? Whatever it was, she could handle it. Giacinta could not understand why he did not tell her what else he wanted.

Giacinta sat by the window and looked down at the family sitting in the garden eating breakfast and laughing. Even Casimiro sat in between Zanipolo and Gunny, laughing. She could not go down there with him, only a chair away from her regular seat. If she moved, they would know something was wrong. Giacinta could not let her family think anything was amiss. She did not want to cause drama on the last day everyone would be in the house together. It would not be right.

Giacinta curled up on the couch and looked down at her family. They were happier without her there to ruin it with her petty problems. She would do them all a big favor by staying in her room until they said their goodbyes. Giacinta pulled the throw over her to cover her face, to hide her tears from everything, including the lingering shadows.

'They're probably talking about how much they miss Amadora... They are probably glad I'm not there... No one gives a damn about me.' Giacinta thought, wiping away a tear. Giacinta's hatred towards Amadora was an act. She was frustrated because she wanted to be her little sister. Everyone loved Amadora, no matter what she did. No one could stay angry at her for too long. There was something about her. Something that warmed even the coldest of hearts. Giacinta wanted the power to melt hearts with only a smile.

Damn Amadora! Only if she was...

Just then a knock sounded on her door. Giacinta looked up at the door and wiped her face with the sleeve of her robe. "Who is it?" Giacinta asked, tossing the throw to the side and fixing her robe.

"It's me, Zanipolo. Can I come in?"

"Sure. It's unlocked."

Zanipolo came in, looked around her room, and then looked back at Giacinta with an eyebrow raised. "Is everything okay? I was worried when I didn't see you at breakfast," Zanipolo walked over and turned her to look at him. Her confusion and pain were clear as she tried to avoid meeting his gaze. "You were crying. Something is wrong. What is it?"

Giacinta threw her arms around Zanipolo and started crying. "Please don't leave, Polo! I need you!"

Zanipolo embraced her softly. "You know if I could do that I would but can't. Tell me what happened."

"I'm confused," Giacinta let him go and looked into his eyes. "There are things happening in my life that I don't understand."

"Like what?" Zanipolo insisted, leaning back on the couch, waiting for her response.

"Did Papa or anyone notice my absence this morning?"

Zanipolo immediately understood the problem and shook his head no. He could see the last bit of light in her eyes disappear. Zanipolo understood the reason she was concerned. It was hard being the misfit child. Zanipolo went down that road twice, so he knew how it felt. It was a confusing time when one felt like no one noticed or cared if they were dead or alive.

Giacinta cleared her throat and wiped her face with her sleeve. "Zanipolo, how well do you know Casimiro?" She changed the subject and turned to Polo with a serious expression on her face.

"Casimiro... I know him well. I guess. I know he's been Gunny's friend since the first grade. Pops took him in as his own child when his parents died in a car accident when he was 12, and he became his consigliere after he graduated college..."

"I know all that. I mean, how well do you know him personally?"

"Personally... Um... Well, I've never talked to him about anything personal. If you want to know that, your best bet is to talk to Gunny," Zanipolo looked at her with his eyebrow raised. "Why do you want to know? Do you like him or something?"

"Like him! Ha! No!" Giacinta laughed nervously, dismissing the thought with a wave of her hand. "Please, Polo. That's ridiculous!"

"Then why are you interested in his personal life?" Giacinta noticed Zanipolo looking at her suspiciously.

"Just a random question," Giacinta smiled before quickly changing the subject. "When is your flight?"

"It leaves in four hours," Zanipolo understood Giacinta did not want to talk about the subject of Casimiro anymore, so he shrugged it off and answered her question while wrapping his arm around her shoulder. "I was worried when you didn't come to breakfast. How do think I would feel if I left without saying goodbye to my favorite sister?"

Giacinta hugged him and walked with him to the door. "Thank you, Polo. Come with me to get something to eat. I'm starved."

After Zanipolo left to the airport, Giacinta went directly to Gunny's room before he left with his family. She knocked on his door and waited. A minute or two later the door opened, and there stood Gunny in his Sunday's best. When he saw Giacinta, he smiled and hugged her.

"I missed your pretty face at breakfast this morning, little sister. Did you stop by to say goodbye before I go?"

"Yes. That was part of my reason for coming, but I also wanted to ask you some questions before you left," Giacinta smiled half-heartedly. She was nervous about asking questions about Casimiro to Gunny since they were close friends.

"What kind of questions?" Gunny stepped aside, letting her into the room and then guided her to the sitting area to continue talking.

"Well, since you are close to Casimiro, I was wondering if you could answer some questions about him?" Giacinta played with the ring on her finger as her nerves raced. Her heart beat faster and her breath grew heavy. She could not believe she was about to talk to Gunny about something so personal.

"About Casimiro? Why don't you ask him yourself?" Gunny asked, confused.

"No," Giacinta shook her head and answered him quickly. "I can't... I just thought since you're my brother and his best friend... Never mind."

"Giacinta... Why do you want to know?" Gunny looked at her softly and sat next to her on the couch.

"No apparent reason... I suppose," Giacinta looked down at her hand and stared at her ring so she would not meet his gaze.

"If there's no reason, then I'm not answering your question," Gunny was about to return to packing until Giacinta grabbed his arm.

"Gunny, please," Once he saw the confusion and warmth in her eyes, he understood. He sighed, closed his eyes, and sat back down. A moment later, he opened his eyes to look at her.

"Okay... What is your question?"

"How well do you know Casimiro? Do you know him personally?" Giacinta asked, returning her brother's gaze with a softer one.

"I guess I know him well. We have been friends for years."

"How is his history with women?"

"Women?" Gunny laughed. "Ever since we were kids, Casimiro was always a prime target for the ladies. But for some strange reason he never seemed interested," Gunny smiled softly and focused on his sister once again. "Are you asking me these questions because you're interested in him?"

"No..." Giacinta blushed. "Maybe... It's just these past days I've seen a part of him that intrigues me."

"These past days? ... He was acting strange this morning," Gunny put his arm around her and pulled her close. "Then you're the cause. You're the mystery girl he's been talking about?"

"He talks about me?" Giacinta smiled as her heart jumped. Gunny nodded yes. Even with that good news, Giacinta was still skeptical about Casimiro. "Even though he intrigues me, he still scares me."

Giacinta ignored the confused look Gunny wore and continued. "I feel as if there's something more he wants from me. More than what he says he wants."

"You shouldn't be scared, Giacinta. Casimiro is an amazing man. He has absolutely no skeletons in his closet, at least none you need to worry about," Gunny reassured.

Giacinta looked at Gunny wide eyed. "I know he's a great guy, but still I have my doubts. There's just something about him. Something that makes him seem too good to be true."

"Little sister, it seems like you're just trying to find something wrong with him. You need to learn how to trust," Gunny spoke softly before turning his head to check the clock on the wall behind him. "As much as I would love to talk more about this, I got to get going."

Gunny kissed Giacinta on her forehead and walked her to the door. He reached down and picked up the last of his luggage along with his jacket and hat. He stopped when they reached the hallway and put his luggage down, then hugged and kissed her again. "Thank you for opening up to me. I want you to come to me more often, even if you can't talk to me in person, you could always write or call."

Giacinta held him while mumbling. "Don't worry, I will."

It took a few hours for Elda to drive from her parents' place to Gugliehno's house. She screeched to a stop as she pulled into his driveway, jumped out of the car and ran inside to her brother's office where Lorenzo waited, ready to brief her on what's going on.

When she rushed into Gunny's office, a dirty-blonde man with large grayish blue eyes stood by the door talking to a few men in dark coats. He smiled when he saw Elda and welcomed her.

"Hey, Elda. You got here just in time."

"Why? Did something happen?" Elda asked, examining the two men across from Lorenzo.

"Yes. But I'll get to that when I fill you in on everything else. It's an urgent matter but must be dealt with delicately," Lorenzo replied, signaling for the men to leave them alone.

Elda crossed the room and looked at the papers on Gunny's desk. "We're alone. Tell me what's going on."

Lorenzo smiled and nodded. "Well, your cousin, Nero, will arrive in a few days. I need to know what you want me to do with him."

Elda's face turned sour when Lorenzo mentioned her cousin. She grumbled and rolled her eyes. "Frankly, I could care less what you do with him. But papa wouldn't be happy if we just stuck him to do lackey work, and he never learned from the experience. Send him to Brock. He's good at dealing with delinquents."

Lorenzo's smile grew as he took down her words in his notes. "Fine. That can be done."

Lorenzo scanned his notepad before looking back at Elda. "The business end of things is good. We're still looking for new recruits who can do the Mancini job, but that's not our most pressing matter now."

"Oh... What's more pressing than securing the Mancinis' loyalty?" Elda asked.

"Jack..." Lorenzo replied.

"What about him? Whatever he does, doesn't concern us unless he steps on our turf. And thanks to the pact between the Rosillis and us, he can't do that," Elda said.

"Well, I don't know if he did this under the order of the Rosillis, but Jack broke the pact, attacked several of our holdings and massacred our men stationed there. Those who didn't die right away were tortured to death then disposed of," Lorenzo answered.

Elda looked shocked when she heard this news. "How long has this been going on? Why are we only hearing about this now?"

"We probably wouldn't have heard about it if I didn't use my family's connections. He's been doing this for some time, three months about, and my father only knows about it because that fool, Jack, went to him bragging about what he was doing to persuade him to do business with him. He didn't know that my family and yours have a friendship."

"Do we know how many they killed?" Elda asked, processing the information as she received it.

"About 30. But that's a rough estimate from how many men we have reported missing."

"If we aren't sure the Rosillis ordered him to do this, then targeting him might open the floodgates to war," Elda said, going over the circumstances out loud.

"But if we do nothing, Jack will continue to target our men," Lorenzo explained.

Elda knew Lorenzo was right, but she wondered if they can stop Jack without pissing off the Rosillis and shitting on their agreement. Her expression became unreadable.

"Fine. I will call my father, Casimiro and Gugliehno and explain the situation. Maybe we can get the Rosilli don to sit and talk with my father during the Autumn Ball. Hopefully, he'll understand my reasoning when we explain why we had to do this. Do whatever you must stop him."

Johnnie pulled in front of the warehouse where he was immediately stopped by a guard. The man wore a black suit and carried a tommy gun. He was taller than Johnnie and built like a truck. The man bent over and examined Johnnie along with his back and front seats.

"Kid, are you lost?" The man growled.

The closer he drew, the more that Johnnie saw the contents of his face. His teeth were a dark yellow. He reeked of alcohol and cigarettes. His black hair was combed back so tight it looked like a tattoo. The man's clothes were also a few sizes too small, which made them look like they would burst with the slightest movement.

"No. I'm here to see Larry Musilli," Johnnie answered, glaring at the guard with no hint of intimidation.

"And who are you?"

"Johnnie Barbone."

The guard turned to a man about the same age as Johnnie and whispered to him in Italian. Johnnie could not catch what they said but as soon as he told him whatever it was the man walked to a trailer on the other side of the gate. He went inside for about five minutes before waving to the guard to let Johnnie in.

The guard stepped aside to let Johnnie pass through the gate. He drove the car to the other side of the gate and parked it. After stepping out of his car, Musilli was waiting for him by a row of crates. By the look on Musilli's face, he was anxious about something. He kept glancing at his watch; and when he saw Johnnie, he waved for him to hurry.

"About time you made it, boy," Musilli acknowledged Johnnie only once before turning around and heading to a small door at the far end of the crates. "Come on."

When Johnnie caught up to him, they entered the first part of the warehouse. He looked at Musilli with his eyebrow raised. "What do you mean 'about time'? I'm early."

As Johnnie followed Musilli, he could not help but look at what went on around them. Men lit cigarettes and talked in Italian about their families and previous jobs. They also had their guns of all shapes and sizes strapped to their sides.

"Why are you in a rush?"

Musilli stopped in front of a door and took a key ring out, scrambling to find the right one. "Well, I just got orders from my boss on a job that needs to be done right away. My only problem is I'm short one man in my crew," Musilli unlocked the door then pushed it open. They walked down the thin corridor. Continuing until they stop at a small arch that led to a large shooting range.

"Who's going to take his place?" Johnnie raised his voice so that Musilli could hear him over the roar of the gun shots.

"You... That's why I told you to meet me here," Musilli answered, stopping in front of one of the empty shooting spots. "Kid, you talk big, but I want to see if you can back up your words."

Musilli turned to the guns on a crate near them. He picked up a small pistol and handed it to Johnnie.

"This job gets dangerous, and I need a sharpshooter. Can't have no useless fools covering my ass."

Johnnie smirked, grabbed some bullets, and reloaded the gun. "I'm no fool. What's the job they want us to do?"

"We got to take care of a minor problem. I'll tell you more about it later. Now, kid, show me what you got."

Zanipolo arrived at his office right before eight. His scheduled dinner with Amadora was at nine. That was only if she accepted his offer. All Zanipolo knew she could be mad at him for trying to keep her out of the business. He really hoped she was not still angry and forgave him.

Zanipolo walked to his window and gazed at the setting sun. The events of that month had been more difficult than ever before. That was why he was not very excited about returning. It held painful memories Zanipolo was not ready to return to. The city of Los Angeles was home to many secrets Zanipolo did not want to surface. Los Angeles was home to Maxine, the object of all his pain and suffering.

Maxine was Zanipolo's ex-fiancée. She broke Zanipolo's heart by leaving him for another man. Ever since they separated, Zanipolo lost all hope to love again. He felt no one could ever make him feel as happy as she did. At least, he used to believe that, until he went back home and saw Sam again.

When he was with her, alone in Amadora's room, he felt inklings of the feelings he thought he had lost. Sam's smile warmed his heart. She was a precious angel because he saw no imperfections in her. Zanipolo put his arm against the wall so he could watch the people walking in and out of the store below.

Zanipolo wanted to return to Jersey, so he could look into Sammy's light-brown eyes once more. He missed talking to her about things, no matter if they were relevant or not. If he heard her voice, that was all that mattered.

Edward Lane saw the door to Zanipolo's office was open, so he peeked to see if his friend had arrived. The office lights were off and the only light coming into the room was the fading light of the sun. Edward noticed a man standing in front of the window. There was not enough light for him to tell if it was Zanipolo, so he snuck inside the office without making a sound. He walked over to the man and right as his hand was about to touch the man's jacket; the man pinned Edward to the desk.

"You're quick as ever. You almost took off my bloody arm," Edward grunted in discomfort while his head was turned to the side, his cheek pressed to the desk, and Zanipolo's arm was pressed against his back.

"Edward... Edward... Edward. Haven't you learned by now? You'll never pull a fast one on me. I'm too good for you, my friend," Zanipolo smirked, letting go of Edward's arm and stepping to the side so he could get up.

Edward stretched out his arm when he finally stood to face Zanipolo. "That's the last time I try doing that. My wife wouldn't like it if I came home without an arm,"

82

Edward walked over to the chair in front of the desk and sat down. "You know your sister is something."

"Did she give you any problems?" Zanipolo asked, walking to his chair and sitting across from him.

"Problems? ... No... she's a sweetheart, but just seems very much like Giacinta. I thought you said she was the polite, down-to-earth sister."

"She is. She must've given you the 'I'm a princess' attitude," Zanipolo laughed and reached into his desk for the bourbon he had stashed in his drawer. "Did she respond?"

Edward reached into his pocket and pulled out the note from Amadora. He handed him the note. Zanipolo snatched it from him and quickly scanned it. When he finished, an enormous smile crossed his lips.

'Eight thirty... A half hour before I'm supposed to meet Zanipolo for dinner, '

Sam sat on her beach chair, curling her toes in the warm sand. She pulled her straw hat over her eyes and closed them as she went deeper into thought. 'I feel so bad for doing this to him, but I know if he even sees me for a second, he'll know I'm not Amadora. I can't be careless with him... especially if the plan is going to work... But I hate doing this.'

Sam kicked the sand at her toes while stretching back in her chair. 'I know someone is going to get hurt by this.... I don't want to hurt him. I want him to find out the truth, so I don't have to lie to him anymore. I hate having to deceive him. I hate the fact I know he's going to get hurt in the end. I also hate knowing there's nothing I could do to ease his pain.'

Sam took a deep breath and held back the tears threatening to fall. 'This month is going to be difficult. I need to be on my guard. I'm no match for Zanipolo. He immobilizes me whenever I'm near him. How am I going to pull this off without someone getting hurt?' Sam pushed up her hat and gazed out to the incoming tides. 'We will both get hurt because of this plan... but who will suffer the deepest blow, me or him?'

Edward brought Zanipolo to Gina's Little Italy restaurant at 9 on the dot. When they entered, Zanipolo walked to the hostess and asked her if his sister had arrived. She flipped through the pages of the book in front of her.

"I'm sorry, Mr. Morelli, but no one by the name of Amadora has arrived yet. Would you like to wait here or be seated?"

Zanipolo looked at Edward, then shrugged. "I dunno, chap, maybe she's just late. I can wait with you?"

Zanipolo glanced outside, then turned back to Edward. "I guess she is. That doesn't surprise me at all," Zanipolo sighed and turned to the hostess. "I guess we'll wait at the bar. Please let me know when she arrives."

Zanipolo and Edward walked to the back of the restaurant and sat at the bar. After a minute or two, a young man about eighteen came over to them and smiled. "Zanipolo.... Edward. Good to see you tonight."

"Frank, I haven't seen you working in a while everything okay with you and your mom?" Zanipolo said smiling softly.

"Mother's doing fine. She just had another baby; so, for a while, I had to help with the babe," Frank was a skinny young man with dark red curly hair and light blue eyes. His voice was kind of high-pitched and raspy. He was not much of a pretty boy like Zanipolo, but Zanipolo and Edward had seen him with different girls all the time.

Edward looked at Frank in shock. "Gina had a baby? How is that possible?" Everyone around them laughed; and as soon as Zanipolo was going to speak, Edward was hit in the back of the head. Edward turned around and was about to yell at the person who hit him until he saw Gina herself glaring at him with dagger-like eyes. "Uh... Gina."

"What did you say, sonny?" Gina formed a fist and was about to slug him if he did not come up with something quick.

Edward smiled sheepishly and reached for her hand to kiss it. "Gina, my darling lady, I was saying how joyous the news is about your new little bundle of joy."

Gina looked at him skeptically and smirked. "Hmmm... Sure."

"Gina, what is the baby? A girl or boy?" Zanipolo asked nicely, trying to change the subject.

Gina turned to Zanipolo, smiling joyously. "The baby is a beautiful girl."

"Of course, she's beautiful. Look at where she gets it from," Zanipolo smiled, complimenting her in hopes she'd calm down and leave. As soon as Zanipolo said that to her, he could see her face grow red from his flattery.

"Aw... Zanipolo, you are a sweetheart. I'm going to fix one of my famous lemon meringue pies just for you. Don't worry, it's on the house," She turned to her son before she headed back to the kitchen. "Frank, give them some drinks on the house."

When Gina left the room, Zanipolo and Frank laughed again as they watched Edward rubbing the back of his head.

"Your mother has a good arm."

"Well, you deserved it," Zanipolo said, patting his friend on the back.

Frank laughed and asked softly. "Who are you waiting for?"

"My sister. She's supposed to meet me here for dinner."

"What time is your reservation?" Frank asked, glancing down at his wristwatch.

"Nine... She's running a little late," Zanipolo smirked to hide his genuine feelings.

He was becoming nervous because there was no sign of Amadora. Maybe she had gotten lost or hurt. Maybe he should have sent Arnold to bring her, but knowing Amadora, she probably wanted to find the place herself.

Frank saw Zanipolo was deep in thought about something, so he just filled up a small glass and passed it to him. "Here. Drink this. Don't worry. She'll be here soon."

Zanipolo took the glass and drank it down. Nine thirty came and went by quickly, and he finished six glasses. When ten o'clock rolled around, Zanipolo was so drunk he could barely walk. Edward put an arm around him, trying to support him as he walked.

"I think you've waited long enough. You can barely see straight. I think it's time for you to go home, my friend."

Zanipolo looked up at him, stammering. "But... But... I... I must wait for...."

Edward cut him off and answered sharply. "You're waiting for no one. You're in no condition to wait any longer. What you need right now is a ton of water and sleep."

Musilli's driver Raphael pulled the car to the front of the warehouse. Musilli, Johnnie, and his other man, Rocko, sat inside. Johnnie put his pistol in the inner pocket of his jacket and some extra bullets in the other.

When the car moved, Musilli talked more about the job at hand. "Three more men are in place checking out the numbers. From what Brock's old lady says, there's four or five of Rosilli's men in the store itself. Me, Raphael, and Rocko can take care of them. You, kid, got to focus on Jack, the owner. Here's him," Musilli pulled out a photo from his jacket and pointed out who he was. "You are going with Brock and the others. They are going to go in first and take out any of Rosilli's men that are in the back. Wait for them to say clear before going in behind them. I don't need you dying on your first job. Your goal is to find Jack and take him out."

Once Musilli told Johnnie his order, his smile faded, and his expression became unreadable. His heart sank and his pulse slowed. 'Take him out! He wants you to take him out! He wants you to kill someone! You can't do that!' Amadora's thought frantically.

'But it's too late to back out now. It's the only way to prove to my father. And if I don't, they'll kill me,' The cool, emotionless thoughts of Johnnie replied.

'But Amadora Morelli doesn't kill, and you will not start now! Amadora Morelli isn't a murderer! You can't do this!' Amadora protested.

A smirk crossed his face as Johnnie thought. 'I'm not Amadora Morelli.... I'm Johnnie Barbone, and I'll kill anyone who stands in my way.'

Musilli looked at Johnnie with his eyebrow raised. "Kid, you are a weird one. I've never seen someone happy to kill someone for the first time."

Before he could answer Musilli, Raphael stopped the car and parked. Musilli took his gun, tucking it away out of sight, so he did not alert any pedestrians. He tapped Johnnie on the shoulder.

"There. That's where we are going," Musilli pointed to a little bar on the end of the block. The windows were dark, and it seemed like it was closed. The only sign that it was open, the few people walking in and out. "Today is its slow day since it's Sunday and people have work. There shouldn't be any casualties on our part. Only drunks and whores are going to be there now."

They climbed out the car and walked as normal as they could down the street. They kept their distance from each other, so no one suspected they were up to something. Johnnie fixed the brim of his hat as they drew closer. He brought it down so people passing would not notice his face. The last thing he needed was a witness who could point him out just because they remembered the look in his eyes.

Musilli, Rocko, and Raphael walked into an alleyway next to the bar. When Johnnie entered, Musilli was talking to a tall man wearing a black suit and hat. Johnnie could tell the man had a very strong build by his broad body and thick arms. His arms reminded Johnnie of two trucks made of muscle and flesh. The man was lighter than Johnnie by complexion and had ice-blue eyes. Johnnie noticed a scar on his neck when he fixed the collar of his coat to his neck and wrapped a dark scarf around his nose and mouth. The man's voice boomed even while whispering. Johnnie sensed a darkness hidden within the depths of his voice as he talked.

Musilli waved to Johnnie to hurry. Johnnie quickened his pace and walked over to where the tall man and two other men were.

"Johnnie, this is Brock. You'll be following his lead for this job," Musilli turned back to Brock. "Remember, wait till' you hear our gunshots before you go in. You want them to follow us. Then you surprise them from behind."

With that said, Musilli left, and Johnnie followed Brock to the back door of the store. Brock and his men pulled out their guns while Johnnie stayed behind with his gun ready in his hand. Johnnie's heartbeat quickened as he waited for the signal for the blood bath to begin.

Moments later, the sound of gunshots and cries of fear and pain could be heard from the front of the store. Johnnie's breath slowed as Brock kicked the door open and he and his men opened fire. Johnnie placed the gun close to his chest, taking a deep breath before following them inside.

When he entered the kitchen, he saw Brock and his men taking cover while Rosilli's men shot in their direction. Johnnie crouched down close to the floor and hid in a pantry by the door. There he waited for the sign to progress further.

The roar of gunfire rang through his ears like fireworks, pounding his eardrums with brute force. A death symphony played when gunfire rang through the air and ended with the cries of death. This seemed like a nightmare instead of reality as the thunder of gunshots echoed around him, shattering any peace of mind he had left.

Johnnie felt the pain and agony as each bullet pierced their bodies. He heard their cries loud and clear, as if they were his own. He looked down at his hand, which trembled because of everything happening around him. He brought it close to him as he pressed his back firm against the wall. He tried to stop his hands from shaking, but that was an impossible task.

He glanced at the doorway, readying himself as much as he could in case someone entered from behind. Nothing but the raging wind came through that door, increasing the smell of blood that hung prominently in the air. Johnnie tried his best not to breathe in too much, hoping the smell of death would leave with the wind. He covered his mouth with his scarf to shield him from the scent, but it still permeated every fiber, suffocating him with the essence of death and despair. He could do nothing until he knew it was safe. He replayed the reason he did this in his mind, trying to focus on the goal.

When the gunshots finally ended, Johnnie peeked out to see the status. There was blood everywhere. The once tile floor had turned into a sea of blood. Johnnie did not want to look at the slaughtered bodies of fathers, brothers, and friends of some person as he walked over to Brock when he signaled. He wanted to close his eyes so he would not have to see those slain corpses; but even closing his eyes could not shield him from the ocean of death surrounding him. But even worse, when he reached Brock, he told Johnnie to stay there in the sea of blood while they took out whoever was left.

Johnnie's heart was now beating faster than it ever had before. He could hear the gunshots, the screams of agony, and then the quietness that followed their deaths. He wanted the horrible dream to end. He did not want to see anymore death and did not want to cause it.

When Brock signaled him at that last moment, Johnnie knew it was his turn now. It was his turn to add another body to the ocean of blood at his feet. As Johnnie walked into the hallway, he looked at the end where more bodies laid on the floor. His heartbeat slowed and resounded in his ear with every step he took. The rhythmic thumping pounded like the ticking of a clock, counting down the moments until Johnnie's hands were stained crimson like the surrounding walls and floor.

When Johnnie reached the door where Brock's men stood, he saw a man on his knees in front of Brock begging for his life. He also saw Brock staring down at him, emotionless.

"Please... Please... Do not kill me. I have a wife and a daughter," Jack pleaded at Brock's feet. Brock pointed his gun at Jack's head as if he was going to shoot.

"I wonder if that was the same thing the Morellis' men said when you slaughtered them like dogs," Brock struck him with his gun, making Jack fall to his elbows. "Did they beg for their lives too? And did you show them any mercy? No! You killed tens of innocent men! They had wives! They had children! They had family and friends! Did you think of that when you killed them!" Brock struck Jack again. That time he kicked him in his rib, causing Jack to spit out blood. "You make me sick! You are nothing but a pitiful little worm! Death is too good for you!"

Jack tried to get back to his knees once more. Sweat fell down his face and mixed with his blood. Then he cried as he noticed the end drew near with every word he said. "Please, I beg you, show mercy.... Please don't kill me."

"Don't worry. I'm not going to kill you," Jack smiled and kissed Brock's shoes. Brock kicked him away, smirking devilishly. "Get off me. I said I won't kill you. That doesn't mean you ain't going to die. Kid, he's all yours."

Brock stepped out of the way, and Johnnie was now in front of Jack. Johnnie was no longer scared or nervous. This man did not deserve to live. He killed more men than he was going to kill. Jack looked into Johnnie's eyes and saw nothing. No humanity or feelings remained in his eyes. His eyes were frigid and soulless. Jack knew right away there was no point in begging anymore. Johnnie raised the gun, aimed it at Jack's forehead and pulled the trigger.

As soon as his finger tugged the trigger, time slowed, and Johnnie saw the bullet's every detail. He saw the residue that flew back on his gloved hand and the path of the bullet until it met its target, splattering blood everywhere. Within seconds, Jack's body fell to the ground motionless.

Johnnie froze as he looked down at Jack's corpse. He could not believe what he did. He brought his arm to his side and looked at the scarlet scene dancing in front of him. Johnnie did it. He killed him.

Brock noticed Johnnie was not moving after he shot Jack, so he walked next to Johnnie and pulled him away from the scene. "Put your gun away, boy, and let's get out of here."

Johnnie did not move an inch. He just stood there. Brock turned him to look at him. "Look, kid. I know you're scared, but we need to get out of here before the cops come."

Brock pulled the dazed boy by his arm. Johnnie ran unknowingly behind him, staring at the door where Jack's body laid... Where his first victim was in a sleep of forever darkness.

5

The Tearing of Hearts

'Johnnie Barbone is just a ruse. He's a mask I wear to get closer to my goal. But why does it feel like he's a shadow trying to devour my soul?' Thoughts of Amadora Morelli.

Amadora stood outside the Morelli Complex's main house wearing a white summer dress. The sky was a depressing gray and threatened rain. She quickened her pace towards the front door. As she put her key in the lock, the door opened. Amadora walked cautiously inside. The entire house was shrouded in darkness and the floor felt wet.

"What's on the floor?" Amadora raised her foot, closing the door behind her and called for the butler. "Barry! Barry!" Amadora tried making her way to the wall by the stairwell, but the water made it difficult for her to cross. As she grew closer, she heard water running.

She mustered all the power in her to tread the rising waters. It took a few moments until she reached the wall. When she finally did, the liquid on the floor was already ankle deep. "Something must have flooded."

Amadora flicked on the light switch. When the light finally dispelled the darkness, it revealed a horrifying truth about the liquid surrounding her. It was not water... It was blood!

"What the!" Amadora screamed at the top of her lungs as her heart raced.

She turned to the stairs to go find her father, but noticed blood poured down the stairs. She fought the rampaging waterfall of blood to reach the top, but its force was too much, causing her to tumble several times before reaching the landing. Crimson blood soaked her entire body, flowing down her face, arms and legs while staining her clothes in its frightening hue. But she fought through her anguish to find her father and make sure he was alright.

Amadora ran to her father's office, fighting through her terror as she opened the door, calling for him. "Papa.... Papa"

When she entered the office, her father was on his knees pleading to his assailant. She had never seen her father, Basilio Morelli, beg in her entire life. It was a nightmare. A terror. A man stood in front of him, pointing a gun to his head. There were tears in her father's eyes as he begged the man to spare him and his family. Seeing this desperate scene brought tears to her eyes.

Amadora froze. She could not remove her hand from the doorknob. She did not want to alert the man threatening her father's life. Amadora could only watch as the man was about to kill her father.

"Papa" Amadora whispered. Her father turned around and looked at her. His horror amplified when their eyes met.

"Amadora, get out of here while you" The man pulled the trigger and her father's body dropped to the floor lifeless.

Amadora fell to her knees, crying uncontrollably. She grasped her chest as her heart pounded ferociously, hurting her with every breath. "Papa!" Amadora lifted her head from her chest and glared at her father's killer with hatred. "Why did you do this!"

The man did not budge. He only faced her father's dead corpse. Amadora slammed her fist on the floor. "Who are you?"

Amadora looked over the scenario again. Her eyes grew wide in fear when she figured out the identity of her father's murderer. She fell back and pushed herself away, terrified.

"No... It can't be... You are not supposed to... What do you want from me!"

The man turned around and put his gun to his side. When he looked at her, she was speechless. Her father's killer was Johnnie Barbone.

"I want you to see yourself. I want you to see the creation you made. You created me so you can prove yourself to that man," Johnnie pointed at her father's body then turned back to her with hatred in his eyes. "I'm the murderer. The cold-hearted killer you created to get what you want. Now, I'm giving it to you."

Johnnie pointed at her father's chair, smirking darkly. "There's your throne. A throne built on the blood of your enemies and your family. Everything you've ever wanted."

"No. I never wanted to hurt my father! Bring him back!" Amadora screamed while her father's blood drenched her body. His blood flowed around Johnnie like a flood engulfing Amadora in its rampage. Amadora tried to fight free from the crimson sea but was dragged to its murky depths by Johnnie until they both drowned in her father's blood and her tears.

Anna heard Amadora crying out from her bedroom. She jumped out of her bed and ran to the living room where Amadora slept. Anna had not even heard her return.

Amadora spread out across the couch, still dress in the clothes she wore as Johnnie Barbone. Sweat covered her face as she twisted and turned violently. Anna kneeled by her side and shook her lightly.

"Dora... Dora... Dora... Please wake up," Anna whispered in her ear so she would not wake her son. "Get up, hun. You're having a bad dream."

Amadora shot out of her dream, sweating, and gasping for air. Her heart pounded so hard that she heard the blood pumping through it. She looked around the room with eyes filled with tears. Fear still held a tight grip on her. It caused her to not recognize Anna when she saw her.

"Where am I?"

"You are at my place. Remember?" Anna said, putting the back of her hand on Amadora's forehead. "No fever. But you're soaked in sweat."

"I'm in Brooklyn? Anna, what day is it?" Amadora rubbed her forehead as she sat straight. She looked down at Anna, who was still on her knees.

"Yes, you are. It's Monday. What time did you get in last night?" Anna rose and sat next to Amadora.

"I think I came back around two," Amadora ran her hands through her hair and sat back. The images of last night replayed in her head nonstop. She wanted them to go away and leave her alone, but they would not.

Anna noticed Amadora's strange behavior. "What did they have you do last night?" Anna asked, concerned.

Amadora looked at Anna, then back down at her hands. She still smelled the blood and felt the gun in her hand. The feeling would never leave her. Would it get worse? Would she grow use to it like her brothers and sister? Or was Zanipolo right? Was she not ready? Amadora wanted to leave, but her pride stopped her as her goal flashed in her mind. She could not give up.

Anna could tell whatever she did was not good. She knew this was not a good idea, but she owed Amadora her life. She could not refuse her wishes. She would protect Amadora like she protected her at her father's party a year prior.

Anna made a stupid choice to agree to go as a date with one of Basilio's men. At the end of the party, she became drunk and made a complete fool of her father and sister, Elda. Of course, that behavior could not be tolerated, so Elda ordered that she'd be taken to the back and 'taught a lesson'.

The men did as ordered by beating her until she was almost unconscious. When they thought her vulnerable, they tried to take advantage of her. Amadora came out to the backyard right as they were about to rape her. She kicked the man who was pinning her down. Then she helped her up and ordered the other two to leave before she reported them to her father.

Amadora brought Anna into her room so she could clean off her wounds. Anna could not believe the kindness of that young girl who risked her life to save her own. Not until she sobered, did she realize Amadora was Basilio Morelli's daughter. That night Anna felt close enough to tell her why she hated mobsters like her father and siblings.

Anna's husband was killed in a crossfire by two rival mafia families. Anna did not care which two families did it because to her they were all the same. They took innocent lives for greed, lust, and blood. They were monsters with no remorse for any other people other than their own. So, to her, she could care less if they all died. At least, that was what she believed before she met Amadora.

If it was not for Amadora, her son might have become an orphan. Anna cared for her; and even though she hated Amadora's strange life choice, Anna would help her because it was what Amadora desired. In Anna's eyes, there was not enough that she could do to repay Amadora for saving her from an unsure fate.

"You know if you don't want to do this anymore, I can help you get out of this."

Amadora just looked at Anna again, then returned her gaze back at her hands without saying a word. She wanted to scream 'Yes!', but she knew that would just prove her brother right. And what if by some fluke they find out she was Johnnie? Anna would be in danger. She could not allow that.

"Have you ever killed a man, Anna?"

"Kill a man? They had you kill already!" Anna grabbed Amadora by her arms and looked her over for any bruises or scares. "Are you alright? You weren't hurt, right?"

Amadora shook her head no and lightly pushed her away. "You're not continuing this madness, are you?" Amadora stayed quiet and walked over to the kitchen to get a glass of water.

"Are you crazy, Amadora! You are going to lose yourself if you keep up this charade! The jobs are just going to get harder and the risk higher! Do you really think that you can handle it!" Anna cried as her fear for her friend took hold. She let Anna's worry and pain make Amadora feel worse. She turned her back from her and filled a glass with water, so she would not see her tears.

"I'm not sure if I can handle it, but I have to try," Amadora grimaced.

"Try to what? Get yourself killed?"

Amadora looked at her hands once more. She could not take her mind off last night. These hands that once embraced others with love had now committed the ultimate sin and killed a man.

'I know he wasn't a good man, but who was I to judge his fate? Who was I to decide whether he lived or died? Did I even have a choice in the matter? If I hadn't chosen to kill him, would that have changed his fate? Would it have affected mine?'

"This is the only way."

Anna wiped her face with her hand and knew there was no convincing Amadora. She knew Amadora would not stop until she reached her goal. And Anna realized there

was nothing she could say or do to stop her.

Brock tucked the envelope his boss gave him containing information on a special job under his arm. He closed his car door and headed up the walkway. He would have done the job himself, but his boss told him specifically that only an outsider could do it. So, since Brock did not have any new recruits, he had to rely on Musilli for someone.

Brock made sure he called Musilli ahead of time to tell him he was coming over, so he could make himself decent and send whatever type of whore he had over away. Since Brock called him ahead of time, Musilli was already waiting at the door when he stepped on the porch.

Musilli stood in the doorway wearing a blue-gray robe and matching slippers. Brock could tell that even though he called, Musilli must have still been in bed when he pulled up.

Brock looked him over and smirked. "Did I disturb you?"

Musilli yawned and let him in. He looked at him with a tired look on his face. "Of course, you did but don't act like you care. I know you don't. You just love waking me up at all different times in the morning. I wonder sometimes if you actually sleep."

Musilli led Brock into his living room and cleared off the couch so he could sit down. "I do sleep. I'm just alert when called for a job. And you wonder why I'm higher ranked than you?" Brock examined the room after he said that.

The place was a mess. He had melted candles all over the place. Some fruit on the coffee table in front of him, wilting flowers and a half-filled bottle of wine sat on the coffee table in front of the couch. "Nice place you have here, Moose. Wilted flowers, melted candles, dry fruit, and a half-drank bottle of wine. Seems like one heck of a party. Wonder why I wasn't invited?"

"Sorry, my friend. It was a party for two."

"I see," Brock laughed before becoming serious again. "Okay. Now it's time to get down to business. I got a visit from Lorenzo this morning. He told me Gugliehno will be out for a couple more days, and he needs a minor problem solved today."

"He wants me to take care of it?" Musilli asked, smiling. "About time the big boss recognized me."

Brock sighed and shook his head, then gave him the envelope. "If that was the case, they would have just asked me. He wants an outsider to deal with this."

Musilli looked at the contents of the envelope. When he finished reading it, he looked back at Brock. "An outsider? Like Johnnie?"

"Johnnie?" Brock looked at him, surprised. It was strange he was the first of his recruits he mentioned. "Yes, like him. Do you like the boy?"

"What makes you ask that?"

"Because he is the first one you mentioned."

"Well, the boy has spunk and fears nothing. I like that, because it saves me time training him," Musilli let out a proud hearty laugh. He sounded like a father talking about his son. "You should have seen him on the shooting range. He was perfect. He has a natural gift for precision and speed. He didn't even jump when he took his shot. He's a natural. He had no feelings at all. He even smiled on the way to the job yesterday."

"Is that true?" Brock raised his eyebrow. "That's not what I saw when we did that job at Jack's. I agree the boy has potential, but he isn't a cold-blooded killer. The boy understands the horrors of taking his first life. I saw it in his eyes after he shot Jack. The boy froze. If I didn't pull him out of there, he would have stayed until the cops came."

"But he seemed fine to me when I saw him after."

"He didn't seem quiet or distant when you were with him?"

"No. He laughed and joked with us in the car ride back."

"Maybe he hid how he felt... Forget it for now. Is Johnnie the one you pick for this job?"

"Yeah. It's a simple job. He'll be able to handle it," Musilli answered, sitting back in the chair and placing the envelope on the end table.

"Then it's settled. If you don't mind, I would like to present this job to him. I have some other things I want to discuss with him."

"Sure. This is your second home, anyway. I don't know about you, Brocky, but I'm famished. Want something to eat?" Musilli offered, standing up before heading to the kitchen.

Brock shrugged and just sat back, recalling the last job. He could not help but think about Johnnie and the fear he saw on his face after. If Johnnie was truly alright, then Brock worried about nothing. However, if he was not fine, then he could be trouble for them later if he was not dealt with.

At noon, Sam sat at her desk staring at a blank piece of paper. She had not touched the lunch her maid brought in, because she was busy trying to figure out what to write to Zanipolo explaining yesterday. She had to make it seem like something Amadora would tell him.

'Maybe I could tell him I was exploring the city and wasn't keeping track of time. How about I was too tired from shopping all day that I fell asleep early? No, that's eventually going to ride his suspicions.... Hm... Damn Amadora for coming up with this crazy scheme. And damn me for going along with this.'

Sam took a bite from her sandwich, then pondered some more. As she was taking

another bite, she finally realized what to write.

After lunch, Basilio and Casimiro discussed the events of the month in Basilio's office. They sat by the unlit fireplace. Basilio smoked his cigar while gazing into the fireplace while Casimiro sat in a chair across from him looking over some papers.

The window was cracked open, and a cool breeze brushed against the back of Basilio's neck. Autumn was coming. He felt it in the air. The temperature dropped and grew cooler by each passing week.

"It's quiet, Casimiro. I can hear the breeze rushing through the empty halls. I miss the days when this house was packed with all my children and grandchildren. I guess that's why I look forward to the end of the month without my Amadora here to bring sunshine to my mornings. That's all I have left for this month. And this end of the month is her favorite. It's when we have our annual autumn ball." Basilio's eyes glowed. He reminisced about when all his children lived under the same roof. It was so full of life and vibrant.

Now, the house was empty and cold since everyone left. He hated that part of the month, especially when there was no work for him to do. Even his own wife wandered to the kitchen with Millie to keep herself occupied.

"The Autumn Ball?" Casimiro asked, surprised. He forgot about the ball at the end of every September. It would be a perfect occasion to ask Giacinta to be his date.

"Yes. Did you forget about it? I'm having the secretary send out the invitations," Basilio smiled softly as he said that. He noticed something or someone else occupied his mind and was why he forgot. "Do you plan to bring a pretty lady?"

Casimiro laughed sheepishly. He felt embarrassed talking to Basilio about that because it was about his daughter, unknown to the don, of course. "I'm not sure. But possibly."

"Don't feel embarrassed, son. Did you ask her yet?" Basilio laughed with pride before taking another long puff from his cigar. Casimiro shook his head no, and Basilio laughed again "Then go ask her. We have no more business today so you can spend the rest of the day with that girl of yours."

Casimiro could not hide his joy. He smiled as he thanked the don before leaving to see Giacinta.

Giacinta stepped outside of her room, closing the door behind her. She was feeling much better today, especially after talking with Gunny the day before. She felt more relaxed and happier now that she had a new bond with her brother. She wanted nothing to ruin her day. All she wanted to do was take a car to the city and go shopping.

As she walked down the hall heading for the foyer, she saw Casimiro heading towards her with an enormous smile. Seeing him caused her heart to stop for a moment before beating uncontrollably fast. She wanted to see him since yesterday but was too scared. She wanted to tell him she was ready to give him a chance; but as he drew closer, her words froze.

"Giacinta, you're breathtaking. Do you have any plans today?" Casimiro brought her hand to his lips and kissed it softly.

The touch of his soft lips pressed against her skin made Giacinta melt and want to have them take hers and claim them as his own.

"You're too kind. There are tons of women better than me. Why do you like me so much? What do you want from me?" Giacinta blushed looking softly into his eyes trying to search for an answer.

Casimiro stroke her cheek softly with the back of his hand and brought her closer to him. Giacinta's cheeks flushed red as his soft gaze captured her with its warmth. "I like the way you are with all your flaws and who you are. Other women don't interest me, only you. Why haven't you realized what I truly want from you?"

When she heard his words, the world became oblivious, and only he was visible. "I don't know what you're talking about. Please tell me what it is."

Casimiro closed the distance between them until she felt his every heartbeat as if it was her own. He smiled as his arms made a protective barrier around her. "How about I show you instead?"

He cradled her face in his hand and pressed his lips against hers. Giacinta's heart jumped in chest.

Then, as if under a spell, she wrapped her arms around his neck. She rose to her tiptoes while he dropped his hands down to her waist and held her tighter.

The feeling from before that she could not identify returned. This time it warmed her chest. She felt weightless and free while in his arms, and the tighter he held her, the safer she felt. Giacinta never wanted their kiss or that feeling to end. But deep in her heart, fear still lurked.

When their kiss ended, Giacinta stumbled slightly, but Casimiro caught her. He smiled down at the beautiful angel in his arms. "I'm free today. Let's do whatever you want."

Giacinta smiled and shook her head yes. At that moment, she felt one barrier surrounding her heart finally break.

When Johnnie arrived at Musilli's house that evening, he saw Brock sitting on the porch holding an envelope. It was obvious he waited for Johnnie, because once he stepped on the stairs in front of the house, he waved him over.

"Johnnie, just the man I wanted to see. How are you feeling?" Brock said, motioning Johnnie to sit in the chair next to him.

Johnnie watched him suspiciously and sat down. Then his expression became plain and unreadable. "I'm feeling ok. Yesterday was just" Johnnie said, looking out at nothing. His words were obvious lies because the images still played repeatedly in his mind. They held him in a world full of blood and horror.

Brock noticed the way Johnnie acted and sighed. "Don't worry, son. The images will go away after a while."

Johnnie pivoted and looked at Brock surprised, wondering if he just read his mind or something. "What?"

"The images of last night. They're still replaying in your mind, aren't they?"

"Yes. They are. How do you know?"

"I was in your position once before. No matter how skilled you are or how prepared you become, you'll never be ready for the mental part of this job. Nothing can prepare you for that," Brock sat back in his chair and sighed.

"Is there a way to calm the nightmares of the blood staining my hands?"

"Yes. Time... Time is the best medicine. It'll help you forget, but unfortunately it cannot erase it from your memories."

"How about with the more people I kill will it feel the same?"

"It's like when you first learn how to drive. At first you are scared, but after a while you get used to it."

"I'll get used to taking people's lives... like some heartless monster?"

"You will never get used to killing someone. That is impossible as a human, but you will learn to deal with it. In this business, it is a fight for survival. Kill or be killed. There is no other choice at times."

Johnnie shook his head in understanding. "Is that all we are fighting for?"

Brock looked at him with a raised eyebrow. "No. We fight for those we hold close to us, some fight for the thrill, others fight because they were born to fight, some fight for greed, and some fight for revenge. But mostly we fight for survival."

"But isn't what we do illegal?"

"Well, it is according to the law, but look at it like this: We are just like soldiers except we protect our people here at home. We are soldiers of the street."

With that said, Brock glanced at his watch and handed Johnnie the envelope. "Time isn't on our side, son. I wouldn't mind talking to you more, but this job has to be done before the place closes at six."

Johnnie opened the envelope. First, he saw an address, then he saw a piece of paper. He recognized the paper from Gunny's stationary at his office at his house and Elda's handwriting. "This mission is important to Gugliehno. If you do everything he says, you will be high in his favor."

Johnnie read the paper and knew right away what job it was. It was the one Basilio and Gunny talked about at the complex. He had to attack the Mancini's store and bust it up with a bat. If Darian Mancini got in the way, then he could mess him up but could not kill him. Finally, the mission he wanted.

"I'm off."

Edward spent most of his day helping Zanipolo with his killer hangover. He took more care of Zanipolo than he did his own wife. He hated that little brat for what she did to her brother. Zanipolo drunk very little alcohol in the past two months. Now that little princess comes, and he's back to going through bottles.

What he hated the most was the little priss did not even call or write a note explaining her absence. Poor Polo was asking every hour if she called or did something come from her. Edward hated having to tell him no, because then he just became silent and stared out the window.

Just as Edward was boiling water to make soup for Zanipolo, a knock sounded on the door. "This better be, Little Miss Princess, now," Edward growled, putting the pot on the fire.

He walked to the door and opened it. To his surprise, it was not her but Arnold. "Arnie, any word from our little princess?"

"Yes. Here, sir," Arnold said, handing him the envelope.

"Ok. I'll give it to him later. Arnie, can you go fetch some sugar? He forgot to buy some," Edward said, putting the envelope in his pocket and giving Arnold some money. Arnold shook his head in understanding and left.

Edward closed the door and walked over to Zanipolo's room. When he reached the door, Zanipolo was sleeping. Edward sighed and closed the door gently. "Poor fellow, well I'll give it to him in the morning."

Johnnie arrived at Mancini's market ten minutes before closing. He snuck into an alleyway near the store and adjusted the black cloth he wore over his mouth and nose. He tucked the bat into the left side of his coat, holding it with his left arm.

His strategy was to go in and act as if he was sick and needed to buy something for his illness, then he would start breaking stuff from the back of the store. When Johnnie was good and ready, he walked towards the store, covering the sides of his face with the collar of his coat.

Inside, a tall man with caramel skin greeted Johnnie. He was fifteen feet away from the door, sitting by the register. "Hi. Just to let you know we are closing in eight minutes, so make it quick." The man inspected Johnnie. "Are you sick?"

"Yes, a little bug. Don't want you to catch it," The man just shrugged it off and continue reading his book. Johnnie walked to the back of the store, trying to see if he could get a better view of the man.

Amadora blushed as she saw how attractive he was. He had short black hair that looked like it was soft to the touch. His eyes seemed to be a light color from where she stood. Maybe green, hazel, gray, or blue. He had an athletic build and seemed strong. He could do some serious damage to her if she messed up. 'This is Darian. He's handsome. Too bad I must wreck his place and possibly him too if he gets in my way.'

Johnnie took the bat out of his coat and readied himself. He brought the bat back, then swung hard. Bottles crashing to the floor sounded through the store. Darian bolted out of his chair and ran to the back of the store.

"What the hell are you doing!" Darian yelled, trying to stop Johnnie before he destroyed more things.

Johnnie did not answer. He just swung randomly at some more stuff. Darian grabbed hold of the bat this time. Johnnie looked back at him and kicked Darian in his stomach. Darian fell back, but the bat flew out of Johnnie's hand, landing in the isle close to the front of the store.

Darian groped his stomach in pain. 'Who is this person? Why are they attacking the store? What do they want?'

Johnnie tried to retrieve the bat, but Darian tripped him. Johnnie hit the floor hard but quickly turned to his side. He kicked Darian once again. That time Darian caught his leg and threw him into an aisle. The isle fell and Johnnie tried his best to get up. When he finally regained his footing, Darian came up behind him and pinned his attacker against the wall.

He choked Johnnie. Johnnie struggled to breathe as Darian pressed against his neck with his massive hands. He desperately kicked him in his private to be freed. Darian let go of Johnnie's neck and hunched over in pain. Johnnie picked up a nearby bottle of wine and smashed it over Darian's head, causing him to fall to the ground unconscious.

Johnnie walked to the front of the store and tried to walk normally to the car, so no one noticed he was in pain. Johnnie closed the car door and drove back to Musilli's to report his progress.

Escalation & Revelation

6

The Worst Enemy–Fear

'Deception... It follows us everywhere, slowly devouring our peace and sanity. It creates a wall between us preventing me from reaching you no matter how much I want to,' Thoughts of Samantha Johnson.

Darian blinked his tired eyes as a throbbing pain paralyzed his body, preventing him from getting up. He looked around the shadow-filled room, trying to remember what happened before his memory fogged over, but his mind went blank. He tried to fight the pain and move around but was stopped by a gentle hand resting on his shoulder.

"Don't move. You need to rest," Darian's expression softened when he saw his father's calm smile while he sat in a chair beside his bed.

"What happened?" Darian asked, lying back against his pillow.

"You don't remember?" Domenico asked, leaning against his cane, and looking at his son with a raised eyebrow.

Darian nodded. "No. My head aches too much to think."

"That's not a surprise. Someone clocked you over the head hard enough to knock you out. They got away before I could get to you, so I don't know who attacked you," Domenico explained.

"How did I get here?" Darian asked.

"I asked Dr. Spreen. He and his son brought you upstairs after he examined you," Domenico replied. "You're lucky you only had minor injuries. Dr. Spreen assured me you didn't have to go to the hospital, just needed to rest for a while."

"My physical injuries might be minor, but the ones dealt to my pride run deep," Darian grumbled under his breath.

"No need to sulk. I told you things like this could happen if we were not protected. You should go to Gugliehno and ask to be under his protection again," Domenico scolded, his feeble hand resting on the dark polished handle of his cane. His faded eyes gently ridiculing his son as he talked.

"I told you I'm not doing that!" Darian snapped. "I refuse to trust the safety of our store to some lawless thugs."

"Calm down, son," Domenico placed his hand on Darian's shoulder. "I know how much you hate the families because of what they do, but we can't be picky. The damage done to the store is too expensive. We can't afford the repairs on our own. We need help. You must ask Gugliehno for help. They will help for little to no cost"

"Even if there's no charge, we're still bargaining our souls to those devils," Darian protested.

"I understand. But we have no choice. The Morelli family is the only one I trust. Please take this and go speak with Gugliehno," Domenico reached into his pocket and pulled out a small eggshell card with fancy gold lettering. He handed it to Darian.

"What's this?" Darian asked, looking over the card.

"It's an invitation to the Morellis' Autumn Ball," Domenico answered.

"Why do I need this?" Darian asked.

"You can go there to speak with him in person. Since he is a busy man, there is no guarantee you will see him if you head to his office. But all the Morellis are obligated to go to this event," His father explained.

Darian flipped the card back and forth, scanning its contents before pressing it to his forehead in defeat.

"I guess if we have no other options, then I'll go."

Domenico smiled in relief but didn't realize his son had an ulterior motive for going to the ball. As Darian sat talking to his father, pieces of the previous night returned to his mind, slowly recreating the image of the fiend who attacked him and destroyed his store.

That man was not a regular burglar from the street. He was calculating. His method proved that. Waiting for the last few minutes before they closed, so no one else was there, not even the cops—who stopped patrolling this area after five.

Darian was certain that person was connected to one of the five families; and if he had to choose which one, then it would be the Morellis. They gained the most from this attack. However, Darian had no proof.

Darian had to uncover the identity of that man and figure out who he worked for. And the only way he could do that was by gathering intel at this soiree. Darian was sure drunk Morelli goons would pack the halls. If he manipulated them correctly, he might get some information from them. However, it was not guaranteed. No matter what, Darian would not stop until he found his assailant and made him pay.

When Zanipolo woke up the next day, he felt much better than he did the day before. Thanks to Edward, who by the looks of it never made it home. Zanipolo laughed silently as he saw Edward draped over the couch next to his bed. He must have been up all night making sure he was sleeping okay. Oh, Edward. He always was looking out for him no matter what and no matter how much trouble he would be with his wife. He has been such a good friend for all these years. Zanipolo could not imagine his life without him.

He would probably be dead. Talking about death, he felt like death the day before. He could not believe how sick he was. The last time he was that sick from drinking was when he was still engaged to Maxine. That girl was such a pain and put him through hell. Maybe that was because she was such a princess at heart.

Maxine Watson was the daughter of Jason Watson and Evalyn Guilden. Her father, Jason Watson, was a world-renowned singer. While her mother, Evalyn, was an heiress of an extremely large fortune. Yes, Maxine was a diva. She loved to perform in front of everyone on stage. He missed her spunk and courage.

However, while recalling the image of her in his mind, it was being replaced by another. The image shone like the morning sun on a clear day. It broke through the pain and hurt left by Maxine. It was the image of Sam.

He sighed turning to rise out of his bed then he noticed a letter sitting on the nightstand. Zanipolo picked it up and opened it. He read it, then smiled. It was from Amadora explaining the night before.

Dear Zanipolo,

My dear brother, I'm sorry about the night before. As absent minded as I sometimes become, I forgot I was supposed to meet you. The warmth and serenity of the beach had me in a deep sleep. And because I went out after the help were dismissed at six, I had no one to remind me of the time. I hope you aren't too mad at me, Polo. You know I would never do this on purpose. I love you so much. Maybe next time.

Amadora

The big band played an energetic melody to rouse the patrons of Calto Club. They clapped along as the lead singer's raspy voice flowed in tune and engaged with the pretty women sitting close to the stage. Everyone seemed to enjoy the performance except one, Marco.

Marco sat in a secluded booth in the club's corner sipping a small glass of bourbon. He paid no mind to the goings-on around him but focused his attention to the man sitting across from him. His long dark coat, the dark scarf still wrapped around his mouth and the broad-brimmed hat covering his eyes obscured the features of the man.

"What are you doing here?" Marco asked, annoyed by the man's presence.

"I heard you're plotting something that could put our entire plan in jeopardy," The man answered.

"What do you mean? I'm doing nothing that concerns you," Marco replied.

"Your pursuit of the Morelli girl does concern me. If she has paid her dues, then leave her alone. We can't afford for her new man to get in our way," The man warned.

"I don't know what you're talking about. I let Giacinta go. I don't care what she does now," Marco snapped.

They looked up and glared at Marco. His dark eyes shot through Marco, making him feel uneasy. "Don't lie to me."

Sweat glazed Marco's forehead as he tried to match the man's piercing gaze and ease his nerves. "I'm not."

The man adjusted his gloves. "Fine. I'll believe you for now; but if your obsession with Don Basilio's middle daughter interrupts our plan in any way, it will be the last mistake you'll ever make."

The man left without another word, leaving Marco stewing in his frustration. Somehow, his boss found out about his little dealing with Giacinta, and they sent out their big guns to try to put him in place, but he would not let his threats deter him. Just because she got her daddy's consigliere involved did not mean he would let her go.

A fierce storm shook the large black windowpanes of Giacinta's penthouse, rattling the small statuettes on their ledges until one fell off the edge and shattered against the hard wood floor. The shattering glass and the roaring thunder roused Giacinta from her sleep. She shot up and drowsily searched the gray shadows for the source of the noise.

She pulled her robe tight around her body and looked at the broken glass scattered across the floor by her window. She groaned as she left to get a broom to sweep everything up. However, before she could retrieve it, the doorbell rang vigorously, breaking the silent interval between the heavy rainfall and booming thunder.

It was almost 1 in the morning, so Giacinta did not know who could be at her apartment door this late at night. Casimiro was away with her older siblings dealing with their cousin, Nero; and none of her friends would stop by.

Giacinta dazedly crossed the shadows and bravely welcomed her unexpected visitor.

The moment the door swung open she regretted her actions as fear stole control of her body, preventing her from reacting to the devil standing before her. The source of all the pain and despair she endured for years stood before her with a devilish smirk and cold entrapping eyes, her ex, Marco.

"You shouldn't be here. Why are you here?" Giacinta asked, fear causing her voice to tremble as she addressed him.

"Gia don't act like that. You know how much you mean to me," Marco pressed forward as he blocked the door and feigned genuine human concern.

"I don't care. I want nothing else to do with you. He paid you off, so we have nothing else between us. Just leave me alone," Giacinta snapped harshly, trying to brush past him and grab hold of the doorknob, but Marco grabbed her arm and pinned her to the wall and whispered harshly ear as she fought to escape.

"Do you really think you can get rid of me that easily?"

Giacinta bit her lip while fighting back her tears. The way he had her pinned, she felt her bones in her arm wretch in pain when she tried to move it. But no matter how weak she was, she could not let him have his way. She made a promise to Casimiro to kick all her bad habits from the past, and that included Marco.

"Yes. I can. I am trying to change, which means I must leave all my baggage behind. That includes you. I no longer need you, so let me go and find another poor soul to manipulate."

"You want me to let you go because you say you've changed?" Marco let out a roaring laugh. "You think someone like you can just suddenly throw away our past and turn a new leaf?"

Giacinta bit her lip as she forcefully fought from his grasp and pushed him into the hall. "Anything's possible."

"Do you think being with your new boy toy will wash you anew and get rid of all the dark secrets from our past?"

Marco grabbed her shoulder and pushed her forcefully against her door. His white teeth flashed as he sneered at her new revelation. "My dear, people like us never change. I'll prove that to you no matter what or who I need to get rid of to do so."

Marco pressed his greasy lips against her trembling ones before letting her go and leaving Giacinta petrified, unable to make sense of the world around her.

Elda played with the pen in her hand, flicking it back and forth as she scanned the long contract in front of her. She exhaled as boredom and annoyance fought in her mind. All this legal jargon made no sense to her. It was Casimiro's expertise not hers, so why did she need to review them by herself.

"This is ridiculous. Why did I get left with this?"

Gunny leaned back in his chair and watched Elda as she grew more impatient by each passing second. He knew the contracts had little to do with Elda's impatience. Ever since they received word from Lorenzo that their cousin settled into his place and would head over soon with Brock, Elda's usually calm temperament vanished, and she became an agitated mess. She disliked the whole situation with Nero since baby-sitting hot-headed brats clashed with her usually cool temper. She reacted the same way to Zanipolo before he straightened out.

"Relax. You can do that stuff later. You need to compose yourself before they arrive."

"I know, but I can't just sit here and wait. I want them to hurry so we can be done with this." Elda dropped the pen on the desk, closed the manila folder, then ran her hands through her dark hair and slouched in her chair. "Nero annoys me."

"Don't worry. They'll be here soon; and once it's done, he'll be Brock's and Lorenzo's problem."

"I guess. I feel bad for shoving more on their plates."

"You're fucking right. I actually was planning to have somewhat of a personal life before you two dumped this man baby on me." A man entered the room, flung his hat and coat over the coat rack, and plopped onto the couch next to Gunny's desk. His grayish-blue eyes sparkled, and a playful grin crossed his lips as he watched Elda's strained expression ease into a more neutral one as he strode across the floor.

"Lorenzo, you're early. Weren't you supposed to arrive with Brock?" Elda asked, completely ignoring his previous comment.

"Yeah. That was the original plan, but I wanted to come talk to you both before I officially become your cousin's glorified babysitter."

"Sorry about that. My father wanted the most reliable eyes watching after him. Since Gunny will be busy with some delicate matters and I cannot stand him, you two were the only ones we thought of," Elda responded.

"I should be flattered, but I would like to know why he needs supervision. What has he done?" Lorenzo asked, taking a seat across from Elda and easing back into the soft cushions.

"We'll tell you about that later. For now, just do us this little favor," Elda said, shooting a slight pleading look at Lorenzo.

"Of course," Lorenzo nodded.

"Thanks for taking on this job for us. I know we're putting you out by having him stay with you, but this is how pops wants it," Gunny sat up straight and looked at the lights flashing past his office window.

Before he could respond, a knock sounded on the door and Brock's towering frame eclipsed the entrance. He stepped aside and placed his dripping hat and coat across the coat rack. He nodded to Gunny and Elda.

"I hope we're not late. We ran into a sudden downpour, making the roads here a little slippery."

"No. You're right on time. We were just discussing the matter at hand," Lorenzo replied, motioning to the seat next to him.

Brock sat down and turned to the door when a scrawny man stood wrestling his coat off before tossing it recklessly over Brock's and waltzing over to a chair across from Elda.

"Miei cugini, che volete con me?" Nero smirked and propped his feet on Gunny's desk.

"Cut the crap! You know damn well why you're here!" Elda snapped, jumping up and pushing his feet off the desk.

Lorenzo and Brock sprinted to her side and held her lightly back before she could strangle the cocky boy.

"Yeah, I remember, zio is worried because I popped some guys talking shit about my mom. He thinks their fat, old boss is gonna kill me," Nero's devilish smirk grew as he shrugged off the reason his mom shipped him here. "I don't get the problem. There's nothing different from what I did or what you do. Why are you going through all this trouble?"

"Running around shooting people for every slight is far from what we do. We don't resort to violence unless it's absolutely necessary," Gunny clarified.

Nero broke into a roar of laughter. "You're splitting hairs."

"You don't believe me? Well then, you'll just have to find out for yourself." Confidence and a dark amusement emanated from Gunny's face, unnerving Nero when he stared at his eldest cousin.

"What do you mean?" Confused and cautious, Nero tried to uncover his cousin's true motive, but he could not decipher the cause of Gunny's newfound cockiness.

"You think we brought you here to be your personal bodyguards?" Elda laughed when she saw the color drain from Nero's face.

"No, silly boy. Since you like to act like a gangster, let's see if your tough guy bravado will last once, you see how our world really is."

"What?" Nero looked over at Gunny for confirmation. Gunny's smile grew and his eyes grew ice cold.

"Elda's right. You're here to work under one of my top men, Brock. He'll decide the extent of your involvement. So, if he tells you to pick up his laundry, you'll be stuck doing just that."

Nero was too dumbstruck to respond, so Elda motioned to Lorenzo and Brock.

"He's all yours. Get him outta here."

Brock nodded and guided Nero out of the office while Lorenzo closed the door behind him.

"Tell me what the point was of dragging him here if you were just going to kick him out?" Lorenzo asked, reclaiming his seat.

"I wanted to see if he's as bad as pops said he is," Guglielmo replied.

"And what do you think?" Lorenzo observed his friend's behavior to gauge his feelings, but his hollow expression was unreadable.

"He's an ass," Elda sniped.

"Yes. He is, but not as bad as pops initially let on. If he's telling the truth about the incident, then it might have been a spur-of-the-moment situation. That's why I want you and Brock to keep a close eye on him," Gunny leaned back in his chair and looked out the window next to him. The rain intensified and beat viciously against the windowpanes, putting him into a slight trance as he mulled over his cousin's situation.

"Fine," Lorenzo redirected the conversation. "Now that we've settled that, what do you want to do about the Barbone kid. He took out Jack and dealt with the Mancini matter. Both Brock and Larry sing nothing but praises about him."

"Isn't it too early to do anything about him?" Elda asked.

"Elda's right. Let's see how he does in the coming weeks. If he continues to prove that he's a valuable ally, then I want you to reach out to him and assess his worth. If you approve, I might have to meet him for myself." Gunny said to Lorenzo.

Gunny read Lorenzo's reports about the rookie, Johnnie Barbone, and was interested in examining him for himself. Both Brock and Larry boasted about his potential, which made Gunny even more curious. He was used to Larry trying to promote his new recruits to get recognition in the business. However, Brock rarely approved of anyone; and when he did, it was only when he believed they had actual skill.

The Tuesday before the Autumn Ball arrived faster than Giacinta expected it would. Her anxiety grew as she watched the servants run from the main house to the ball room preparing for the festivities. The Autumn Ball was supposed to be a joyous, light-hearted occasion because all the family reunited, which meant she would see Polo again but also would not be alone this year.

Every year she attended the ball by herself because she never found someone, she would feel comfortable coming with. But this year she thought that could change since she had Casimiro, but Marco destroyed those hopes.

Weeks had passed since her encounter with Marco. Since then, she had not heard from him, even though she went to great lengths to make sure he could not reach her. She returned to the complex, which was heavily guarded, and went nowhere by herself. When Casimiro was busy, her maid, Nanette, remained close by her side.

Even with all these extra precautions, Giacinta feared it would not be enough to keep Marco at bay. Giacinta was not sure if he would make good on his threats, but she would not take a chance on it.

Giacinta was not sure when he would strike, but she had a feeling it might be soon.

Giacinta paced back and forth in her room as every dark, despairing moment with Marco replayed in her mind. Her mind raced as she lazily scanned the room, but her focus returned when her eyes fell on a small note on top of her desk. She picked up the note and the bright red rose lying next to it. She opened the note and read its contents.

"My dearest Giacinta, I know I have spent little time with you because of work, but I hope to make it up to you tonight. I have a special surprise for you. Meet me by the fountain at 7pm."

All negative thoughts weighing on Giacinta's mind disappeared as she brought the flower to her nose and inhaled its soft, mesmerizing aroma. Casimiro's cologne mingled with the rose's sweet fragrance. His scent aroused the precious memories from the few times they spent with one another, along with an anxious feeling that this precious illusion could disappear at any moment.

When Giacinta entered the garden, her eyes beheld a most enchanting sight. Small iron lily lamps aligned the brick path winding throughout the garden. The dark fuchsia petals glowed softly, painting the path in a soft, warm hue. Their intricate designs of these lamps mesmerized Giacinta. She stopped in front of one and ran her hand along the details of the stem of the lily lamps. They were exquisite and lifelike. Each flower differed from the other. They looked like little blooms of light that brought a comforting air to the garden.

Giacinta enjoyed the feeling they gave off as she made her way to the fountain. She stood in front of the stone stairs leading down to the fountain was supposed to be and looked towards it. When she saw no one was there, her smile faded. He promised he would be there. She wondered where he was.

Giacinta walked to the fountain and sat on the edge. She turned towards it, sighing softly to herself. "He's not here. I hope he didn't forget about me."

As she ran her hand across the surface of the water, someone's hand caressed her cheek from behind. Giacinta put her hand over theirs and turned around. When she turned to face them, there was Casimiro standing behind her, smiling lovingly.

"I would never forget you," Casimiro embraced and kissed her softly. "Did you like the lamps I added to the garden?"

Giacinta looked up at him, smiling courteously. "They are absolutely beautiful. But did you tell my mother before you did that? You know she'll have a fit if you change her garden without asking her first."

"Of course, I did. Millie and your mother were the first ones to see them. She loved them," Casimiro laughed, guiding Giacinta back to the fountain. He motioned Giacinta to sit next to him on the edge of the fountain.

"Casimiro, why are we here? What is the surprise you have for me?" Giacinta looked at him wide-eyed with wonder. He laughed softly at the way she looked at him. Her expression was innocent and sweet.

"I wanted to talk to you," Casimiro reached down, grasping her hand in his own. His gaze was warmer than ever before. "Remember when you asked me what I wanted from you, and I told you I'd tell you when you were ready. I think it's time to let you know my true intentions."

Those words caused the fear lying in the depths of her heart to surface. Her heart dropped, afraid of the words that would soon leave his lips. She wanted to know what his intentions were; but if they were bad, she did not want to hear them. She did not want to ruin the one thing in her life that was going well.

"Giacinta, we've known each other since we were young, and I've always been fond of you. As the years went by, my fondness for you grew, and I adored you. I adore your smile and laugh. I adore your poise and grace," As Casimiro talked, Giacinta's cheeks blushed slightly as he continued to compliment her. She enjoyed every word he spoke, but the more he revealed the greater the fear inside her grew. "I adore everything about you and have always felt this way. That's why I helped you."

"I don't understand. Why do you feel like that? What do you want from me?" Giacinta asked, looking at him confused. She did not understand what any of that had to do with what he wanted from her. It must be something important if he went through all this trouble to woo her.

Casimiro looked at her with an eyebrow raised and smiled. "You don't know by now?" Casimiro brought her closer to him, gazing gently into her eyes. Giacinta could feel the warmth in his gaze. Her cheeks grew rosier the closer they got. "The only thing I ever wanted was to love you, Giacinta. I want to share my love with you. That's all I want and have ever wanted."

Casimiro's confession cut through Giacinta like a knife. At a time that should inflame her with joy, but an incurable bout of fear and anxiety struck her down. A dark emptiness swallowed her as she froze in his arms. The warmth of his love was not powerful enough to free her from the mental spiral she was embarking.

As she looked into his anticipating green eyes, she felt the world grow dark and a treacherous voice echo through her mind.

"Go ahead, Gia. Tell him how you feel," A dark shadow appeared behind Casimiro and brought its cold shapeless arm up his body until they hovered by his neck.

"Let him know everything. Do you think he'll accept you?" The shadow rested its head on his shoulder and brought its hand across his neck. "Do you think I'll leave him alone just because you told him how you feel?"

The shadow disappeared and reappeared behind her and ran its hands through her hair.

"I told you I'd destroy anything that gets in my way. Do you want to risk his life to see if I'm telling the truth?"

Her heartbeat raced as the surrounding air thinned and she struggled to breathe. She felt trapped and wanted to escape. Giacinta could not be selfish and let him share something so pure with someone like her. She would rather him hate her than let him risk his life protecting her from the monsters plaguing her. The fear in her heart took over. She pushed him away as she fought the threatening shadows engulfing her.

Casimiro saw the scared look on Giacinta's face and became worried. When she tried to back away, he grabbed her to calm her down. He held her close and tried to hide his concern while trying to return sense to his beloved.

"Giacinta, tell me what's wrong!" Casimiro held her tight, but she squirmed viciously. Fright filled Casimiro. He became confused. He did not know what to do or say anymore. He did not know what upset her or why she was acting like this.

"Let me go!" Giacinta shouted, banging on his chest. Darkness completely consumed her, and escape was all she desired. Casimiro could not understand what was happening, but he just let her go. He watched, his heart aching as she ran from him.

The past few weeks were the hardest in Sam's life. She hated the amount of lies she fed to Zanipolo every day. With each lie, she saw she was slowly killing Zanipolo inside while also killing herself. She hated seeing Zanipolo's face as her maid told him she was not available. She felt his heart sink when he left the porch to return to his car. She saw the fury and pain he had as he drove away.

Sam wished all the deceit would end soon. She hated lying and the pain their little charade caused. She hated Amadora for convincing her to do it, but she hated herself even more for agreeing to help. If Samantha knew how much pain she would cause Zanipolo, she would have never agreed to it.

How much longer could she keep it up before Zanipolo became suspicious? How long before he wanted to find out what is really going on with his little sister? How long could she keep him at bay? Eventually, he was bound to notice something was not right. If that happened, she would have no choice but to tell him the truth.

Sam brought her hat over her eyes, concealing the tears falling down her cheeks from the servants. She rushed to her room, shut the door behind her, and leaned against it while her tears fell and she sank to the floor.

"I can't do this. I will not lie to him. I am going to tell him tomorrow. Even if it means both Amadora and him hate me then sobeit."

Zanipolo sat at his desk in his office finishing his last bottle of juice. He could not stop thinking about Amadora and the way she acted. Something was not right. Zanipolo did nothing to upset her that much, so there must be another reason behind her behavior. But what could it be? What was she doing that she did not want him around? What was she hiding?

Edward told him he worried for no reason, but Zanipolo could not help but be suspicious. But he wondered if his reservations were correct. Did she really have some crazy plan in action? If so, what was it?

According to Arnold, Amadora never left the house except to go to the beach or the garden. So, that meant whatever she hid must be in the house. But what if Edward was right? What if he was over analyzing the situation and there was nothing going on? Maybe she really wanted to be alone to relax, but why was she deliberately keeping him at a distance. Amadora was not a loner and always needed someone with her. She would not hide herself unless there was something going on that she did not want him to know about.

Zanipolo poured the last of the apple juice into his glass, drank it, and then put the cup down before leaning back in his chair and propping his feet on his desk. He needed to find out what his sister was hiding so he could put his nagging suspicions to rest.

As night neared and the sun set, Sam tied back her hair and headed out to the garden for some fresh air. She walked over to the orange trees lining the front of the garden. She sat on the wooden bench under the trees, watching the wind as it danced through their leaves.

All she needed was some time to just sit back, relax, and enjoy the beauty surrounding her, to forget all the dangers and deceit plaguing her. She deserved that much. Sam closed her eyes and let her hair down, feeling the wind as it blew through it.

Zanipolo arrived at the vacation house around five o'clock. Zanipolo informed Arnold to let him know when Amadora was in the garden, so he could surprise her. He walked to the front door and rang the doorbell to wait for Arnold.

"Mr. Morelli, you are just in time. Your sister just went to the front of the garden. Come see for yourself." Arnold smiled, guiding Zanipolo to the gate where the orange trees grew.

Zanipolo smiled graciously. "Thank you for doing this."

When they reached the gate, Zanipolo could not believe his eyes. That girl was not his sister! Fear struck his heart at the fact something might have happened to Amadora. That girl looked almost exactly like her from afar, but she was too light skinned to be his sister. And the girl's hair was a little shorter than hers.

Zanipolo was not sure if one of the rival families was behind this and if any of the staff was working with this imposter. He also was not sure what they did with his actual sister. Was Amadora kidnapped or worse? He was uncertain, but he would figure out what was going on even if he had to beat it out of the imposter and her accomplices himself. God help her, if that girl had anything to do with his sister getting hurt, he would slit her deceiving throat himself.

Rage mounded inside him. He needed to know the truth. Zanipolo gritted his teeth before recomposing himself and turning back to his car to leave.

"Mr. Morelli, didn't you want to talk to her?" Arnold asked, confused when he saw Zanipolo leaving.

"I want to surprise her later. Don't tell her I stopped by today," Zanipolo said, smirking crookedly.

The Truth Revealed

'Just like the sun dispels the shadows of the night each morning, embracing your heart's true desire is the only way to dispel fear and doubt,' Thoughts of Giacinta Morelli.

A strange creaking noise echoed through the late-night rousing Sam from her sleep. She looked at the clock on top of the nightstand. It was three in the morning. No servants should be here for a few hours. She wondered if they left a window open and the early fall winds caused this late disturbance. No matter what it was, she would not know for sure unless she checked it out.

Sam reluctantly rose from her bed, threw on a robe and slippers, and went to check the house. All the windows in the library and extra bedrooms were locked, which meant the sound came from the first floor.

The first floor was dark and quiet from where Sam stood at the top of the stairs. The eerie silence made her heart skip a beat. Sam paused, took a deep breath before descending the dark stairs into the shadows of the night.

When Samantha reached the bottom, she grabbed an umbrella from the closet underneath. She turned around and made her way to the hallway. She pushed open the door and peered out. There was nothing. Maybe she was just getting worked up about nothing.

Samantha saw something unusual on the floor by the kitchen. It was a can of coffee beans. Sam smiled, relieved when she found the cause of the sound, putting her fear to rest.

Samantha walked over and picked up the can, then placed it back inside the cabinet where it belonged. While closing the cabinets, someone grabbed her from behind.

Samantha tried to scream, but the intruder pressed their hand firmly over her mouth. She tried to struggle but was too afraid to move. Her heart froze in her chest while her breathing grew heavy as they covered her nose and mouth.

Was this the end? Were they going to kill her? Fear paralyzed Sam. She did not know what to do or how she could fight back. The assailant did not seem to have a weapon. But as soon as that thought formed, the assailant took out a knife and pressed it against her neck. There was nothing she could do.

"I'm going to remove my hand. If you scream, I won't hesitate to slit your throat," The intruder whispered harshly in her ear.

'No. It's Zanipolo. He must have noticed I wasn't Amadora. What should I do?' Samantha tried to calm her racing nerves after she realized the identity of the intruder. But even after knowing, she still was not safe, because he did not know who she was. Sam followed his orders as he locked her arms at her side with his own, preventing her from breaking free.

"At least you're obedient. Maybe I'll spare your life if you tell me what I want to know," Zanipolo tightened his hold around the woman and whispered harshly in her ear. "What did you do with my sister? What's your plan?"

"Zanipolo, let go of me. You're hurting me," Sam begged, trying to wriggle from his grasp.

Shocked, Zanipolo released her and tried to get a better look at the shadowy figure before him. When she turned around, he finally realized who she was.

"Sa... Sam?" Zanipolo stuttered in confusion. "What are you doing here? Where's Amadora?"

"She's busy at the moment," replied Sam, biting her lip to prevent from revealing the truth.

"Busy doing what? When did you get here?" Zanipolo demanded.

"I can't tell you," Samantha refused.

"What do you mean? This isn't a great time for silly games. I need to know that she's safe and where she is," he pressed worry and desperation visible on his face.

Samantha could not stand seeing the dismay in his eyes.

"She's fine. You don't need to worry about her. She's in New York with a friend," Samantha reassured.

"What's she doing in New York?" Zanipolo noticed Sam's defiance to tell him the entire truth, so he grabbed her arms and pleaded with her once more. "Please tell me."

"She's undercover as a man working her way into Gunny's circuit. She had me pose as herself so everyone would think she was in California and wouldn't connect the two," Sam thought revealing the truth would make her feel better, but the weight of her guilt from the charade only grew. She could not maintain eye contact with Zanipolo because she felt too shameful.

Zanipolo grew enraged, turned to the wall, and punched it as hard as he could, leaving a gaping hole in its wake. Sam jumped when she turned around and yelled at her. Her heart sank and tears threatened to fall. "I knew something was up! You two are so stupid! Do you know how much danger she is in! Do you realize the damage you've caused me and whoever else you've roped into helping you with this farce!"

"I understood the danger very well and have tried to convince Amadora against this. But you know how stubborn she is when determined to do something, she won't let anyone stand in her way or try to convince her otherwise," Samantha answered.

"But why did you go along with it?" Zanipolo moved closer to her and lifted her head so she could look him in the eye. He wanted her to see the pain he felt over the weeks. He wanted her to see the pain she caused him.

"I am loyal to your sister and would rather help her with this dangerous charade than let her face it alone," Sam averted her gaze, because she did not want to be reminded of the distress that she caused him.

"I knew people would end up getting hurt. That's what I was afraid of. That's why I stayed inside the house. I was tortured every time a word of deception left my lips to the maid. Or when I wrote you a letter that was not in my own words," Samantha remained distant. She held back her urge to cry in frustration. "I'm sorry for deceiving you, but I had to do this for Amadora."

Zanipolo grimaced "Is that all? You had no choice, because Amadora needed you to do this. Are you stupid? Can't you think for yourself, or will you do anything just because my sister tells you to?"

"I guess I can't," Samantha shrugged him off and walked back towards the hall. "Now you know everything. It's your turn to decide: will you help us or rat us out to your father?"

Tons of large trucks drove in and out of the tall black gates of the warehouse. Each driver flashed their credentials to the guards as they inspected the contents before directing them into which loading area to drop off their goods.

The happenings in the yard below seemed more exciting than what went on in the supervisor's office. The phone barely rang; and when it did, it was either Lorenzo or Brock checking up on random things in the yard. Nero yawned and kicked back in his chair while looking at the pile of papers stacked on his desk.

This kind of work was meant for women not able body men like himself. He should be in the yard helping unload the trucks. He hated the mundane simple jobs they gave him all because his cousin did not trust him enough to join the 'real' business. He was afraid he is too much of a loose cannon to give a more interesting job to; and he was wrong.

Nero's situation was bittersweet. He loved being away from his shabby Italian country home and moving to the hustle and bustle of American life. Ever since he was young, he dreamed about the luxurious lifestyle that his uncle and cousins lived. But after one row with his stepbrother and his political thugs, now he was stuck being babysat by his cousin's goons and having his entire life controlled and micromanaged.

Nero believed his uncle overreacted about his situation. He needed to turn his situation around to his advantage. He had to get closer to either his cousin or his men and show them his usefulness. If he was going to be exiled here for the foreseeable future, then he wanted to have some fun.

The heat from the early morning sun's rays burned Giacinta's body as it crept through her bedroom curtains. Drenched in sweat, she pulled at her clothes and wiped away the increasing droplets. Sharp aches and pains cascaded through her thin, frail frame as she tried to force herself on her stomach to fight a sudden urge to vomit.

Giacinta's current state was a product of her own making. Late nights drinking back copious amounts of alcohol became the new source of entertainment she needed. The temporary pleasure of intoxication to mask her new harsh reality. But the pain of each hangover, the following morning reminded her of the hurt she held inside.

Giacinta was back in her room at the compound. Locked inside, she tried to hide from all the regret and sorrow she bared, but unknowingly trapped it with her.

Giacinta hated herself for how she treated Casimiro. She should not have let her fear take control of her like that. She should not have given Marco's threat such power over her heart. Giacinta was not sure if he would act on it, but she was a heartless fool for letting it influence her mind and cloud all consideration for his feelings.

Giacinta wondered what impact her foolish actions had on Casimiro. She avoided seeing and talking to him, because she was not sure what she would say to justify what she did. She wondered day and night about the suffering and confusion she must have caused him. Giacinta forced herself off her bed, walked over to her bathroom and looked into the large golden mirror hanging over her sink. She grimaced at the pale, bony mask glancing back at her. She was a terrible beast, manipulated by fear trampling on the heart of the one man she cared for the most.

Giacinta wanted to fix it, but she did not know how to without revealing everything. She needed to tell him the truth if she did not want to lose Casimiro; but if she told him about Marco, she knew he would not hesitate to go after him. She did not care if he got rid of Marco, but she did not want to risk his life to do so. It would be an internal struggle that could destroy the best treasure she ever possessed.

After Samantha revealed Amadora's plan, Zanipolo stayed at the vacation house with her until he could sort through this mess. Zanipolo could not sleep after last night's antics. He reviewed different solutions to resolve this foolishness quietly and quickly before it grew out of hand.

When Samantha woke up and went to the first floor, she ran into Zanipolo who was leaning against a window in the hall and staring outside deep in thought.

"Zanipolo, I didn't know you were up this early. Did you sleep?"

"Of course, I didn't. I'm worried sick because my little sister is out parading as an associate in New York. Everyday she's in danger by each new threat that'll come her way, and I must figure what I should do to best protect her," Zanipolo snapped coldly.

"You still haven't decided on whether you're going to help her see this through?" Sam pressed slightly unnerved by Zanipolo's mood.

Zanipolo shrugged and returned his focus to the window. "I can't promise that. I don't agree with this little scheme of hers and want to get her out of this as soon as possible. However, I will help her until I can speak with her to figure out what's going on."

"Speak with her? Do you want to call her?"

"No. I want to speak to her in person. What name is she using, anyway?"

"Johnnie Barbone," Samantha replied.

"Johnnie Barbone! You gotta be kiddin' me!"

"What's wrong?"

"There's no way out for her now, because Barbone is about to become one of Gunny's soldiers. If he leaves now, suspicions will rise, and his disappearance will be investigated. They might think it's foul play from a rival family and could cause an all-out war. There's nothing I can do to get her out without exposing her; and that has a worse fallout than just making her leave."

"So, what do you want to do?"

"For now, I'll make sure her cover isn't blown. But we need to hop on the first thing smoking to Jersey so I can have a chat with my sister," Zanipolo grabbed his hat and started towards the door. "I need to tell Edward to make arrangements for our return home. While I'm gone, give my sister a call and tell her to meet us at the complex tomorrow. Otherwise, I might spill the beans about her little scheme to Gunny."

Zanipolo's expression was frigid and unreadable. Samantha became uneasy when their eyes met because she saw all his conflictions raging inside. She felt bad for playing a hand in putting him in this predicament and wished they chose another way to do so. But she could not alter the past and needed to focus on maintaining her part for the sake of Amadora.

Giacinta searched high and low for any sign of Casimiro around the complex but came up empty-handed. The complex was like a ghost town because most of the staff had the day off to prepare for the long day ahead when they dealt with the final arrangements for the autumn ball. Her mother and Millie were in the hall finishing some preparations for the ball. To her knowledge, she was probably the only one left at the complex. But even if that was true, she could not help but wander around the main house looking for someone she knew would not be there.

Giacinta wander around the guest wing heading towards the one place she had not searched yet, her father's office. As she walked down the silence-filled second-floor hall, she paused when she saw a faint light coming from one bedroom by the landing of the side stairwell. The door was cracked open; and as she drew near, she heard hushed whispers coming from inside.

Giacinta tiptoed over to the door, pressed against the wall next to it, and peeked inside. She could not see anyone from her position, but the intelligible whispers became slightly louder. She pushed the door open and entered the room, hoping the deep voice she heard belonged to the man her heart longed for. But as soon as she entered the room, her hopes vanished and disappointment crossed her face when she saw the actual owner, Gugliehno.

Giacinta's sudden appearance startled him, making him almost drop the phone in his hand. He gestured for her to wait as he finished up his call.

"Thanks for keeping me up to date. Keep up the good work. We'll talk soon," Gugliehno spoke softly into the receiver before hanging up and turning his attention to his younger sister.

"Giacinta, what's wrong? Did you need something?"

Giacinta shook her head. "No. Sorry for interrupting. I thought you were someone else."

"No need to apologize, I was just finishing up," Gunny smiled.

Giacinta tried to hide her disappointment behind a painted smile. "It's a surprise to see you here so early. I thought you and the girls were supposed to come later today."

"That was the initial plan, but Susie brought the girls to see her parents while I came early to take care of some important business matters," Gunny replied.

"Business matters? So, you came early to see father and Casimiro?"

"Yes, but it seems they've stepped out for a bit," Gunny noticed Giacinta's smile drop in reaction to words. "Is something wrong? Were you looking for one of them?"

Giacinta was too emotionally exhausted to hide her feelings anymore. "Yes."

"You were looking for Casimiro, weren't you?" Gunny asked.

"How did you know?" Giacinta looked at him, shocked.

Gunny sat down in the chair next to the phone and motioned for her to sit across from him. "Did you forget he's one of my closest friends? We tell each other everything. Of course, he told me about you two. Tell me what happened."

Giacinta sat down across from him and tried to fight the tears threatening to fall while recalling all the events surrounding her and Casimiro. "It's my fault, Gunny. I'm a coward."

"A coward? What do you mean?" Gunny asked sympathetically.

"All this confusion is my fault because I was too cowardly to face my fears."

"Fears about what?" Gunny asked.

"I can't tell you," answered Giacinta weakly.

"Why not? If it's something important, you can tell me," Gugliehno pressed, trying to get his younger sister to reveal what was bothering her. He knew they were never close, but seeing how disturbed she was in this moment bothered him and he wanted to help her.

"I can't! If I tell you the truth, I'll just cause more problems for you! I don't want to get you involved!" Giacinta cried, trembling in fear of the dark secrets she held deep within.

"Don't you know who I am? I'm the righthand of 'Don' Basilio Morelli. There's nothing you could say or do that'll cause me trouble," a comforting smile crossed his lips as he tried to calm his sister down. He placed a gentle hand on her shoulder, reassuring her everything would be okay; but even with his warm touch and encouraging words, Giacinta could not speak. She was too afraid to reveal anymore, so she withdrew and moved farther away from him.

Gugliehno noticed her peculiar behavior. "Does this have to do with Marco?"

"You know?" Giacinta looked shock when he mentioned that name.

Gunny nodded. "No. I only suspected since Casimiro mentioned he paid off your debt to him a while back. I thought you cut ties with him."

"I did, but he refuses to go away," Giacinta responded.

"Wait. What do you mean? Start from the beginning."

Giacinta calmed down and took a deep breath to soothe her racing nerves. She told him everything that happened between her and Marco since the day their father refused to pay her debt. As she retold every grizzly detail between her exchange, Gunny became unnerved and furious. He held his tongue until she finished, then and hid his rage behind a cool, even facade.

"Why didn't you come to us sooner?"

"I was afraid if you did, that he might hurt you," Giacinta replied.

"No low-level bookie can hurt us," reassured Gunny, forcing a soft smile as he patted her hand. "You need to tell Casimiro the truth about everything."

"But what if he wants to retaliate against Marco?"

"Tell him not to worry about it. I'll deal with everything and show Marco what happens when you mess with my family."

The constant ringing of Anna's phone woke her from her slumber. She fought the berating high-pitched noise, hoping whoever was calling would give up and try again later. But the deeper she buried herself into her blankets, the louder the incessant ringing echoed through the room. She sat up, yawned, and stretched her arms before tossing off the covers, sliding on her slippers and heading over to the dresser to answer the phone.

She wobbled over hungover and tried searching the shadows for the phone. A pile of clothes covered it. She picked up the receiver and greeted the caller on the other end. "Hello. Who is this?"

"Anna... It's Brock. How are you?"

"Brock... Hey. I was doing fine until the annoying ringing woke me up... Not that I don't enjoy getting a call from you, but why are you calling this early in the morning?"

"I'm sorry for disturbing you, but I really need to talk to Johnnie. It's important."

Anna rubbed her temples as she tried to remember who Johnnie was. Then she remembered that was Amadora's alter ego's name. "Oh Johnnie... Hold on, I'll go get him."

Anna placed the phone on the table and headed to the guest bedroom. When she reached her room, she pushed the door slightly open to see if Amadora was awake. To her surprise, she could not see a thing because the room was completely dark. Anna stepped inside and ran her fingers along the wall until she came to where the windows were supposed to be and yanked at the thick fabric covering them, letting them drop to the floor so she could see where she was.

Once the light poured through the windows, Amadora stirred. When she opened her eyes, she saw Anna standing over her with her hands on her hips and an annoyed expression on her face. Amadora sat up and yawned.

"What's wrong with you?"

"What's the matter with me? Well, you know how I love getting early wake-up calls from your thug buddies. Brock is on the phone for you. Get up and go talk to him. He says it's important," Anna growled, glaring down at Amadora in agitation.

Amadora looked confused. She wondered why Brock would call so early. He might have another mission for Johnnie, but what mission could be so important that he would call so early. She just shrugged and headed to the phone that was on the floor by her closet. She reconnected it to the wall and picked up the receiver.

"Hello?" Amadora said, talking like Johnnie Barbone.

"Johnnie? Hey. Did I disturb you?"

"No. Not really... What's up?"

"Lorenzo wants to meet with you at two."

"Lorenzo?"

"Yes Lorenzo, that's my boss. He's also Gugliehno's right-hand man."

"And where does he want to meet me?"

"He wants to meet you at Donny's. His brother's nightclub on the east district of Gugliehno's territory."

Salvatore Lorenzo was one of Gunny's and Elda's closest friends and the eldest son of the Lorenzo family, one of the Morellis rivals. He was initially supposed to take over for his father; but because of his loyalty to Gunny, his father allowed him to stay by his side and work for the Morellis as a sign of good faith between the families.

Ever since Lorenzo worked as Gunny's right-hand man, he mostly laid low and only got his hands dirty for the most difficult and covert jobs. He fulfilled all his tasks, leaving no evidence behind and making them look like an accident. His ability to mask his actions and produce results gained him the nickname, The Chameleon.

"Hey boy, you still there?" Brock said when he noticed the prolonged silence on the other end.

"Yeah, I am. Sorry. What does your boss want with me?" Johnnie asked, trying to mask the sense of worry and concern in his voice.

"I have no clue, kid. He just told me he has an important message from Gugliehno for you. You must find out what he wants when you go see him today. Just make sure you're on time, kid. Lorenzo doesn't like to wait." With that said, Brock hung up the phone, and Amadora did the same.

Amadora did not turn around right after hanging up the phone. She kept her back turned towards Anna because worry was still embedded deep in her eyes. She knew if Anna noticed something was bothering her, she would ask too many questions. She also would worry herself; and if it turned out to be nothing to worry about, then she would waste time and energy worrying about her.

"What did Brock want?" Anna asked, sitting in the scarlet armchair by the window. She stretched her arms behind her head and focused her gaze on Amadora.

"Nothing, really. He just wanted to tell me his boss wanted to meet me," Amadora turned around and smiled, erasing the worry on her face.

"You mean Lorenzo. Don't you?" Anna said plainly, closing her eyes.

"Yes. How did you know I meant him?" Amadora asked, surprised.

"Because I heard from some other soldiers Gugliehno left earlier to the main house. Lorenzo is the only one he could be talking about," Anna looked Amadora over and could tell by the way she acted something was bothering her. Because mostly after she getting a call like that, she would throw herself back in bed and fall right back to sleep. But she just stood there with a weird smile, trying to act as if everything was alright.

"Are you nervous about meeting Lorenzo?"

"No. Of course not," Amadora tried to act as if everything was perfectly fine, but when she saw Anna's face, she knew she was not believing a word Amadora said. She plopped herself on the bed in defeat and sighed. "Yes. I've heard stories about him that put me on my guard. That's all."

"I've heard the same stories, but you shouldn't worry about them. He would never let you know ahead of time if he was going to bump you off that's not the Chameleon's style," By Anna's attitude, Amadora could tell she was not the least worried about her meeting with him. If Anna did not care, then she should not worry either. "You never know, he probably just wants to give you a special job. One from Gugliehno. It's nothing you should worry about."

"Maybe you're right. I don't know why I was worried. Maybe all these jobs are finally taking their toll on me. Maybe they're making me a little paranoid." Amadora put her hands on her head and tried to relax. She could not because of the constant headaches those jobs were causing.

She could barely sleep without the frequent nightmares every single night. She thought she had seen the worst of it, but they just kept growing worse by every new job. No wonder why it seemed like she was going out of her mind. It became a normality for her these past weeks. She wanted to know when those feelings and headaches would finally go away. She needed to find some way to mask the pain she caused as Johnnie Barbone.

"Maybe you just need to relax," Anna said, worried. She walked to her side and put a hand on her shoulder.

That was the first time Amadora ever mentioned anything about what they had her doing there. Anna wanted to tell her if she wanted to give up now there was a possibility that she still could, but she knew she would waste her breath. Amadora made it very clear last time she would not give up until she reached her goal. It was also probably too late to do anything about it, anyway.

"I'm going to leave you alone but try not to stress yourself." Anna hugged her gently, then made her way to the door. Anna put her hand on the knob to open it. Before she left, she turned back towards Amadora. "You're in charge of the phone now. If anyone calls for me, I'm not available."

Amadora smiled and watched Anna leave. Once she was gone the phone rang, Amadora smirked at the irony. She picked up the phone and pressed it to her ear.

"Hello? Amadora?"

Amadora smiled. It was Samantha. Talk about great timing. "Sammy, how are you? How are things in Cali?"

"Not good, Dora. Not good at all."

"Why? What happened?"

"The worst," With that said, Amadora knew something bad happened. "He knows, Dora. He knows about everything."

Edward arrived at Zanipolo's apartment after receiving a call from him, ordering him to get two plane tickets to New Jersey. He thought it was strange since he told him the other day; he was not planning on returning this month since he had to watch his sister. But now, even though he made the arrangements, he wanted to know why

the sudden change.

When Edward pushed open the front door of Zanipolo's apartment and walked inside, two large, gray suitcases stacked against the wall in the corridor greeted him. He looked around the apartment and saw it was a complete mess. Zanipolo's coat rack was on the floor, clothes were scattered all around, and still there was no sign of Zanipolo. Edward stepped over the piles and made his way to Zanipolo's office.

The door was wide open, and, inside, Zanipolo rummaged through his desk drawers looking for something. Edward did not move from behind the door so he could see what Zanipolo was desperately searching for.

Zanipolo pulled all his files from his top drawer, reached inside, and pushed a wooden button. Moments later a faint click sounded, then a small compartment on the inside of the desk appeared. Zanipolo reached inside the compartment and pulled out a medium size leather box. He smiled, placing the box on the desk.

"Alright, my old friend. I thought I'd never have to see you again. But with the present conditions my sister caused, I might need your services," Zanipolo opened the box, pulling out a gold pistol.

Edward stood there behind the door and just watched when he saw the gun in full view his mouth dropped. He knew Zanipolo and his sister had some differences, but he never believed that it would be bad enough that pistols would get involved. Edward immediately pushed open the door and walked in.

"What happened? Did the little she-devil finally pissed you off enough to make you want to blow her brains out? Or is there something else going on?"

Zanipolo jumped, startled by the sound of the doorknob hitting the wall. He looked surprised by Edward's intrusion. He could tell by his look that he misunderstood his statement.

"You got it all wrong," Zanipolo explained with a smirk. "I'm not using this on my sister, no matter how angry I am at her. It's my lucky pistol. I always take it with me when I travel on important business," Zanipolo put the pistol back in its container and put it in his coat pocket.

"I've known you for too long, Polo. You wouldn't bring a pistol unless you knew you'd have to use it. Is there something you aren't telling me?"

"Nothing's wrong. The only problem is that you are here when you are supposed to be making our flight arrangements," Zanipolo snapped defensively. Edward could tell by Zanipolo's tense behavior there was more to his visit than he was telling.

"I took care of that already. But I'm your business partner, not your secretary. Tell me what's really going on," Edward sat across from him behind the desk and glared at him. By Edward's expression, Polo knew he was not leaving until he knew the truth.

"I guess if it's the only way you'll leave, then I must tell you. But you must promise, you'll keep your mouth shut about what I'm about to tell you. You can't tell anyone, not my father, my brother, and definitely not Elda."

"Is it business related? What the hell did you do this time?"

"Nothing. It's not about what I did. It's about what Amadora did."

"You mean that little brat at the house. I don't know, chap. I don't think I can pass up a chance to see her get in trouble," Edward said sarcastically.

"You can, especially when you hear the severity of this situation," Edward saw the seriousness in his friend's face, so he just sat back and listened. "The girl at the beach house isn't my sister. Actually, that's my sister's best friend Sam pretending to be her."

"But why would she do that?"

"It's all a part of my sister's plan. She had Sam masquerade as her, so my father would think she was here. While she's in New York pretending to be a man trying to enter our family business from the bottom and work her way up without suspicions."

"But why the hell would she do that? Doesn't she know how dangerous that is?"

"Yes, she does, but she took the risk anyway so she can show everyone she can handle all the dangers this business offers. She's doing well so far, but I don't know how long her luck is going to last. That's why I'm heading back home with Sam to help her."

"She's doing pretty well. Which associate is she pretending to be?" The ingeniousness of her plan marveled Edward. The girl was smarter than he thought. She must have planned this for months before pulling it off. There's no way it was just a spur-of-the-moment idea.

"Johnnie Barbone."

"Johnnie Barbone! There is no way you can pull her out of there now. She's too far in."

"Don't you think I know that already?"

"My friend, be very careful," Edward could tell by Zanipolo's look that he had already lost hope. Knowing his current fragile relationship with his father, he knew Basilio Morelli would not hesitate to put blame on Polo for his sister's mess if the truth came out. The only way Edward could help his friend was by keeping quiet and helping him with the business here while he was gone.

"You know the risks of this escapade. With the cunning and training you and that little Napoleon of a sister possess, you can keep her safe and reach her goal with no problems. I can help from here, so don't hesitate to call."

Zanipolo's smile returned to his face. "Thanks. You don't know how good it feels to have someone on my side."

Edward reached out and shook Zanipolo's hand. "I'm always here for you, brother. I will always have your back."

The cool autumn air wrapped around a mysterious figure as he crossed the early morning shadows and ran along the side of Glory house. He remained agile and swift as he quietly pried open a window and climbed inside. He searched around the small room and looked behind a large canvas bag stashed in the corner. He slid his hand in a slit in the bag's rear and pulled out a large cannister and a small wooden box.

The man unscrewed the top and poured its contents throughout the first floor of the house. When he was done, the shadowy figure ascended the tall winding stairs and continued pouring the clear liquid on the nice, polished stairs. His steps were soft and swift as he moved from one room to another.

The man paused in front of the master bedroom and peered through the crack in the door to make sure its occupant was still fast asleep. To his luck, he had not stirred since the last time he checked. He was in such an alcohol-induced stupor that he did not hear the mysterious intruder when he entered the room and withdrew his gun.

The shadow shot four times, injuring the slumbering man in each of his limb. The excruciating pain jolted the man from his comatose state and into one of uncontrollable misery. He yelped as he tried to make sense of his new hell. Blood soaked his bed; and no matter how much he wanted to move, agony immobilized his body. His dark eyes traveled the darkness and fell upon a shadowy figure in the far side of his room. The dark room and blood loss blurred his vision, so he could not see any features of his assailant.

"Who are you!" Marco demanded through the elevating pain.

"That doesn't matter," The shadowy figure trained his gun on him again.

"Then what do you want? Why are you here?"

"I'm here to collect a debt."

"What debt?" Marco asked, terrified.

"The debt you owe Giacinta."

Color drained from Marco's face when he heard his ex's name. He knew right away who he was and why he was there. "I don't know what she told, but it's all a misunderstanding. I just wanted to make her sweat to be spiteful. I never intended to do anything."

"We have to make sure there are no more misunderstandings."

The man pulled the trigger once more and shot Marco in the groin. He ran back to the first floor, struck a match, and dropped it on the floor. The room went ablaze one after the other while he escaped through the back door before getting caught in the fiery inferno.

"What do you mean he knows everything!" Amadora's heart raced in fear when she heard Sam say those words. Zanipolo knew. What was going to happen now?

"Zanipolo knows everything. He knows the entire plan, Dora."

"How!"

"He found out I wasn't you and broke in this morning. I didn't know it was him at first, so I went to investigate a noise coming from downstairs. I saw a can of coffee beans on the floor and immediately went to put it back. As I was putting it back, he grabbed me from behind and told me if I made any noise or if I didn't answer his questions, he would kill me. When he let go of my mouth, I immediately told him it was me and from there I told him everything that was going on."

"My god. What did he say?" The fear of embarrassment glowed more than death at that moment. At least with death, the pain ended after a while; but with embarrassment, she would have to carry that pain forever.

"He won't say anything as long as you follow his terms."

"What terms?"

"You must return this weekend and meet him at the Autumn Ball. He wants to talk to you. If you don't come, then he won't hesitate to tell Gugliehno. Otherwise, he'll help you keep your secret and reach your goal."

"Alright. I'll do it. Is that it?"

"Yes, but, Amadora, please be careful."

"Of course, I will be. Don't worry, Sammy. See you tomorrow. Bye"

"Ok. Bye."

Johnnie arrived at Donny's fifteen minutes before his appointment. When he entered the place, it looked like it had just opened because there was no one inside. He looked around. There was no one there except the bartender. Johnnie headed to the bar and sat down.

The bartender was a tall, heavyset man with slick, black hair and green eyes. He wore an enormous smile when he saw Johnnie. He placed the tumbler he was cleaning down on the counter and reached out his hand to shake Johnnie's.

"Hi, Johnnie. I'm Donny, Lorenzo's brother. We've been waiting for you," Donny let go of his hand and walked around the bar. Then he motioned for Johnnie to come over. Johnnie stood and followed him.

As Donny walked through the double doors leading to the back of the bar, the light dispersed when they entered a long, narrow hall. Johnnie's initial gut feeling of caution returned. They continued until they came to a small stairwell leading to the second floor of the building. When they reached the top landing, cigar smoke lingered in the air along with loud music and a chorus of laughter. They walked to the door of the source of the commotion. When Johnnie crossed the threshold, he saw a bunch of Gunny's men talking on all sides of the room.

Johnnie did not recognize any of the men they passed until Donny brought him to a small table in an adjoining room where Musilli and Brock sat talking to a tall, lean, dirty blonde man with bright gray eyes. He was a young and handsome man, no older than Gugliehno. He recognized him immediately as Gugliehno's right hand, Salvatore Lorenzo.

"Brother, here's Johnnie Barbone," Donny said to the man who was sitting with Musilli and Brock. When he said that, Lorenzo turned to Johnnie and smiled.

"Ah yes, Johnnie Barbone, I've heard a lot about you. Please sit down. Relax. Enjoy yourself. This day is about you after all," Lorenzo motioned Johnnie to a chair across from him. Then he turned to his brother and smiled. "Donny, do you mind getting us another round of drinks?"

"Sure. Coming right up," Donny turned and walked away, leaving Johnnie, Lorenzo, Musilli, and Brock alone at the table.

Johnnie was still stuck on what Lorenzo said earlier. The day was about him? What did he mean? It seemed to be a positive statement. Lorenzo turned to Johnnie, smiling.

Johnnie could not put his finger on it, but something about Lorenzo's smile seemed unnerving. Malice lurked in his smile. It was as if Johnnie saw all the blood and lives that he had taken just by his grin. It sent Johnnie into a state of caution.

"Johnnie, I've heard great things about you from both my men. You're a prodigy among their recruits. There's no job you're not willing to take. They say you're courageous and cunning. With all this praise, I'm very honored to be in your presence."

By the way Lorenzo talked, Johnnie could tell he was sort of eccentric, but he did not know if that was good. Like it was said, the weird ones were always the best for a life like this. "Thank you, Lorenzo. But I am envious of those who have witnessed your own unique skill. Maybe I can accompany you on a job next time."

Lorenzo took a sip of his drink. He smirked and turned to Brock. "You were right. He is a very smart boy." He turned his gaze back at Johnnie and his smile grew. "I must decline that offer for now. I prefer to work alone, but I like you, boy. Maybe I can make your wish could come true soon once I fulfill my current engagement."

Lorenzo brought his cup to his mouth, then looked at the red liquid swirling around. "Red wine, the liquor of the gods. We might not be gods, but we sure as hell try to be. Man does nothing but fight constantly for what they want, even if it means they could lose their own life. You, my boy, I can tell are fighting for something. What it is only you and the heavenly father knows? I see a lust in your eyes for some secret desire and that intrigues me. I like that. That's why it's my pleasure to say this on behalf of the Morelli family. Welcome, Johnnie Barbone. You are now a soldier, a brother. From this moment on, your fate rests on the wings of your angels. May you get whatever it is you desire."

When he finished, Brock, Musilli and the other men clapped, welcoming their new brother. Johnnie smiled as he thought to himself. 'He did it. He was one step closer to

his goal. One step closer to her goal. One step closer to their goal.'

Shortly after the claps stopped, Donny came over with glasses filled with wine. He set the glasses in front of them and they toasted to Johnnie. Johnnie thanked them and took a sip.

"Gugliehno really wishes he could be here, but important matters keep him away. But he sends his congratulations," Johnnie wondered what was so important that Gugliehno would not be here. He hoped everything was okay at the compound. "Well boys, I have a minor task for one of you to do. I need one of you to take a team to the north warehouse and be on guard duty during the Annual Autumn Ball. So, who wants the job?"

Lorenzo looked at Johnnie and he shook his head no. "Sorry, Boss, but I have another engagement. Otherwise, I wouldn't hesitate to do this."

Lorenzo said nothing. He just turned his head towards Musilli. "Larry, I guess you are the next candidate. So, will you take this job? I would ask Brock, but he is already doing something for me."

Musilli shrugged his shoulders in agreement, and Lorenzo smiled. "Now that that's taken care of. Let's enjoy ourselves with a game of Poker."

As they dealt the cards, Johnnie felt an icy breeze sweep past his heart. It slowed, and time stopped capturing that moment forever.

The Annual Autumn Ball

'Peace can only be achieved when we're united under one common cause,'
Thoughts of Basilio Morelli.

Smoke billowed around Johnnie as he played another round of poker. He scanned his opponents, seeking any clue of what was in their hands, but their cards covered their faces. He recognized three out of the four players as Brock, Musilli, and Lorenzo. But the fourth mysterious player he did not remember seeing at the table before. The player sat next to him on the right, but Johnnie still could not make heads or tails of the face hidden behind his cards.

Another icy chill crossed Johnnie's heart as they laid down their cards. First, Brock huffed and groaned as he tossed his cards on the green, suede tabletop. His lips moved, but his words were intelligible. Lorenzo laughed and patted Brock on the shoulder as he tossed his cards in the center of the table. Only Johnnie, Musilli, and the mystery player remained.

Musilli and the other player kept their cards close to vest. They did not move an inch, just waited for Johnnie to make his play. Johnnie folded and waited to see the outcome of this standoff.

The mysterious player went first. He placed his cards face up on the table, revealing his face. Shock paralyzed Johnnie when he came face-to-face with the player, Darian Mancini.

"Hi Johnnie," A cynical smirk crossed his lips. Vengeance and rage radiated from his eyes as he focused his attention on his adversary. "Two pairs."

"Whew! It must be my lucky day!" Musilli whistled in glee. "I'm sorry, Darian, my boy, but I think a royal flush of spades beats that."

Johnnie's body grew rigid with terror when Musilli finally removed the cards from in front of his face. Nothing was there. An empty void replaced his head. Johnnie jumped away from the table. He tumbled over his chair, fighting to get far away from the horrific sight, but the farther he moved the closer the table got. Musilli and the others laughed.

Escape was impossible. Their laughter turned into a dark chorus summoning large flames surrounding Johnnie. Hacking and coughing, Johnnie buckled to his knees. He grasped his throat, fighting for any pocket of air, but salvation never came. His eyes glazed over as he fought the flames consuming him. His dying scream drowned out the chaos surrounding him as he delved into the dark abyss.

Soaked in sweat and shaken, Amadora shot up in fear. She scanned her surroundings as she tried to regain her bearings. An old man next to her grunted and flipped the pages of his newspaper. She was on the bus back to Jersey. It was only a nightmare. She grumbled, covered her head with her hat and slumped into her seat. She felt uneasy ever since Musilli received that job. Maybe she worried about nothing. It was not a dangerous gig, just guard duty.

Signs for Newark airport popped up more frequently as the bus raced down the highway. She needed to redirect her focus on more pressing matters, Zanipolo. She was not sure what he had planned now that he knew the truth. He promised to keep his mouth shut if they met, but he did not trust he would keep that promise. She was no fool. She knew about his history with their father and his gambling addiction. Ever since his recovery, he has fought to stay on their father's good side. This made her skeptical that he would keep his word. She would have to stay on guard until she fixed this unpleasant kink.

Lola Germaine, the best nightclub diva in Manhattan, was an American jewel. Her glossy raven hair glistened in the spotlight as she danced and sang on the large red velvet draped stage. She seduced the crowd with each swing of her hips and her powerful, sultry voice echoed through the high walls of the club. She scanned her sea of admirers until her dark eyes fell upon Nero. Her ruby lips curled and blew a kiss into his direction. Nero ignored the jealous glares from her fans because all he could see was her.

When she finished her set, Lola walked over to Nero's table and sat next to him. She brushed back a few strands of her hair and trained her eyes on him.

"I haven't seen you here before. Is this your first time?"

"Yeah. It is," Nero replied hopelessly drawn into her sweet smile.

"That accent... You're not from here?"

Nero nodded and drank from his wineglass. "No. I'm a pure-blooded Italian. Does that bother you?"

Lola moved closer to him and ran her fingers along his tie. "Not at all. I love foreign men. I hope you'll be staying here for a while."

"That's the plan whether I want to or not," Nero laughed.

"Good. I hope you'll come visit me more often." Lola pressed against his body and gave him a flirty peck on his cheek.

"Cool it, Lola. You need to focus on the paying customers."

Nero snapped out of the lovely diva's spell and looked up at the massive figure towering behind her. His dark eyes glowered at them, causing the singer to scurry off backstage.

"Sal, I found your lost pup. Why don't you put a leash on him before I have to put him down?" The man stormed off behind the billowy curtains leading backstage.

"You stay making friends, don't you, kid?" Lorenzo sat across from his ward and laughed.

"Who was that? And what did I do to him?" Nero asked, confused.

"That was my brother, Donny. This is his place, and that was his girl you were messing with."

"His girl is Lola Germaine. I didn't know that. Besides, she was hitting on me, not the other way around."

"That's not what it looked like to us. Just be careful when you're around them in the future. My brother might look like a gentle giant, but he's known for keeping his 'promises'."

"Why are you here, anyway?"

"One, saving your life. Two, I need you to be my partner at the autumn ball."

"Sorry. I must pass. You're not my type."

Lorenzo struck him on the back of his head. "No, you idiot. We're going on official business."

"Doing what?"

"Being undercover guards and just making sure everything goes smoothly."

"Why me? Can't Brock help you?"

"Sadly, he's busy doing something else for Gunny. You're my last resort."

Nero ignored Lorenzo's slight because he was glad that he needed him for this. It was still grunt work, but it was much better than pushing papers at the warehouse. Also, it was a perfect opportunity to show Lorenzo his reliability.

The Autumn Ball was only twelve hours away and servants packed the main house scramming to rearrange the decorations and preparing the food for tonight's festivities. Everyone in the family who was here helped except Gunny and his father.

Gunny and Basilio had a couple of matters to deal with before they could lend a hand with the remaining preparations. Gunny was not sure what urgent business his dad needed to do that day. His father ordered him to bring his car to the front of the house and wait. Being the obedient son he was, he did exactly what he wanted and waited by his car.

He smoked a cigarette and looked at the cloudy, gray sky. It seemed like it would rain soon. Gunny hoped it did not, so they could avoid canceling the event and dealing with his mother's disappointment.

His mom and Millie worked themselves to the bone to make this ball the best one yet. They even made all the food for this year instead of hiring a caterer, which was strange since Millie disliked cooking for large events. Maybe something important caused this change of heart.

Gunny worried if it rained before any of the guest arrived, then some might not attend; and if that happened, all hell would break loose. He would hear for months on about his parents' disappointment. The only reason his father cared about the ball was because it was important for business. It acted as a peace summit where all five families put aside their differences and came together to discuss matters that would promote peace and also work out any grievances between them.

Gunny took another pull from his cigarette and watched the commotion surrounding him. It has been a twelve-year-old tradition that started as a deterrent for a war that shook the families to their core after several tragic incidents following Gunny becoming his father's second-in-command. One of them robbed his best friend of his life.

As Gunny put out his cigarette, he watched his father leaving the main house in his black overcoat and matching hat clutching onto a long yellow folder with the New Jersey seal stamped on the front. Gunny did not know what its contents were, so he laid his concerns to rest, climbed inside his car and waited for his father to get in.

"Pops, where are we headed?" Gunny started the engine and drove the car down the driveway.

"We're paying our friends, the Johnsons, a visit," Basilio replied tucking the folder out of his son's eyesight.

"Why do you want to see them?"

"I need to catch up with my old pal, Malcolm," Basilio smirked.

Gunny was not an idiot. He knew Malcolm and his father were far from being pals. If it was not for his mother's bond with Malcolm's wife, the families would not have met, and he would not have known one of the greatest friends he ever had.

As the car turned down the Johnsons' block, Gunny's heart sank. He had not been there in years. Returning now and not knowing why, made him feel uneasy, because the last time he did was to tell Joey's parents about his death.

The memories of Joey raced through his head when he pulled in front of the Johnsons' house. The agony of their reemergence increased as they approached the front door of the joyful looking home. Gunny knew better than most that its appearance was just a mask to cover the void Joey left behind.

Basilio rang the doorbell. After a moment, the door opened, and Malcolm stood in the threshold with an agitated expression. He did not acknowledge Gunny, because he was too busy glaring at his father. Hatred and rage emanated from his eyes.

Whatever the reason for their trip here, it was clear that his father already reached out to Malcolm, and the contents of that folder was the cause.

"What's wrong, Malcolm? Won't you let an old friend inside to catch up on old times?" Basilio ignored the intensity radiating from Malcolm's eyes and grinned.

"You're a piece of shit. You know damn well what's bothering me. If it wasn't for..." Malcolm stopped and stepped back into the house. He waited until Gunny closed the door before continuing. "If it wasn't for those papers in your hand, I wouldn't have even bothered letting your ass inside."

"Now... Now... Malcolm, all of this hostility isn't good. You shouldn't get worked up over these papers," Basilio held up the folder and opened it. "I wonder why they're so important that you would try to hide them?"

Malcolm gritted his teeth and curled his fingers into a large quivering fist while he fought his intensifying frustration. "I have done nothing to you. Why would you go through all this trouble to get this information?"

"Normally, I wouldn't care about this charade, since it's not my place to interfere with matters like this. But when Mr. Baldemar begged for my help, I couldn't resist."

Gunny looked on confused by the entire situation as his father's even tone grew more aggressive.

"You should've known he'd ask for my help eventually."

Malcolm stood frozen. Basilio turned to his son and smiled gently. "Gunny, you're probably wondering why we're here today. Well, out of all of your siblings, with intense matters, you're the most rational and level-headed. Also, your ties with the Johnsons made you an ideal candidate to accompany me to take care of this matter," Basilio started. "When you were out with Casimiro the other day, a German gentleman about your age stopped by the manor. Normally, I don't take requests right before the ball; but since he knew about our ties to the Johnsons, I heard him out. Never in a million years would I suspect this man was actually Malcolm's illegitimate son."

Shook, Gugliehno could not move after hearing his father's word. He could not believe the same man he saw when he left was Joey's blood brother.

Basilio knew about how much Gunny cared about Joey. He also knew how much guilt he carried for years because of his death. Basilio understood that by bringing his son here and revealing this news would rehash some painful memories, but he was the only one strong enough to withstand the awe and see the bottom line. Gunny's loss of his peace-of-mind was a risk he had to take.

"Diederich is your son, Malcolm. I don't get it. After losing one child, I'm surprised you would shamefully shun him from a chance of having a proper family. Joey wouldn't have let you get away with this."

"You killed him! You of all people shouldn't even dare say his name or act like you know what he wanted!"

"Get your head out of your ass and think about the people surrounding you. You're not the only one in pain. Your wife and daughter have suffered for years. Stop blaming everyone else for his death and using it as a crutch. Step up and be a man. Do the one thing that could bring your family together."

"I beg you. Keep what you know to yourself. I'll deal with this situation on my own. You won't have to worry about Diederich bothering you in the future."

Before Basilio replied, Gunny rushed at Malcolm, grabbed him by his collar and slammed him against the wall.

"Is that it, you damn coward! You just want us to keep quiet about this, so you can drag your feet while you decide what to do! Do you know how much this could help Samantha? Just do the right thing!"

Basilio pulled Gunny off Malcolm and walked him over to the threshold before he accidentally strangled Malcolm.

"Fine. We'll give you some time to sort everything out; but if you wait too long, I can't promise Gunny won't tell Samantha himself."

The return trip to Jersey was silent as the distance between Samantha and Zanipolo grew. He did not interact with her except to hold doors open and help her carry her bags, but the moment they arrived at the main house of the Morelli Complex, he dropped her bags in the main hall and went off into the surrounding chaos.

Samantha did not try to stop Zanipolo when he walked away. It was better if she left it like this and let him sort out everything on his own. Besides, she was more concerned about what Amadora's next move would be now that her brother knew about her ruse. She wondered if these circumstances would change her mind and try to end this charade.

Samantha took her bags and hurried off to Amadora's room until she returned. She sat on her bed and ran her hand under the pillows until she found the box from earlier. She desperately wanted to know what it hid inside. When she was about to search for the key, someone turned the knob and pushed open the door. The sound of the doorknob clanking against the wall as they struggled to lug in some bags made Samantha jump in surprise. She left the box in its place and smiled towards the sudden visitor. Once the person dropped the bags and turned around, her pulse settled as she came face to face with Amadora.

When Amadora saw Samantha's smiling face, she ran over to her friend and wrapped her arms around her.

135

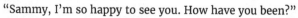

"Sammy, I'm so happy to see you. How have you been?"

"I'm fine, Dora. I'm just a little tired after traveling in a plane without sleep," Samantha replied embracing Amadora and patting her gently on her back.

"I'm to blame for how you feel. You can head home and rest. I can handle the rest on my own," Amadora released Samantha to follow her into a room next to her bathroom. She flicked on the lights closed the door and sat on a couch on the far side of the room.

"I want to stay here. I promised to help you reach your goal. I can't turn back now." Samantha sat across from Amadora.

"Are you sure? Now, that Zanipolo knows things could get a little hairy from now on."

"I understand, but I don't care. I want to help you 'till the very end in case you need me."

Amadora was stunned by her friend's support. It was not too long ago when she tried to convince her to give up her goal and just live normally.

"Thank you. You don't know how much that means to me."

"Are you nervous about your meeting with Zanipolo?"

"Yeah, I know I have no choice but to see him; otherwise, he'd make good on his threats."

"Do you really believe he'd tell your father or brother what's going on?"

"In the beginning, yes; but now, I'm not sure what to think."

"What are you going to do?"

"There's nothing I can do now because I'm too far in. I need to accomplish my original goal if I want to get out. That's why I came back to hopefully convince him to keep it a secret," Amadora replied.

"We knew this wouldn't be easy going in, so how are you handling it?"

Sam's words made the events of the last month replay in Amadora's mind all at once causing the room to spin and a prickling pain pulsate through her brain. She fought the growing ailments of her weakening body and closed her eyes to regain control of her senses.

Amadora wanted to tell her friend all about her life as Johnnie Barbone, but she could not bear dragging her farther into this dangerous mission. This was her desire. Amadora agreed to do whatever it took to gain her father's attention, but she did not want Samantha to muddy her hands by knowing more than she should.

"Of course, it's difficult. It's mentally and physically exhausting, but it's worth it. I've made a lot of progress in a small amount of time. I can't slip up now. I can feel it. I'm getting close to reaching my goal."

When the sun fully set, muffled music echoed through the night. Zanipolo crossed the enormous crowd surrounding the entrance of the grand ballroom. Socialites, movie stars, politicians and other members of the social elite lined outside patiently waiting to be vetted so they could enter the booming party.

His father was extremely strict about the security at the party. Since his rivals attended, some of them with vendettas against him and other families, he wanted to make sure they did not sneak weapons inside and caused a ruckus. This event was a night for peace and compromise. Weapons had no place in an environment like that. His father refused to have anyone ruin it, no matter who they were or what connections they had.

Two doors surrounded by his father's men split the entrance. Long, golden velvet ropes divided them, splitting the elites from the small business owners and common guests. They gawked as Zanipolo walked past the starlets and entered the building without hesitation, but he ignored the sea of fleeting glances directed at him.

Zanipolo marveled at the lush, forest-like display surrounding every corner of the hall. Trees sprinkled with yellow, red, and orange leaves lined the towering walls. A colorful mosaic of fallen leaves spread out on the floor underneath his feet. The warm tones of the gold and red decorations highlighted the true majesty of autumn and immortalized it in this isolated dome, creating a peaceful atmosphere.

Zanipolo wanted to sit back and enjoy the festivities, but he was stuck trying to clean up the mess Amadora got herself into. He made his way through the crowded first floor and walked over to the large golden stairs leading to the upper levels. He scanned the clusters of elites scattered throughout each floor until he found a secluded, dark cove on the third floor, hidden by long red drapes. Sitting in the gold booth was the source of this new inconvenience in his life, Amadora.

Amadora peered through a small opening in the drapes surrounding her and watched the movement of the crowds. Her eyes wandered over the colorfully dressed people, but her mind fixated on why she hid in this isolated corner on the highest floor of the ballroom. She promised Zanipolo she would meet him here to discuss her situation and what their next steps would be now that he knew everything.

She wondered why he chose this spot. It was secluded, but they were still on the floor where all the families gathered. The heads of each family were in a meeting at the moment, but she noticed a lot of their men and family spread throughout the floor, including her own. It was too risky to talk about her matter here. Someone might overhear them, and that could have some dangerous repercussions.

Regardless, when they finally talked, Amadora needed to convince her brother to agree to cover for her. She was getting close to her goal and too far in to jeopardize it now. It would take all her charms to convince Zanipolo, and even that was not certain. Polo was harder to persuade than Gunny. Once his mind was set on something, it was near impossible to convince him otherwise. If he wanted to expose her, there would be nothing she could do to change his mind.

Amadora rested her chin on her hand while she watched guests laughing and dancing. She envied them in a way. If only she did not have this intoxicating drive propelling her, she might have been among them. She could have enjoyed the trivialities in life and made them her sole worries in life. What it must feel like to be so free to do what you want and act any way without worry of the consequences leading to your demise. But this was what she wanted more than anything. This was the path she chose. She should not feel envious because this world was her heart's genuine desire.

Distracted by her thoughts, Amadora did not notice someone enter her cove until they tapped her on the shoulder. She forced a large welcoming smile to mask her concerns. When she turned around, though, her heart sank, and she struggled to maintain her pleasant demeanor. "Polo"

"Amadora," Zanipolo wrapped his arms around his sister and pulled her in close. "Long time no see. How have you been?"

Amadora hugged him back hesitantly. She knew something was off about his actions, but she did not want to alert him as he let go and faced her.

"What's wrong, Dora?" Zanipolo asked, noticing the confusion pasted on her face.

"I'm fine. I'm just surprised by your affection."

"Come now," He closed the space between them once more and whispered in her ear. "There are too many eyes and ears around. We can't draw attention by acting out of character."

"You're right. Do you have a safer place where we can talk?"

"Yeah. I spent the last day scouring the grounds, but I found a place that's perfectly isolated from the ruckus of the guests and staff that we don't have to worry about someone overhearing us. Follow me."

Zanipolo grabbed Amadora's hand and led her through the chaos of the grand hall. They descended to the ground floor and followed the staff as they disappeared behind an enormous tree trunk. They waited until the activity going in and out of the truck stopped, then they snuck inside and left out the door hidden there.

Surrounded by tall maze-like bushes, Polo guided Amadora along the cobblestone path until they wound up in a vast grove of trees sprawled around a small ivy-covered building. Zanipolo ran his gloved hands along the vines until he found the doorknob. He yanked on the rusted door until it broke from its frame and cracked open. He held it while Amadora entered, then shut it behind him and flicked the lights on so they could see.

Cobwebs, dead plants, cracked dirt, and rusted tools decorated the room. This greenhouse was a relic of Amadora's childhood. Her mother had not used it ever since they expand the grounds when she was a child and they left everything like it was. Amadora was surprised Zanipolo found it since the wild growing trees and bushes concealed it from the rest of the world.

"This is an excellent location. It's perfectly hidden in the brush that it's almost impossible to see what's going on from the ballroom," Amadora said.

"That's why I chose it. I couldn't risk someone overhearing our conversation in that booth. I needed to speak freely about how I feel."

"So, how do you feel?"

"I'm pissed, Dora! What you're doing is crazy! Do you even realize the danger you're putting everyone involved in!" Zanipolo scolded.

"Of course, I understand and have taken every precaution to protect those who are helping me out. But this is the only way to prove to father that I can handle this world on my own."

"You are a damned idiot. I get that much, but what I can't understand is your lack of empathy towards those you've roped into your façade like Sam. I thought she was an imposter, part of some devious plan to kidnap you to use as leverage against the family. I could have killed her if she didn't tell me who she was. What would you have done if I hurt her?"

"But you didn't," Amadora noticed the frustration brimming on Zanipolo's words, so she counteracted it with a calm and rational façade. She did not want him to know the truth, that she would have died if something happened to Samantha. Amadora did not want her to see even a glimpse of how she truly felt in fear he would see it as a weakness.

"That's not the point! Maybe you're too far in, because you're losing your human-ity to this world! I could have killed her, and you wouldn't have felt a thing! Her death would have just been an unfortunate risk to reach your conceited desire, wouldn't it?"

"No! You're wrong! Sam's safety was one of my top priorities! I wanted to do this on my own, but she insisted on helping me," Amadora's voice trailed off and she averted her gaze.

"Do you know why she agreed to help you?"

Amadora remained silent, causing Zanipolo to shake his head in disappointment. "She understands the dangers and wouldn't let you face them on your own. She'd do anything to protect you," Zanipolo sighed and calmed down before he continued. "Everyone who gets wrapped up in your perilous game probably feels the same. You give them no other choice, and they willingly risk their lives to help fulfill your cause, just like me."

"Like you? What do you mean?"

"No matter how I look at it, I have only one option now that I know everything. I can't turn away and ignore what you're doing. I also can't rat you out to pops. That would just increase the risk since we couldn't control how he'd react. So, the only choice left is to help you safely navigate this scheme until it reaches a satisfying ending."

"Polo, thank you," Amadora said concealing her surprise.

"Don't thank me yet. If I'm helping you with this, everything is going to be on my terms. First, tell whoever you've been staying with to plan a small vacation to the beach house in Cali. All expenses are on me. I want to reduce the calamity in case this gets hairy. We'll use their place as our base while they're gone. Second, we must come up with some kind of strategy on how you can maneuver as Johnnie Barbone to reach your goal. But for tonight, I want to focus on getting you familiar with the operatives of the other families. You might cross paths with them later down the line and need to be prepared if you do."

Zanipolo turned off the lights and motioned to the door. Let's get out of here before someone spots the lights."

Faint noises from the ballroom faded as Elda, Casimiro, and Lorenzo descended into a dim corridor. Elda tried to remain expressionless as she entered the large bunker where members of the rival families and her father sat around a large rectangle table, but she fumed on the inside. Normally, every leading member of their family business was supposed to attend the annual peace summit with their father, but this time, it was only Elda. Zanipolo ran off somewhere at the beginning of the ball and had not been seen since, so they just left him alone since they did not need to discuss anything regarding his territory. However, Gunny was more important.

He was the second-in-command and needed to be here, but he refused to attend for reasons Elda understood the moment she looked across the table at the representative for the Rosilli family, Lana Rosilli. The second-in-command of the Rosilli family was a terrifying figure and her short temper and altered reality of honor dragged the meeting longer than it needed to be. Elda understood why anyone would want to skip, especially with the escalated tensions between his men and hers; regardless, it was not fair he left Elda to pick up his slack once again.

Sometimes, Elda wished she could be just as irresponsible as her siblings and dump her duties on someone else, but she could not do that to her father and Casimiro. Dealing with two delinquent leaders was enough of a burden for the family. Someone had to be the rock and hold everything together and that, unfortunately, was her job.

Don Lorenzo stood at the head of the table and raised a glass of water at the other representatives.

"Welcome, my brothers. Don Morelli, Don Canora, Don Borcini and Lana Rosilli.

I am glad you could make our annual summit. Sadly, Don Rosilli could not meet with us again this year because of his health. I pray he swiftly recovers and meets with us once more around this table in the coming years. Now, let's get down to business."

Don Lorenzo crossed off something on the paper in front of him and scanned its contents before moving on.

"Let's deal with some of the smaller grievances between us," Don Lorenzo looked at the Don Canora and Borcini. "It seems a small feud has sparked between the two of you because your children are romantically involved."

Don Borcini leaped to his feet in anger, cutting off Don Lorenzo before he could continue. "Tell Canora to put a leash on his son before he defiles my sweet Isabella!"

"Sweet... tsk... If your daughter wasn't such a seductive harlot, my son wouldn't be caught in this mess," Don Canora retorted coldly.

Don Borcini jumped across the table to grab Don Canora, but Don Morelli, Casimiro and some of his men held him back. Tensions rose viciously in the room as the two dons continued to hurl insults at one another. Don Lorenzo watched carefully, then he interrupted them with a booming demand.

"Sit down!"

Both dons stopped arguing and sat back down.

"You're acting like madmen over a situation that's very advantageous. Just like my family's bond with the Morellis, by forming this union on their own, your children have formed a bond between your families that can create an alliance instead of wasting time, energy and resources in a feud," Don Lorenzo scolded.

"I guess you're right," Don Canora reluctantly agreed.

"I didn't think of it like that. I guess I can support it if it's put that way," Don Borcini echoed.

Don Morelli flashed a relieved smile at Don Lorenzo as he sat back down. It was clear this problem was resolved and no need to continue any farther down this messy road. However, when Don Lorenzo glanced at the next item on the list and looked back at his friend, his expression was more worried than before. Don Morelli did not need to be a mind reader to figure out what was on his mind.

"Now, we move onto the biggest matter affecting our peace. The recent tensions elevating between the Rosilli and Morelli families. We hoped to address these concerns directly to Don Rosilli, but because of the current state of his health I know that will be difficult," Don Lorenzo started.

"I'm here as my don's voice and ears until he's fit to come on his own. Address me with any concerns you have, and I'll relay it to him," Lana's smooth voice broke through Don Lorenzo's words, carrying an icy chill with it.

"Fine. I understand there have been a series of unfortunate events between the two families that warrant this animosity, but you must not let these incidents escalate tensions any farther," Don Lorenzo replied.

"I agree. If things progress more, it could affect all of us and draw us into a need-less war," Don Borcini added.

"We have no problem with the Rosillis even though their man, Jack, brutally butchered our men," Don Morelli responded.

"You're a liar! I know you're the ones behind both Jack's and Marco's deaths!" Lana yelled in frustration.

"Watch it! My father wouldn't lie about something like that! There's nothing link-ing us to their deaths, so you need to be careful where you fling your accusations!" Elda stood up and moved closer to the table, defending her father from Lana's fury.

Lana stared down Elda for a moment before returning an unbothered smile to her lips. Everyone could feel the tension rise between the two strongest women of the opposing families. Don Canora, who sat next to Lana, interjected.

"The deaths of the Rosilli's men are unfortunate, but it's dangerous to wave around those types of allegations without proof. Until we know more about the iden-tities of the culprits, you need to tread lightly, Lana, and not act so brazenly to prevent anymore unnecessary bloodshed."

"You're right. We don't know who's behind their deaths, but we will find out." Lana's dark smile widened as she looked over to Lorenzo, Elda and Casimiro. "But we will act once we do."

"Alright then. In the meantime, can the Morellis and Rosillis propose a brief ceasefire?" Don Lorenzo looked relieved when it seemed they could quell Lana's fury reasonably easy this time.

"Of course," Don Morelli smiled.

Lana Rosilli did not say a word. She just smiled warmly and nodded. And as they continued with the meeting, she remained quiet and attentive. Her actions worried Elda, who snuck out of the room once they discussed the important matters and dragged Lorenzo into a crevice in the corridor.

"Elle, what's wrong?" Lorenzo whispered, checking to see if anyone else was around.

"I don't trust that bloodthirsty bitch. She gave up too quick without a fight, which is unlike her. She must have something planned. I want you to use some of your men to monitor her and her people. I want to know about every interaction they have and every move they make. I have a bad feeling about this."

Lorenzo smiled and nodded. "You got it."

After the meeting with the heads of the rival families adjourned, Lana Rosilli re-turned to her booth on the west balcony of the third floor and watched the other guests in discontent. She did not expect to get much from the summit. She knew they would not let her get revenge for her men's deaths, but the way old man Morelli made it seem like they were the sole problem and deserved what happened to them pissed her off. She knew both Jack and Marco had their quirks, but that was no excuse for the way they were brutally murdered.

Lana did not have any proof linking the Morellis to their deaths, but she knew they had motives to kill them both. She also knew they would not leave a trail if they wanted to get rid of them, but still leave a warning for anyone else thinking to cross them. They were behind the deaths of her men, and Lana would get her revenge no matter what. She waved her hand to summon one of her men guarding the opening of the cove. She motioned him to sit across from her.

"Mistress, how can I serve you today?"

Her crimson lips curled as she whispered.

"Let them know it's time."

"Are you sure you want to do this?" He warned.

"Yes. Be careful not to be followed. I'm pretty sure they're keeping tabs on us after that meeting. I refuse to let Jack's and Marco's deaths go unpunished.

Zanipolo brought Amadora to an empty table on the ground floor of the ballroom with a view of the balcony on the third floor. He moved in close to her and spoke low, letting the music from the band shroud their conversation so no one nearby could eavesdrop.

"Amadora, look, if you're going to delve into this world, you need to know some of the key players you might encounter," Zanipolo motioned over to a large table in the center of the top floor where their father dined with three men. "You might have noticed pops never sits with the rest of the family during the ball but sits with those men up there."

"Yes. I noticed, but I understand why. Those men are the heads of the other families, and he must sit with them for diplomatic reasons, right?" Amadora scanned the men sitting around the small circular table with her father.

"Correct," Zanipolo replied. "This ball plays two important roles in strengthening our family's power. One reason is to strengthen our ties with those we protect, and the other—most important—reason is to quell any grievances held between the five families."

Zanipolo looked over at a man in a gold suit, wrapping his arm around their father and laughing. "There's only one among the heads who pops trust and that's the one sitting next to the one in the gold suit, Don Lorenzo. You're probably familiar with our history with the Lorenzos, so I won't rehash it now. But pop's goal for holding this event isn't to become friends with them but to keep them at bay for the sake of business. He knows dealing with petty feuds while trying to run a profitable business is near impossible and would be damaging for all of them. So, if the families could have one night to come together, air their grievances and find some common ground, they could continue unbothered for the rest of the year on their own separate goals. Luckily, the other dons, Don Borcini, Lorenzo and Canora, think the same."

"What about Don Rosilli? Doesn't he think this summit is helpful?"

"Who knows? He used to attend every year like the other dons a few years ago, but he suddenly stopped coming and sent his second-in-command in his place."

"Second-in-command?"

"Yeah... The black widow, Lana Rosilli," Zanipolo motioned to a cove off the edge of the west balcony of the third floor where a woman sat talking to a man wearing a long, dark coat and large-brimmed dark hat.

"Black widow, huh? Why did she get that nickname?" Amadora asked, watching her carefully to see past her delicate features for a glimpse of her true nature.

"She's the deadliest and most reckless of the second-in-commands of the rival families. Lana seems like a gentle beauty, but that's a mask hiding her true nature, one driven by bloodlust and despair."

"Do you think she is the reason her don doesn't come anymore?" Amadora asked.

Zanipolo shrugged and grabbed a glass from a tray of a passing waitress. "I doubt it. The official reason he doesn't attend is because he's too sick to come to a crowded event like this. No one doubts that since he's much older than all the other dons and didn't look good at the last meeting he attended. Besides, Lana hates taking on the spokesperson role. She's a brute who acts based on her own whims. She's not good at diplomacy from what I've seen in the last meeting I attended."

"Then, should I worry about someone like that?" Amadora turned to Zanipolo and smirked.

"Don't get cocky, Dora. Lana might not be diplomatic, but she isn't stupid. Try your best to avoid her at all costs. If you cross her, then she can become a formidable adversary."

Amadora looked back at Lana, and this time, she caught her gaze and smiled softly. Chills shot down her spine when their eyes met. Amadora smiled back, matching her look of intimidation with one of confidence. For that moment, Lana seemed impressed, and her cordial smile transformed into something else before she stood and walked away from her table.

Amadora was not sure if the most feared woman of this world would remember this moment, but Amadora would. She was not sure if she would ever cross paths with Lana again; but knew if she did, she would have to learn how to banish all emotion and be prepared to endure whatever Lana threw her way.

144

Casimiro pushed his plate away and downed the rest of his wine as Elda informed Gugliehno about the events from the summit. Too many things raced through his mind to focus on their conversation. He knew this meeting did not come to a peaceful resolution for them and the Rosilli family. He feared the effects of Jack's and now Marco's deaths. Casimiro knew about their involvement with Jack's demise, but he was not sure about their connection to Marco.

Basilio informed him about Marco's death this morning when they gathered for a private meeting before coming to the hall. At that moment, Casimiro did not care about the effects it had on the Rosilli family, but his mind wandered to the person who he knew had a connection with him, the one who left his heart and him stranded in the cold, lost and confused, Giacinta.

Casimiro resolved her deal with Marco, and she promised to never have contact with him after. To his knowledge, she kept that promise and told no one else about their past. So, their family did not have any reason to go after him. Clearly, Lana's blame for his death was misplaced. He worried what a misdirected, vengeful Lana would do to satisfy her vengeance. If she found out about Giacinta's debt with Marco, she might use that as reason enough to go after them, or worse, she might turn her wrath onto Giacinta.

After weeks of avoiding Giacinta and keeping himself busy with work to prevent any glimpse of her in his mind, Casimiro felt himself slowly fall into the dark rabbit hole of her essence. The memories of the pain and confusion caused by the last time he saw her faded, and he remembered the precious moments they shared. Thinking about Lana possibly targeting her ignited the love he tried to conceal. A part of him wanted to know why she ran away, while another wanted to keep his pride and move on, not wanting to give her such control over his reality. Either way, he would not let his pride jeopardize her life. Casimiro would protect her with his life even if he could not return to her side.

Fate must have eavesdropped on Casimiro's thoughts because just when Gunny refilled their glasses, a small blonde teenage girl wearing a brown dress walked over to their table. She nodded courteously to each of them before handing a small note to Casimiro and leaving.

"Was that Nanette? I wonder what she wants with you." Elda watched as the girl hurried across the crowded floor and dashed down the stairs.

"Who knows? If you need to go, you can go ahead. We can't do much until Lorenzo returns, so go have fun," Gunny patted his friend on the back and flashed one of his infectious smiles.

Casimiro read the note carefully. It was from the one person he did not expect to hear from tonight, Giacinta. He crumbled up the piece of paper, stuffed it into his pocket and rushed off. "I must deal with something. I'll be back soon."

"No hurry," Gunny smirked, waving Casimiro away.

Giacinta stared at the large, dark billowing clouds hanging in the sky searching for answers behind the threatening storm. She sat on the edge of the bridge's wooden banister and stared at the hall's brilliant glow as it dispelled the night's lingering shadows. She clasped her hands tightly together as she held onto the last bit of hope left in her heart while waiting for fate's answer.

Gunny took care of the problem weighing on her heart, and she could finally express it freely to the only person she wanted to share it with, Casimiro. However, Giacinta wondered if he would even show up after the way she treated him the last time they met. She would not blame him if he was too upset to be near her, but she hoped he would come even if he had not forgiven her yet. She wanted to explain herself and apologize. Giacinta did not want to lose the one meaningful relationship she ever had because of her pathetic cowardice. She needed him to know how she truly felt.

Casimiro rejected all his sanity and hushed all the warnings from his head to embrace the desires of his heart. He crossed the dimly lit brick garden path until he reached the bridge. Tall willow trees blocked the bridge from his sight. But once he stepped on the wet stone lining its entrance, he saw the source of his desires and nightmares.

She stood as a radiant light in the vast shadows while she looked to the sky. Her long, flowing ivory dress glowed as the bridge lanterns illuminated her body in a marvelous aura. When she heard his footsteps, she turned towards him, brushing back the long, wavy strands flowing with the brisk breeze. She flashed a warm smile when her mesmerizing blue eyes met his gaze. In that moment, it took all his strength to keep his distance and not scoop her into his arms, because despite all the pain she caused him, a part of him longed to be close to her again.

Giacinta saw the way Casimiro looked at her, and her heart raced. She could not believe he came. All the anxiety that built inside her poured out, causing tears to form. She bit her lip, fought them back, and smiled.

"Casimiro, you came. I'm glad. For a moment, I thought you wouldn't." Casimiro did not respond when she called him.

"Were you scared that I would do the same thing you did to me?" Casimiro's anger and hurt shone through his eyes as he spoke. "I wouldn't do that because I don't run from my problems. I face them even if I don't want to."

"I know you wouldn't," Giacinta looked away sadly while she wrestled with her emotions and tried to find the right words.

"Giacinta, why did you ask me to come here?" Casimiro did not move from where he stood. He just observed her.

"I want to apologize for how I acted last time we met," Giacinta replied.

"You don't need to do that. It was my fault for forcing you into something you weren't ready for."

"That's not it," Sorrow weighed on Giacinta's heart as she turned back to Casimiro. She moved closer to him, but he took a step back for each step she took. The distance between them stirred the pain hiding inside her chest and caused the tears she tried so hard to conceal to flow freely.

When Casimiro saw the first tear drop fall, he wanted to wipe it away before another fell, but his own broken heart paralyzed him. He could not control the cold persona that took over every time he spoke. "Why did you run then?"

"I put everything I love in danger because of the reckless decisions I've made in my life. If I told you how I really felt then, I'd put you at risk too."

Casimiro softened his demeanor, closed the distance between them and wiped her cheek with his hand. "Don't be silly. What danger could you possibly put me in?"

The wind howled as it whipped past them, drowning out Giacinta's words as she told him about her encounter with Marco. Even though the moment was long gone, the fear was still fresh in her mind. Her tears blinded her while the wind muffled her cries. Before she could regain her composure, she felt someone grab her tight. The security of their embrace helped her break the hold of her past fears.

"You're safe now. I'm not going to let anyone hurt you," Casimiro replied, holding her tighter.

"I'm sorry for letting my fear of Marco stop me from telling you how I really feel. I was weak and hurt. Please forgive me," Giacinta nuzzled her head into his broad chest.

"There's no reason to be afraid anymore. I'm here and not going anywhere. Just tell me the truth. Tell me how you really feel."

"I love you with all my heart and never want to be apart from you again. Please, tell me you still feel the same," Giacinta placed her hand softly over his heart and looked up at him, letting a few hopeful tears escape her eyes.

Casimiro wiped away the tears from her flushed cheeks and smiled. "Giacinta, of course I do. I never stopped loving you."

With those words, he ensnared her lips with his, calming the world around them. Their blissful reunion lasted only for a moment until the soft pummeling of the sky's tears interrupted them. They stopped for a second, looking up at the sky as the rain gently fell upon them. Casimiro then looked at her, smiling.

"Let's return to the ballroom before we get soaked."

Giacinta shook her head no, smiling back at him and gazing lovingly into his enchanting light green eyes. "I don't mind staying out here in the rain as long as I'm with you. This is where I want to be... in your arms forever."

Casimiro pulled her in close to use his body as a shield while the rain engulfed them. Ignoring all logic that told him to go inside, he listened to his heart that told him to stay here and kiss the lips of the one person he desired above all, letting the rain wash away their pain while their love shone through the dark night.

Darian glanced at the card he held in his hand and scanned the tables scattered on the sides of the dance floor for table 29. He wanted to skip the fancy dinner and just go straight to the big man upstairs and settle the matter immediately so he could return home, but he was one of the last business owners to meet with the don because he arrived late. While Darian waited for his turn, he needed to find something to do to pass the time.

When he finally found his table, it was not empty. A young woman in a gold dress sat watching the band play a lively song. Darian could not see her face from behind her long, wavy, dark hair. He searched the area to see if her party was nearby, but no one came. She seemed to be all on her own.

"Nice song, isn't it?" Darian walked to her side and smiled courteously.

When the girl turned around, Darian could not help but stare at her charming looks. Her enormous eyes grew as if he startled her.

"I'm sorry for scaring you," Darian smiled.

The woman's expression softened and turned into an inviting smile. "No. It's fine. It's my fault for not paying attention."

"Why is a pretty gal like you sitting all alone? Are you waiting for someone?"

"No. I'm just enjoying the ambiance."

Darian looked at her suspiciously. "You came alone to this ball just to enjoy the scenery?"

"Not exactly. I had to come."

"I understand that feeling. Are you here to meet with Basilio Morelli?" Darian sat in a chair near her.

The woman looked away and returned her focus to the musicians.

"No. I'm here to support my mom and aunt. They spent a lot of time and hard work in putting together this event."

"They did a great job. Were they hired by the Morellis to decorate for this ball?"

"Actually, they did it for free since this is their ball." The woman turned back to him and chuckled. "Let me introduce myself. I'm Amadora Morelli."

Darian stared at the enchanting woman next to him. He could not believe this sweet creature was the spawn of the man he hated the most. Darian hid his real thoughts and painted a warm expression to respond to his question.

"You're Don Morelli's daughter. I'm Darian Mancini. It's a pleasure to meet you."

Darian reached out his hand. "You shouldn't waste your night sitting alone. You deserve to have some fun. Come dance with me."

Amadora was hesitant at first; but after a moment, she took his hand and followed him onto the dance floor. In the bright light of the chandelier lit dance floor, Darian saw the details of her extravagant features. Her dark eyes sparkled like crystal, illuminating her subtle features. He became mesmerized by her gentle touch and heart-warming laugh as they glided across the floor. But the more he gazed into her eyes, the more familiar she seemed.

"Amadora, have we met before?"

Amadora paused before flashing a playful grin while following his lead.

"No. You're mistaken. This is the first time we've met."

Darian looked her over with a raised eyebrow. "Are you sure?"

"Yes. I'm sure," Amadora seemed a little annoyed by his perseverance. He dropped the subject and flashed a charming smile. Maybe she was right, and he was confusing her with someone else.

"I must be wrong. I would be an idiot to forget a gorgeous face like yours."

Amadora became flustered as Darian spun her around and complimented her. Darian enjoyed seeing her innocent reaction. The more time he spent with her, the more he wanted to know about this Morelli princess.

After a few drinks, Gugliehno burned as if he was set aflame. He needed to step away from his family and cool off outside, but a vicious rainstorm raged. The only place safe from the vicious downpour was the third-floor outdoor balcony, which was hidden by the elaborate decorations behind them. He snuck outside, tucked his hands into his pockets and watched the rain pound the yellow haze now surrounding the garden. A brisk breeze brushed against his face and cooled his rising anxiety.

This misty night reflected his heart. Each raindrop reflected a tear he could not show. Gugliehno wanted to leave and go elsewhere especially after the news he learned today. He could not handle the chaos of their business while he was absorbing the information about Joey's brother. If it was not for how this revelation could affect Samantha, he would not even get involved. But he had to. He made a promise to Joey to watch over his sister. He needed to reach out to Mister Baldemar and figure out what was his angle.

"Something on your mind, Gugliehno?"

Gugliehno froze the moment he heard that voice. Years passed since he heard her voice. He tried his best to avoid them, to avoid the terrible memories they invoked, but this night he slipped up, and here they stood in the soft light surrounding them.

A breathtaking woman wearing a crimson gown smiled at him. Her light-colored curls were pinned into a fashionable bob. Her delicate heart face glowed with a mask of concern. Her sharp sea-green eyes sparkled with dark amusement of his reaction. Her small scarlet lips curled into a smile making him feel uneasy.

"Lana," Gugliehno grimaced.

"Come now, Gunny. Why do you hate me so? When we were together, I gave you nothing but joy. Didn't I?" Lana purred, cutting the shadows and moving closer to him.

"The only good things I got from you were my two beautiful daughters. The rest was nothing but a bunch of heartache." Gunny turned from her, disgusted.

"At least you came out with your life," Lana laughed, covering her mouth with her delicate gloved hand. "If you listen to all these ridiculous rumors, you'd think I was a monster."

"You are a monster," Gugliehno said coldly.

"If that's so, why did you have two children with me?" Lana glowered.

"You were different then."

"Open your eyes, Gunny. I'm the same woman you loved and married."

"You're delusional if you think you're the same! You lost everything that made you beautiful when you succumbed to the darkness of your family's world!" Gunny snapped. "I would be shocked if you even have enough of a heart left to feel the slightest tinge of love!"

"Look at you assuming the worst again! You think you understand me, but you don't! I wanted to embrace the trivial pleasures I once enjoyed! Peace, Joy, Love. The three things I cherished more than life itself were robbed from me!" Her tone remained soft, but it trembled with anger.

"Don't try to play the victim, Lana. They weren't stolen from you. You threw them away to pursue the path you're on now."

"I didn't throw away my children! You took them from me!"

"No. You're wrong. I shielded them from the monster you've become."

"How could you say that? They are my daughters, too. They deserve to know their actual mother." Lana clenched her hand to fight her growing fury. "You're no saint, Gugliehno. Blood stains your hands too. You can taint them just as much as I can."

"That's true; but unlike you, I never let my business corrupt me. I can maintain my sanity while around my kids. Tell me, Lana, can you say the same?"

Lana faced the ballroom door to hide her boiling rage. She was nearing her breaking point and about to do something she might regret to her children's father. She took a deep breath and exhaled to release her building aggression. She forced a grin across her lips.

"You've put me in a tight spot, Gunny. Don't get cocky. I'm not giving up just yet. I will get my daughters back. Just you wait and see."

Lana's last words made Gunny feel uneasy. He was not sure what she had planned,

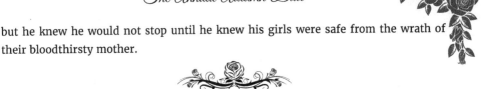

but he knew he would not stop until he knew his girls were safe from the wrath of their bloodthirsty mother.

Musilli walked into the second-floor office in the main warehouse. He sat down at the desk and cleaned his gun. He hated being stuck guarding the warehouse. This warehouse sat in the center of the Morellis shipping community. Everything along these docks belonged to them and their allies. It was also impossible to get inside the community without being thoroughly inspected by their men stationed at its gates and the one surrounding the warehouse.

Musilli understood the purpose of guarding it; but he did not take this job because of that. He had more selfish reasons.

This job was given to him directly from Lorenzo instead of telephoned through Brock. That was a privilege few men got, and Larry would make use of it. If he fulfilled this meager task, he would gain his boss's respect and finally get some traction on his waning career. Musilli hated being one of the lowest soldiers. He worked for this family for years but could never catch their eye. Even his own protégé, Johnnie, gained more attention in a few weeks than Larry did in his entire career.

Larry had to admit that the kid was impressive, but he could not help being a little jealous of his success. It took him years to get to his current position, and that was mostly with the help of Brock putting in a good word for him. Maybe Brock was right. Maybe he grew too comfortable and slacked off too much. If he wanted anything to change, he needed to step up his game.

As Musilli took a part his gun and reassembled it, he sighed. He did not know why he brought it. He doubted that he would even need it tonight. The chances of someone breaking into this warehouse were very slim. There was nothing important here.

Larry knew this would be just another long, boring night, but he needed to suck it up and deal with it. Even though it seemed meaningless to him, it was important to his boss, and that was all that mattered.

A small truck pulled up to the warehouse's gates. The guard walked over to the driver and pointed a gun at his head. He could not see his face because his coat's collar covered it.

"Who the hell are you?" The guard pressed the mouth of the gun against the driver's temple, causing a tiny drop of sweat to fall. He slowly raised his hands and turned to face him.

"Come on. Is this how you greet all the truck drivers who come to your warehouse?" The driver smiled as the guard looked him over indifferently.

"Only those I don't know. Who sent you?" The guard demanded.

"I'm just delivering a shipment of goods from the Southshore Docks in Atlantic

City. I was supposed to arrive earlier but got caught in some traffic on the way here."

The guard scanned the truck and peeked at the passenger seat, then he called over to his partner. "Barney, check and see if any shipments haven't come in yet."

His partner went into the gatehouse and picked up the logbook. He flipped through the pages until he found the page for the incoming loads.

"Hey, Marty, his story checks out. One shipment hasn't come in yet."

Marty lowered his gun and motioned for the driver to enter. Some men inside the yard guided the driver to the loading zone in the back. When the truck parked, the men opened the back of the truck. But before they let go of the door, a thunderous chorus of gunfire echoed through the yard, and they fell motionless on the ground.

Men covered in black outfits and wearing masks jumped from the trunk, clutching their various weapons. About twenty men, excluding the driver, surrounded the back of the truck. One of the tall men went to the driver, accompanied by four other men.

"It's your job to make sure they don't shoot up the truck. We need it for a clean getaway. Four of my men will stay behind to help you." The man handed the driver a gun. "Use this. Get rid of anyone who tries to stop you."

The tall man's men took positions surrounding the truck while he returned to the others.

"Grab all the ammo and explosives you can. We're razing this entire complex to the ground. No survivors. Those are our mistress's orders."

The man pointed in different directions and his men fanned out in groups.

The guards heard gunshots echo through the air, coming from the loading docks where the truck went. They grabbed their guns and went to check out the ruckus. They stealthily crept along crates and boxes until they came close to where the truck went. With their guns pinned close to their sides, they crept around the rows of crates and boxes to check out the situation.

Under the yard lights, their comrades laid motionlessly on the crimson-stained ground and over them were a hoard of men. They dragged their bodies to a clearing, poured some liquid on them, then a few moments later a large flame engulfed them.

Marty counted the men surrounding the truck. "This isn't going to be pretty. There's too many to outrun and warn the others. We need to let them know what's happening." Marty whispered to Barney as he prepared to shoot at the intruders.

"Any ideas how? They've already killed half of our men and have us outnumbered twenty to two. We can't outrun them."

Sweat formed on Marty's brow as reality struck. The odds were against them. No matter how he went over it in his mind, the outcome was always the same... death.

"The only way we can alert the others is to send out some warning shots. Luckily, we have some dummies to help us with that. If we're going to die, we might as well

bring some of these bastards down with us."

The whole mess with Amadora zapped Zanipolo of all his patience. He needed to take a breather and put all the complications to the side. He was not sure how he would handle this new challenge his sister forced him into.

Zanipolo's life became ten times more difficult thanks to Amadora. He was not sure how he would handle her little secret. If they were going to reach her goal, he must deceive everyone in his brother's crew, including Gugliehno. That was where things got tricky.

Zanipolo and Gunny did not have much of a relationship. Gunny was always closer to Elda and his friends than Polo, and he did not mind that. They were polar opposites. Gunny's innocent, infallible smile was a perfect ruse to throw onlookers off his true nature. It made him seem foolish, but he was far from it.

Gunny was the most talented of them all. Gunny was very observant and could spot a change in someone's manner in a matter of seconds. If Zanipolo was going to suddenly work by his men, Gunny would notice something was up almost immediately. Polo needed to find an excuse to help his crew without stirring Gunny's suspicions.

Zanipolo exhaled and leaned against the gazebo's railing, staring at the rain hitting the ground. He wished Amadora could be more like Giacinta. Polo could handle a materialistic brat focused on partying and gambling over Johnnie Barbone. Only Amadora would obsess over a desire that tests the boundary of life and death while dragging everyone around her into it.

Zanipolo's mind lingered as the rain intensified. The patter of footsteps running across wet stone shattered his thoughts. He turned to the mushroom-shaped, ghastly figure gliding through the fog and over to the gazebo.

"Polo... Is that you?" The figure hurried to the refuge of the gazebo and placed an umbrella against the railing.

"Sam, what are you doing out here?"

Samantha pulled the flaps of her jacket shut to shield her soaked body from the chilly air. She smiled hiding her discomfort and replied.

"What do you think I'm doing here? I'm looking for you."

"Why were you looking for me?"

"You talked to Amadora, right? I wanted to check and make sure you're alright."

"I'm okay. You didn't need to check on me."

"I guess you're right. I didn't have to check on you, but I wanted to." Samantha turned from him, ignoring the tension between them.

"Why do you want to do that?"

Samantha bit her lip holding back what she really wanted to say. "I wanted to see what we should do next now that you're on board with her plan."

"We're not doing anything. Amadora and I will take it from here-on out."

Sam looked at him, confused. "What do you mean? What about me, Polo? I'm helping Amadora too."

"No, Sam. This is too dangerous. I don't want you anywhere near this part of her plan."

"I don't care what you want. I'm not going to be pushed out of the loop. I made a promise to Amadora to help her see this through until the end, and that's what I'm going to do."

Samantha remained steady while her eyes brimmed with a bustling fire. Zanipolo did not react when their gazes crossed paths; but basked in the rays of her determination and courage. Over the years, Samantha was always the sheepish shadow following his sister, with no real voice of her own. She did everything Amadora told her to do without hesitation, and Zanipolo thought she did that because Amadora told her to. But that was not the case at all. Samantha followed along with his sister's commands because that is what she wanted.

As the music faded, Darian spun Amadora around one last time. Amadora blushed when their eyes met once more. She could not believe how much fun she was having with him. However, getting close to him would be dangerous. Amadora was pretty sure he had not forgotten about the person who ransacked his store. If he ever found out she was the one who did that, who knows what he would do to her?

When their dance ended, Darian let go of her and smiled. "Thanks for the dance. I enjoyed every moment."

"No. I should be the one thanking you. I had lots of fun." Amadora blushed.

"You did?" Darian's smile grew. "I'm glad. I wish I could stay with you longer, but it's almost my turn to speak with your father. Can I see you again?"

Mesmerized by Darian's enchanting blue eyes, Amadora felt light-headed and giddy inside. She fought all the warnings from her sanity screaming in her head to turn him down.

"Yes. I wouldn't mind that. Give me your number, and I'll call you."

When those words escaped her mouth, Amadora's heart skipped a beat, then plummeted into oblivion. If they met again, the stakes would rise drastically. She would tag him onto the long list of people she must hide her double life as Johnnie Barbone.

Darian's face lit up as he grabbed a pen and scribbled his number on the back of the seating ticket. He placed it gently in her palm, then kissed the back of her hand.

"I'll wait for your call."

Amadora watched Darian rush off into the crowd, heading towards the stairs. She

placed her hand over her heart and breathed deeply. From this moment-on, if she followed this strange desire, then she might lose everything she worked so hard to accomplish. But there was something about Darian Mancini that made her want to risk everything just to see him again.

The echo of gunshots roused Musilli and the guards inside into action. Musilli quickly ordered them into the main loading zone, hoping to lure the enemy into a trap before they reached them. While his men headed to different advantage points throughout the loading zone, Musilli grabbed a young recruit named Mark and took cover by the door opposite them. Mark was young, but he was agile and a skilled marksman.

All entrances leading into this warehouse were blocked off ahead of time as a precaution for an event like this one. The small door leading into the main loading zone was the only entrance and exit. It was a significant advantage and disadvantage if things got hairy. They had one chance to even the playing field and defend the warehouse with their lives intact.

Mark and Musilli ran to their positions, preparing themselves for the bloodbath that was about to begin. The intruders busted through the door, entering in small groups. With one wave of his hand, Musilli and his men open fire. The scent of death lingered in the air as their enemy fell, one by one.

Victory seemed imminent when the enemy retreated, and the zone fell into a deafening silence. Musilli scanned the entrance to find any clue of their adversary's whereabouts, but nothing. A second before Musilli retreated to his hideout, three sticks of explosives hurled through the air. One aimed straight for Mark and Musilli. Musilli grabbed Mark and pulled him away from its path. But when it exploded, the blast sent them flying through the glass walls of the loading zone security office.

Bruised and cut up Musilli's body could barely move when he fought to stand. His left arm smashed against the ground during the blast and was shattered and useless. He fought the excruciating pain and the sea of blood at his feet to find Mark.

Disoriented from the blast and blood loss, Musilli searched through the debris until he found Mark's lifeless body skewered by a large shard of glass.

"Poor kid, you didn't deserve this," Musilli closed Mark's eyes with his blood-covered hand.

There were casualties on both sides, with no signs of life among his comrades. Musilli picked up a gun and snuck out into the zone yard. He crossed over to the garage opposite the loading area and snuck into one car. Luckily, his men were too lazy to remove the keys, making taking the car easier.

With only one working arm, steering the car was near impossible, but Musilli did not let that stop him. He drove across the yard as fast as he could through the garage doors.

The collision alerted the rest of the intruders. Bullets flew at the driver of the car from all sides. Musilli ducked down to avoid the barrage of bullets. Before he could celebrate nearly escaping death, his car swerved into the side of the main gate, knocking him unconscious on impact.

"Is Amadora so important you'd recklessly risk your life for her?" Zanipolo asked.

"She is," Samantha looked away.

"You're an idiot, Sam. Even though my sister is your best friend, you must watch out for yourself," Zanipolo walked over to Samantha and placed his hands over her arms, forcing her to face him. "Please reconsider. I don't want you to get hurt."

"I can't do that. Please respect my decision," Samantha replied.

Zanipolo released her and turned away. "Sure. I get it. You'll do anything for Amadora. She *is* the only one you care about."

Samantha eased her expression and gently grabbed his arm. "No. You're wrong. She's not the only one."

Zanipolo looked surprised as she wrapped her arms around his body and pulled him into a warm embrace.

"I don't want to lie and hide how I feel anymore... Not to you."

Samantha's words cracked as she spoke. Hearing her confusion and pain, Zanipolo wrapped his arms around her and pulled her into the security of his chest.

"Then don't... I want to know everything."

Samantha nuzzled into his chest and held back the tears threatening to fall.

"I want to stay by your side. If you're going to jump into Amadora's dangerous quest, I want to be with you every step of the way."

"Sammy... What am I going to do with you?" Zanipolo ran his hand through her hair and pulled her tighter into his protective embrace. "If you get hurt or worse, I will never forgive myself."

Samantha was not sure if this moment was a dream or reality. Regardless of which one it was, she refused to leave his arms. She let go of his waist, caressed his soft cheeks, and submerged into the comfort of his gaze. Their heartbeats ebbed and flowed until they mirrored each other.

Samantha could not see the future and what it had in store for them. They could disappear tomorrow. Now was all she had, and she refused to leave him. She would risk it all if it meant she could stay in his arms.

"And what do you think would happen to me if something happened to you when I'm not there? I would rather risk my life fighting by your side than slowly die of worry without you."

Zanipolo smiled in defeat. "Fine. Have it your way. You're too stubborn to argue with any longer."

Zanipolo closed the final distance between the determined beauty in his arms and kissed her small, soft lips. The passion of their lips touching excited their hearts and sealed their promise to encounter the rest of this journey together. The sweet sensation it created made Zanipolo want her more than ever before. He wanted to protect her and shield her from any obstacle thrown their way. Samantha was his and nothing will ever harm her as long as he breathes.

9

The Aftermath

'Blood begets blood. It's a never-ending cycle of agony, despair and ultimately vengeance.' Thoughts of Elda Morelli.

Amadora's mind swirled with thoughts of Darian Mancini. She admired his persistence when she did not show interest at first. She also adored his sweet manner, that captivated her when they glided across the ballroom floor. Even though he was a son of a grocery store owner, he carried himself like a prince. But the one thing that drew her in the most was not his charms or persistent nature, but those diamonds he called eyes. Just one look immobilized her and shattered the world surrounding them. Never did someone impact her like he did. With just the memory of their meeting, everything in existence vanished.

Amadora wanted to see Darian again, but understood the risks attached to that decision. Johnnie Barbone was probably on the top of his hit list. If she met him again, she must work hard to hide every connection to her other side. Amadora did not want to find out what he would do if he learned the truth. She wanted to learn more about him and desperately wanted to see him again.

Amadora drew back the curtains to let the sunshine in and fight the gray, dreary shadows. The sun's warm kisses against her skin awakened memories from when she was young and the stories her grandmother used to tell her.

On a sunny summer's day at her grandparents' farm in the hilly countryside of Sicily, Amadora sat in her grandmother's garden playing cards. She enjoyed the sweet fragrance of the chamomilla blossoms braided into her hair. The soft sounds of gentle breeze rushing through the tall colorful trees and the intoxicatingly sweet scents from the blooming flowers reemerged in her mind, recreating the events of that day as if they happened at that very moment.

Amadora loved dancing and playing with her grandmother while drinking tea and eating freshly baked cookies. Her grandmother planned their entire day together just for her. Her parents and siblings were in town with their grandfather, so her grandmother stayed behind to watch over her until they returned. Amadora did not remember why she remained on the farm. She just knew the sadness and loneliness disappeared the moment she stepped into her grandmother's garden.

The vivid canvas of blooms spread across the land surrounding them consoled her and quelled all ill will. Her grandmother softly hugged her as she told old myths. One myth she told was called "I Regali degli Dei" or "The Gift of the Gods".

"Dora, my youngest bambina and my heart, are you ready to hear another story?"

"Yes, nonna. I am," Amadora shook her head excitedly. Her grandmother got into character as she began retelling the story of her family's blessing.

The story surrounds their great ancestor in the days when people still revered ancient gods. She was so favored by them that each of them gave her a gift when she was born.

The first God to bless the babe with a gift was Mercury. He gifted her ultimate knowledge or extreme analytical ability and using it to overcome any obstacle. Then the god of war, Mars, gave her a warrior's heart, which increased her ability to survive. Neptune gave her a temperament like the sea, which meant she could be calm and composed or powerful with rage. To help control the rage, Pluto gave the babe a gift of shadows that could quell it and increase her serenity. Next was Jupiter, who bestowed great strength and courage to her. After that, Uranus gave her free will and determination.

Juno gave her the blessing of one day becoming a wonderful mother and wife. Diana blessed her with brilliant weapon control. Apollo blessed her with the gift of music, allowing her to play any instrument she came across. Vesta's gift was a great love towards those she considered family. Minerva blessed her with great wisdom and medical knowledge. Ceres granted her with a green thumb capable of growing plants unlike any ever seen before, along with unbreakable patience. Helios provided her with a special warmth that attracts any person to her, no matter what. Finally, the gods, Venus and Vulcan, bestowed her with two of the greatest gifts.

Vulcan gave the babe a gold and silver box with a carving of his wife on it, which granted any desire she wished for. The goddess Venus loved the babe more than any other god, so much so she gave the ultimate protection and hid it somewhere no one could ever find it... in her eyes. This gift was special and could not be inherited by just anyone in her lineage. It could only manifest in one who possesses "L'innocenza della Speranza" or "Hope's Innocence". This type of innocence was one that granted the person the ability to maintain a pure outlook on their world, regardless of the situation. It helped them from being corrupted by despair. This innocence was the only one compatible with Venus's gift.

Her gift prevented harm from befalling the babe if they looked into her eyes, no matter what. This gift reflected a bit of the goddess's own power. It immobilized the person in an allure of attraction and love, preventing them from harming her, but even such a magnificent gift had its flaws.

"It has a flaw? What kind, nonna?"

"Love is a crazy thing. Forcing someone to love you can be dangerous. They might become obsessed and want to receive the same feelings in return. And if they are not reciprocated, they'll come after those you love the most, since they can't harm you." Her grandmother smiled and hugged her. "Our ancestor used these gifts to become a well-celebrated soldier in the Roman army. But when she realized the danger of Venus's gift, she fled with her family to a small village in the mountains and spent the rest of her days tending to her garden or protecting her family since they matter more than all the gods' gifts."

"Do you have the gift?"

Amadora remembered the smile on her grandmother's face grow exponentially. "Yes. I do. Your grandfather is under my spell." Then she tapped Amadora's nose with her finger. "You have the gift too, Dora. I see it in your eyes."

Tears fell down Amadora's cheek after reliving her past. All she had left of her grandmother were memories. Sometimes, she wished she was still here to guide her. In times of confusion and uncertainty, she needed her now more than ever before.

A soft rapping sounded on Amadora's bedroom door; she wiped her face with the back of her robe. She crossed the room and opened the door, greeting the surprise guest on the other side of the door, Samantha.

"Sam, you're here early. Did you stay in one of the guest rooms?"

Samantha still wore her dress from last night. It was dirty and wrinkled from the hem all the way up her thighs. Her dark, frizzy hair was sloppily tied into a loose ponytail. Even in her homely state, she looked vibrant and relaxed.

"This is not the time to worry about where I've been. What's important is that Johnnie Barbone is needed," Sam said, handing Amadora a piece of paper.

"What do you mean?"

"I was just on the phone with Anna. Lorenzo called her house, looking for Johnnie. He needs to speak with him immediately." Samantha looked around the room. "The phones in this house are on the same line. You can't call him here. Someone might overhear your conversation. Is there somewhere else you can call him?"

Amadora paced back and forth, looking down at the floor as she assessed the situation.

"There are three separate lines. One is in my father's office, but I can't use that one because he might come in while I'm on the phone with him and that would be terrible. The second line is in the servants' house. But everyone's resting from the ball, and there's the risk of someone walking in and overhearing me while I'm making this call. The only place that might be safe to call from is the one in the guest house. The only one staying there is Zanipolo, so it should be safe."

"Great! What are you waiting for? Run over there and call him back," Sam said, thumbing through Amadora's clothes.

"By the way, I'm going to borrow an outfit. You don't mind, right?" Sam smiled sheepishly back at Amadora while she grabbed several outfits and mentally tried them on.

"Of course, I don't. Take what you want. Just don't make a mess," Amadora smirked and ran out of the room.

The cool, misty air nipped at Amadora's face as she stepped into the east garden. She pulled her robe tighter around her body to trap what little warmth she could. She walked up the stone path, avoiding the puddles scattered along her way until she arrived at an ivy-covered gate. After crossing the threshold, she saw a small brick house beyond a grove of wisteria trees.

Amadora rushed down the path, through the tall, blue front door and into the shadow-filled parlor, where the main phone sat on a desk in the room's corner by the window. Amadora picked up the white phone and dialed the number Samantha gave her. The phone rang a few times before the other end clicked and someone answered.

"Hello. Who is this?"

"Lorenzo, it's Johnnie. Anna told me you needed to talk. What's up?" Amadora replied, masking her voice to speak like Johnnie.

"Johnnie, I'm glad you called. Something horrible happened last night. The warehouse was attacked."

The mere utterance of those words made his blood run cold and his heart drop. His hand tensed around the phone, preventing him from pulling it from his ear until he heard everything.

"The one you had Musilli guard?"

"Yes. I'm afraid so."

"Did anyone survive?"

"I don't know. I just arrived a little while ago and have not checked things out, because I wanted to call you and Brock first. Since everything is destroyed, I had to come to a shop nearby to call you. We need to find out what happened and who's behind this. I need you to hurry over here. I'll need your help."

An icy chill traveled through Johnnie's body when he realized the bitter truth. The meaning behind that strange dream was a warning that a tragedy might have manifested in reality. Johnnie agreed and hung up the phone.

When Zanipolo woke up the day after the ball, it was not of his own accord. Casimiro walked into his room at five in the morning, forced him awake and urged him to go to his father's office for an emergency meeting. Zanipolo reluctantly rolled out of bed and dazedly looked around the room. It was empty.

Zanipolo walked over to his sitting room to see if she fell asleep on the couch. He flicked on the light to dispel the shadows. Once they lifted, no one was there. Zanipolo scratched his head and shrugged.

'That's weird. She left without saying anything... Maybe she went home to change?" Zanipolo thought, walking back to the main hallway to head over to the main house.

As Zanipolo entered his father's office, three pairs of sleepy eyes who were less than happy to see him walk through the door greeted him.

"Oh, Polo. It's only you," Elda sighed and looked away, disappointed.

"Well, good morning to you too, Elda," Zanipolo snarled while sitting in a chair opposite her and Gunny.

"Sorry to be a grouch, but I was really hoping you were Papa. I didn't mean to offend you."

"Forget it, Elda. I'm already used to your crude remarks," Zanipolo looked at Casimiro, then at Gunny. "Neither of you know why we're here, do you?"

"Nope. Don't have a clue. Pops probably wants to bitch about last night," Gunny replied, kicking up his feet on the ottoman in front of him and relaxing.

"I doubt that's it. I think he was on the phone with Lorenzo before ordering me to gather everyone." Casimiro placed his finger under his chin while recalling the events after Basilio came knocking on his door.

"Lorenzo?" Gunny shot up and looked at Casimiro, surprised. "If he called, then there could be a problem in my district. I wonder what happened."

Just then, Basilio came rushing into the room. The anger and tension emanating from him resulted from whatever Lorenzo told him. "He called because they attacked the main warehouse on the northern docks!"

Shock riddled through everyone at the sudden news. Fear penetrated deep into Gunny's gut. "When did this happen?"

"From what the locals told Lorenzo, it happened between 10-12 last night," Basilio toss the heavy paperweight on his desk at the wall, creating a tiny hole in the plaster. "Those bastards had the balls to sit in my house, eat my food and enjoy my hospitality just to send men to destroy one of my properties! I'll kill them!" Basilio pulled out a pistol and aimed at the wall. Before he could pull the trigger, Casimiro stopped him and confiscated the weapon.

"Please calm down. You don't want to cause a panic through the house."

"Listen to him, papa," Elda said calmly, taking the gun from Casimiro, emptying its bullets onto the desk, and placing it on the mantle behind her. "You have every right to suspect one of the other families, but which one could it be?"

Basilio took a deep breath, reached into the cigar box, and took one out. "Lorenzo is a trusted friend. He would never betray our family. That leaves one of the other three families, but the two on the top of my list are Canora and Rosilli."

"But why those two? Borcini is just as capable of betraying us as them," Elda questioned, returning to her chair.

"Because in the past month, Gunny's men ran into trouble with both families," Casimiro answered while lighting Basilio's cigar.

Gunny nodded in agreement. "That's true. But if we're judging off that alone, then Rosilli should be number one on that list. We've crossed paths with them more than Canora."

"That makes sense. I just hope you're not just suggesting them because of some petty personal grudge. You wouldn't want to start a war over a pestering vendetta," Elda's words were sharp and steady with harsh reason.

"No. I never let my personal feelings corrupt my judgment. Rosilli could not keep a handle on his men, who targeted my best men and killed them. We had no choice but to retaliate."

"I heard about your troubles with Rosilli and his men. If that's what happened, then it makes sense to have them on the top. That also explains the odd encounter Lana Rosilli had with one of her men," Zanipolo said.

"Encounter? What did you see?" Casimiro pressed.

"I saw Lana briefly speak with one of her men before immediately leaving," Zanipolo started. "I mean, it could have been nothing but her setting up a fling for that evening. Or she could've been arranging a car to meet her outside to leave. Who knows? After hearing about the attack, though, I'm a little skeptical."

"I had Lorenzo follow that man. He led him nowhere of interest, but that doesn't mean she was behind it. Lana could have easily used him as a diversion," Elda added.

"Regardless, Lana is a cold-hearted, psychotic broad. I wouldn't put it past her." Gunny's rage grew deep in his eyes when he mentioned her name. Zanipolo was surprised by how strong his hatred was for Lana. "If the Rosillis are behind the attack, then it was Lana who ordered it."

"You have no argument here. After watching her at the summit, I wouldn't be surprised if she did this to get payback for the grievance that she feels Gunny's men inflicted," Elda said coolly.

"You all make brilliant points, but we aren't sure. We shouldn't do anything until we learn more. We can't risk a rupture of the peace pact between the families based on hunches," Casimiro said calmly, guiding the room to reason.

"How are you going to do that? The cops probably cleared out the place. I doubt there's any evidence left." Elda asked.

"On the contrary, Elda, my dear, our friends in the local police department over there are holding off their investigation until we finish ours," Basilio responded taking another puff on his cigar.

"Who will do our investigation?" Elda asked, stretching her arms behind her head and leaning back in her chair.

"Lorenzo will head the investigation with two of his best men, Brock and Johnnie," Basilio answered.

"Johnnie?... You mean the golden boy, Johnnie Barbone, will assist in such an important matter? Do you think it's wise to send someone as green as him?" Elda looked at Gunny, slightly concerned.

"I must admit I had my concerns at first since I never met him and couldn't make an opinion about him on my own. However, I trust Lorenzo and his judgment," Gunny replied.

"Once this matter is settled, you need to meet this promising boy. You need to see with your own eyes where his loyalties lie," Basilio added.

"Well, in the meantime, I want to volunteer to help your men investigate this matter," Zanipolo interjected.

Everyone looked at Zanipolo, surprised. "I'm grateful for the offer, but don't you have to get back to Los Angeles?" Gunny looked at his younger brother wide-eyed confused.

"Ed has everything handled over there for now. Besides, it would be better if one of us took part in the investigation in case foul play within your men played a part in this tragedy."

"Zanipolo makes a brilliant point. I see no reason why he shouldn't overlook the process and be our eyes and ears." Basilio agreed.

"Fine. Just make sure you keep me updated with every new development," Gugliehno said.

"Got it," Zanipolo hid the confident smile threatening to cross his lips as his excuse to work with Johnnie Barbone became a reality.

When Johnnie arrived at the warehouse, it was after ten thirty. The destruction was worse than he initially thought. A car was entangled in the left gate. Ash and debris scattered the grounds. The buildings were blackened hollow shells adorned by black scorch marks. The moment Johnnie stepped into the yard, he was transported into a world of despair and death. Charred corpses surrounded Johnnie as he watched his comrades struggle to look over the unrecognizable shells in search of their fallen brethren.

The real-life horror show surrounding him grew worse as he walked inside what remained of the main warehouse. The main building was caved in and only the charred frame of the wall holding up the main door stood somewhat intact. Johnnie tapped the wooden door, and it crumbled to dust.

Even with the roof caved in, the main loading area was well preserved. Fragments of flesh and bone were scattered amongst the debris. Johnnie tied his scarf tight around his mouth protecting him from the lingering stench of scorched flesh. He stepped over the graveyard of bodies and walked to where the loading deck office was and peered inside. The windows for the office were shattered resulting in large shards of glass paving the ground below his feet.

In the corner of the small room was a charred body skewered by a large piece of glass. The agonizing expression frozen on his face even with his eyes closed killed Johnnie's focus. The stench of death increased as he drew closer to the body, making it near impossible to examine the area without wanting to vomit.

Johnnie covered his scarfed mouth with his gloved hand to prevent his repulsion. He squatted next to the body and examined it. The glass impaling his body was clearly from the broken windows. Only a powerful force could propel glass with such precision to impale a body in this way. No human could cause this. Only some kind of explosion would create a scene like this one.

Johnnie walked over to the windows and examined the remaining shards. Bits of blood soaked into its edges, but it was not just one window involved. Two shattered windows had blood along their frames.

"There should be two bodies here, not just one," Johnnie said softly to himself. He turned back towards the body and searched through the debris for another corpse.

"Johnnie, what are looking for?" Johnnie turned to the voice coming from behind him to see Brock fixing his own scarf to shield him from the foul odor.

"I'm looking for a second body. If you look close at those two windows over there, they have small traces of blood on their edges. I found a body, but one is missing. Were there any survivors?"

"There was only one." Right away Brock saw a gleam of hope embedded in Johnnie's eyes. Brock looked down and shook his head. "It's not Larry."

All of Johnnie's hope vanished and his expression became unreadable.

"Where is he?"

"Kid, follow me."

When Johnnie and Brock went into the yard, there was a group of men surrounding a car stuck in the front gate. Lorenzo stood, ordering some men to place a corpse on a gurney, but Johnnie's attention drifted to a young man standing next to Lorenzo. His curly, dark hair and confident stance were too familiar. He was Amadora's cousin, Nero.

"What's he doing here?" Johnnie asked partially to himself.

"Who? Nero? Do you know him?" Brock asked.

"No. I've never seen him before. Are we just letting anyone deal with this sensitive matter?" Johnnie answered.

"He's Gunny's cousin and for now Lorenzo's protegee, so he goes wherever he goes," Brock replied.

"Ah... Johnnie, I didn't see you come in. I know this tragedy hits close to home for you, but I really need your help to sort out this mess," Lorenzo called out to Johnnie, waving him over.

When Johnnie reached the car, his heart dropped when he finally made sense of the scene in front of him. The whole car was burned to a crisp. A body slouched over the steering wheel and merged with the melted seat was burned beyond recognition. Johnnie could not believe this was his mentor, Larry Musilli.

"Are you sure that's him?" Johnnie asked, stepping back from the car to collect his senses.

Lorenzo placed a hand on his shoulder and nodded sadly. "Yes. It's true."

Brock pried the car door open as far as it could and pointed at the body's wrist.

"See that wristwatch? There is only one like it in the entire world. His mother gave it to him when he turned eighteen years old. His parents were watchmakers. They made that watch and engraved on it a message for him. There's no doubt this is him." Brock turned to Johnnie and saw the shock embedded in his eyes. "I'm sorry, kid. He's gone. There's nothing we can do now but bring his murderers to justice. Will you be okay to work?"

"It's just a part of the job, right?" Johnnie said emotionlessly, turning his head from Brock and whisking away Lorenzo's hand. They scanned him for a sign of his genuine emotions, but he was unreadable.

"It's sad, but I won't let it affect the way I work. How many people were on duty last night?"

Brock opened the notepad he kept tucked under his arm. "According to the log, there were about thirteen, including two guards at the front gate."

"Thirteen? That doesn't seem right. I counted all the bodies, including Moose's. There were only eleven. Are you sure?" Johnnie looked back at Brock with an eyebrow raised.

"Yeah. There are thirteen names on the log. See for yourself," Brock ran over, got the log from the guard house and brought it back to Johnnie. Johnnie flipped through the pages, then tucked it under his arm.

"Someone else survived and got away before we arrived," Johnnie removed his gloves and tucked them in his pocket. "Was the survivor conscious when they took him to the hospital?"

"Yes. He was, but he was messed up pretty bad. It was a miracle he survived so long with his wounds," Lorenzo said, taking the log and passing it to Nero. "You two should head over and see what he knows. We can handle things here."

Johnnie and Brock nodded in acknowledgement. They knew Lorenzo was right. This man could be the only key they had to uncover the events of last night and the identity of the missing person.

Shadows danced across the sparsely lit rooms of Cyclamen manor. Its dusty, cold halls echoed in silence from its lack of inhabitants. The only sign of life on the entire grounds was a small flicker of light from the south tower. As the sun settled in the eastern sky, footsteps echoed through the halls. Their casual stride grew louder as he walked up the towers winding stairs.

The owner was a man hidden in the dark. He paused in front of a gigantic wooden door and stealthily entered. He avoided the streams of light shining through the holes in the curtains.

The man placed his hand into his coat and clutched something inside as he glided into the parlor. There stood a woman glowing in the soft morning sun. She watched the dew fall from the pine needles while the wind howled past the window. Her long strawberry blonde hair draped over her white nightgown. The man crept slowly behind her, basking in the beautiful sight in front of him, and reached for her. Before his hand brushed against her skin, she turned around, pulled a knife from her sleeve, and pressed it to his neck.

"Viper, you disappoint me. I heard you coming."

Viper chuckled, pulling out a scarlet rose from his pocket. "I wasn't trying to hide, Mistress." He handed her the rose. "I got this for you."

Lana replaced the knife into its holder and laughed. "My dear Viper, you always flatter me. Thank you." Lana accepted the rose and kissed his bony cheek. "Please tell me you have returned with some good news."

Viper fixed his coat and scarf, then nodded. "We did what you wished. There were some casualties, but their warehouse was destroyed."

"Good," Lana smirked softly, pressing the flower to her nose inhaling its soft aroma. "Did you find any information regarding my other task?"

"Yes. I did. I got it from our informant. According to him, Jack's killer was a boy named Johnnie Barbone."

Confusion painted Lana's face as she looked at Viper. "A boy?"

"Yes, a kid about eighteen, who just became one of Gugliehno's new soldiers."

"Can we trust your source's intel is reliable?"

"Yes. We can. I double-checked with some of the Morellis men before killing them."

"How long has this boy been an associate?"

"Only a month."

"A month, huh? And Gunny promoted him that quick. That's unlike him. He must be good to weasel his way up Gunny's ranks in such a short time," Lana bit back the intrigue growing inside her about her ex's new prodigy.

"He's supposed to be. Some members of the other families are keeping a close eye on him. They think Gunny's new secret weapon could leave them at a great disadvantage if war broke out."

"I see. They're crowning him as Gunny's new little toy. I'm surprised the other families are fawning all over a newbie." Lana chuckled. She stroked the petals of her rose as she gazed at the groggy day.

"What do you want me to do with him? He killed Jack."

"I know. But I don't want to do anything rash. I want to know more about Gunny's little pet. I am a little skeptic and want to see if he's worth all the praise he's receiving."

"How do you plan to do that?"

"First, I want to see how he looks for myself. Find him and take his picture."

"But how will I know where he'll be next? He's hard to track down."

"We don't need to know where he'll be, because we know what the Morellis will do next. They probably already started investigating the attack. It's just a hunch; but if he's as good as you say, they'll have him be a part of that team. Hopefully, they'll learn about our source."

"But Mistress, if he finds out what our source knows, won't they come after us next?"

"That's correct. I want Johnnie to figure it out. I want him to come straight to me and show me how good he is in person."

Elda, Casimiro and Gugliehno went to the observatory while they waited for a report about the progress of the investigation from Lorenzo. Elda and Casimiro sat in the wicker chairs while Gugliehno paced back and forth. He nervously cracked his knuckles and stared into the nothingness as if in a trance.

"I know this is a pressing matter; but if you don't calm down, you won't be able to deal with this problem rationally," Casimiro tried to soothe his companion, who seethed in anger.

Gugliehno stopped for a second in front of the stained-glass windows. He gritted his teeth, formed a fist, and tried to control his rage.

"You don't understand! No matter what they find out, I already know the culprit!"

Casimiro and Elda looked at him skeptically. "And who do you suspect is behind this?" Casimiro asked, even though he already knew the answer.

"Who else could it be other than that bitch, Lana!" Gugliehno took his fist and drove it into a nearby wall.

"Oh, please, Gunny. Are you positive it's her? What proof do you have?" Elda asked.

Casimiro and Elda knew the history between Gugliehno and Lana. Aside from Lorenzo and their father, they knew about the unique feelings he still had for her. They knew about his desperation to finally rid himself of her, but they wondered if he would risk an all-out-war to target her for something she might not have done.

"The only proof I need is the fact that I talked with that bitch last night where she vowed to get Aniela and Loretta back no matter what!" Gunny roared as he cleaned his knuckles of wall fragments.

"I highly doubt that. Lana is reckless, but she wouldn't risk a war just to get her kids back," Elda replied.

"Elda's right. If Lana wanted to get her kids back, why would she attack the family instead of targeting you or Susan?" Casimiro added.

"No. This is an attack against the family and purely business related. I'm not sure if Lana's to blame or not, but we must look at all the possibilities and evidence before making our next more," Elda input.

Gunny's anger skyrocketed after hearing their words. He knew who was behind the attack. If they just let him head back to the city, then he could uncover the truth and prove them wrong.

"That's a waste of time! We know she did it! Let's just bust down the doors of Cyclamen and drag the truth out of that conniving bitch!"

"And what if you're wrong? Your personal vendetta would put us all at risk!" Casimiro snapped.

"You will wait with the rest of us until Lorenzo reports their findings from the investigation! Until then, calm the hell down and regain your senses! You're useless when you fly off the rail like this!" Elda added.

Gugliehno sighed and pressed his hand on his forehead. He had to ignore the itching feeling in his gut if they were going to sort this out.

"You're both right. I'll try to calm down, but I promise you my gut isn't wrong. Lana is behind this, and you'll realize that sooner than later."

Rumbling of tires rushing through small puddles scattered over the cobblestone drive of Woodburrow General echoes through the sparsely crowded area. Brock grabbed the door handle as Johnnie slammed on the brakes. Once the car safely stopped, Brock gathered himself and followed Johnnie outside.

"God, Johnnie, you drive like a crazed broad. Who taught you to drive?"

Johnnie smirked. "Anna did. Why did I scare you?"

"That explains everything," Brock chuckled, heading towards the entrance. "Scared of your driving. Never. I'm just thinking I should drive on the way back. You know it's funny your driving is like..."

Brock snipped his words short, because he was not sure how Johnnie would react from just the mention of Larry's name. Johnnie noticed his withdrawal; and the awkward hesitation that followed. Johnnie paused and turned back to Brock, smiling.

"You can say his name. I won't cry, throw a tantrum or break. It's okay if you talk about Larry," Johnnie turned away and continued. "Larry was my mentor and taught me more than I could've learned on my own. And I'm thankful to him for giving me a chance. But I'm not going to let my grief control me. I need every bit of my sanity if I'm going to hunt down his killers and make them pay."

Brock stared at Johnnie, astounded. He could not tell if it was wisdom or apathy that motivated him on this mission of vengeance.

"Okay. Good," Brock's shock transformed into pride.

After listening to all Larry's gushing over his prodigy, he realized he was right to put his faith in him. In all the years he has worked for the family, he never found such a dedicated and loyal recruit. Also, he never saw a recruit Larry grew attached to like with this kid. Johnnie was truly special.

Brock quietly entered the hospital lobby with Johnnie and walked over to the nurses' station. An auburn, curly-haired, stout woman sat behind the desk, flipping through a stack of papers. She did not react when they stepped in front of her station. Only when Johnnie politely introduced himself did she notice them.

"Sorry to interrupt you, miss, but we're here to..." Johnnie started, but was cut short by the gawking nurse.

"You must be here to see the new patient?"

"Yes, we are, but how did you know that?" Brock asked.

"I got a call from the owner of the warehouse that burned down. We prepared for your arrival," the nurse replied.

"Prepared for our arrival? Is that why it's so empty here?" Johnnie asked, scanning the solemn, vacant halls.

"No. Not at all. We're a small hospital that barely gets traffic, so we don't have a lot of staff on hand at the moment." The nurse twirled her pen nervously as she scanned the two men in front of her. "I'm sorry, but the patient's still in the emergency room. You can wait over there until the doctor comes."

The nurse pointed at a small sitting area a few feet away from the station. They followed her instruction and waited. Johnnie sat in a chair with a clear view of the nurses' station and kept an eye on the anxious nurse.

"You noticed it too?" Brock whispered secretly, following the nurse's actions. Johnnie nodded in agreement. "What do you think is her problem, kid?"

"I'm not sure and not positive her behavior has anything to do with us. But I want to keep her in my sight," Johnnie responded, briefly breaking his focus on the nurse and turning towards his partner.

"I guess you're right. Do you want to watch her, or you want me to do it?" Brock asked, checking his coat for his holster.

"I don't understand what you mean."

"The emergency room is on the opposite side of the hospital. If we both go, we can't keep track of everyone else around us. One of us should stay behind."

"If that's the case, then I'll stand guard here while you go."

"You don't want to question him?"

"Yes. I do, but I want to observe her. Since I'm smaller than you, I can blend in better with these current surroundings and monitor her."

"You're right. That makes sense," Brock responded.

Twenty minutes passed before a doctor came to give them the okay to see his patient. Johnnie reclined in the plain, gray chair, cupping his head in his arms and watching the doctor and nurse while Brock went to the survivor's room. His eyes wandered along the grainy ceiling for a few minutes before returning to the nurses' station.

The doctor, who once seemed calm and rational, became slightly irritated and turned towards the nurse and called her into the office behind the nurses' desks. Johnnie could not hear their words or see anything more than their frosted silhouettes.

The doctor seemed agitated, pacing back and forth for a few seconds before stopping in front of the nurse and gesturing intensely. The nurse remained still and just looked down as the doctor reprimanded her about something. Johnnie could not hear what their argument was about, but he had a feeling that judging by the timing between the meeting and his little excited display that it was likely about them.

They argued for a few minutes before the doctor rushed out and left to go make his rounds. Johnnie sat up and observed the nurse. She was not shaken up by their disagreement but seemed more paranoid than before. Johnnie grabbed a magazine and pretended to read it shielding himself from her probing gaze. When she was satisfied with her scans, she left the nurses' station, and Johnnie followed a few minutes after.

Johnnie walked down the long, empty halls while keeping some distance between them so not to rouse her suspicions. Johnnie ducked in every doorway and shadowed crevice to shield his presence from her constantly wandering eye. His chase lasted a few minutes until they reached a set of large double doors in the back of the hospital leading to the parking lot.

Johnnie ducked behind a screen and waited until she made her next move. The nurse scanned her surrounding then went through the doors and crossed the parking lot. Johnnie dashed over to the doors and peeked out their small windows. He saw the nurse enter a small black car. The car did not pull off when she went inside. Instead, it sat there for a while until a man in long black clothes emerged.

As the man adjusted his coat while conversing with the nurse. A light reflected off something attached to the inner lining of the man's coat. Johnnie knew he was not a cop since they rarely concealed their weapons unless undercover. Johnnie pulled his own gun out of its holster and raced over to the E.R. to find Brock.

Brock tipped his hat, turned to the door to leave but was stopped by a wheezing Johnnie holding a gun and nervously looking over his shoulder.

"What's going on?" Brock whispered, trying to rouse the sleeping man behind them.

"A man is coming this way packing heat. I don't know if they're here for us or him, but I don't think we should stick around to find out," Johnnie turned towards Brock then looked at the man sleeping on the cot. "Did you get anything useful out of him?"

"Yeah. He told me everything he could remember about last night during the raid." Brock took out his pistol and guarded the injured man. "They might be after him. The traitor probably sent them to silence him before we got to him."

"Traitor?"

"You were right. There was a second survivor, one of the guards. He saw everything." Brock motioned towards the unconscious man on the cot. "He saw the guard pretend to help his partner fight off the intruders before shooting him in the back and running away."

"If that's true, then I wonder how he found out about the survivor. Did he see him before he escaped?"

Brock shrugged. "Who knows? This hospital is in the center of several families' territories. That nurse was probably in cahoots with one of them and warned them when he was brought in."

"Now, he's trying to cover his tracks," Worry washed over Johnnie's face. He only had a few minutes to come up with some way to protect this man's life. "What should we do? Do we stay and fight?"

"No. There are too many innocents here. We need to get him out of here," Brock replaced his gun in his holster, went over to the man and hoisted him into his arms. In a groggy, doped up state, the man stirred from his sleep and began flailing his limbs around. Brock forced to look at him and whispered harshly. "Calm down. I'm not here to hurt you. Your life is in danger. If you want to live, we need to get you out of here and move you somewhere safe, so keep still and don't say a word."

The man stopped his frantic movement and nodded in understanding. Brock carried him to a side door hidden behind a divider. When Brock opened the door, he saw Johnnie rearranging the bed.

"Come on, kid. What are you doing now is not the time to tidy up."

"I'm buying us some time. Go ahead and I'll meet you at the car shortly."

"I don't know what you've got up your sleeves, but just hurry."

Brock followed Johnnie's orders and carried the survivor through the next room and out into the hallway. He dragged him to the front door. Once they crossed the threshold into the warm sunlight, the booming thunder of gunshots echoed through the halls. Brock looked back briefly before rushing to the car, placing the injured man across the back seat and hopping into the driver's seat.

Brock started the car and anxiously waited. He clenched his hand around the steering wheel, preventing him from running back inside and searching for Johnnie. He could not lose the kid too after losing Larry, but he needed to trust him. Johnnie was resourceful. He would not die after vowing to bring Larry's killers to justice.

Before Brock could rethink, grab his gun and step out of the car, Johnnie dashed down the hospital steps with his gun tucked away in its holster and jumped into the passenger seat.

"What the hell happened in there, kid? I told you not to attack them!" Brock yelled, speeding down the streets.

Johnnie moved his scarf from his mouth and smirked. "I didn't. I just made them think someone beat them to the job they were sent to do."

"How did you do that?"

"A little creative trick to fool the mind's eye."

"What do you mean?"

"I bundled up some blankets and pillows under the sheets to look like a body lying in the bed. Then I used some of the spare blood packets in the cooler of a nearby laboratory, placed it on the dummy and shot it a few times to cause a huge blood splatter. The illusion should be enough for them to think someone else already shot him dead, and they'll leave before the cops arrive."

Brock could not help but laugh. He was stupid to believe someone as sly as Johnnie would die that easily. He was becoming a useful asset to not just him but the family as well. Maybe Larry's late-night boasting was not entirely crazy. Maybe he could rise higher than any outsider has before.

Nightfall arrived sooner than Zanipolo expected it would by the time they arrived at Anna's home. The ride over was draining, because he could not stop thinking about the lies that he told his father to get this far. He told his father fibs before, but nothing like this. This time his lies carried a heavy burden and hid a perilous gamble.

Zanipolo put his pops through hell because of his own selfish antics when he was younger and tried to make up for it a little at a time. Now, his sister's secret threatened to destroy all the progress he made to repair their bond. Zanipolo had no other choice but to assure her charade lead her to victory.

Anna waited outside the front door, leaning against the stone banister and smoking a thin cigarette. She tugged on her thin blue jacket and watched them as they crossed the cracked blacktop. Anna's chilling eyes scanned Zanipolo as he greeted her with a subtle smile. When he extended his hand, Anna tossed her cigarette to the ground and gently clamped her hand around his. Her expression warmed once their hands united into a friendly embrace and her large gray eyes sparkled in amusement.

"Zanipolo, nice to see you again. Please come in," Anna greeted, releasing his hand and guided them inside.

Once they reached her apartment, she motioned for them to sit while she went over to the kitchen and put on a pot to boil.

"I see your sister roped you into this little death scheme of hers. At first, I thought the girls' ruse would work on you. It seems I underestimated you."

"You wouldn't be the first to do that." Zanipolo closed his eyes while a large, triumphant grin crossed his face.

"You should've known I'd figure it out sooner than later. Give me some slack here. I'm smarter than you give me credit for."

"Okay. Don't get cocky. It had little to do with smarts, but luck."

Zanipolo glared, irritated and snapped. "I see you're still carrying a chip on your shoulder. I don't have time for your petty games. There are more pressing matters to focus on. When are you leaving, exactly?"

Anna roared with laughter. "You're a funny boy, aren't you? I'm staying right here."

"Don't be stupid! It's too dangerous for you and your son to stay here!" Zanipolo exclaimed, clenching his hands around his keys.

"You don't have to worry about us. I sent my son to stay with his grandparents once Dora said we'd have two more roommates. As for myself, I can't leave Amadora in the protection of a hot-headed thug like you."

Through Anna's bitter words, there laid a sliver of concern that Zanipolo could not decipher its origin. There was not much he could say or do to convince her otherwise, and his fatigue was too intense to try anymore. He closed his eyes, trying to contain his rising frustration. He had to accept his new reality. He was trapped in a small apartment with a bunch of stubborn women driven by death wishes tied to their pride and loyalty.

"Fine. Do whatever the hell you want. Just know there's no turning back after this."

"Too late for that kid. I've already been too far in since your sister arrived at the bus station a month ago. There's no point backing out now. I made a promise to Amadora to help her see this through until the end."

Samantha's eyes sparkled after hearing Anna's words. She knew too well how hard it was to turn your back on Amadora, especially when she did something so damn dangerous. She was relieved to meet someone who felt the same way she did.

Anna turned off the whistling kettle, filled two mugs with hot water and tea leaves and brought them over to Samantha and Zanipolo. She set them on top of two tiled coasters, then pulled out another cigarette and lit it.

"This should help with any fatigue you have from your drive. I'm going to head out for a bit. Try not to wreck the place while I'm gone."

Zanipolo waved her off and looked down at the brown, murky liquid in front of him. His face crinkled in disgust as he scanned the small room.

"Out of all the people Amadora could partner with, why did she choose this bitch?" Zanipolo grumbled.

"What's her problem? Why is she so hostile towards you?" Samantha asked.

"She's not hostile to just me, per se. Anna has a vendetta against anyone in my line of work."

"Why is that?" Samantha said, taking a sip of her tea.

"I heard some random thug from a small gang killed her husband. She doesn't know which one, so she treats everyone in my world like shit. I don't blame her but can't help wondering why she'd agree to help Dora with this charade. It goes against everything she believes."

"Maybe she will change once she gets to know you. It shows she has some deep wounds that will be near impossible to heal. Who knows, maybe our current predicament will be the chance you need?" Samantha replaced her cup on the coaster.

"I'm not here to make friends. I'm here solely to help Dora with her crazy scheme," Zanipolo retorted sipping his tea.

"I know, but it wouldn't hurt, especially if we're going to be staying under the same roof for a while," Samantha stood up and grabbed her suitcase. "It's getting late. I should unpack. I don't need to eat tonight. I'm not hungry."

Zanipolo stood and grabbed her arm. "Sam, wait. I don't get it. Did I do something wrong?"

"What? No, of course not. Why would you think that?"

"This morning you left without saying a word and barely spoke on the entire ride over here. Did I upset you?"

"That's not it," Samantha replied, combatting the confusion in his voice with calm empathy.

"I never thought we would ever grow as close as we did last night. And even though I loved every moment, right now I can't afford to be selfish. We should focus solely on Amadora. I'm scared that if we grow too close, we might forget why we're here, and someone might get hurt or worse."

Zanipolo pulled Samantha closer. "Look, Sam. You don't have to worry about that.

I won't forget why we're here, so don't ignore me." He gazed deeper into her eyes and cupped her small cheek in his hand. "The only way we'll make it through this nightmare is if we work together. We don't have to lie and hide how we feel anymore."

Zanipolo kissed her softly, then smiled. "I guess you're right. We don't." Samantha blushed as his lips escaped hers.

Before Samantha could continue speaking, the door opened, and a strange man walked inside. His scarf shielded his face, so they could not recognize anything about him. His black hat hid his hair and left a gap between it and the scarf, showing only a sharp pair of dark eyes.

The man walked over to Zanipolo, then paused a distance from him. He was not as tall as him, but he was a bit taller than Samantha. He removed his scarf with his gloved hands, revealing a charming, young man. He smiled softly.

"How do I look?" Amadora's voice resonated gleefully from underneath her disguise. "You couldn't recognize me, could you?"

"I must hand it to you, Dora. You had us fooled for a moment there until you opened your mouth. I hope you're as good at disguising your voice as you are your appearance when you're parading around as Johnnie," Zanipolo said indifferently.

"Of course not. I use this voice," Amadora changed the depth and inflection of her voice to match Zanipolo's. Samantha and Zanipolo gawked in awe.

Zanipolo could not believe how much he underestimated her. Why was he surprised she could imitate his voice? Amadora was known for calculating every single step of a plan so she could attain her goals. He was not surprised she could create a fool proof plan to prevent someone from finding out the truth. Maybe she might reach her goal after all. If she could fool him, then she could probably fool Gunny, too.

"You make an enchanting young man, Dora! You completely had me fooled!" Samantha exclaimed, clapping her hands in applause.

Zanipolo scanned his sister and tucked his hands inside his pockets. "Your disguise is impressive. But as second-in-command of this investigation under Gunny, I need to know how everything is progressing. Did you learn anything useful?"

Amadora's expression faded and turned unnervingly grave. It was an expression neither saw on her before nor even knew she possessed. They watched her as she walked over to the window on the other side of the room and glance up towards the cloudy sky.

"It's going well, I suppose. There were only two survivors." Amadora took off her hat and scarf and pulled her hair out of its binding. "One of them is a traitor who helped the enemy get onto the grounds."

"Who do you mean?" Zanipolo asked, confused.

"The guard helped orchestrate this massacre," Amadora elaborated.

"Do we know which one?"

"Yes. The other survivor identified him. He saw everything."

"Can we trust him? How do we know he's not a traitor too, just trying to save his own hide?"

"I'm sure of it, since the real traitor sent some men to silence him this morning."

"Is he still alive?"

"Yes. We got him out of there in time and tricked his assassins that someone already killed him."

"Where is he now?"

"In a hospital deep in Gunny's territory," Amadora looked at Samantha, then returned to Zanipolo. "He's heavily guarded. He should've been taken there earlier but his wounds were too extensive, so they brought him to that one."

"What did he tell you?" Zanipolo asked.

"The name of the traitor is Barney. He lives south of Park Avenue and thirty third. We know which building he lives in just not the exact address. Brock and I are going to check it out tomorrow."

"That's an expensive area. I'm surprised a guard could afford it on his salary. He must have been working with them for a long time," Zanipolo mumbled, thinking aloud. "It sounds fishy. I'm going with you tomorrow. He had to ally with someone with deep pockets and connections to cause all this trouble. Besides, you'll need all the help you can get."

Amadora shrugged and walked over to her bedroom. "Do whatever you want. You're the boss, remember?" A dark smirk crossed her lips. "I only have one stipulation."

"What's that?"

"I'm the only one who gets to interrogate those bastards. I have a score to settle with him and his cronies."

Worry grew in the depths of Zanipolo's heart after hearing her words. Bloodlust lingered in her eyes and fed off her vengeance. Such darkness would corrode her very essence and tear her apart.

No matter how deep rooted her vengeance was, he would not let it destroy what little innocence she had left. He had to protect her from that fate and put that urge to rest forever.

Amadora lost a lot in a day, but she also gained something of great importance. Her eyes trailed along the moonlit room and landed on a piece of paper resting on her nightstand. The sadness she fought to conceal faded, and joy replaced it. It was the paper Darian gave her with his number.

Amadora picked it up and held it close to her chest, debating whether she should call him. If she did and they met again, then she would enter another treacherous

path. Darian was Johnnie's victim. If he learned the truth about him and her, Darian might repay the treatment she gave him. However, she wanted to see him again. Amadora longed to know everything about him. She did not know why she felt like this, but she just knew he was worth the risk.

Amadora walked over to the phone, reached for it and then withdrew her hand. Fear momentarily disabled her, but she took a deep breath to regain her senses as she mulled over whether she should open this Pandora's box.

Amadora closed her eyes and let her heart decide. Her hand moved on its own and picked up the phone. She opened her eyes, dialed the number, and brought it to her ear. The moment she heard the first ring it merged with the beating of her heart and trailed on forever until a glorious song broke the unyielding, monotonous wait, the sound of *his* voice, the voice of an angel.

The True Enemy

'His touch... His kiss... His embrace... Everything about him threatens my dream, but I can't give him up. He's a toxic addiction I can't and don't want to quit,' Thoughts of Amadora Morelli.

Dawn's warm rays glowed brighter than they ever had before. Darian opened the window and embraced its invigorating touch against his skin. These last few wintry days were brutal on him. He disliked going out into this freezing weather. That's what made a warm day like today perfect, because he would see her again... Amadora Morelli.

Darian went to his kitchen in search of something to fill his stomach before beginning the long day ahead. His search was not long because his father laid out some food for him on the table. As he sat down to eat, his pleasant thoughts about seeing Amadora faded as reality struck. He could not forget who she was, the daughter of that monster, Basilio Morelli.

Darian could not forget the vagrant who destroyed his shop and knocked him out cold. He did not doubt Basilio Morelli was behind it somehow. Darian was supposed to find some answers about his assailant's identity, but because of her, he forgot about it entirely.

Darian slammed his hand on the table in frustration. His fixation on that girl distracted him from the real reason he went to that ball. Now, what was he going to do?

That was probably the only chance he would get to find out more information about his attacker. He could not get any of the Morellis' lackeys to talk now. He could not use his police contacts, because he was not sure which ones were still loyal to their oath and which were loyal to those thugs' deep pockets.

Darian needed to find someone who might know something about their identity. Darian's annoyance faded slightly as his mind flashed back to Amadora's shining face. Her soft, brown eyes occupied his thoughts, but not because of their beauty. No. Those dark eyes flashed in the profound trenches of his memory. He saw them before, but he could not remember from where and needed to find out why she plagued his mind.

As he fought that nagging concern, Darian thought of a way he could eradicate this unusual feeling and possibly uncover the identity of his attacker. Amadora was more valuable than he initially thought. She was a Morelli. And even though she was not a part of the guilty party he despised with his entire essence; she might have overheard something linked to the incident. He must make her trust him enough to extract any useful information from her. There was one problem. He really liked her. However, his obsessive yearning for revenge against his attacker was stronger than his interest in Amadora Morelli.

His name is Giuseppe Vulcano. He worked at the warehouse for years as a simple shipping manager. Giuseppe took the job to get a good paying job to support his elderly parents. An unmarried man in his late thirties with no kids may never work again or find a woman. While at Woodburrow General, Johnnie did not notice the extensive burns on his face and half his body because his bandages shielded them well in the dim light. Now, in the sunlit room at Halmore Hospital, the damage from the attack was clear.

Johnnie concealed his anger as he watched Giuseppe struggle to answer Zanipolo's questions through his bandaged mask. He knew they needed this information to find the traitor and get justice for that tragedy, but Johnnie wanted Zanipolo to hurry and conclude his questioning so he could stop torturing this man. Even on a slew of medications, Giuseppe winced in pain and discomfort.

Johnnie needed to find the traitor, so he could pay for all the pain he put this man through. He ruined many lives all for the sake of this man's greed, and he could not let that stand.

After getting the exact location from the victim, Zanipolo, Johnnie, and Brock pulled into the parking lot of a large mahogany brick building called Cedar Tower. They entered through the large golden framed glass doors and into its massive marble and cedar wood lobby. They walked over to the manager's office and knocked on the glass door.

A pudgy, pepper-haired man sat in the far corner of the room whistling a jolly tune. The man, who reeked of alcohol, sat back in his chair with his feet propped up on his desk. He turned towards them when he heard Johnnie rap louder on the door with his knuckle. Once he saw them, he jumped up and tried to stash a bottle somewhere out-of-sight.

The man flashed a set of golden teeth at them and acted as if he was not higher than a kite. He focused on Zanipolo, scanned him carefully before laughing.

"Mr. Barney, it's just you. Did you lose your key again?"

Zanipolo, Johnnie, and Brock exchanged confused looks before Johnnie motioned to Zanipolo to play along. It was clear this man was too drunk to tell the difference between Zanipolo and Barney. From the few times Johnnie saw Barney, he did not notice any resemblance between him and Zanipolo but drink enough whiskey and anything is possible.

"Yeah, I must have misplaced mine at work. Do you mind giving me the spare?" Zanipolo said, masking his voice in a raspy undertone, so the drunk manager would not realize this was not the owner of his apartment.

"No problem, Mr. B," The man reached into his desk drawer, pulled out a key on a small ring, and gave it to Zanipolo. "I know this isn't my business, but you should take it easy. You don't sound good. It's good that you're a real workaholic, but you must watch out for your health."

"I'll try to do that. Thanks," Zanipolo pushed past Brock and headed over to the elevator. He pushed the call button then turned to Brock, who now stood beside him.

"This is turning out to be a fine day. I got health tips from an alcoholic. Who the hell drinks this early in the morning?" Zanipolo grumbled.

"Just be grateful he was too soused to realize the real reason you didn't sound like Barney. If he was even a slightly more sober, we'd be in a tight spot," Brock replied, stepping into the elevator once its iron doors opened. "But it's weird he'd confuse you with Barney. You two look nothing alike."

"I was thinking the same thing. But I think there might be a simple explanation for that. Barney must own a suit of a similar color as Zanipolo. It would explain how he could mix you two up. If you can only see a foggy silhouette, the color of Zanipolo's beige suit would be the only thing that stood out."

Johnnie pressed the floor button while Zanipolo looked at his reflection in the chrome walls. He placed his hand over the holster hidden by his jacket.

"I guess it will be easier to spot Barney. I doubt he's here now but stay sharp. He's not stupid and probably has eyes on this place, too."

"Yes, boss," Johnnie and Brock said in unison.

Johnnie and the others were not sure what traps Barney might have left behind to cover his tracks. All they knew, the drunk manager was just a ruse to lure them upstairs to be ambushed. Johnnie pressed his back against the side wall, glancing between Zanipolo and the floor indicator. His blood grew cold, and his heart froze as the penthouse floor drew closer.

They did not know what dangers lurked on the top floor. Maybe Zanipolo was right, and he was not home yet. But there was also a possibility the lush downstairs was only a ploy to send them to their doom. The suspicions gnawing at the back of his mind ripped away his peace of mind.

Johnnie was used to unpredictable situations like these, but that did not mean he had grown accustomed to the anxiety they caused. He hated going through unfamiliar situations but had no hesitation confronting them before, so he wondered why this time was different. His nerves trembled, and he became riddled with uncertainty. It was only when the elevator stopped, and the unknown became clear, did his fears vanish. The blinding rays peering through the tall, rectangular windows lining the halls momentarily interrupted his vision as they stepped off the elevator and onto the rich auburn and gold carpet. Two large, pearl white doors trimmed in gold stood at the end of the small hall. Zanipolo and Brock walked ahead and checked the doors. They were locked. Zanipolo took the key, unlocked them, and walked inside.

Johnnie warily followed them inside, but his nerves settled when he saw the dusty air and unkempt room. By the condition of the room, he could tell it was some time since Barney returned to this location. Johnnie circled around a stack of papers left by the fireplace and was going to look through them until Zanipolo stopped him and motioned to a room next to the fireplace.

Johnnie withdrew his gun and quietly made his way over to the door. Before he opened the door, a glimmer sparkled in the corner of his left eye drew away his attention. The source was a silver platter sitting on an end table by the window.

Johnnie picked up the platter, walked over to the door and slid it halfway under the gap of the door. He crouched down and looked closely at the reversed reflection on the plate.

A bed, mirror, some drawers, and a large wooden wardrobe lined the walls of the room. It was hard to see what was inside, but there was no evidence of anyone hiding inside. Johnnie pushed the platter to the side and went inside to verify his observation.

Johnnie searched through every crevice of the wall bedroom. Every drawer, corner and even the trash was void of anything of importance. Barney cleaned out every drawer and the closet of its contents. Wherever he went, it did not seem as if he planned on returning here.

Johnnie left the bedroom to see if Brock or Zanipolo fared better. As he passed the kitchen, he found Zanipolo ripping through drawers, scanning any piece of paper he found. He only stopped briefly when he saw Johnnie and waved at him to come over.

"So, little sister, did you have any luck?" Zanipolo teased, darkly nudging her arm. By the cool tone in his voice, Amadora realized Zanipolo had not gotten over the fact that she was going ahead with her plan and pulling it off flawlessly.

"Are you crazy, Polo! What if Brock overheard you!" Amadora hissed, glancing behind them, worried.

Zanipolo turned away from her and continued sitting through the mountain of papers he pulled out from his drawers. "Don't worry, Dora. I sent him to check the other side of the penthouse. At a quick glance, I gather there are about three or four more rooms over there. He won't be back for a while."

"Don't call me by my real name while I'm dressed like this. You never know who's listening. Besides, Brock is an old fox who isn't easily fooled and catches on quick. I'm surprised I held it together this long around him, so be careful when we're around him," Amadora whispered coldly while closely monitoring the door.

"What's wrong? Don't you trust him, Johnnie?" Zanipolo looked at her with an eyebrow raised in caution.

"Of course, I do. I trust him with my life... so far. But his loyalties are deeply tied to Gugliehno. I doubt he'd hesitate to tell him the truth if he found out who I was." Amadora looked back at Zanipolo and masked her voice with that of Johnnie's.

"You make a good point. I'll keep that in mind for the future," Zanipolo closed the drawer he searched through and pouted in disgust. "I've never known a person to have more papers in his kitchen than cookware or utensils. All of which are useless garbage with nothing of interest on them. I'm guessing if you're here, then your search was just as fruitless."

"Yes. The room was completely cleaned out. Everything that was left behind was useless garbage," Johnnie replied disappointedly, fixing his black gloves.

"Well then, let's help search the remaining rooms on the other side."

They left the kitchen and walked over to the rooms. They split up and searched the two rooms he had not yet reached.

Johnnie searched the room at the end of the hall. Just like every other room in this place, it was just as vacant and dusty. The only light illuminating the dense shadowy room was a small rectangular window on the back wall across from where Johnnie stood. Johnnie holstered his gun as he trekked around the large, bookshelf-lined room and made his way over to the huge black desk in the center of the room.

Johnnie dug through each drawer, carefully analyzing everything he came across, but found nothing of worth. He was going to give up and check the next room when he kicked a small, crumpled ball of paper. He scooped it up, unraveled it, and examined its gray, ashy corners. It was obvious Barney tried to destroy this piece of paper, but the flames were smothered out somehow. A confident grin crossed Johnnie's lips. Finally, it seemed like they might have stumbled on something useful.

"B," Johnnie started reading the note softly to himself.

"We went over your concerns and believe it would be best if you didn't stay at your current residence, especially with the *Day* drawing near. We have a small cottage hidden by marigolds that would be a perfect spot for you to lie low. The address is on the back of this letter. Thanks for your alliance. You will be highly rewarded for it... V."

"A cottage hidden by marigolds... Aren't marigolds just flowers? How can they hide an entire house?" Zanipolo said, entering the room with Brock.

"I don't think they meant that literally. It says there should be an address on the back of this letter. Is it still there, kid?" Brock added.

Johnnie turned the note around and examined the back. There was no sign of any writing. He raised the paper into the stream of sunlight when he saw the truth. "Found it. I believe it's time we go pay him a visit. Don't you?"

Amongst the dried earth and wilted plants of Cyclamen manor's garden, Lana Rosilli transformed into the physical embodiment of Eris as she basked in all the discord and chaos she reaped. Her malicious smile grew as she stared at the clear sky above her while plotting her next challenge for her new rival, Johnnie Barbone.

For years, a single man never piqued Lana's interest as much as Johnnie Barbone, not even her wretched ex, Gugliehno. Something about this reckless newcomer, Johnnie, lured her in. He was consistently expanding his horizons and adapting to every situation thrown his way and coming out unscathed. He was driven to succeed, no matter how much despair and danger he faced. These qualities drew her in more. He even made her wonder if he could be the first man to best her at her own game.

Johnnie Barbone became Lana's new obsession. She needed to find out everything about him. Lana needed to uncover the source of his drive and determination before she dismantled him and brought an end to one of Gunny's new shining stars.

Lana needed to observe Johnnie up close, but that would be near impossible. In a few hours, she would be on the top of the Morellis' hit list. She would sign her own death warrant if she openly tried to follow her new pet now. She turned around and made her way back to the manor.

Lana glanced at her watch while she placed her desires on the back burners until the nighttime came. She paced back and forth in the sunroom, checking her watch periodically.

"Where is he? It's been over an hour, and he hasn't returned. Damn that V…"

"V… what? You know patience is a virtue. You should practice it some time, Mistress." Viper replied, walking across the smooth wooden floors and kissing her hand.

"Even though I love spending my time with you, I need to know what is so urgent."

"I'm sorry to interrupt your more important plans." Lana snipped.

"If this was disturbing my plans, I wouldn't care, but I'm in the middle of doing a quick errand for the Don."

"The don… huh? I wonder what else the don has planned?" Lana pondered partially to herself. "Well… I won't worry about that. I have more pressing matters. Viper, I need you to get rid of Barney."

"Are you sure? I thought you wanted him to lead them to us."

"Yes. I want him to lead them to us, but once he does, I'll no longer have any need for him. You can get rid of him as soon as he gives them our names. I don't want him to reveal too much. I want Johnnie to find me on his own."

Confused, Viper tipped his hat and left. He did not understand what Lana had planned, but he was worried about her determination to get him involved in this mess. Her rash obsession with Johnnie Barbone would damage the family and their allies if word leaked that they turned on one of them when they are no longer useful. Now, he had to decide. Should he follow her orders? Or take him out before revealing the truth?

The afternoon sun's warmth kissed Lorenzo's cheeks as he lounged on a lawn chair in Gunny's backyard watching Elda's son play with his cousins. Elda and Gunny faked smiles in front of their spouses as they conversed in polite chitchat. Lorenzo's eyes traveled from his friends over to the bored lump of skin hiding in the shadows behind him.

With Zanipolo leading the investigation, there was no need for Lorenzo to get involved, especially with this leach tagging along. Besides, Lorenzo did not need to be psychic to tell who was behind this attack. After Lana's man tried so hard to distract them, Lorenzo knew immediately who was behind everything. Lana made it perfectly clear at the meeting that she wanted revenge. The question was only when she would exact it. He was just surprised she did it so soon.

Lorenzo wondered how all this affected Gunny as well. If he reached the conclusion that she was behind everything, then he was sure Gunny realized the same thing. Lorenzo wondered how Gunny was holding up. He did not send his family away yet, so it was clear he did not suspect that she would come after them just yet.

"Why the long face, Ren? Seeing all the kids around finally inspiring you to settle down and make some of your own?" Elda joked, plopping down on the seat next to him.

"Don't be ridiculous. You know I gave up on that years ago. The bachelor's life is too enticing to throw away now," Lorenzo laughed.

"I guess you'll never change," Elda smirked.

"So, tell me. How's Gunny dealing with everything?" Lorenzo's smile faded as he looked over at his friend, who was jesting with Elda's husband.

"As well as you'd expect. Gunny has always been good at hiding how he feels, especially with matters dealing with her; but this time, even though he's trying to perfect a smile around Susan and the girls, he rants and raves about what's going on when he's alone with us," Elda replied.

"I guess that makes sense," Lorenzo said. Before he could continue, one of his men walked over and whispered something in his ear.

Elda watched quietly as the man exchanged a few hush words with him then left after Lorenzo sent them away.

"It seems they've made a huge break in the investigation. Grab Gunny. We need

to talk."

Viper drove to the thick woods overlooking the clearing where Marigold cottage stood. He parked his gray car behind some bushes, stepped out, opened the trunk, and pulled out a large golf bag. He unzipped the thick leather case and whipped out a long rifle. He quickly assembled its pieces, then shoved the bag in the trunk and closed it shut.

Viper scanned the surrounding area to make sure no one saw him arrive. When he was sure the coast was clear, he settled in the heavily forested area, finding the best vantage point to focus on his target. Barney was alone and unguarded in the bedroom reading. He steadied his gun as he followed his prey's every move. He rested his finger on the trigger and waited for the perfect moment.

Elda, Gunny and Lorenzo gathered in Gunny's office, so Lorenzo could tell them the news he just received.

"My men made a lot of progress they found out who's behind the attack and tracked down the location of the traitor. They're now enroute."

"Where are they going?" Elda asked.

"Marigold Cottage," Lorenzo replied.

"Marigold... I see," Gunny said faint-heartedly.

"Do you know that place?" Elda interrogated.

"Who cares if he knows about that place? If we know where the traitor is, then why are we sitting around doing absolutely nothing?" A sharp voice broke through the brief silence and cut off Gunny's words. Elda turned towards the door in frustration.

"Nero! What the hell are you doing here?"

"Lorenzo brought me against my will. Don't worry, cousin, if it was up to me, I would be out there with Polo chasing down this scum."

"Look at you. A month shadowing Ren and you think you're a full fledge gangster," Elda sneered.

"Don't fuck around with me, Elda. I'm just as ready as your new soldier, Johnnie Barbone. Why is he out there getting all the action while I'm stuck sitting on the sidelines?"

"Your cousin has a lot of spunk. I like it," Lorenzo laughed.

"More like a lot of stupidity if you ask me," Elda grumbled.

"I appreciate your enthusiasm, but this mission is too dangerous to send you out there. Your inexperience would jeopardize yours and your team's safety. Johnnie Barbone has proven that he has enough skills to complete this task without a problem and produce favorable results," Gunny explained, suppressing his growing annoyance.

"Fine. If I'm not needed, I'm heading out for a drink," Nero rushed off, slamming the door behind him.

"Good riddance," Elda snapped.

"If I didn't know better, I'd say he reminded me a lot of Zanipolo when he started. But even Polo couldn't escape maturity and is taking his role more seriously," Lorenzo observed.

"I must agree. When he volunteered to help with the investigation, I was shocked. Normally, Polo doesn't get mixed up in any matters outside his territory. I wonder what sparked this change."

"That's true. Maybe he finally wants to take a shot for father's heir," Gunny responded.

"I highly doubt it," Elda retorted.

"Maybe he simply wants to check out the new soldier catching everyone's attention, Johnnie Barbone, up close and personal." A slick grin crossed Lorenzo's lips. No one uttered a word in response, because out of all their theories, his was the best.

The sun was setting by the time they found Barney's hideout. They parked far enough from it, so no one by the cabin heard them approaching. With secured bullet-proof vests, guns and ammunition ready, they walked over to the boundary between the woods and the clearing housing his base. They ducked behind the thick brush and surveyed the perimeter of the cottage.

From their vantage point, only two men armed with tommy guns stood guard outside. Once they had a good idea of the outdoor surroundings, Zanipolo motioned to Johnnie to take out the guard on the right while Brock trained on the door, and he got rid of the other. Johnnie unstrapped his rifle and aimed at his target. He peered through the thin eye scope and searched for the man's heart. Once he found it, he nestled his finger on the trigger and waited for Zanipolo's signal.

After settling into his own position, Zanipolo motioned to the two unsuspecting targets, and they opened fire. The thunder of their shots rang through the valley, and the moment their bodies collapsed to the ground, two more guards busted through the door.

The two men cautiously scanned the scene. With their comrades brutally slain before them, they withdrew their weapons and checked their buddies' conditions.

Johnnie watched their every movement through the thick branches he lurked in. He used this moment to take his shot at the man kneeling next to the body, but his partner noticed the gleam from Johnnie's barrel and immediately dragged him back inside.

The men shouted swears, then the roar of gunfire thundered through the air, causing Johnnie to hit the ground. He covered his head from wood chips and tree fragments scattered by the bullets.

Johnnie set aside his rifle, pulled out his automatic and analyzed their firing pattern. Keeping his body low and his chin pressed deep into the cool earth underneath him, he peered through the leaves and tried to find where his enemies fired from.

Zanipolo and Brock ducked for cover and returned fire while Johnnie analyzed the situation. Glass broke, and a man fired from the window. His bullets whizzed through the air missing Johnnie and hitting the trees behind him.

The man became Johnnie's target because he was the easiest to reach. He purposefully kept low and only brought out his right arm when firing. If they were going to make it inside, this would be the only way to make it happen.

Johnnie monitored how long he kept his arm exposed, then he aimed his gun at the approximate spot it would appear in. Johnnie took a few deep breaths before pulling the trigger and severing his elbow.

The man roared in agony, but his comrades ignored him, stepping aside when Barney emerged from the bedroom to see what was going on. The wounded guard bellowed, grasping his arm. One of his comrades dragged him away from the window so they could try to stop the bleeding. The rest of his guards took cover and shot out the door.

One guard shooting by the door, ordered him to return to his room, but Barney was paralyzed in fear. His sight was fixated on the blood pouring from his guard's arm, and his ears transfixed on the thundering roar of gunshots. His pulse slowed as time stopped around him and the steady stride of the angel of death neared.

Barney ran back into the bedroom, locked the doors and barricaded the door with the dresser and desk before retreating into a secluded crevice in the room's corner. He glanced over at the windows and debated whether he should risk escaping through there. He crouched on the floor and crawled over to the window. He peered outside to the grassy clearing leading to the lake behind the cabin. Everything seemed quiet, and the lake made it impossible for them to ambush the rear of the cabin. The only possible vantage points were the forested towering cliffs on each side. The thick brush made it difficult to see if any hidden assailants lurked nearby. His best bet was to wait and hope his guards triumphed over these intruders.

Time did not favor Barney. As he listened to another of his men fall victim to his assailant, he realized it would not be long until death claimed him, too. He had nowhere to go or hide. The angel of death was there to claim his soul as payment for his treachery.

Barney's men fought diligently until their very last breath; but as they faded one by one, Barney took a deep breath, bit his lip and hid deeper in the crevice in the far-thest corner of the room. During all the commotion, he left his gun in the other room, leaving himself vulnerable to his advancing enemy. He clung onto the cross around his neck, praying for some sort of salvation for his pathetic life. But as the minutes passed, a clamor of footsteps crossed the wooden floors of the other room, and some-one fought his barricade to get inside. Barney realized his time was up.

To save his life, Barney scrambled to the window and struggled to open it. His sweaty palms made it impossible. After several fruitless attempts, the door was busted open, and several gun barrels aimed at him.

"Barney, you've been pretty difficult to find," Zanipolo said darkly, cocking his gun and training it on the nervously trembling form in front of him.

"Zanipolo, please. Let me explain," Barney pleaded, falling to his knees before him and fighting the threatening tears of fear and uncertainty of his fate.

"That depends on what you tell me."

"I'll tell you anything!" Barney begged fearfully.

"Why did they attack the warehouse?"

"They told me they wanted revenge against Gunny and the family for the attacks on Jack and Marco!"

"Who's they?" Anger ravaged Zanipolo while he watched the sniveling coward grovel at his feet. Zanipolo could not tell if this was the same man who had the balls to help the enemy attack one of their strongholds and betray his partner by shooting him in the back.

"Viper, Lana's man!"

"Where are they?"

While Johnnie watched Zanipolo's interrogation, he noticed a small sparkle glint in the corner of his eye from some bushes on the cliff outside the window behind Za-nipolo. Instinctively, he pulled Zanipolo down to the ground.

"Get down!"

A loud cascade of thunder and breaking glass broke the sudden silence. Brock jumped out of the way while Johnnie and Zanipolo fell on the floor far from where they originally stood. Zanipolo rolled off Johnnie and looked down at his once beige suit, now splattered in a dark, goopy substance. He followed the crimson trail back to where the traitor stood. A gruesome scene appeared before them as Barney's lifeless body laid motionless on the floor. What was left of his brains was splattered all over the ground in front of him.

"I guess we aren't the only ones who wanted him dead," Zanipolo signaled for them to stay low while they retreated from the scene.

"It seems that way. We need to get out before we end up the same. I think we got enough information to move forward. We just need to find out who this Viper person is and where he's hiding," Johnnie responded, following Zanipolo out of the room.

"That might be a problem. He's one of the best hitmen in the game. No one knows Viper's identity or where he is since those who meet him rarely come out alive," Brock replied, crawling over to the door behind the others.

"I'll see what I can find out when we get back. There's gotta be someone out there who knows something useful about Viper. For now, we should listen to Johnnie and focus on getting out of here," Zanipolo said.

The clear night sky revealed the brilliant form of few powerful stars strong enough to break through the soft glow surrounding the city. The subtle, unusual warmth settling in the fall air blended with the occasional crisp breeze. It was the perfect atmosphere for a night like tonight.

Darian expected this moment all day long. He could not wait until the clock struck eight to make his way to Je'adore. Even though his reasons were selfish, he could not stop thinking about the beauty he was about to meet, Amadora. He longed to see her again, so he could become captivated by her charming smile; but as he neared the amethyst and gold awning and the roped off red carpet leading to the restaurant, he realized he might be risking much more by trying to get close to her.

Je'adore was one of the most expensive French restaurants in New York. This was a popular place for the social elites and stars to frequent. He could barely buy an appetizer at a place like this without putting another mortgage on the store. They were from two completely different. How was he going to convince her to go somewhere else without upsetting her?

Darian hoped she would understand. He was a retired vet and the son of a grocery store owner. He could not afford to please her extravagant taste.

Darian paused under the awning and looked for any sign of Amadora. Young women with their partners packed the surrounding sidewalks, but Amadora was nowhere to be found. He turned towards the entrance and looked past the line of people waiting to be checked in by the doorman. Darian sighed reluctantly as he walked closer to see if she was already inside. He wanted to save the embarrassment that would surely come if he had to explain why they could not stay in front of all these wealthy patrons.

Darian took his time walking to the door as he mentally embraced for the humiliation to come. However, when he reached the man in front of the crystal and gold entrance, he felt a tug on the back of his jacket. Relief washed over him when his eyes met the beauty of the subject of his thoughts: Amadora.

Amadora flashed an infectiously warm smile when their eyes met. In a flowing blue lace dress with an ornate matching band settled in her long curls, Amadora's innocence brilliantly multiplied. Her fairy-like appearance bewitched him, wrapping him in an uncontrollable longing. He wanted to scoop her in his arms and steal a kiss from her heart-shaped lips, but he refrained from doing so and reached for her hand instead. However, when he reached for her hand, Darian noticed it was full, holding a medium-sized wicker basket covered with a light green scarf.

"Amadora, what's with the basket?"

"It's too beautiful a night to be crammed in a crowded restaurant. I thought it would be perfect weather for a picnic. Who knows when we'll luck out and get another night like tonight with winter just around the corner?" Amadora answered.

"If you wanted to do that, why did you tell me to meet you here?" Darian asked, confused.

"Because we are having it here."

"Here?" Darian looked over to the restaurant door, then bent over and whispered in her ear. "Won't we get in trouble if we do that?"

"Of course not, because we're going to have it in their garden." Amadora's smile grew in reaction to Darian's confusion. She watched him scan the premises searching for the place she spoke of.

"Follow me."

Amadora took his hand and guided him inside. They turned into the grand foyer opposite the restaurant, crossed the black marble hall, and climbed the stairs until they reached the second-floor landing. Amadora guided him down the gold and ivory hall until they stopped in front of a black iron gate guarding a black void.

Amadora pressed the call button and soon a loud mechanical hum filled the hall. The grinding gears lasted a few moments before a silver box emerged from the darkness and opened its doors. They stepped inside, waited for the doors to shut, then Amadora pressed another button before turning to him anxiously exuberant.

"Gardens are my favorite places. I hope you'll like this one too."

"Why do you like them?"

"Ever since I was little, gardens were a separate world where I could escape the troubles in my life and just drown in its ever-changing wonders," Amadora noticed the strange way Darian stared at her. She blushed and averted her gaze. "I'm sorry. You must think I'm spouting weird nonsense."

Darian chuckled. "No. You have no reason to feel sorry. I'm surprised by your passion for gardens. That's all."

Darian grabbed her free hand when the elevator reached their destination. "I want to know about all your favorite things. Show me everything you like about this garden."

By just the touch, caught in his possession, Amadora's face grew wider than before. For the first time in a while, she felt safe; so, when the elevator doors opened, all her fear flew out of her and soared into the stars above.

Amadora tightened her grip and guided him onto a red brick path leading to a golden gate. Roses woven into the intricate lace arch framing the entrance greeted them as they crossed the threshold into this floral world. She watched, amused, as her guest gawked at the overflowing greenery and flowers surrounding them. Seeing his interest in her hideout as they walked farther inside filled her with joy.

Even in the city's subtle haze, the stars and moon looked close enough to pluck right out of the sky. The air was cooler than before, but that did not bother Amadora because the closer she was to Darian, his warmth sustained her. Amadora guided him into a small moonlit space in the center of the garden. Small hydrangea bushes encircled a small iron and glass table decorated with a small, round yellow candle and a thin white rose and tulip filled vase.

Amadora released Darian's hand. She placed the basket on a chair, covered the table with the scarf, and set the table while Darian surveyed his surroundings.

"You know this breaks the golden rule about first dates," Darian sighed, returning his attention towards Amadora.

"Golden rule? ... What rule?" Amadora asked, confused.

"Guys are supposed to pay for the first date, but you went and planned all of this."

"I've never heard that before," Amadora smirked devilishly. "But the first thing you'll learn about me, Mr. Mancini, is that I never follow rules. I enjoy living spontaneously."

Darian chuckled. Amadora stared at him as she became entranced in his charming laughter. As her gaze traveled along the contours of his face, Darian's eyes fell upon her and captured her in their warm, unwavering grasp. Grinning from ear to ear, Darian moved closer. It was clear he knew the effect he had on her and enjoyed every moment as he softly caressed her cheek with the back of his hand. For the first time in her life, Amadora felt helpless and did not regret the feeling. The closer he grew, the more she longed to remain lost in this paralysis.

The increasing drumming of their hearts drowned out the calm night's noises. Amadora placed her hand over his, letting it linger for a moment before gently grabbing his and setting it to the side.

Reality struck, triggering her slumbering head and subduing the wishes of her foolish heart. Why did she do this? Inviting him here was a much more dangerous risk than she expected.

This place just helped solidify his possession over her senses. Amadora stepped away from him and turned back towards the table. Shocked by her withdrawal, Darian's smile faded as concern took hold.

"I'm sorry. You look so irresistible under the soft moonlight I couldn't help myself. I hope I didn't offend you."

Amadora turned back towards him and smiled softly. "No. You didn't. I think it's better if we sit down, drink some wine and get to know each other first."

"You're right." Darian nodded and sat in the chair across from her. He waited until she finished pouring the wine and setting out some snacks before saying anything.

"What would you like to know about me?"

"What do you do for a living?" Amadora asked, popping a grape in her mouth and focusing on her guest.

"I'm just a retired marine and ex-cop who runs my father's shop."

"Why do you run it all by yourself?" Amadora asked.

"My father's old and can't tend to it on his own. I'm an only child, so there aren't many people who can help my dad out. My aunt used to help him out while I was deployed, but she left a year ago, and I had to leave the police force to help maintain his business," Darian replied.

"It must be difficult to deal with all the responsibility on your own."

"Not really. This was my father's dream. I just want to keep it alive. I'm just getting used to how he does things around there."

"Your father's business was why you were at the ball, right?" Amadora sipped on her wine.

"Yes. Before I took over, my father joined Morelli's protection. I withdrew from it once I took over; but after some recent events, I had to reverse my stance." Darian ate some treats Amadora served, then scanned their surroundings. "I'm surprised the youngest daughter of one of the richest men in New Jersey has such a romantic, earthy disposition. When did you have time to arrange all of this?"

"I just threw it together at the last minute. If the weather didn't hold, I wouldn't know where we would have met, because I don't enjoy going to busy restaurants for first dates. They make it hard to have a decent conversation without yelling over a bunch of noise," Amadora responded. "I didn't want my first moments with you to be drowned out by random chatter."

Darian looked at her, surprised, as she stood up and extended her hand. Her infectious smile and flamboyant personality radiated from her. He took her hand and followed her to an area where the flowers and moon intertwined. Amadora stopped when she reached the gold brick circle path, then twirled around to face Darian.

Gazing into his glistening blue eyes, she grabbed his other hand and moved in closer.

"I want to share every moment of this beautiful night with you." Amadora swayed and drew him into a soft spin in rhythm with the music of the night. The wind, chirping of animals and little critters were all they needed to dance.

"I never thought this would happen," Darian said softly.

"What would happen?" Amadora asked, surprised.

"That I would spend this beautiful night with an angel like you."

Amadora's smile faded as she closed the space between them and sunk deeper into his embrace. Amadora placed her head against his chest. Her heart fluttered uncontrollably as she wrapped her arms around his neck.

Darian did not know how wrong he was because she was not the angel... he was.

Reflection & Obsession

Memories of a Lost Love

'Suppress her, and she re-emerges. Run from her, and she follows. Hate her, and I remember all the reasons why I loved her,' Thoughts of Gugliehno Morelli.

Steam billowed through the thick, tropical scenery cradling the hot springs. The fluffy white mist shrouded the hot waters producing a vague silhouette of a man's shape. The man sat dazed and alone as he tried making sense of his surroundings.

The mist obscured his vision and shielded everything in its white shroud leaving only subtle outlines of the unknown. He could not tell if it was night or day, nor did he know where exactly was. He sloshed around the warm, navel-high pool. The man frantically searched for some means of how he arrived in this current place and how he wound up in his current naked state.

The man felt around the water looking for a way out; but when he found a ledge, a hand brushing against his arm from behind stopped him. He whirled around slightly disoriented and collapsed into a woman's embrace. While trying to regain his senses, he nestled into her bosom. He opened his eyes and glimpsed at his savior.

Striking sea-green eyes peered through the mist. Her silk skin became a remedy for his bewilder state. He found pleasure in the effect her beauty had over him and caressed his face as she whispered.

"Gugliehno, you silly man, you need to be more careful. You could've gotten hurt if I wasn't here."

"Sorry. I was trying to find the exit," Gugliehno said giving into the satisfying warmth of her possession.

"That's fine. Just try not to be so reckless. I couldn't go on if something happened to you," The woman drew him in closer running her hands through his hair as he wrapped his hands around her waist. Her soft lips traveled along his cheek until it stopped right by his mouth.

"Lana…" Gugliehno whispered into the mist before she seized his lips with her own. Her warm touch and subtle kisses incited a longing Gugliehno thought he banished from his heart. All the pain they endured vanished and all that remained was his eternal desire for her.

Gugliehno regained his footing, picked her up and pressed her against the nearby rocks. His hands traveled along her body taking in every pleasure of her silky frame. She egged him on with sweet proclamations of affection. Lana wanted all of him as much as he wanted her. Gugliehno bended to the will of this beautiful seductress and began his entry into her body.

Lana grabbed hold of his back while joining his gentle rhythm. As their passionate union deepened, Gugliehno's resurrected feelings grew stronger and the hold she had over his heart strengthened. Every utterance of love that left her lips triggered tears of joy. He fought them back while love completed its spell over him bounding him to his past desires as he kissed the lips, he longed for many years to possess once more. All doubt melted away leaving behind only his true feelings.

Love, the mischievous vixen, seized his tongue as he produced the three words, he once kept sealed away deep inside his heart. He spoke to them fully aware of the consequence of his actions. Those foolish words betrayed him as he was yanked from the source of his bliss and thrown on the wet stone ground. Paralyzed in pain, he was too weak to open his eyes but knew he was no longer in the springs. The cool misty air caressed his naked body. He fought his pain and touched its source. A thick oozing liquid poured out of his side and enveloped his hand. He fought to muster what little strength he could to open his eyes.

Gugliehno looked down at his side and saw a gaping wound. Blood covered him and the surrounding ground. As he moved and more blood poured from his wound, his life slowly slipped away with each drop. He knew he should stay put until help came but he could not. He needed to find Lana and make sure she had not suffered the same fate. He crawled through the dense mist hopelessly searching the unknown for Lana leaving a little of his life behind.

The minutes dragged on forever as he suspended what little energy he still possessed. When death came to ease him of his pain, the mist faded in an area far from his grasp and revealed his worst fear came to pass. Lana and their daughters laid motionless on the ground. An unknown assailant slaughtered them. Gugliehno desperately called their names until his last breath, but there was no answer. As his trapped tears fell, he screamed to the heavens as they disappeared in an encroaching shadow. When the darkness began devouring him, Gugliehno did not fight back and just gave in to the abyss.

The echoing song of the clock striking the hour snapped Gunny out of his slumber. Sweat poured down his body as he frantically tried to make sense of where he was. He sighed in relief when he saw the clock and fireplace from his study. He leaned back in the chair, took a deep breath and glanced up at ceiling.

It was only a dream. Everything felt real. Could his mind really manifest something that lifelike?

The heated water, cool stones pressed against his skin and even her touch felt realistic. Her silk body, every word she spoke, the warmth of their growing passion and even that feeling that coursed through his veins. Everything could not be only a figment of his imagination. Gugliehno refused to believe his mind would trick his heart like that.

Gugliehno glanced down at his desk and replayed the images from his dream. He saw their specters reenacting every detail further blurring the line between reality and fantasy. In a world where he was now married to a kind wife, who was caring for his daughters along with their own, he wondered why his subconscious still drifted to Lana. Nothing made any sense.

A soft rapping echoed through the room breaking him from his delusions and yanking him back into reality.

"Did you pull another all-nighter again?"

Zanipolo stood in the doorway watching the disheveled figure moping around in the shadows. It jumped upright in its chair and tried fixing its appearance before acknowledging him.

"Polo, you have news for me."

"Yeah. I do. But why is it so quiet? Where's Susan and the girls?" Zanipolo looked at the empty, dark hall behind him.

"Susan took them to visit her sister in upstate New York. Things are getting too hairy here to keep them around. They'll return when I'm satisfied it's safe." Gugliehno motioned to a chair across from him. "Come in and tell me what you found out."

"You were right. It seems Lana Rosilli was behind the attack."

Those few words turned Gugliehno's skin pale and sank his heart. The moment his father told them about the attack, he realized the truth, but he wanted to be wrong. He kept a bit of hope that Lana was not responsible. He hoped she would stop herself from crossing this line. Now, it was out of his hands. His father clarified that he wanted those behind the attack to pay for what they did.

Gugliehno noticed Zanipolo watching him and analyzing his hesitation. He whirled his chair around facing the window to conceal his true feelings, but it was too late. His sharp-eyed, younger brother caught on to the disturbance plaguing his mind.

"What's wrong? I thought you of all people would jump for joy at the news. You told us from the beginning that it was her. Now, you know that it was true, you don't seem satisfied."

"I'm partially satisfied at being proven right, but that's not what I wanted at all. I was hoping it was only paranoia; and the investigation would prove me wrong,"

Gunny answered.

"Why would you want to be wrong? Now, we have an excuse to put that psychotic bitch, Lana, in her place and get her out of our hair for good," Zanipolo sat in the chair across from his brother trying to get a better glimpse into his reasoning.

"Don't you dare talk about her like that!" Gugliehno exploded angrily glaring at Zanipolo.

Surprised, Zanipolo sat back and crossed his arms. "What's wrong with you? Normally, you're spewing a lot worse about that bitch. But when I state the truth, you bite my head off."

Gugliehno calmed down and returned to the window. "Sorry, Polo. It's complicated. She wasn't always like this." He trailed off watching the rain hit the windowpane.

"How do you know?" Zanipolo asked.

"Because I was married to her."

"Married? When?"

"Years before my girls were born."

"How come I didn't hear about this?" Zanipolo looked at his brother shocked.

"Pop wanted it that way. We kept it a secret for years, because we knew our fathers wouldn't approve. And when we finally told pops, he detested the union and refused to be involved."

"Could you blame him? You know his checkered past with old man Rosilli better than any of us. He was probably worried her father's crazy was hereditary, and he wasn't wrong," Zanipolo leaned back and processed the information he just received before continuing. "Wait! What about the girls? Whose kids are they?"

"Roselia is my daughter with Susan, but Loretta and Aniela are my kids with Lana."

"I don't get how you could marry her. Were you drunk?" Confusion riddled Zanipolo's face while trying to understand his brother.

"I told you before she was different back then. That person was the one I fell in love with and would later marry."

"I'm surprised that thing can love. I guess you learn something every day," Zanipolo chuckled at him annoyed.

"Come on act seriously, Polo. This is one reason I didn't tell you in the first place," Gugliehno grumbled annoyed.

"Sorry, Gunny. This is difficult to swallow. I want to know more. Go on," Zanipolo flashed a remorseful smirk.

"Fine." Gunny turned away and looked out at the increasing rain while he collected the memories in the back of his mind.

"Three years before Loretta was born, we met in Naples. She was a college student, and I was traveling with my friends. From the moment we first met, I fell in love with her witty charm, warm heart and mesmerizing beauty."

"Wait. Did you know she was a Rosilli when you first met her?" Zanipolo interjected.

"Of course, I did. She told me who she was, but I didn't care. I loved her and only wanted to be with her. That's why after three months I proposed to her."

Gugliehno stood and walked over to a tall file cabinet in the room's corner. He opened one of the bottom drawers and took something from it. It was a small piece of paper. He stared at it for a moment before continuing.

"The imposter we know as Lana is not the same woman, who I loved years ago. She is a dark shell filled with bitter hatred and petty vengeance. My Lana was a silly, hopeless romantic, who dreamed of traveling the world with a loving husband and a hoard of kids. She could be a brainy jokester one moment and a gullible ditz the next. She was just the type of gal worth risking everything for."

"Did you tell pop about your engagement?"

"Yes. I did. I wanted to share that joyful moment with the whole family, but Casimiro advised me to tell pop first, because she's a Rosilli. He understood that insignificant fact would have a greater impact than everything else," Gunny handed the paper in his possession to Zanipolo. "This reflects the happier times, before she slowly started her transformation into the blood thirsty loon now inhabiting her body"

Zanipolo glanced over the sweet picture of Gunny in his younger days twirling his blushing bride around in the air.

"I'm guessing pop wasn't pleased when he found out about your new fiancée's lineage, right?"

"You guessed right. At first, when he came to our villa in Italy, my beautiful catch impressed him, but once he found out who her family was, his pride turned to disappointment quick. He immediately withdrew his blessings, ordered me to break my engagement and return home. Pop used every tactic he could to try to convince me, but I was determined to be with her and refused to buckle to any obstacle that stood in our way, even pop," Gugliehno retook his chair and smiled.

"You and Giacinta weren't the only rebels in the family. Each of us clashed with him. This was my time."

"I feel slightly relieved. Who knew pop's golden boy was an ungrateful delinquent just like the rest of us?" Zanipolo laughed.

"I wouldn't take it that far. But I'm pretty sure pop's thought pattern wasn't too far from that. We fought nonstop for days until finally he caved and accepted my decision only if we met a certain condition. We could marry but had to keep our disgraceful union—his words not mine—hidden from everyone else."

"I can't believe he disowned you over something like that. That's ridiculous. I thought he's always the one preaching about family above everything."

"You know all logic goes out the window when Rosilli comes into the picture. If you deal with anything related to him, he sees it as a betrayal. I wasn't surprised by the outcome just disappointed that he'd let his hatred for Rosilli outweigh his love for me," Gugliehno ran his hand through his messy locks and sighed. "I accepted his terms and married Lana in Naples at the plaza where we first met. She had all of her friends and some family members there, but I only had Lorenzo and Casimiro."

"I want to apologize for our father's selfish actions. If I knew about all of this then, I would've been there for you. It's not right how he treated you." Zanipolo gritted his teeth while trying to suppress the anger growing inside him towards his father.

"Thanks. That's good to know. However, I'm past all that now. I ignored all of it and embraced the joy I felt being with the woman I loved. After our wedding we lived in Hawaii for a little while before moving to Lana's childhood home and beginning our new married life."

"How long did your marital bliss last?"

"Not long. A few months after Aniela was born, our actual problems began. Lana wasn't part of her family's business when I met her. She actually did not know about the true nature of it until she started helping at her aunt's request," Gunny replied.

"Wait. Her aunt works in their business?" Zanipolo interjected.

"No. By that time, they knew that old man Rosilli's health was deteriorating, and Lana's aunt worked as his caretaker since he was too paranoid to hire a professional. Her aunt, Hilara, acted as the don's middleman to relay messages to Lana. He is a very paranoid man and refused to contact her through the phone," Gugliehno leaned back in his chair. "I still wonder 'till this day if I should've tried harder to convince her not to do it; because once she started helping with the formal aspects of their business, the pitfall into the darker aspects occurred not soon after. I didn't know then how much helping her family would change her. That's why I didn't see anything wrong when she first agreed to help."

"Do you think her aunt knew that having her help would lead to her present state?"

"I doubt it. Like I said, she was just her brother's caretaker. Besides, she was a religious widow, who was in denial of the true nature of their business. When she noticed Lana was changing, she tried to convince her to leave but failed."

"How did she change?" Zanipolo questioned.

"It was a subtle change. About six months after accepting her aunt's request, I noticed a significant change in her personality. She isolated herself from us and avoided being close to our daughters. It took a little while before I could calm her down and get her to enjoy her life outside work. My efforts worked a little too well. Not only did she sharpen her edge, but she also grew a little too comfortable with her new power. Lana transformed into the vessel we see today. She became cruel and demanding when she didn't get what she wanted. Sometimes, her attitude transformed into rage making living with her unbearable."

"Did she act like that around the girls?" Zanipolo asked surprised.

"Strangely, she didn't. Lana returned to her warm motherly roots when around the girls. As if torn into two different people, she flipped between insanity and reality when interacting with Roselia and Loretta. At first, I thought it was a phase that would pass with time, but it just got worse. That's when I made the hardest choice for the sake of my daughters. I took them and left."

"Where did you go?"

"I stayed with Lorenzo until our lawyers hashed it out over the details of our separation. Other than Casimiro and pop, he was the only one who knew about our situation.

After winning full custody of the girls, I went to pop to decide how to break the news to the rest of the family. He was happy over our split but dealing with the aftermath was a new challenge. Pop's grudge prevented him from telling Mom that she had other grandchildren aside from Angelo. He wanted to lessen the shock for the family so he decided it was best to hide the whole affair and find a suitable woman who would go along with the ruse. That's when he found Susan."

"Why would anyone agree to be a part of this mess?"

"I don't know exactly why she agreed. Casimiro said our union would benefit her family but didn't tell me how. I could care less. In my eyes, she was just a pawn in my father's scheme, and I was desperate to see my family again. I already spent years away from them all for Lana and didn't want to spend another moment away. I wanted my kids to experience the loving environment I grew up in."

"How did you get Aniela and Loretta to go along with this ruse?"

"They were both young enough that they had a vague memory of their mother, and Susan was close enough in resemblance that they confused her Lana."

"That's bizarre. I can't even image going through such a convoluted plan just to wipe one person from existence all for father's sake."

"It wasn't just for his sake. I went along with it for the sake of my family as well."

"I get it. But after hearing your story, I can't believe how much of a prick dad could be by micromanaging every aspect of your life. With all the lovey-dovey crap he spews, you'd think he'd leave our love lives alone," Zanipolo grumbled.

"If Lana wasn't a Rosilli, pop would have treated her differently. Sometimes it's just better pleasing his wishes," Gunny hissed.

"Like hell we don't! We sacrifice a lot for this old man and our world. You'd think we could at least have the freedom to do what we want with our hearts," Zanipolo snapped. "I don't care who you are. Whether it's you, our parents or God, I will never let someone tell me who I should be with or love. If it turns out I'm making a mistake, then let me make it so I can learn from it. I would've told pop to shove it once he came up with that charade."

"I guess you're right. I should've done that. There's a lot of things I should've done differently, but there is no point in wallowing in those past mistakes now. I told you about this, so you'd understand why this next ordeal is troublesome for me."

"I'm glad you trust me enough to confide in me such a personal aspect of your life," Zanipolo replied.

Gugliehno turned towards the desk picked up a piece of paper and pen. He scribbled a few words on it then handed it to Zanipolo.

"You're my brother. I should've told you since the beginning. Take this. It's the address for Lana's childhood home, Cyclamen Manor. This was our home when we were married. I'm not sure if she still goes there, but it's very possible."

Zanipolo took the paper and read it before standing to leave. "Promise you won't tell anyone about what I told you!" Gugliehno added.

"Don't worry. I won't. You can trust me."

Gunny, who was stunned by Zanipolo's words, just smiled as he watched his younger brother leave baring the secret burdens that once weighed down his heart for many years.

As if etched in marble, the thought of Darian Mancini was forever engraved into Amadora's memory. His handsome features, warm smile and powerful presence flooded her mind, but they were not the only things occupying it. Last night colored the gray mosaic of the person she desired. He differed from her in every way. Other than being the son of a shopkeeper, who was fine with his simple, unexciting life. His past tour as a marine and later a cop gave him a sense of self-righteousness that was almost infectious. Darian gave up his dreams for the sake of his father. Amadora could never honor the same sacrifice.

Amadora fell back onto her pillow and closed her eyes. Why was he the only thing on her mind? Every touch they shared and every word that escaped his lips became the only things she knew. How come after one night with him she felt she would be lost if they never saw each other again? Why did she feel like this especially after knowing who he was?

Underneath the enchanting words, attentive gaze and handsome looks, one fact remained true. Darian was one of Johnnie Barbone's victims. He was a poor pawn in his selfish scheme to rise higher in Gunny's ranks, and Amadora was certain a man like him probably hated him for doing so. She had not confirmed her suspicions just yet but remembered the hatred radiating from his eyes when he had his hands around Johnnie's throat.

Amadora understood the risks involved with this little tryst. Darian did not seem like a person who would forgive a betrayal easily. She had to make sure he never connected Barbone to the attack, and never found out that Johnnie Barbone was really her.

Dread swept over her as thoughts of revelation seeped in. Amadora wrapped her hand around her neck as the specter of every callus of his firm grip imprinted her skin. She squealed as air escaped her lungs and his pressure against her throat increased.

In that instance, where unconsciousness lingered, another emotion crept inside her: pleasure.

Amadora gasped for air, breaking the powerful, arousing spell that enveloped her, and smiled. She was glad she had the strength to escape. She could not let an attractive brute like him stop her before he reached her goal, but she longed to see him again... not only because she enjoyed his company. But because Amadora enjoyed this teeter totter between bliss and danger. She enjoyed the thrill of this romantic hide-and-seek with the one man who could make everything she desired come tumbling down.

Once the rumblings of her mind calmed, Amadora grabbed her robe from off the closet doorknob, wrapped it around her, and left the room. She walked into the kitchen in a daze, ignoring two shadows sitting in her peripheral.

Samantha and Anna sat at the round wooden table in the corner of the tiled kitchen floor. They watched Amadora quietly as she went from the fridge to the cabinets, caught in a trance. They exchanged worried looks waiting for her to notice them, but time marched on without a single acknowledgement.

Anna placed her cup on the table before breaking the suffocating silence.

"Good morning, Dora. I didn't see you come in last night. They're really working you like a dog. What time did you get in?"

Amadora jerked back, spilling orange juice on the counter in front of her.

"Shit. Anna, you scared me. When did you get there?" Amadora grabbed a rag from the sink and wiped up the mess.

"We've been here talking for quite some time until you waltzed in. You seem out of it. Did you have a rough night?" Anna sipped her coffee while her sharp eyes monitored Amadora's every move.

"Not really..." Amadora replied.

"Where did you go? You left your Johnnie Barbone get up here." Samantha asked. "Did you go on a date?"

"A date? Don't be ridiculous, Sam," Amadora turned away, blushing.

"I guess you normally get all dolled up while traipsing around with a picnic basket just to go for walks?" Anna smirked.

"No. But..." Amadora bit her lip, trying to concoct some excuse, but she could not find one. "You're right. I went on a date last night."

Anna and Samantha glanced at her, smiling from ear to ear. "Come on. Tell us. What's his name? When did you meet? And why haven't you mentioned him before?" Samantha pried.

"His name is Darian. We first met at the ball and last night was the second time we spent time together." Amadora stared at the counter before continuing. "I was worried about what you'd think about us if I mentioned him, so I didn't even bother saying anything."

Her friends burst into a fit of laughter until their lungs ached after a while.

"You're a queer one, Dora. You come up with this crazy scheme and rope us all in it. But when it comes to finding a boyfriend, you're terrified to let us in. That just doesn't make sense," Anna chuckled.

"I'm not terrified. I was worried you wouldn't accept the news well," Amadora corrected meeting Anna's gaze.

"I don't get why you would be. We're friends. We want you to be happy and wouldn't judge you for trying to find some normalcy in all this chaos," Samantha said.

"I know that, but still wasn't sure," Amadora replied.

"But why?" Anna asked, concerned by Amadora's avoidance.

Amadora bit her lip, trying to create the right words to soften the blow of her paramour's identity. She preferred to keep this information to herself but knew if she did, her friends might find out on their own and this bit of deception could rupture their trust in her. That was a risk Amadora could not afford. As long as Johnnie Barbone existed, she needed them to help her get through this.

"I wasn't entirely honest about how Darian and I met. The first time I met him wasn't at the ball but as Johnnie."

Samantha and Anna looked at one another, confused.

"What do you mean?" Samantha asked.

"Did you work together?" Anna added.

Amadora laughed sheepishly. "No, not exactly. He was my target."

"Oh god, Dora! What did you do to that poor man?" Sam exclaimed.

"Nothing too bad. They ordered me to trash his place. During the debacle, we scuffled, and I knocked him unconscious while barely escaping in one piece," Amadora explained.

"Let me get this straight. You trashed his placed, knocked him out, cost him a lot of money in damages and now you're dating him. Yeah, that sounds like quite the love story to me, a perfect union between a sadist and her victim," Anna's lips curled. "I'm not surprised by this revelation. I just can't tell if you're just doing this out of some sick thrill or because you might actually like him."

"I'm not that cold-hearted, Anna. Of course, I went out with him only because I like him," Amadora pouted.

"Even if that's the case, do you think that's wise? God forbid he finds out the truth. Do you know this man well enough to trust he wouldn't try to harm you?" Samantha cautioned.

"I understand that. I've struggled with that fact ever since I met him again at the ball." Amadora leaned on her hand, contemplating the moments they shared.

"Struggle with what? It shouldn't be that hard, since all you must do is stop seeing him," Anna stated plainly.

"It's not as easy as that."

"What do you mean, Dora?" Sam stopped Anna when she noticed Amadora's withdrawal.

"Don't tell me you're falling for him?"

Samantha wanted to go to her friend's side to see for herself if her nagging suspicions held any truth, but she could tell by Amadora's behavior she did not want to say any more about the topic.

"Don't worry. I'm not falling for him," Amadora smiled while turning from them and walking over to the refrigerator for more juice. "Sometimes you can be ridiculous, Sam. How could I fall for someone I barely know?"

Amadora pulled out a fresh glass. "I'm hungry. What do we have to eat around here, anyway?"

Samantha quietly watched Amadora as she pretended the feelings pasted on her face were nonexistent. She wanted to say something but knew Amadora had her reasons that she did not want to admit them. Amadora understood the danger this man brought. She probably also understood that eventually she must choose between him or Johnnie.

The tension around the breakfast table was so heavy it lingered in the room long after everyone left. During breakfast, no one said a word and just quickly finished up so they could go their own way. Anna went to the store while Amadora went to shower and got ready for the day. Samantha volunteered to clean up so she could dismiss all the awkward energy swirling around her.

Samantha watched the bubbles in the sink pop one after the other and sighed. The murky reflection staring back at her stirred the image of Amadora's confusion from earlier. Samantha hated seeing her friend in that state but could not do anything. Amadora made it clear she had this situation under control; but Samantha knew that was not true. Amadora was in denial and until she realized it, there was nothing Samantha could do but worry.

Samantha could not understand why Amadora would do this. First, she came up with this ridiculous charade and ropes everyone near her to play along just so she could get into her father's business. Now she had the audacity to fall for one of Johnnie's victims. How could she do such a thing?

Amadora, whose only obsession has been winning over her father's approval, was now willing to jeopardize her entire plan. Samantha never thought something like this could happen. Amadora had a one-track mind. When she wanted something, she never deviated from her desired path or let anything stand in her way. But what was different now? Why did she go against everything she believed in for some random guy?

Samantha grumbled in frustration. She could not believe Amadora would make everyone's lives more difficult than they already were because of her foolish desires.

"You must really hate doing dishes?"

Samantha broke from her thoughts and looked over towards the door. Zanipolo stood in front of the door, smirking. She was so caught in her thoughts that she did not even hear him come back.

"I guess you can say that." Sam said softly to herself. "Polo, you left early this morning. Where did you go?"

"Were you worried about me?" Zanipolo teased.

"No. I was only wondering..." Samantha blushed and returned her focus to the sink.

Zanipolo's smile faded. "I went to report what we found out yesterday. I'm back because I need Amador- I mean Johnnie. We have something we need to take care of."

"Well, 'Johnnie' was in the back taking a shower. 'He' might be in his room already getting dressed," Samantha replied.

Zanipolo tipped his hat to her and made his way to Amadora's room.

A soft rap sounded on the door while Amadora brushed her hair. She called to whomever was on the other side.

"It's unlocked. Come in."

The door opened and her brother entered. Concern cracked his usual charming mask. His expressions faded as he focused on Amadora. She knew immediately that he received their next orders from Gunny. She tied her hair back so she could change into Johnnie.

"You received new orders from Gunny. What did he tell you?" Amadora asked.

"He told me a lot..." Zanipolo said softly, remembering the information he learned about Gugliehno. "He gave me a probable location to where Lana might be."

"A location?" Amadora asked. "I guess I shouldn't ask how he knows for sure this is the right place."

Zanipolo turned back to the door, clenching his teeth to help conceal the secret Gugliehno entrusted to him. He lingered in silence for a moment before finding the right response.

"You're right. You shouldn't. Just get ready. Gunny wants results as soon as possible."

Amadora did not press the matter any further. She turned away and waved him off so she could get ready.

A loud pounding noise broke Casimiro from his slumber. He sat up in his bed and paused, trying to figure out where the noise came from. As it persisted, he jumped from his bed, taking care not to wake Giacinta, who, by some miracle, slept soundly through this annoying racket. He grabbed his robe and dashed out of the bedroom.

As he rushed down the hall, he frantically searched for his belt. He fought the booming ruckus growing louder as he neared the source. At the door he fumbled through the locks and chains, unlocking them as quickly as he could, but his groggy state and the dark hallway made it difficult to see what he was doing. The knocks increased as he struggled through the locks.

"I'm trying to unlock the fucking door! Quit your obnoxious banging already!" Casimiro snapped while unlocking the final lock.

When he opened the door, he was greeted by a sour faced Gugliehno, and a sheepish Lorenzo still dressed in his night clothes.

"About time. I thought we'd have to kick in the door. What took you so long?" Gunny growled, pushing past Casimiro and walking inside.

"Sorry that I didn't rush over here and open the door like a little lapdog, but I was sleeping like most people at this hour," Casimiro said, closing the door behind Lorenzo.

"Sorry for the intrusion, but Gunny needed to vent about the current findings of the investigation," Lorenzo apologized, fixing his disheveled hair with his hand and following Gugliehno as he walked into Casimiro's living room.

"I see. That's why he's in this wonderful mood this morning," Casimiro grumbled, closing the living room door and sitting in a chair next to Lorenzo.

"Zanipolo visited me this morning," Gunny began coolly.

"Oh. So, you know?" Casimiro said.

"I see. He told you," Lorenzo grumbled to himself.

"You two know already? How?" Gunny snapped.

"Of course, I know. Brock filled me in on everything," Lorenzo replied.

"Zanipolo told me directly when he came to the main house last night to report to your father. He was furious by the news and declared war on the Rosillis. However, I convinced him against retaliating publicly and proposed a more discreet approach. I told him that striking in the shadows would be the best plan since they wouldn't expect it and could prevent a massive bloodshed on our part."

"That's an excellent idea," Lorenzo added.

"Can you stop acting so casual, as if this is a war against just any family? This isn't simple!" Gunny yelled.

Casimiro noticed this was harder on Gunny than he expected it would. Until now, he protested his hatred for her, so Casimiro was not sure about the true factor motivating his sour disposition.

"Sorry for being insensitive. We didn't realize this would still affect you," Lorenzo said, leaning on the arm of the couch.

"We should've known as your friends how you really felt," Casimiro added.

"No need to feel sorry. It's true I'm affected by all of this, but not because of any reserved feelings. I'm worried about my children. This affects them more than it affects me. I could keep this from them, but one day they will find out the truth and the role their father played in their mother's demise." Gunny collapsed into the armchair across from his friends. He cradled his head in his hands.

"You came rushing in a fit over the fact your ex-wife was behind the attack on your main warehouse. Now, you want me to believe your anger stems from what your children might think about you in the future. Please stop the bullshit, because it's not convincing me. No matter how you try to spin it, you won't convince yourself either," Casimiro scolded.

"He's right, Gunny. Eventually, you need to admit that you still have feelings for that insane woman and hate that you might take the life of the one woman you ever truly loved," Lorenzo added.

Gugliehno glared at his friends, annoyed but softened once he realized what they said was true. He took off his hat and ran his fingers through his hair.

"I hate that you might be right. I just don't understand why. There is a gentle whisper that echoes through the deep corners of my heart that still cares about her. And no matter how hard I try, I can't silence it." Gunny shook his head in aggravation. "I understand pop wants revenge for that incident, but I don't feel comfortable being the force behind her demise. I don't think I could handle it."

"Don't worry yourself about this just yet. We may still avoid it," Casimiro walked over to Gunny and placed a hand on his shoulder.

"Also, it's too early to count your wins. Lana is very crafty and won't be found easily, even with our best men searching for her. Don't underestimate her," Lorenzo pointed out.

"That's true. Besides, no matter the outcome, we will try to protect you from any pain that might come," Casimiro added.

The support from Gugliehno's friends quelled his concerns. He had no words left to respond. He placed his hand on top of Casimiro's in thanks. Casimiro accomplished one of the most difficult feats ever satiating Gunny's worries.

However, Casimiro knew it would not be the end of them. They would return; and Casimiro hoped when they did, they would not return stronger than ever before. He prayed they would not cause Gunny to do something he would deeply regret.

Zanipolo swerved down the long driveway leading to the tall, black iron gates of Cyclamen Manor. He stopped behind two black cars parked on one side of the road. Zanipolo left to check them out while Johnnie followed cautiously behind. Zanipolo circled around one car and examined it. Johnnie withdrew his gun while covering Polo's back.

The cars did not have any license plates. Johnnie walked to the front door and tugged on the handle. It was unlocked, so he opened it. Zanipolo motioned towards the car, giving Johnnie the okay to check it out.

Johnnie kept watch outside while Johnnie searched inside. After a few moments, he came out and tucked away his gun.

"What are you doing?" Zanipolo asked.

"These cars are okay. They're Brock's," Johnnie replied plainly.

"How do you know that?"

"Ever since Larry died, Brock keeps his watch tucked underneath the front passenger seat. If you look, you'll find it wrapped in a velvet cloth," Johnnie pointed inside, stepping aside so Zanipolo could check for himself.

Zanipolo rummaged under the front passenger seat cushion. Just like Johnnie said, there was a piece of cloth wrapped around a hard substance.

"You're right, but why does he keep it here?" Zanipolo unraveled the cloth and examined the charred watch before wrapping it back up and replacing it in its original spot.

"That used to be where Larry sat when they worked together," Johnnie answered simply.

Johnnie tensed while fighting back his own looming anger and guilt. Zanipolo noticed the intensifying conflictions inside Johnnie.

"You miss him, don't you?"

Johnnie glared at Zanipolo, then looked away.

"I... I don't allow myself to get close enough to anyone here to miss them."

"Cut the crap. It's okay to miss him. You're human, after all. Things like this happen in our world. You must embrace it, then move on."

"No!" Johnnie snapped. "It's not okay. That's not how you make it in this world. You can't let a weakness like that overtake you. You must tame your heart along with your head. Those who can't end up the ones who don't survive. I won't be one of them."

"You're partially right. However, it's not a weakness to show your emotions. It's alright. You just must know when and where. Also, concealing your feelings and never dealing with them can just be as deadly. They can be used as leverage against you if discovered. They also can impair your judgment as they build up inside you like a ticking time bomb," Zanipolo warned.

"I can handle it a little while longer. Once I sort this out, I'll deal with my feelings then." Johnnie scanned their surroundings.

Seeing his sister dressed as Johnnie Barbone for just the briefest moments, Zanipolo could no longer recognize her. She transformed into a completely different person. She had no fear or emotion. Amadora became the perfect soldier, who Zanipolo would admire if he did not know the high price that she paid for this new being she created. Zanipolo wondered which she wagered: her humanity, innocence, or heart.

Silence washed over them before Johnnie interrupted it.

"Brock and his men must be checking the estate's perimeter. It's your call, boss. What should we do? Do we go look for them or stay here and wait?"

Zanipolo closed the door and leaned against the car. "No. Let's wait. There's no sign of foul play, so we don't need to be hasty."

Johnnie nodded in understanding while scanning the area. Zanipolo walked over to the large iron gates and examined the entrance. The tall, pointed roof and towers looming over the vast yard created a gloomy aura. It was empty, with only a few stray critters calling it home.

"Come, look at this," Zanipolo waved Johnnie over.

"What is it?"

"I don't think anyone has been here for ages. It seems dead, doesn't it?" Zanipolo looked back at the manor.

"Maybe that's what Lana wants us to believe. You should know that looks can deceive," Johnnie smirked. A cunning woman like her could orchestrate a simple trick of perception with ease. If I was a top Rosilli dog, I would lie low in a desolate place like this to avoid my enemies."

"That makes sense. We should stay on our guard while inside." Zanipolo returned his attention to the house. This time, he envisioned his brother with his eldest kids sharing a life with that psychotic woman. He still could not grasp that that demon was once human and capable of love.

A tap on his shoulder interrupted his thoughts.

"Brock and his men have returned," Johnnie said, pointing to the far end of the gates.

Zanipolo nodded and returned to reality.

"Just in time. Once they get here, well go inside."

Brock reported their findings to Zanipolo. They confirmed Zanipolo's initial suspicions. There were no signs that anyone was or had been there for a while.

"Boss, what should we do next?" Brock asked.

Zanipolo scanned the area once more. He did not see any point in continuing their search, but Johnnie was right. Lana was a master at covering her tracks. It would not surprise him if she would hide in plain sight. He could not underestimate her.

"Let's split into groups to cover more ground. We'll see what clues we can find about her whereabouts. Once we're finished, let's meet in front of the house." He turned to Brock and continued. "Pick two of your men to stand guard in the front while we're inside searching."

While Brock and his men entered the manor, Zanipolo stopped Johnnie from going any farther. His strained expression alerted Johnnie to his intentions.

"When we go inside, stay close to me," Johnnie nodded in agreement and followed Zanipolo through the gates.

Walking to the mansion, a lonely presence swept over Johnnie with a cold, steady breeze. The towers' tall shadows lining along each side of the building transported him to a world surrounded by sorrow and despair. It slowly drained what little joy he had as he drew close to the large black doors.

Passing through the threshold, his heartbeats slowed and thumped loudly in his ear. Johnnie followed Zanipolo down the dark corridors, searching each room they passed. They found nothing but dust.

At the end of the corridor, they ended up in a gigantic dome, glass-enclosed room. White flowers decorated the large stained glass surrounding them. The frosted light that passed through them cast over the marble floor and white iron benches. Book-ending the enormous marble fireplace across from the benches stood two massive statues. An ethereal figure adorned in long, flowing garments danced on a round scene of earth. The marble figure's long wavy hair and joyous expression eased the gloomy atmosphere of this vacant manor, but all her calming radiance vanished when they looked at the menacing figure on the other side of the fireplace. Brandishing a large spear and shield, stood a beastly form sparsely draped in robes and hidden beneath a fierce helmet ready for war. His intense presence played as a warning to anyone who came upon it.

Johnnie's eyes drifted from the structure and fell upon the fireplace's mantle. Under the heaps of dust, a square outline peered from underneath. Johnnie retrieved a handkerchief from his pocket and wiped away the dust, revealing an old picture.

The scene portrayed in the picture was of a young mother and father smiling happily on the grounds of the manor as they played with their little daughter. Their attire was pretty dated about twenty years out of style, but the little girl's features caught Johnnie's attention. She seemed familiar, but he could not put his finger on how.

Johnnie grabbed the picture and showed it to Zanipolo.

"Look at this photo, Polo. Doesn't this little girl look familiar?" Johnnie pointed to the child in the photograph.

Zanipolo's jaw clenched at the sight of the girl. She looked exactly like their niece, Loretta, but it was clear from the type of clothes she wore in that picture was at least thirty years old. Such an uncanny resemblance only left one possibility. The child must have been Loretta's mother, Lana.

"Put that down. It's not relevant to why we're here. Try to stay focused," Zanipolo scolded coolly.

Zanipolo's mood shifted once seeing the picture did not go unnoticed. Something about the picture bothered him. Johnnie waited until Zanipolo turned his back and looked closer at the picture. He opened the frame and removed the picture. He examined the back of it and found some writing that read:

"The best moments of my life spent with my wife, Olivia, and my daughter, Lana."

Confusion washed over Johnnie as he reread the caption. Why did this old picture of Lana create that reaction in Zanipolo? This was from a time before she turned into the crazy bloodthirsty monster she was today. She was only a child and not the least threatening.

Curiosity burned inside Johnnie. He needed to know everything Zanipolo knew about Lana to understand why he reacted like that. He stuffed the picture into his pocket, then continued uncovering the pictures on the mantle. Each picture was similar, except for one with only the father. In this scene, he pulled the lever of a gigantic machine. Tools and some antique wall sconces covered the stone room it stood in.

"Polo, what do you know about Lana's father?" Johnnie called over to Zanipolo, who was searching on the other side of the room.

"Not much. To many, old man Rosilli is her father since he's taken care of her for years. Her real father was a brilliant inventor with no ties to the Rosillis' business. He made a bunch of contraptions for the government. Why?"

Johnnie shrugged. "No reason. Just curious and wanted to get some insight on how she turned into the person she is now. What about her mother?"

"She was a very popular musician in her day. Other than that, there's not much known about her."

"What happened to them?"

"I don't know how, but they died when she was an adolescent, and she became the don's ward." Zanipolo answered briefly. "Come on. I want to check out the rest of this floor before moving to the next ones."

Johnnie followed Zanipolo while his mind drifted back to the information he just learned. Every room was empty, with no sign anyone ever entered them in years, but still they searched. Once they cleared every room on the first floor, they preceded to the stairwell and climbed to the next floor.

Searching the upper floors produced similar results. Zanipolo gave up hope in finding any clue by the time they reached the top floor of the manor. He lost all expectations for finding a clue as they searched the last few rooms. After finding nothing relevant, Zanipolo was about to give the order to return outside, but a subtle glint in the corner of his eye caught his attention. He followed the glistening light until he reached a sharp corner where a small wall sconce flickered, illuminating the tall shadow of the wooden door. The door looked out of place compared to the rest of the ones throughout the mansion. This one was made from heavy driftwood fastened by bulky, iron hinges that groaned in a husky, rustic voice when they moved.

Fear glanced about him, triggering his caution. He checked the long, spiraling hall for any traps, but the ascending stairway was free of any. They climbed the stairs until it opened to a large circular room bathed in darkness.

Zanipolo ordered Johnnie to remain where he stood while he searched for a light switch. He felt along the walls for a few moments before he found something that seemed like a switch and flicked it up.

Light rushed over the room, chasing away the darkness and illuminating the unknown. Smiles crossed their faces when it appeared their search finally bore some fruit. The room was free of dust and cobwebs. A few articles of women's clothing hung in the closet and the vials of makeup and perfume sitting on the vanity were evidence of a woman staying here recently.

The living quarters were separated into several rooms. They stood in the main bedroom, but there were several other doors leading to unknown places.

"We might make some headway if we split up. I'm going to look through this room and those doors over there. See what's behind that door over there? Maybe Lana left something behind that might hint at her whereabouts," Zanipolo stated.

Johnnie did as commanded and checked out the small door opposite the bedroom. When he pushed open the door and walked inside, he entered a dark parlor. He flicked on the light and searched every shelf but found nothing of importance there. It was not until he searched the desk until he found something of interest.

Johnnie rummaged through the top drawers and found nothing. As he rustled through the papers in the bottom drawers, he found a stack of photos. Johnnie flipped through the pictures, then froze in shock after seeing their contents.

The photos contained playful scenarios of a young, happy family, but this time, it was not Lana with her parents. The ones in the photos with her were Gunny, Loretta, and Aniela. Johnnie finally understood why Lana's baby picture looked familiar and the meaning behind Zanipolo's reaction. Lana resembled Loretta in those pictures because she was his nieces' birth mother.

Johnnie faded as Amadora seized control. Confusion raced through her mind. She could not understand how Gugliehno could have hidden a separate life with another woman. By the looks of the photos, this was before he introduced Susan and the girls. They could not have been taken more than a few years prior. Why did her brother keep this secret from her?

What Amadora could not understand was how the two oldest kids acted like Susan was their actual mother and seemed to completely forget about Lana. There were several times when Lana and the girls were in the same area, and they never acknowledged her even once. Aniela was probably too young to remember her, but Loretta was not. How were Gunny and Susan able to alter their memories?

Amadora had a lot on her plate at the moment, but her curiosity was getting the best of her. She needed to know the truth behind these photos and find out why Gunny never told her about it. The thought crossed her mind to ask Zanipolo and find out what he might know, but she doubted he would know much. Gugliehno and him were not that close, so he might know very little. Besides, approaching him now would not be ideal.

The best source would be Gunny himself. However, if Amadora approached her brother prying about his past relationship, Gunny would wonder how she discovered the truth. That would unleash a whole can of worms she was not prepared to encounter.

The only way Amadora would uncover the truth was to investigate the matter herself.

With no clues, Johnnie and the others left Cyclamen Manor unaware their biggest link was there the whole time, watching their every move. Tucked away within some hidden passages, a deadly creature lurked, watching its prey closely, driven by its deepening blood lust. Its unflinching gaze followed every man who entered the grounds, but only one caught its attention: Johnnie Barbone.

It watched Johnnie as he rummaged through his master's belongings and slowly pieced the puzzles of his theory. It waited until Johnnie stood in front of the desk, then pressed a button on one of Lana's father's contraptions that was built into a painting and snuck back into the shadows. He got exactly what his mistress wanted, and no one suspected a thing.

The small, red brick building housing the Green Isle Pub became clearer as Darian walked down the narrow alley. Drunken bums lined the surrounding walls, slouched over the corners, throwing up, pissing on the walls, or yelling incoherently. The intensifying stench of foul alcohol made Darian nauseous while he fought past to enter the bar.

This bar was owned by his close friend and former fellow service member Riley McGinny. Darian used to live with Riley before his father's health worsened, forcing him to return home. After leaving the force to help his dad, he needed to talk to his friend about all the chaos plaguing his life but never had the time to visit him since he lived all the way in New Jersey, and Riley's paranoid ass did not believe in phones. But after recent events, he desperately needed advice from his close friend.

Darian pushed through the rustic wooden, stained glass-embedded door and entered the smoke-filled bar. He brushed past hordes of alcohol-infused patrons, tossing darts and chuckling over pints of beer, and walked over to the long, L-shaped bar. He smiled at the pretty barmaid as she greeted him.

"Welcome to Green Isle Pub! I'm Fiona! Sit down and take a load off! In the meantime, let me know what I can get ya!"

"I'm not thirsty, Fiona. I'm just here to see Riley." Darian smiled.

"Riley…" The barmaid racked her brain for a moment. "He was here a moment ago. I don't know where he ran off to."

"Don't worry. I'm here. Just fixing something in the kitchen, but I'm back." A blonde man in a grungy looking apron came rushing in from a gray door behind the bar. He wiped his hands on his apron and smiled when his eyes fell upon Darian.

"Darian, my friend, so good to see you! It's been a while!" The man extended his hand and shook Darian's in an anxious embrace. "I know it's been a few years, Riley. How have you been?"

"Nothing's changed. I'm still running this old joint on my own. If it wasn't for Lady Fi here. I'd be lost," Riley's thick Irish-accented voice reverberated with joy.

"Still living the bachelor life, I see?" Darian smirked.

"Yeah. Much like yourself," Riley winked, poking fun at his friend.

"I guess you're right. But who knows, maybe that might all change?"

"What? Don't tell me you've found a little lass to give up your wild ways for?"

"Possibly..."

"Come now. Tell me all about her," Riley pried.

"She's a fresh breath of air in a world filled with so much darkness."

"What's her name?"

"Amadora Morelli," Darian answered.

"Amadora? Basilio Morelli's daughter?" Riley looked shock by this news.

"Yes. Don't remind me," Darian grumbled.

"I see... Good thing the love of the youngest daughter of New Jersey top mafia kingpin hasn't completely tainted you."

"Of course not. No broad could kill my hatred for those thugs," Darian growled. "The main reason I like her is because she's not involved in her family's world, but close enough that she might have overheard something useful to me."

"I see, so you're using the poor lass to exact revenge on whoever trashed your shop?"

"Not entirely," Darian replied.

"Be careful, my friend. I don't know much about Amadora Morelli, but I know her father and brothers won't take kindly to you if you trample over her heart," Riley said.

"Let's hope that never happens."

"I heard about the incident at your store. I sent some money over to help. It wasn't much, but I hope it helped a little."

"Yes. Thanks. It helped some."

"Darian, you're always so modest. Don't be afraid to tell me the truth that my pitiful donation didn't help at all," Riley chuckled.

"No. I couldn't do that. I'm truly thankful for your help. Don't worry too much about it. It was hard at first, but soon everything will be fine."

"Really? How exactly?"

"I got a small loan to help buy supplies to repair the damages from the attack.

Once the supplies arrive, I can start fixing up the place."

"Where did you get the loan?"

Darian hesitated and gritted his teeth.

"By your reaction, I guess you didn't get it from the bank."

"Unfortunately, no. I didn't. But before you judge me, I want to point out that it wasn't my idea but my father's. He trusts the Morellis more than he does banks."

"I bet there was a steep price to pay for asking for their help."

"Yup. If relinquishing all my pride and morals counts. They're not charging interest on the loan if we pay the protection fees again."

"Well, that's not too bad. Some of the rival families are much more ruthless to defectors."

"You sound exactly like my father. Why are you so optimistic about the Morellis?"

"Unlike you, I don't have a problem with them. Basilio is an old friend of my father. Compared to the other crime bosses, Basilio is the most rational and humane."

"Comparing him to other criminals is setting a low bar."

"He can't be that heartless if he raised a charming enough daughter to lure you in and make you fall head-over-heels for her."

"I haven't fallen for her."

"Are you joking? You're completely smitten with her."

Darian smirked in defeat. "Am I really that transparent?"

"Like water. I enjoy seeing you this way, and don't want you to risk everything by betraying your new love's trust. You want to know who sent the man who destroyed your store, right?"

"Yes."

"Fine. I can see what I can find out. I still have some old contacts who are actively engaging with the rival families. Just leave poor Amadora out of this mess. Don't make her a martyr in your personal vendetta. Even though she's her father's favorite, she has nothing to do with his world."

"You're right. I wouldn't dare hurt her."

Riley's words rang true through his heart. Amadora was not like many girls her age. Her kind and innocent heart intoxicated him while her warm beauty further enveloped him in its soothing embrace. How could he even think about using someone like her to satisfy his own selfish desires? She did not deserve it. Who knew a devil like Basilio Morelli could create an angel like Amadora?

Darkness blanketed the land covering Lana's dimly lit room in shadows. Draped in a flowing silk robe and her long wavy hair falling freely over her shoulders, Lana paced the room impatiently. She did not give a damn about the results of Gugliehno's

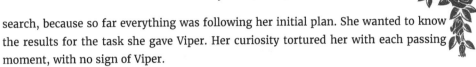

search, because so far everything was following her initial plan. She wanted to know the results for the task she gave Viper. Her curiosity tortured her with each passing moment, with no sign of Viper.

Lana checked the clock multiple times, cursing Viper for his delay. She desperately wanted to know who Johnnie Barbone was and what made him tick. She needed to know the face of one of her greatest adversaries.

Lana did not completely blame Viper for his lateness, because her new hideout was at the top of the mountains hidden in thick woods miles from the closest neighbor and even those homes were owned by executives of the Rosilli family. This old rickety manor was what remained of her grandparents' home. The roads leading to it were a treacherous drive unless you took a four-legged beast. It was the perfect spot to lie low until the next phase began.

Lana huffed and spun around the bed post until she collapsed onto the soft cushions. Her blood pressure was at its peak as her longing for Gunny's prodigy intensified. She grabbed a small decorative pillow and prepared to scream her frustrations into its soft bosom, but she was stopped when a dark figure glided into the room and kneeled at her feet. A thin, bony arm extended out to her, holding a small rectangular paper.

"Sorry for the wait, mistress. This is for you."

"Finally! Give me that!" Lana snatched the picture from him and pressed it against her chest. "I have to see him."

Lana brought the photo up to her face and scanned the image engraved there. She stared at it for a long while emotionlessly. She turned it in different directions to see it from other angles before collapsing on the bed and tossing the picture to the side.

"Leave me. I want to be alone."

Viper nodded and slithered out of the room, leaving Lana to bask in a state of sweet satisfaction. Johnnie Barbone was young and handsome. His boyish face created an innocence that lured Lana into desiring him more.

This picture was not enough. She needed to see him in person. Lana wanted to understand the brain nestled behind those alluring eyes. She wanted Johnnie Barbone all for herself so she could find out how manly he was, both mentally and physically.

12

A Promise of Forever

'When the wounds on my heart heal, their scars will remain. But I don't care, because even if more wounds form, I'll never be afraid if you're by my side,' Thoughts of Giacinta Morelli.

Curiosity prevented Amadora from entering the land of dreams. Endless questions replayed nonstop in her mind. She could not understand how the brother she once believed told her everything could hide an entire life from her.

Amadora always ran to Gunny for everything. Whether it was about a fight with one of the neighbors' kids or something trivial like not getting what she wanted from their parents, Amadora came to her older brother about anything and until recently she believed he did the same Amadora could not help but feel betrayed, but soon simmered down. Was Gunny any different from her right now?

Gunny kept his life with Lana secret, because he believed he was doing what was best for the family. Amadora could not say her reasons for withholding her secrets were the same. In this regard, they differed. If she accomplished her goal, she did not worry about the possible collateral on the way. Regardless, Amadora was determined to uncover the truth. She needed to know more about their relationship. She needed to know more about their relationship. She needed to make sure Gunny's past would not interfere with Amadora's future.

Amadora debated the various ways she could use to uncover the truth. She could ask him about their marriage, but Gunny would demand to know how she found out about it. Amadora did not know who knew about the affair aside from Zanipolo, so she could blow her cover if she took that route.

Amadora pulled out the picture from the manor. She could use it as an excuse for how she knew about it, but that might intensify his suspicions. It would not take long until he realized the only place where she could have gotten it and put two-and-two together about her identity. Even Amadora's usual pleas of ignorance and creative stories would not fool Gunny. He was far from gullible enough to fall for that and would know she was lying.

Amadora was too close to her goal to deal with any complications, but her curiosity was killing her. She needed to quell her nagging concerns without alerting her brother's suspicions by listening in when Polo reported to Gunny.

Amadora went out to Zanipolo's car and snuck under the black tarp covering his backseat. She laid flat, slowing her breath while trying to calm her racing heart as she waited patiently. After finding nothing useful at Lana's manor, Zanipolo said he would meet with Gugliehno to report their findings and get their next orders. This meeting was the only chance Amadora had to get the answers to her questions.

Amadora did not make a peep once Zanipolo got into the car and drove off. Being tucked underneath the thick tarp laying as stiff as a board for a long period was uncomfortable. The gentle rumble of the car as it swerved down a series of winding roads. Amadora's pulse pounded through her skin and her heart painfully throbbed in her ears.

Amadora snuck through the shadow-filled halls until she reached Gunny's office. She ducked aside while listening to their conversation through a small opening in the doorway.

"We found nothing leading us to Viper or Lana. Although there were signs, she used the house as a safe house recently," Zanipolo informed, trying to mask the weariness in his voice.

"What signs?" Gunny asked, with a hint of anticipation.

"There was a large bedroom in the west tower..."

"West tower?" Gunny's voice faltered as those words escaped his mouth.

"Yes. Exactly. But..." Zanipolo responded, slightly surprised.

"Remember, we lived there for years. I know that estate like the back of my hand. That room I know especially well, because it was ours."

These words pained Gugliehno. Amadora heard it in his voice. She never heard Gunny sound like this before. He was always so cheerful that she forgot anything could hurt him. She wanted to ease her brother's pain, but she knew there was nothing she could do to help him.

"I searched that room. It was clear that someone used it recently," Zanipolo continued.

Gugliehno did not know how to process that information. He wondered why she would stay there with those shadows of their former life. Maybe she stayed there to bask in memories of a happier time, or possibly she stayed only because it was a great hiding place.

Like fire trapped in an airless room, his hope quickly vanished as he thought about the slew of men who defiled their bed. Anger rushed through his body, tensing every muscle. Zanipolo noticed Gugliehno's strange behavior.

"Gunny, What's wrong? If there's something bothering you, tell me."

Gugliehno's eyes grew wide as he stared at his brother for a moment before letting out a sigh and averting his gaze.

"Ever since I found out about Lana's involvement, my head has been spinning in emotional circles. At first, I suspected she was involved; but after realizing my suspicions were true, I prayed it was all a lie. A small part of me hopes she hid somewhere the remnants of the woman I once loved in her heart. Only if that was true, maybe I could save her once and for all."

Zanipolo held back, criticizing Gunny, because his brother was opening up and showing what little faith remained inside him. The last thing he needed was criticism.

"I don't know what to say. At times like these, hold onto that belief. Hopefully, it'll help you as this situation progresses. I wish I knew the version of Lana from when you were together; maybe, I would have a better view about her. The only things I know about her are based on rumors, so my advice might not be much..."

Amadora pulled away from the door and ran back to the front foyer before hearing the rest of their conversation. She could not take any more of Gunny's pain. Its intensity shot through her body and filled her with helplessness. She hated leaving, knowing there was nothing she could do to help him.

When Amadora was in her hiding place, she did nothing but conceal the pain and sadness she absorbed from Gunny. She wanted to know the truth but could not bear listening to it anymore. Maybe this was one secret that was better off remaining unknown.

Who would have ever guessed Giacinta Morelli would finally find true happiness? Who would have thought she, of all people, could find peace after so much chaos? She never believed someone would want to get close enough to her to love her; and never in a million years would she have believed that she could love someone in return.

No one believed this could happen, not even Giacinta. Even now, everything seemed like a fantasy. The woman staring back at her in the mirror was unrecognizable. That infectious smile plastered on her face that never faded, no matter what she did, was foreign to her. How could one man make her feel like that? He awakened feelings she forgot she possessed, an innocence and freedom she forgot she had, the freedom to love.

Even though her feelings were still new to her, she loved the joy created by his love's warmth. Giacinta loved seeing herself grow more with each passing moment they shared. Every moment with him was more precious than all the riches she possessed. Casimiro was unlike any man she ever encountered. His sweet and caring heart was more addictive than any drug she ever enjoyed, but aside from their romantic moments, they never acted on their passions.

Sometimes she slept at his place because it was too late for her to return home. But Casimiro did nothing she did not want or try to pressure her. Even though she wanted him, they could never reach that point. Something always interrupted them or Casimiro would stop before going any farther. She did not understand his hesitation. It was obvious he wanted her too, but something held him back. She wanted to know what, but how could she find out the truth?

If Giacinta asked him right out, he might misunderstand her and be offended. It is a delicate matter and did not want to think she was slighting him. But she wanted to know what she was doing wrong, and why he was not giving her his all.

Giacinta gazed at a silver pearl bracelet dangling from her wrist. She played with the small silver cross dangling from it and drifted into thoughts of him.

"Giacinta, you have a beautiful gift from your beau," Fiorella beamed, placing a large colorful bouquet on the table next to Giacinta.

"Mama, I didn't hear you come in," Giacinta looked at her mother, surprised. "How do you know he sent those?"

"They must be from him. Who else would send flowers to your doorstep?"

"When did he bring them?" Giacinta asked excitedly. She ran her finger along the soft petals of the flower, then picked up the card.

"What's with all the questions, Giacinta? Just read the card."

Giacinta scanned over Casimiro's words quietly to herself. She gushed over the card.

"He invited me to dinner."

"Oh, that sounds romantic. You better get ready. This might be a special night for you," Fiorella said lovingly.

Giacinta held the card in her hand and brought it close to her cheek to feel what bit of his warmth still lingered. God must have overheard her prayers and gave her the perfect chance to talk to Casimiro about her concerns. A comforting feeling washed over her.

Amadora walked around the neighborhood near Anna's place. She was not going anywhere in particular. She only wanted to clear her mind before confronting Zanipolo. Amadora had a lot to review in her mind and needed to regain her composure.

An hour passed before she returned to the apartment. The lights inside were off and everything was quiet. Everyone seemed out; but when she looked at the windows in the living room, she saw Zanipolo. She could not tell if he noticed her, because he was staring into a cup cradled in his hands. However, when she walked behind him and tapped his shoulder, the surprised expression that followed confirmed her doubts.

"Amadora, there you are. Where did you run off to?"

"I had a lot on my mind, so I went for a walk," Amadora replied, sitting in a chair across from him.

"Traipsing around as Johnnie Barbone must be finally wearing you out," Zanipolo chuckled.

"Yes. It's finally taking a toll on me," Amadora sighed.

"If that's the case, why do you insist on continuing this charade?"

"I'm too close to back out now," Amadora sparred with her brother's annoyed gaze and grinned. "I can admit this job is affecting me, but I can endure it. Until I reach my goal, I must. If I give up now, then everything I've done until now would be for nothing, and I won't let that happen."

"Be careful, Dora. That pride of yours might become the death of you if you don't rein it in," Zanipolo grumbled, returning to the mug in his hands.

"Maybe, but I'll just hope for the best before then," Amadora smirked mischievously. "Now, enough about me. What about you, Polo? It's not like you to be so grossly unaware of your surroundings. What's distracting you?"

"Nothing's bothering me. I'm just still tired. It's still early," Zanipolo said, taking a sip of his coffee.

"That might fool some random off the street, but I'm your sister. I know you too well and can tell when something's wrong. Did Gunny say something about our results?" Amadora asked softly, hoping Zanipolo might let the truth about Gunny's relationship with Lana slip.

"That's not it. Gunny didn't have much to say about that. Something else is on my mind," Zanipolo shook his head.

"Could it be the actual nature of Gunny's relationship with Lana that's bothering you?" Amadora baited.

Zanipolo did not respond immediately. He looked back at her and examined her, then he returned to his coffee.

"They did not have a relationship."

"Don't play dumb. I know they were once married."

"How did you find out?"

"I found some old photos of them and his oldest girls while searching the office at Cyclamen," Amadora answered. Amadora knew she hit a nerve by the fear plastered all over his face.

"Don't look at me like that, Polo. I'm not planning to tell Gunny about this. That would do me more harm than good. Besides, I'm less concerned with his past as I am about how well he's taking the news."

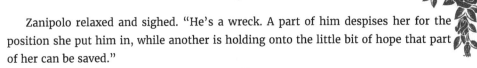

Zanipolo relaxed and sighed. "He's a wreck. A part of him despises her for the position she put him in, while another is holding onto the little bit of hope that part of her can be saved."

"I guess you don't believe that's possible."

"What I believe doesn't matter. I'm more concerned about how Gunny feels. No matter how you look at it, sooner-or-later he'll have to let her go. Pops is absolute in his decision. He wants revenge, and I'm afraid he'll take it no matter the repercussions, even if that means shattering his son's heart."

"Is there anything you could do? You're leading the investigation. We don't have to kill if we find her, right?" Amadora asked.

"It's not that simple. Even if I defied Pop's wishes, I can't guarantee Lana will give us the option to let her go freely. We might be put in a tough position where killing her is the only way we can escape with our lives."

Giacinta sat still as she whisked down the dark woods to Casimiro's secret location. She wrapped her hands around herself, trying to subdue her anxiety. Excited to see him again, she could barely contain her concerns. She did not want to spoil this mysterious night he planned, but her desires burned ferociously and would not settle until she got answers.

Anticipation flowed through her being, fueling her body with a profound longing for the man she loved. Giacinta watched as the city faded from the rear window and a sea of trees took its place. She did not know where they were going, but the calming woods flooding the sides of the road calmed her frustrated mind.

An hour passed before they reached the location. A large lake sparkled under the moonlight. Next to it, a small wooden cottage sat on its edge. At first sight, it was not much but a quaint little hovel; but it meant something to Casimiro, then it must be special. Giacinta wondered why?

Giacinta stepped out of the car and scanned the small wooden structure. She swatted a few bugs that brushed past her face, and immediately, regretted her decision to come here all dressed up. She rushed over to the porch to escape the pesky creatures and knocked on the front door.

A second barely passed before it swung open and Casimiro scooped her in his arms. He held her tight to calm her down, nestling his chin on her head.

"Everything's alright. Come inside quickly."

Casimiro ushered her inside, closed the door and pressed her close to his chest. He kissed her softly on the forehead. His secure embrace quelled Giacinta's anxious mind as she settled deeper into his chest and wrapped her arms around his body.

"Why did you want me to meet you here in this horrid place? You know I'm not an outdoorsy type of girl."

Casimiro lifted her face in his hand and kissed her pouting lips.

"I know, my dear. I'm sorry, but I had to bring you here."

"You had to? How come?" Giacinta asked.

"Because this place is special."

"It's special? Well then, I guess I'll have to suck it up and try to enjoy myself," Giacinta averted her gaze, hiding her flushed cheeks.

"Thank you, my darling," Casimiro tightened his embrace and rested his head by her ear. He exhaled deeply, releasing all worry and relaxing in her soothing scent. "We've been apart for only a day, and it feels like a lifetime. You don't understand how happy I am that you are here. I am helpless without you and want to spend every waking moment with you in my arms."

Giacinta melted into his embrace, hiding her flustered cheeks in his shoulder.

"If you feel that way, then why do you tease me so, you cruel man?"

"Tease you? How have I done that?"

"You always profess sweet words of love and shower me with kisses, but that's all. If you truly want me, then why have you waited so long to make love to me?"

Casimiro paused and looked at Giacinta, surprised. "Giacinta, I didn't know that bothered you. I'm sorry. I never meant to cause a misunderstanding."

"If that's so, then help me understand. What's wrong? Don't you want me?" Giacinta looked at him, determined to get the answers she sought.

"Don't be silly. Of course, I want you. You're the only woman I ever wanted," Casimiro replied.

"Then, tell me why." Giacinta demanded.

"After everything you have been through, I didn't want to rush you."

"Rush me? What do you mean?"

"You're used to dealing with low down dogs who only used you for your body while trampling on your heart. I wanted to prove to you I was different by cherishing your heart and only partaking in my desires when you became mine officially."

Casimiro placed his finger under her chin and stole another kiss from her lips. "I'm sorry for making you suffer."

"Casimiro..." Giacinta exhaled softly, trying to make sense of his gentle words as her whole body became overwhelmed from his warmth.

Casimiro gently took her hand and guided her through the room. "I planned this whole evening just for you. Let's not wait any longer."

Giacinta relinquished any protest left in her heart and followed her beloved into the candlelit hall outside of the foyer. The moment they crossed the threshold felt like she crossed between the realms of heaven and earth.

The soft glow and sparkling white roses weaved around the banisters welcomed them as they proceeded down the hall to the stairs. Red petals lined the light-colored carpet all the way to the top of the stairs. With each step past the romantic display, Giacinta's heart raced faster. She could not believe he prepared all of this for her. Over all these months, he took care of her debts, protected her heart by withholding his desires and showing her what genuine love felt like, and now, he put together this wonderful display all for her. She knew that she should know why he did this for her, but his kindness was too much for her to comprehend.

Her dumbfounded expression grew as he guided her through a flower and gold covered arch at the end of the hall. The trail of petals spread out like a velvet, red carpet surrounding a small, white iron table set in the middle of a large balcony overlooking the small lake behind the cottage. Four white marble goddess lamps decorated each corner, surrounding them. Their whimsical garments and soft expressions seemed to rejoice in the subtle light.

Casimiro pulled out a chair for her, but Giacinta was too fixated on her surroundings to sit down.

"Why did you do all of this?" Giacinta asked, surprised.

Casimiro smiled, motioning for her to sit. "Don't you like it?"

"Yes. I do. But why did you do all of this for me?"

"Don't you know that there is nothing in this world that I wouldn't do for you?"

"I know I'm being silly, but I'm not yet used to your actions," Giacinta glanced out at the soft embers reflecting off the lake. "I know I complained about being here earlier, but now, I think I see its charming attractions."

"I'm glad you're coming around. This place means a lot to me, and I hoped you grow to appreciate it too."

"You mentioned that before. Tell me why this place is so dear to you?"

"This place is where my parents began their lives together."

"I see... This is a perfect place to escape the hustle and bustle of the city and just enjoy a peaceful life with the one you love," Giacinta mumbled half to herself while surveying the shadow-blanketed forest surrounding them.

"That's probably what my parents thought when they bought this place." Casimiro smiled. "Before I reminisce about the past, I'm going to bring out dinner and drinks. We have all night. There's no need to rush."

Before Giacinta protested, Casimiro left to get everything. She stared at the faint remnant of where his shadow once stood and drifted in the swaying will-o-wisps. Hot tears threatened to fall as her crimson lips curled and her heart swelled from his lingering warmth. She placed her hand over her heart and succumbed to the bliss-infused atmosphere.

"You never fail to surprise me, my love. Your hand created all this beauty just to impress, a bratty, spoiled, good-for-nothing, who does nothing but cause you trouble. I don't deserve your kind heart. You're a blessing I never asked for but will cherish until my ill-fated luck destroys our wonderful dream."

When Casimiro returned to the balcony, Giacinta did not notice him until he finished placing everything on the table. Casimiro sat across from her and gently caressed her hand.

"Are you mesmerized by the scenery, or is something else occupying your mind?"

Giacinta rubbed his hand with her thumb and smiled. Concerns and doubt filled her mind, but the moment he touched her, they vanished. She had no reason to worry, because she knew his heart. So, if his feelings never changed, their happiness would not fade.

"Don't worry. I'm not thinking of anything bad. I am only enjoying the moment."

Casimiro's smile widened as her words soothed his anxious heart.

"I'm glad. I thought you lost interest."

"Lose interest? Never!" Giacinta responded, serving the food. "This is more than I could ever imagine. I love it."

"Wait. You're my guest. I'm supposed to serve you." Casimiro tried to stop Giacinta, but she playfully swatted away his hands.

"My love, you're too slow. You promised you'd tell me more about the memories lurking in these walls once we got our food. Now we have it, thanks to me." Giacinta cheesed mischievously. "Now, start talking."

"Fine. But why do you want to know about my past?"

"If this place is special to you, then I want to know why it is? I want to know about every precious moment, so I can share a pale shadow of the joy it brings."

"I don't have many memories of my parents, because they died when I was very young. However, the few precious moments I remember were all made here in this house by that lake."

Casimiro exhaled and looked out at the black water glistening in the moonlight.

"My father was a hotshot lawyer who fell in love with a simple small-town girl. This place was a peaceful refuge in his chaotic world. It was the closest thing to paradise he could offer her. They spent every waking moment together enjoying their simple life in bliss. They got engaged, married and even gave birth to me here. We spent many peaceful, loving years living in this cabin until they died when I was twelve years old."

Casimiro tensed as his last words struggled to leave his lips. Giacinta cupped his hand in hers and smiled lovingly.

"Thank you for everything. I couldn't ask for a more perfect evening. However, it's clear that being here and recalling your memories are painful. So, tell me. Why did you bring me here?"

"I don't mind sharing those memories with you or bringing you here, even if it causes discomfort. I want to share every moment of my life with you, no matter how painful they are."

Casimiro stood from the table, walked out of the room and returned with a rose-bud. He dropped to his knee and offered it to her. Confusion stained Giacinta's face as her heart raced and her body grew numb. His smile grew while he waited for her to take the bud.

"I longed for this moment my whole life, when you accepted my heart and gave me yours in return. Each moment we spent together only nourished my growing love. Ever since our first meeting in the garden, I dreamed of when I could officially make you mine, this moment."

Dumbfounded and speechless, Giacinta watched as the bud's petals unraveled one by one until it revealed a sparkling diamond ring in its center.

"Giacinta Morelli, will you marry me?"

Those few foreign words resonated in her heart, releasing her captive tears. She could barely breathe, and everything became a misty blur. Her words traveled from her lips without a second thought.

"Yes, Casimiro! I will marry you!"

Giacinta did not wait for him to place the ring on her finger and just threw herself in his arms, kissing him wildly. She never believed this moment would come for such an unlucky soul like her. But now that it had, she wondered if this was a sign that she will finally be granted the blissful life she always dreamed about.

The brisk breeze transformed into frigid winds, and still there were no new leads regarding Lana. Zanipolo knew finding her would not be easy. She was the second-in-command of the Rosilli family. She might be an evil bitch, but she was also clever. Unlike other high-ranking officers from other families, Lana was not driven by her ego and would not let overconfidence lead to her downfall. Every step she took until now was calculated. This was nothing but a game to her. If they found her, it was not because she slipped up, but because that was what she wanted.

Zanipolo sipped from his mug of hot cocoa and watched the passersby navigating piles of slush. January was nearing its end, and still they had nothing. Even with their combined resources, they could not find even the smallest clue hinting to her where-abouts. It was as if she vanished into thin air.

Finding Lana was their top priority. They carefully surveyed every Rosilli front and stronghold. They even used insiders to give them an idea of what was going on within the Rosilli ranks; but even they were clueless. It was business-as-usual. None of their other high-ranking members or even the don acknowledged her disappearance.

Every day that passed without a development intensified Amadora's and Gunny's obsessions to hunt Lana down. Amadora spent most of her time as Johnnie searching for anything that would lead her to the Rosilli's second-in-command. Zanipolo understood why Gunny wanted to find her but did not know Amadora's reasons.

Amadora turned into a vicious hunter driven to trap her prey. This time, her determination was not fueled by her goal to prove herself to their father. Vengeance seeped through her efforts; but from where it originated, he was not sure.

A swift chill, whisking through a cracked window, foretold the outcome of this manhunt. They could gain nothing good. Only misery and misfortune waited for them if they followed Lana into the unknown shadows. It was inevitable.

Zanipolo sighed and walked around the room. Whatever happened was out of his control, but he would make sure no one he loved got hurt. A high-pitched ringing interrupted Zanipolo's thoughts. He placed his cup on the counter, raced over to the phone, and picked it up.

"Hello?"

"Johnnie, kid. Is that you?"

"No, Brock. It's Zanipolo."

"Sorry, boss. You sound a lot like the kid. Why are you at his place?"

Zanipolo hesitated after realizing his mistake. It would look strange if they thought he and Johnnie had a special relationship. Gunny's men would grow suspicious of Johnnie and rivals might emerge causing unnecessary problems. The last thing Zanipolo needed was some low-level grunt with a grudge, putting Johnnie on a hit list. He had to do immediate damage control to prevent anymore complications.

"I needed his help with something. Not that it should concern you, but why are you calling this early?"

"I was calling Johnnie because we need to check out a potential lead."

"A lead? What lead?" Zanipolo pressed, trying to avoid showing his growing interest.

"I found a hideout for her assassin, Viper. He meets some of his clients in an abandoned building in Newark."

"Are you sure? Who gave you this information?"

"Yes. I trust my sources. They've dealt with the famous psychopath many times. Lorenzo wants us to check it out just in-case."

"Okay. I'll let him know. Also, I'm coming with you. We can't be too careful when dealing with Viper."

Zanipolo hung up the phone, smirking in excitement. This lead could be the thread they needed to find Lana and end Gunny's misery.

Winter was Samantha's least favorite time of year. She hated going outside during this cold, desolate time. Sometimes, she wanted to wrap herself in her comforter and hibernate until spring. There was only one thing that made this dreary time bearable and that was the time she spent with Zanipolo.

Unlike Samantha, Zanipolo enjoyed this time of year. He took her ice-skating, sledding and to play in the snow. Despite her deep resentment of the cold, she enjoyed all those moments with him.

Samantha loved seeing how childlike and carefree he became while skating upon the ice or racing down hills in their sleds. Ever since Zanipolo joined Amadora's little masquerade, he grew serious and tense. He seemed to stress over whatever business concerns plaguing him now. Neither he nor Amadora shared what was happening. No matter how much she asked, they would not tell her anything. They avoided her questions entirely by changing the subject or acting like they did not hear her. Samantha gave up trying to find out the truth. Even though she could not help him overcome his worries, Samantha would use these precious moments to divert him from everything on his mind.

Around noon, Samantha finished getting ready for the day. She walked down the hall to the living room where she found Zanipolo huddled over the kitchen counter with Anna whispering. She could not hear what they discussed; but whatever it was seemed important, because they did not notice her when she entered the room.

Samantha clenched her teeth as her blood rushed through her body. She could not understand why he confided in Anna about their business but left her in the dark. He promised they would go through this journey together. Did he forget?

Samantha could not take it anymore. If they were going to keep everything secret, then she would get out of their way. She dashed to the closet, grabbed her coat, put it on, and headed to the front door. The turning knob drew their attention to her presence.

"Sam, where are you going?" Anna asked, surprised by Samantha's sudden appearance.

"I'm going home," Samantha snapped, remaining fixated on the door.

"But why?" Zanipolo asked, confused.

"Well, you don't need me here. Why should I stay?"

"Why do you think that?" Zanipolo asked.

"Lately, you've been keeping me in the dark. When I ask you what's going-on, you ignore me and treat me like I'm invisible. At first, I thought you were just withholding information from those not involved in your work; but now, I catch you whispering to Anna about God-knows-what. If you're going to avoid me and treat me like I'm not here, then I'll leave." Samantha glared at Zanipolo, aggravated.

Anna did not have to be a psychiatrist to know this little spat was not going to end well. Before the tension between Samantha and Zanipolo grew worse, she snuck away.

Zanipolo did not react how Samantha expected. Instead, of getting annoyed or

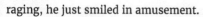

raging, he just smiled in amusement.

"You think this is funny? That's it! I'm leaving!" Samantha turned back to the door; but before she could open it, Zanipolo grabbed her arm.

"Sammy, please don't go. I'm sorry."

Samantha avoided his mystifying gaze, so it would not cripple her defiant heart. He would not get off easy for how he treated. Not this time.

However, he thwarted her attempts when his hands cupped her cheeks and forced her to look at him. As soon as their eyes met, her frustration melted away and a sole tear fell down her cheek. No matter how hard she tried maintaining her composure, she was weak around him. His magnetic eyes destroyed any barrier she conjured.

"You lied to me. Didn't you promise we would endure this together?" Samantha cried.

Zanipolo cradled her head in his palms and wiped away her tears with his thumbs. "I didn't lie. I meant every word I said. Sorry for excluding you. I didn't mean to. I've just had a ton of things on my mind."

"Don't you see? If something's bothering you, why don't you confide in me? I can't do much to help, but maybe talking about it can ease some of the burden."

"You're right." Zanipolo kissed her softly. Maybe you can help. Since you're wearing your coat, let's drive to Central Park. We can talk more there."

Samantha winced at the thought of sitting in the cold for a long time but forced a smile and nodded in agreement.

When Samantha was four years old, she came with her older brother, Joey, to Central Park one cool spring day. He brought her there to drive through the park in a horse-drawn carriage. She could not remember much from that day other than her feelings.

Sandalwood lingered in her mind as he pressed her close to his body, shielding her from the chilly air. His voice was soft and light-hearted, but his words remained a cloudy mystery. Slowly, minor details from that day emerged. Tears crept down her cheeks as they entered the park. Her memories of her brother resurfaced, and she did not know how to handle them.

'It's all my fault. I killed my brother.'

Zanipolo heard her sniffle and looked down at her, worried.

"What's wrong, Sam?"

Samantha wiped her face without making it obvious. "It's nothing. I might have caught a cold."

"A cold? Maybe we should head back?"

"No. I'm fine. Let's stay and talk."

"Okay. If you say so; but if I hear even one more sniffle, I'll carry you back and place you in quarantine. We can't afford to get sick now," Zanipolo teased playfully poking Samantha while continuing their stroll.

"You can be mean," Samantha sighed.

"I'm not mean, just realistic. It's my duty to speed up Amadora's scheme to a decent conclusion. That means I must protect against anything that could slow its progress. If I even think you spread some unsightly germ to Amadora or myself, then you'll have to live the rest of your days with us as a leper until this madness ends."

"You're right. You're not mean, just cruel," Samantha pouted.

Zanipolo hugged her and kissed her gently on the cheek. "Sammy, I'm only cruel because I care."

Samantha giggled, enjoying the warmth of Zanipolo's embrace as they wobbled down the path going deeper into the park. They walked for twenty minutes until they neared the lake's shore. She looked up at him while they rested by a large boulder and sat down.

Zanipolo wore his usual boyish grin; but when his eyes surveyed the lake's ripples, she peered behind his mask and saw the secrets he hid. All her anger dispersed after realizing the truth behind his behavior. Maybe he avoided telling her everything not to hurt her, but because he had not yet figured it out for himself. His smile concealed his reservations from the world, but only she noticed the truth.

"Now, you have my attention. Tell me what's going-on," Samantha placed a hand on her arm.

Zanipolo took a deep breath and rustled his hair roughly before smoothing it out and explaining the web of madness spun by Lana Rosilli. He relayed everything to her except the tidbits about Lana's ties to Gunny.

"No wonder why you and Amadora have been preoccupied lately." Samantha turned to the lake. "I'm sorry for giving you a hard time. This is obviously stressful for all of you. Hopefully, you'll find her so you can all relax."

"Relax, huh? I don't know if it will be that easy. Too many people will get caught in the aftermath."

"What do you mean?"

"Capturing Lana won't get rid of all our problems. I won't name names, but she has history with someone I care for. Ever since that person found out about her in-volvement, they've been out of sorts."

"I see. Try not to worry about that now. Things can change for the best, and they can both find peace." Samantha smiled.

Zanipolo roared with laughter. "You're always the queen of optimism. Aren't you, Sammy? That's my favorite part about you. I hope you're right. The happy ending would be a pleasant change of pace."

Zanipolo wrapped his arms around her and pressed her close. "Thanks for listen-ing. I needed to let it out." He caressed her cheek. "You're a marvelous gal. Don't ever change."

Samantha blushed when he closed the final distance between them to kiss her. Time always slowed when she was with Zanipolo. As if straight out of a romance novel, the tips of their noses touched before he claimed her lips. Samantha froze in his arms as the heat of his passions overcame her. However, her sweet fantasy did not last too long, because a soft voice interrupted their blissful serenity.

"Zanipolo, is that you?"

Zanipolo tensed pulling away from Samantha to see the owner of that voice. The voice was sweet as a harp's note but shot thorns through his body. He froze at just the sound. As he slowly turned to the source everything surrounding them became a hazy wonder transporting him to a dreamlike place. Zanipolo tried to snap back to normality where only Samantha existed; but when he scanned the poise, raven hair beauty standing in the path wrapped around the arm of another man, his hopes shattered. Fate's cruel humor struck again as it turned this sick dream into a reality.

"Maxine..." Zanipolo tried to bury the shock on his face.

Samantha noticed Zanipolo's strange behavior towards this random woman. She was stunning to look at. Her white fur coat accented her porcelain skin and stunning, light-brown eyes. When she smiled, a strange aura radiated from her, briefly distracting Samantha from her concerns.

"Fancy meeting you here. It's been a while, hasn't it, Zanipolo?" Her carefree tone mesmerized him, seizing his senses and drowning out his internal conflictions.

"It has," Zanipolo replied softly.

Samantha did not recognize this woman, but it was clear by the dumbfounded expression plastered on Zanipolo's face that he knew her. Samantha was shocked by this woman's effect on him. One moment they were entangled in a passionate kiss, and the next Samantha did not exist. Who was this bitch?

"Where have you been hiding? I haven't seen you around LA lately." Maxine smiled.

"Haven't had the time. I've been here dealing with some family matters."

"I see. I hope everything is alright." Maxine looked concerned by his words.

"Yes. Everything's fine. Just business." Zanipolo's lips curled unwittingly in tune with hers. He wanted to stop but seeing her prevented him from doing so.

"What are you doing here?"

"Just attending a few events and parties here and there. I needed a change of pace. We should catch up. I'm attending a party thrown by Marty Lenoir. I can add you and your friend to the list." Maxine smiled at Samantha. Even though her expression seemed sincere and inviting, Samantha still did not trust her. Something about her demeanor did not seem right.

"Maxine, I want to introduce you to my friend, Samantha," Zanipolo turned to Samantha and motioned to Maxine. "Sammy, this is my ex-fiancée."

"Nice to meet you," Samantha stifled her irritation and cordially responded.

If she was only a friend, then maybe everything between them was just a dream. Was she the only one who had feelings? Maybe his feelings were just a figment of her imagination. Maybe they were misguided and meant for her. Zanipolo did not care for her at all. Samantha was just a distraction until he got Maxine back.

"Thanks for the invitation. It sounds like a pleasant diversion. Where is it?"

"Nice to meet you, Samantha. Regarding the party, Lenoir's penthouse is at the top of Madison Towers. You remember where that is, don't you?"

"Yeah, I do. When is it?" Zanipolo nodded.

"Wonderful. It's this Thursday. It was nice seeing you again. I'll see you then."

Maxine smiled and waved goodbye. Zanipolo watched after her, caught in a mystified state, unaware of Samantha's gaze or her aching heart. Everything was ruined. That woman shattered her sweet dream with Zanipolo; and their colored pieces transformed into a gray nightmare.

Samantha rushed through the front door of Anna's apartment, sighing in relief. After a long, awkward drive with a mindless puppet version of Zanipolo, she was happy to escape. Zanipolo dropped her off in front of Anna's building and drove away. Samantha was not worried about where he was going, because she wanted to find Amadora and find out what she knew about Maxine.

Samantha did not have to search far, because Amadora sat on the back porch flipping through the pages of a book, scanning each line. Samantha strolled past her, plopped down on the wicker cushioned bench next to Amadora, and kicked up her heels on a nearby ottoman.

"I see you're back early from your romantic getaway. Do I sense trouble in paradise?" Amadora poked fun, playfully nudging her arm.

"I guess you could say that. Have you ever heard of a woman named Maxine?"

"Maxine. Do you mean that snooty socialite who briefly dated Zanipolo and used him for tabloid fodder years ago?" Amadora placed her book in her lap.

"What about her? If you're worried about her, don't be. They broke up a while ago. Besides, he's crazy about you."

"Do you think so?"

"I know so. It's obvious from how he treats you." Amadora grew worried as Samantha's expression darkened. "Did something happen?"

"No. Nothing," Samantha smiled, redirecting the conversation. "How about you? How are things with Darian? They must go well, since you've spent most of your free time these past months with him."

"Everything is great. He helps me forget everything and remedy all my stress from work," Amadora smiled.

"Are you falling for him, Dora?" Samantha cooed happily.

"No. Of course not. I wouldn't do that," Amadora snapped.

233

"Don't lie. It's written all over your face," Samantha teased.

"You're wrong. I have all my emotions in check. You know very well I cannot afford to fall for him." She turned from Samantha to hide her reddening face.

"That's absurd. Why can't you?"

"If I do that, I'll be vulnerable, and he'll have access to the one thing I can't afford to lose right now... my heart."

"Do you think he'll break it?"

"I'm not sure. I trust he won't for now. But who knows how he might change if he ever found out the truth? He hates Johnnie Barbone. If he found out that we're the same, he'd despise me too."

Samantha relaxed, mulling over her friend's predicament.

"That's likely a possibility, but you really like him, Dora. It shows. There is a lot of risk involved with loving him, but there is a greater risk if you run away from how you feel. Doing so would guarantee the loss of your heart."

Amadora smirked and laid her head on Samantha's shoulder.

"Maybe you're right."

Love of a Fallen Angel

'I want to unravel the mystery surrounding her and open the heart she tries to hide.' Thoughts of Darian Mancini.

Sweet aromas of vanilla and rose danced through the air as Fiorella poured hot water into three cups on the small, round table in front of her. Basilio grabbed a cup and handed it to the shaken figure beside him. Her frail fingers folded over the porcelain cup as she expressed her gratitude.

"Thank you, Fiora. I'm too much of a wreck to navigate the stove."

"It's no trouble. That's what family is for. We're here to check on you and help however we can." Fiorella placed the pot on a coaster and sat beside her sister-in-law.

"I appreciate you both for coming here just for me. Things have gotten worse since your last visit. But first please tell me how my Nero is adjusting. I hope he's not causing you too much trouble."

"Not at all. My nephew has been a big help to Gunny," Basilio replied, smiling and patting her hand.

"I'm glad. I was certain that he could harbor some resentment about having to move away soon after the Bruzzano situation."

"There's nothing to worry about, sister. Nero is fine. However, regarding that incident, I need to know the details about everything that happened."

"The Bruzzano family, my daughter-in-law's family that's led by Gaetano Bruzzano, is one of the most influential families in southern Italia. Owning most of the commercial ventures and dappling in several key figures of the political and underground worlds give them the ability to say and do whatever they want. And if someone dares cross them, they'll crush them under their might." Tears welled up in her eyes while recalling the event that ripped her son from her arms. "My Nero is a good boy. He's only caught up in this mess because he was protecting me."

"Protecting you? Why did you need to protect you? Did they hurt you?"

"I'm not sure what they told my excitable boy, but it was bad enough for him to attack both of Gaetano's sons and wind up on their hit list. I tried vouching for forgiveness on my son's behalf, but they refused to listen."

Basilio tried to conceal his rage behind a warm smile directed at his sister. "You don't need to worry anymore. I'll talk to Gaetano myself. Now that I'm here, he's not the only one with connections in Napoli."

Basilio left his sister with his wife while he prepared for his meeting with Gaetano Bruzzano. He went into the salon where his assistant, Gio Cianchi, sat by the phone, penning a memo in his notepad. Since Casimiro was tied up with Rosilli matters, he sent his secondary advisor and assistant to help him with this matter.

"Gio, I'm glad I found you. Arrange a meeting with the head of Bianchiola Industries, Gaetano Bruzzano. We need to have a chat."

"Yes, sir. Right away. However, before I do, I have some news from back home." Gio updated Basilio on the progress of the investigation and some exciting news about Casimiro and Giacinta.

Basilio smirked. "My Giacinta is finally engaged and to Casimiro, no less. I'm glad. At least, some good blossomed from this mess."

The news of Giacinta's engagement spread quickly through the Morelli household. Joy and shock echoed through most. No matter how they reacted, the news lifted the darkness left by the attack. Everyone was excited for the prelude to this precious union and the subsequent celebration, even Amadora.

Amadora had many reasons to rejoice. One: Giacinta finally found love, and it was with an amazing man like Casimiro. Two: her parents were visiting her aunt in Italy, so she could stay at the house in their absence without raising suspicions. Amadora missed being in her own bed and having the free time to tend her garden whenever she pleased. Staying away from it for so long had a negative effect on her mind.

Even though it was winter and most of their plants were dormant, Amadora still longed to see the blanket of snow illuminating the gray winter day with its sparkling crystals. Sitting in the gazebo and basking in the calm serenity of her winter wonderland were the welcoming pleasures she yearned for. After all that happened, she desperately needed to indulge in its peaceful security.

Amadora's face lit up as road lamps flashed by, indicating the end of her journey. With her home in full view, she could not wait to see Darian and share her wintery world with him. She invited him over to share all the secrets her earthy Eden held along with some secrets of her heart.

236

Tires rolling over the cobble stone driveway echoed through the great hall. Amadora's pulse raced when she peeked through the curtains to get a glimpse of the new arrival. The clunk-clunk of an engine of a worn-out green pickup drove her to her feet immediately. Amadora rushed outside and stopped short of the truck.

Amadora watched as a tall figure wearing a dark brown coat and matching hat emerged from the driver's side. She suppressed her growing excitement until his enchanting blue eyes found her among the snow-covered evergreen bushes.

"Darian! I'm glad you came!" Amadora ran to him and threw her arms around his neck.

Surprised, Darian smiled and swung her around. "Of course, I would. There's nothing in this world that could keep me away from you."

When he placed her down, Amadora grabbed his hand and guided him towards the garden.

"Good. I planned a lot of things for us to do; but first, I want to show my garden to you."

"Your garden? Is this the best time for that? Isn't it buried under snow and too cold to walk along a barren wasteland?"

"Don't be such a worrywart. Now is just as good a time as any. Just because a little snow is on the ground, doesn't mean there isn't anything to see."

Darian did not argue. He followed behind her while she navigated through the white garden and into a small octagon patio. When they reached the railing, Amadora let go of his hand and admired her surroundings.

"Isn't it beautiful?" Amadora smiled.

Darian scanned the garden, looking for what caught her eye but did not see a thing.

"What are you talking about?" Darian asked, confused.

"Everything around us. Isn't it enchanting?" Amadora responded.

Darian shrugged. "I don't see it. It just looks like a frozen wasteland."

Amadora laughed softly. "You're looking at it the wrong way."

Darian looked at her, confused, raising an eyebrow as he reanalyzed their surroundings. "How so? I'm just telling you what I see."

Amadora turned back to the snow and smirked. "If you only look with your eyes, you will never see the surrounding beauty. You must use your heart as well."

Amadora turned to Darian and extended a hand. "Here. I'll show you what I mean."

Darian grasped her hand and stood beside her. "For just a second, look at the snow and then close your eyes." Darian followed her instruction while she continued. "Now listen, forget about all your troubles. Once you do that, open your eyes and look at the snow crystals. They should twinkle like stars in the night sky. Their mesmerizing dance should calm your body and immerse you in pure serenity."

While Darian open his eyes following Amadora's instructions word from word, he understood Amadora's adoration. The snow crystals glistening playfully under the sun's beams cast a spell over his heart and mind, tranquilizing all his worries and setting him at ease. The cool air around him faded, and only the warmth of Amadora's hand remained.

"You're right. It's lovely here." Darian smiled lovingly. "You have a knack for finding hidden pleasures. Where did you get that ability?"

"It's a talent I've had since birth," Amadora shrugged. "Who knows, maybe I was just blessed by the gods?"

"Gods?" Darian asked, confused.

"Amadora giggled. "Yes. It was a silly tale my grandmother told me as a child."

"What tale? You've piqued my interest. Tell me more."

Amadora blushed. "If you're interested, I guess I have no other choice."

Amadora recanted the tale of her ancestor and each of the gifts she received from the Roman gods. As she retold the legend, brief memories of her grandmother replayed in her mind.

Darian observed Amadora while she told her unusual story. Gods, magic, blessings... It all sounded ridiculous and normally something like this would make him burst into laughter, but this time, he could not laugh. the gentle passion lurking in Amadora's eyes warded off all his skepticism and opened his heart to believe in her legend.

The intensity of Darian's ice-blue eyes focusing on Amadora snapped her out of her trance and made her blush in embarrassment. She could not tell if he stared because he was confused, surprised, skeptic or amused. He was unreadable.

A momentary pause fell upon them. Darian did not change his expression, which left Amadora wondering about the thoughts running through his head. She longed to hear what they were to spare her any future embarrassment.

Her fears disappeared when his blank stare transformed into a warm smile. "That explains why I'm drawn to you. You must be enchanted."

"Are you teasing me?" Amadora pouted turning from him to hide her embarrassment.

"Not at all. Your story impressed me. It's a beautiful tale. You truly are pure. The gods were right to bless you, because you're something special, Amadora."

Darian's words made Amadora's body numb as he drew close. A fire pulsated from inside her, surrounding her in a radiant aura of security. She uttered a few words of gratitude. However, her whispers barely reached his ear.

Amadora's pulse raced as Darian closed in the distance. Breathing became difficult as confusion and fear filled her. She did not know what to say or do. For the first time in her life, Amadora was afraid of something. She feared his advances. She thought she was ready but was wrong. Without revealing her doubts, she needed to escape.

Amadora stepped back, smiled, grabbed Darian's hand and pulled him towards the house.

"Come with me. Since you liked the story, I'll show you the box. It's truly a mar-velous sight."

Darian noticed something was off with Amadora but did not see her fear. He did not stop her or voice his concerns. He held on tight to her hand and let her guide him wherever she pleased.

Darian waited for Amadora in the observatory while she retrieved the box. He strolled around the large room, taking a glimpse into the world of the filthy rich. To his surprise other than the glass dome ceiling and the large stone fireplace roaring in front of him, this place looked no different from any family room with its quaint, plain furniture covered by a hand-knitted throw and little trinkets of precious family moments displayed all over the room.

Darian walked over to a chair, placed his coat on the back, and sat down. He stretched out his hands and warmed them by the flames. Amadora... the cheerful girl he adored struck his mind in awe. How could a girl born into this world of luxury and privilege turn out like her?

Amadora was more intriguing than he ever believed. She was an innocent creature blind to the world outside of her own bubble. How could someone filled with a heart soaked in vengeance and hate dare feign to be worthy enough to fight for the heart of an angel like her?

For the first time in Giacinta's life, everything was going her way. It was still hard to believe that only a few months prior; she was the plague of her family, just a trou-blesome parasite. Now, her fate changed and once again she found herself in God's favor.

Giacinta no longer had doubts in her heart. She finally found peace. High off the pure ecstasy of her turn of fortune. Giacinta could not see any end to her bliss. Every-thing would just continue getting better.

Giacinta frolicked down the halls. Finally, she made her parents proud. Even though she had not told them the news, Giacinta was certain the news would reach them in no time. She could finally right all her wrongs to her parents.

As Giacinta danced down the east hall, she saw a faint glow chase away the gray shadows. She composed herself and snuck over to the large glass doors leading into the observatory. Giacinta peeked inside, curious of the mysterious occupant since her family and servants were away.

A dark figure hunched over the fireplace, gazing into the prancing embers. Giacin-ta could not make out all their details in the dim light; but from the features she rec-ognized, she did not know who this strange visitor was. Powered by her new bliss and authority as Casimiro's fiancée, Giacinta strutted inside and confronted the intruder.

"Excuse me. What are you doing here? If you're here to see Casimiro or my father, please come back at another time."

The man jumped, stood up straight, and politely acknowledged her. "I'm sorry, miss, but you've misunderstood. I'm here to visit Amadora, not them."

Giacinta looked over at this handsome, tall and dark man standing before her, confused. She found it unbelievable that someone like him would wait for that homely little urchin.

"Amadora? I had no clue she came back. What is your relation to her?"

"I'm just her friend. I'm Darian Mancini. It's a pleasure to meet you, miss," Darian answered sweetly.

"I'm Giacinta Morelli."

"Giacinta? Ah, I see. Are you Amadora's older sister?"

"Yes. I am. But how did you know?"

"Amadora talks a lot about you."

Giacinta's blood pressure surged, and her jaw tensed while she spoke. "Did she now?"

Darian caught onto the growing tension emanating from Giacinta and immediately recognized the misunderstanding.

"Please don't worry. Your sister admires you a lot and always brags about you."

Darian's words could not pierce Giacinta's ears because her growing irritation at the mention of Amadora drowned everything out.

"Well, Darian. It was a pleasure talking to you, but I must go. Maybe we'll meet you again."

"My sentiments are the same. Goodbye, Giacinta," Darian smiled respectfully and escorted her to the door.

Amadora tightly clutched onto a velvet wrapped box while racing down the halls towards the observatory. All was in silence until footsteps interrupted. As soon as they sounded, a poised glimmer of Giacinta pushed past Amadora and faded into the darkness behind her. Giacinta did not acknowledge her, which did not bother her much because she usually treated her that way. However, after the announcement of her engagement, she expected her sister would be in higher spirits. Worry colored her face as she raced to the observatory.

"Darian, did my sister just come from here?"

"She did. We talked briefly, then she left. Why?" Darian answered.

"What did you talk about?" Amadora huffed, trying to regain her breath.

"Not much. We only introduced ourselves. What's wrong? Why are you in such a panic?"

"No reason." Amadora turned away to regain her composure before focusing on the package she carried.

"I brought the box. Here it is."

Darian took the box from Amadora and examined it carefully. Amadora watched him, amused at his astonishment. His attentiveness unearthed some memories from her childhood when her grandmother first showed her the box.

Darian looked like a boy stumbling through a toy store. He gawked and fiddled around with the mechanisms around the lock. She did not interrupt because she enjoyed seeing him this way. It was a side of him she never saw before.

Darian felt Amadora's gaze upon him. Embarrassment colored his tan cheeks a soft red. He averted his eyes and placed the box gently on a table nearby.

"Why are you staring at me?"

"I'm sorry. I couldn't help it. Your expressions were too precious."

"Precious? How?" Darian asked, confused.

"You looked like a kid stumbling on buried treasure. I enjoy seeing you that way," Amadora smiled.

Amadora touched his arm and inched slowly to his hand. Her sudden actions surprised him. He took her other hand and stared into the dark depths of her eyes. She was nervous, but slowly closed the gap between them.

Being so close to him paralyzed Amadora in a fiery aura originating from her chest. The subtle vibration of his heart echoed to hers, filling her with an intoxicating desire. Its strength rivaled her goal. She wanted Darian all for herself.

Amadora was not sure Darian understood the power he had over her. She wished she was brave enough to share her true feelings with him.

"Do you want to know why I'm really like this? It's because of you, Amadora."

Trapped by his words, Amadora could not avoid her overwhelming emotions.

"It's fine if you don't say anything. I just want you to listen."

Amadora blushed and obeyed.

"You're different from any girl I've ever encountered. Your sweet innocence refreshes my heart and helps me view the world differently. Every day with you is an intriguing adventure. I've never felt this way about another woman and don't think I ever will."

Darian's hands wrapped around her waist before continuing. "I want you, Amadora. I want to spend every day of my life with you and enjoy the pleasures of your lips, your touch, and your heart. You're the only one I want and love."

Amadora's head spun as she tried to make sense of Darian's words. Her heartbeats pounded rapidly and fueled her body into action. She wrapped her arms around his neck and let her lips deliver her heart's answer.

Her kiss was enough of an answer for Darian. He accepted her offer willfully. The heat of their kiss sealed their love, transforming it into an addictive dream that was as dangerous as it was beautiful.

Zanipolo needed time to gather the goings-on of his mind after his encounter with Maxine the other day. Everything raced in a frenzy, warding off any logic. Pale shadows of feelings he thought were dangerous. Having them would only lead to an unnecessary headache. He did not need that stress. He just needed some time to sort everything out.

Zanipolo left Anna's apartment to hold up at Gunny's Harlem house. It was the most private location he could find near their primary base of operations. It was above a family-owned bar run by a friend. After a long day, it was a good place to drown his confusion in booze.

Tonight was no different except instead of going straight to bed after splurging on several glasses of bourbon, he called Edward. As soon as Edward picked up the receiver, he gave Zanipolo an earful about not calling sooner to update him directly about what was happening. A sincere apology and bringing him up to speed calmed down Edward. He was the only person familiar with Zanipolo's relationship with his ex-fiancée and understood his friend's conflicts.

Even through intoxication, Zanipolo recalled every word exchanged with that woman as he relayed the incident to his friend.

"You saw that shameful woman again. Unless you say she has finally found the error of her ways and begged you for forgiveness, then there is no reason you should let that tramp occupy your mind."

"No. She didn't do that. Instead, she acted as if nothing happened. I don't know if she's putting on airs, because I wasn't alone," Zanipolo replied, stretching across the couch.

"I highly doubt it. But you said you weren't alone. Who was with you?"

"Sam."

"Little Miss Princess? You've spent a lot of time with her. How are things between you two?"

"Sam and I have grown close during all this madness. But that has nothing to do with this situation."

"What do you mean it doesn't? Your status with Miss Samantha has a lot to do with this situation. Because if you're serious about that girl, then why are you bothering with Maxine?"

"I don't know. Ever since we met again, my mind has been bombarded with a flurry of mixed emotions I can't make sense of."

"You shouldn't let her get under your skin. Throw any feelings you have for her in the rubbish, where anything dealing with that witch belongs. It's not like you'll ever see her again."

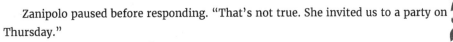

Zanipolo paused before responding. "That's not true. She invited us to a party on Thursday."

"And you declined, right?"

"No. I couldn't."

"Have you gone mad? What do you mean you couldn't! Of course, you could! Saying 'no' is very simple. It's only two letters, N.O!"

"I know, but all common sense went out the window whenever I'm around her."

"Be careful, chap. Did you forget the hell she put you through? Do you want to go through that ordeal again?" Zanipolo understood his friend's concerns. However, all logic disappeared when his old emotions resurfaced.

"Of course, I remember. Catching the love of your life in the arms of another isn't something you'd easily forget. But I need to go to this party to talk to her."

Edward sighed. "I hope it works out, and you get the closure you desperately need so you can finally move on. Otherwise, you'll risk everything for nothing. You don't want to do something you'll regret."

Something he'll soon regret... Edward's warning echoed through Zanipolo's head, draining all his energy. His friend's words seemed meaningless. Zanipolo could handle himself around Maxine. No matter what foreign feelings drudged up, he would not let her trick him again. Things were different now. He knew what he wanted in his life, and Maxine was not one of them.

Zanipolo groggily popped two aspirins and looked over at the clock on the end table. A quarter past one... Zanipolo scrambled to his feet, grabbed the water on the end table, gulped it down, and dashed out the door.

Zanipolo raced through the streets, skillfully maneuvering through traffic until he reached Anna's place. His car screeched to a halt when he reached her building. Zanipolo sprung from his car and sprinted to the apartment.

He rushed through the door and down the hall towards Amadora's room to wake her up. Anna blocked his path when he approached her.

"Polo, where's the fire? Don't you know better than to run indoors?" Anna grabbed his arm.

"I need to get Amadora. She's sleeping, right?"

"No," Anna shook her head. "She returned to the Morelli complex for a bit."

"The complex..." Zanipolo turned away and dashed back out the front door.

Everything in Giacinta's life was now perfect. So, why did it irk her that an immature, pesky brat like Amadora could find a halfway decent guy like Darian? What did he find so special in that little urchin?

Giacinta strode slowly into the main foyer. It was empty. Usually, it was like that, except on holidays or at the end of the month, but this was the first time she noticed the emptiness. At this moment, it was clear as day seeping deep inside her and feeding a misery and loneliness she never knew she possessed. Giacinta wanted to know how she could feel this way after all the blessings in her life. What bothered her so?

The wondering inquiries faded when echoing footsteps rushed towards her. A shadowy figure cloaked in a dark overcoat and matching fedora. Only when they brushed past her and their scarf fell from their face, did she recognize them.

"Polo, it's you. I'm so happy to see you. I missed you," Giacinta threw herself at him, cooing in excitement.

"Giacinta, I missed you too," Zanipolo briefly hugged her back before lightly pushing her away and looking around.

"I hope you're not going to rush off without spending a moment to catch up," Giacinta said, noticing his anxiety.

"I'm sorry, Gia. Not now. I have some work to do; but, first, I must find Dora. Have you seen her around?"

The mere mention of Amadora's name made Giacinta's blood boil. Another man came for her. Giacinta could not tolerate this one and withheld her growing desire to scream.

"If you have work to do, then why are you looking for Amadora?" Giacinta pressed.

"I need to talk to her. Just tell me where she is," Zanipolo replied, trying to avoid the questions growing within her. However, it did not work, because Giacinta noticed his strange change in behavior, but he could not concern himself about that now.

"She's in the observatory with her boyfriend, Darian," Giacinta gritted her teeth.

"What boyfriend?"

"I don't know or care. If it interests you so much, go find out for yourself," Giacinta pouted and stormed away.

Zanipolo did not react to Giacinta's tantrum and rushed over to the observatory to uncover the truth about Amadora's boyfriend. He could not believe amidst all this chaos that Amadora had time to fraternize with a stranger. Zanipolo strolled softly down the hall, cautious in alerting them. He did not want them to notice him before he got there. He wanted to meet the man Amadora was willing to risk everything for.

When Zanipolo walked into the room, the lovers were busy, wrapped in a passionate embrace. They did not notice his presence, which was helpful to Zanipolo. He observed the large man draped over his baby sister. The more Zanipolo looked at this man, the more familiar he became. Zanipolo just could not figure out from where he knew him.

Zanipolo cleared his throat. "Ahem. Hope I'm not interrupting, but Amadora, I need to talk to you about something very important."

Amadora's beautiful dream crumbled from an unexpected source. She broke from

Darian's embrace and faced the intruder. Her heart stopped the moment she saw her brother. His annoyance was evident. She was in trouble. During the many moments that she shared with Darian, she had never worried about her brother's reaction until now.

"Polo, I didn't see you there," Amadora said, forcing a smile to conceal her worry.

"Of course, you wouldn't. You were preoccupied," Zanipolo looked from Darian to Amadora.

Darian read the tension in the room and started his exit. "It's time I take my leave." Darian kissed her hand. "I can't wait to see you again."

Amadora blushed and nodded in agreement. "I can't wait either."

Amadora watched Darian as he grabbed his things and left. Her heart drifted deeper into her chest as he walked away. Watching him leave was hard for her to do. Each time they parted ways, she longed to bring him back and bury herself in his arms. She wanted to immerse herself in the exhilarating sensation of his possession. It was a captivating danger she did not want to avoid. However, reality was a cruel, formidable foe, because it gave her the pleasure of a pure, compassionate kiss just to interrupt it by having them be discovered by the last person in the world she wanted learning about her secret affair.

Amadora could not say or do anything to change Zanipolo's mind. She kept a brave face and avoided saying anything unless he brought it up.

"You can probably tell by the look on my face that I'm pissed about finding out about your new boy toy like this, but that is the last thing on my mind. I'm more concerned about why you're here."

"Since mama and papa are gone, I thought it would be alright to stay here for a while."

"Have you lost your mind? You can't stay here!" Zanipolo shouted.

"I'm not crazy. Since everyone's gone, there shouldn't be a problem if I stay."

Zanipolo looked shocked and was not sure if she was serious or not. She concocted this crazy plan and now toyed with the levels of risks that were already high.

"You must be kidding, Dora. I can't believe you, of all people, would risk being exposed. Did you know Giacinta and a few of the servants are still here?" Zanipolo stopped short of her and whispered harshly.

"Yes. I know. I saw Giacinta earlier," Amadora answered, slowly backing away.

"Why are you being so foolish? If Giacinta or the servants see you masquerading as Johnnie, that could cause unnecessary problems. What if they're not easily fooled? We can pay the servants off, but do you think we can easily persuade Giacinta?" Zanipolo cast a piercing glare laced with anger. "It's dangerous. I won't let you stay here."

It was no use trying to persuade Zanipolo because he was right. Staying here was perilous to her goal, even if it made meeting Darian much easier. Amadora swallowed her stubborn pride and placed her hand on his arm.

"You might be right. I'll stay at Anna's place, but I will continue to come here occasionally."

"Why?" Zanipolo asked, partially relieved that she reconsidered her decision.

"I enjoy bringing Darian here and spending time together."

Zanipolo bottled up his annoyance towards her new romantic liaison. He clenched his teeth and sneered.

"I'd love to waste more time trying to drum more commonsense in your dense head, but we're short on time. There's a lead we need to check out. Just watch out for that Darian guy. Something about him makes me uneasy."

Amadora bit back her initial protest and nodded in understanding.

"You don't have to worry. I will. Let's go before it gets any later."

Zanipolo and Amadora left from the direction he entered, never noticing a shadowy figure hidden behind the draped doors on the other side of the room. Someone who was just as dangerous as the vixen of blood they sought after. A flash of white teeth in a stream of light cast a menacing aura over the room.

"So, the perfect child has been poking her nose in places daddy told her not to. Finally, I have enough to bury that little bitch. These truly have been the best days of my life."

Fluffy billowy steam clouds filled the empty corners of the white-tiled walls, drowning Basilio in its intense calming aura. He sank deeper into the warm opaque liquid surrounding him and nestled into its healing embrace. Sweet aromas of mint, sandalwood and vanilla danced past his nose, feeling him with serene ecstasy.

"You're enjoying yourself, aren't you, Don Morelli?" An elder man with short, peppered hair entered the bath across from Basilio.

"It's very pleasant here. These mineral baths remind me of the hot springs up north."

The elderly man roared in laughter. "Great eye. That's exactly what I was going for when I built this resort. You see. I was raised in Tuscany, not too far from the hot springs. My goal was to bring the healing atmosphere of the natural springs to Napoli." The man stretched his arms behind his head and sunk deeper into the steaming water.

"What a wonderful way to pay homage to your hometown, Gaetano. I'm honored you invited me here."

"The pleasure is mine. It's not every day that I get a visit from a notable man like yourself. I'm curious to what I owe this pleasant meeting."

Basilio sat up straight and ran the warm water through his hair. "I wish my only goal for coming here was to enjoy these soothing facilities, but I'm here to discuss an incident between my nephew, Nero, and your sons."

"An incident, you say? What incident could that be?" Gaetano looked confused as he washed his wrinkled body.

"I heard about a scuffle between Nero and your sons because of an argument dealing with my sister. Normally, I wouldn't take such slights against my sister lightly. But since her only desire is to have her son come back safe without worry, I want to settle the matter. I want to apologize on my foolish nephew's behalf and hopefully put this all behind us."

"I accept your apology. But there is no grudge between your nephew and me. I will convince my pig-headed sons to set aside their grudge, but they can be quite difficult. If I'm going to succeed in this venture, I'll need a proper apology from your nephew as well. Do you think he'd be up to the challenge?"

"No. But I will try my best to convince him."

"I hope your efforts succeed. I would love to put this nonsense behind us; so, hopefully, we can build our own lucrative friendship."

There were no guards lurking around the perimeter of the old Schwartz office building. Ever since the Schwartz company pulled out of New Jersey and focused on their properties in New York, most of their old buildings were vacant. They were perfect for discrete hideouts. Johnnie was not surprised when their lead brought them here.

Every sign of human life was long gone. Wild grass tangled in weeds overran the grounds, with only a few footprints and tire tracks etched into the few spots of flaky dirt. Johnnie did not think much of it since a secluded place like this was a perfect hangout for drug dealers and random hoodlums.

Brock's men ripped away the loosen boards blocking the entrance and led the way inside. The area by the entrance was almost pitch black. Only a few strands of sunlight sprinkling a massive lobby a few yards away made it barely possible to navigate the covered junk by the door. The stale, musky air choked Johnnie as he entered the building. He quickly took his scarf and pulled it over his face to filter the invading pathogens obstructing his breathing.

Zanipolo trailed off into the shadows, running his hands along the walls, following the faint streams of light for the object of his desire. A light switch. He flicked it up and down multiple times, but nothing happened.

"The electricity must be out," Zanipolo grumbled.

"That's not a surprise. If this is where Viper meets his clients, then it makes sense he'd keep it shrouded in darkness," Johnnie surveyed the room and looked at the tower of balconies outlining the sky above them. "A place this grand has plenty of vantage

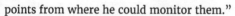
points from where he could monitor them."

"This place is enormous. It's going to make it harder to find any clues. Use your flashlights to navigate through any dark areas of the building. Just remember, we're in enemy territory now, so be on guard. We don't know what else is lurking here," Zanipolo returned to their side and then continued.

"We'll split into four groups. The first three will comprise of Brock and your men. Investigate the lobby and the offices on the three opposite corners. Johnnie and I will investigate the front left ones. Once you're done, meet back here so we can touch bases and move on."

They followed Zanipolo's orders, splitting into their groups. Johnnie and Zanipolo forced open the doors to the left offices. Dust sprayed out, increasing the difficulty of breathing even more. They fought through the cobweb canopies, searching for anything useful. But the more they traveled through the gray room, Johnnie realized there was not anything of importance.

"Polo, why are we wasting our time here? There's nothing here. From the look of it, no one has been in this office for a long time," Johnnie whispered, maneuvering over the piles of junk to reach Zanipolo.

"Stop complaining and check every nook and cranny. Do you think a slippery snake like Viper would leave an obvious trail behind?" Zanipolo said, checking the floors and walls for any secret doors or traps.

"I guess not, but didn't Brock's source know where exactly their meetings took place?"

"No. It seems Viper knocked them unconscious before and after the meetings; so, when they woke, they were in a different location."

"If that's true, then how do we know their meetings even took place in this building?"

"Luckily, one of them wasn't completely unconscious. They remembered being drugged while searching one of the first-floor offices and was dragged along the floor. They never saw the sunlight, so they were sure their assailant didn't bring them outside. That's why we need to investigate this place from top to bottom. If he uses this place for his meetings, there might be other clues leading to his primary base of operations and possibly even to where Lana is hiding."

"We got here a little late. Do you think we'll find it before it gets dark?"

"Aren't you Mr. Optimistic? You know we could've gotten here earlier if I wasn't chasing you around Jersey." Zanipolo answered.

"Sorry about that," Johnnie chuckled nervously.

"Anyway, to answer your question, we should be fine. We have enough men to scour this whole place. If we search in our groups, we could cover three to four floors easily."

Nothing became a trending factor as they rummaged through the lobby before ascending to the upper floors. No secret entrances connecting the ground floor to the higher ones existed. There was just dust and old furniture the Schwartz company left behind Johnnie reluctantly searched through the executive suites of the uppermost floors. But once they reached the tenth floor, a strange feeling swept over his body, wrecking what little peace remained and fueling his anxiety. Someone else was there; however, no matter where he looked, there was no sign of another.

The persistent aura followed them as they reached the higher floors. As they rummaged through one vast room to another, Johnnie wondered how Viper navigated through this building without leaving a trace. Even if he used secret compartments or passages, dragging adult bodies from floor to floor without the use of the elevator would be a hassle. After carefully examining it, the elevator was useless without power. Johnnie needed to uncover Viper's secret.

The feeling of someone watching them intensified when they stepped onto the twelfth floor. This floor differed from the others. The corridor was almost pitch black from the absence of windows. Even when the faint light from their flashlight could not illuminate the true form of their surroundings.

Johnnie remained close to Zanipolo as they progressed farther. He placed his hand over his gun while focusing the flashlight with his other in front of them. Fear once again loomed over Johnnie, strangling his heart with each step closer, as they neared the hall's end.

After opening the door, they walked into a gigantic room filled with rows of shelves and boxes. Zanipolo signaled them to split up and searched different sides of the storage room.

Johnnie's anxiety grew worse as he checked some rows of shelves. Most of them were empty, but by an aisle close to the wall, a faint light sparkled from underneath a section of the wall. Johnnie examined the wall for a way to open it but did not find anything. His hands floated down to some large shelves covered in dusty packages and dug behind them, searching for some sort of lever or switch. But while digging through the never-ending pit of trash, someone grabbed him from behind and pressed a cloth to his mouth. Within seconds, Johnnie fell unconscious, unable to fight back against his mysterious assailant.

When Zanipolo finished checking out his side, he went over to Johnnie to see if he had any better luck.

"Johnnie, did you find anything?" Zanipolo called, examining the aisles. "I had no luck on my end."

After looking down all the aisles, Zanipolo's pulse raced. Johnnie was missing. He ran up and down the rows to see if there was a hidden room, but his search was meaningless. Zanipolo settled down, redirecting his mind on his next moves. Johnnie would not leave without telling Zanipolo. What happened to him?

Zanipolo rushed out of the room and ran to the areas they already searched. His breathing grew heavy because of his frantic sprints here and there. Zanipolo overturned every sheet and piece of furniture, calling Johnnie's name until his voice went hoarse, but nothing. Not a single sound except his desperate cries.

'Crap. Why isn't he responding?' Zanipolo ran to the lower floors and regrouped with Brock. Brock met him when he rushed down the stairs to the 8th floor.

"Boss, Where's Johnnie?"

"I don't know. I was hoping he'd be down here, but he isn't. Damn it." Zanipolo clenched his hand, trembling fiercely.

"Why would he be down here? You two left together." Brock asked, concerned.

"I know that. But he vanished while we were investigating the 11th floor. We need to find him, even if we must tear down this entire building."

Brock nodded and ordered his men to scour the building for Johnnie. He was surprised by his boss's determination to find Johnnie. Maybe it was from a feeling of responsibility towards losing one of his men. Brock knew Zanipolo for years, and he rarely inserted himself in matters outside of his jurisdiction or broke face for anyone other than family. What made Johnnie different? What was his relationship with Zanipolo?

Darkness welcomed Johnnie once he opened his eyes again. Cold concrete pressed against his body, rousing his heavy muscles. He could swing his arms and legs freely, but shadows buried his surroundings. He stayed put until he could better grasp his situation. Johnnie moved his arms around to gauge the height and width of his new prison. It was roomy. He could not feel the ceiling or walls.

Johnnie checked his body for any injuries, but everything seemed fine. Although, when he checked his boots and holster, his gun and the two knives hidden in his boots were gone, along with a pocketknife he kept tucked in his cuff.

"Polo! Brock! Anyone! Can you hear me?" Johnnie called out while wandering around this shadow filled dungeon. His voice bounced off the walls, but no response followed.

Johnnie continued to call out at the top of his lungs; but no one answered, only the soft whispers of a subtle draft. Desperation for freedom raced through his body. He battled the darkness, being careful not to fall into a trap.

"Help! Is anyone there!"

A faint echo of grinding metal against concrete sparked Johnnie's attention. He cautiously turned towards the noise and demanded.

"Who's there?"

"No need to be afraid. I'm not here to hurt you." A deep male voice echoed through the shadows, making it hard to pinpoint the location.

"Who are you? Where am I?"

"Don't worry about trivial things like that. You will return to your comrades once I've told you what I need to tell you. As for my identity, you'd think someone who spent hours searching for me would know who I am right away."

"Viper," Johnnie snarled. The ominous presence from before surrounded him once more. "You are nothing like your reputation. I wouldn't peg you for the talking type."

"Don't fool yourself, child. I could kill you now if I pleased but won't. My mistress has taken a liking to you, so I won't go against her wishes."

"Do you mean Lana? Why is she interested in me?" Johnnie demanded, trying to adjust to the shadows, hoping to get even a glimpse of Viper.

"I'm not sure. You're her new obsession." Viper's voice moved closer, causing Johnnie to retreat backwards until his back hit the icy wall, and there was nowhere to run.

"Why me?"

"I don't know or care but be careful. Once my mistress obsesses over something, she will do anything to get it. She will break you down in her pursuit and destroy everything you love to isolate you. In that regard, she can be more dangerous than even I."

Before Johnnie could reply, Viper pressed a cloth over Johnnie's face. He struggled for a moment before collapsing and giving way to the darkness.

When Johnnie came to, Zanipolo and the others surrounded him. He groggily tried to speak, but the drug prevented him from doing so. Everything was hazy and surreal as he drifted in and out of consciousness.

"He's alive, but someone drugged him. Let's get him out of here." Johnnie heard Brock's voice through his distorted mind.

Everything after fused with the deep crevices of his distorted mind. The blur between reality and make believe disappeared as he drifted into a deep sleep.

14

A Sister's Scorn

'Even with all the love and happiness in the world, I can't get my mind off Amadora. Her deception bothers me,' Thoughts of Giacinta Morelli.

Zanipolo watched a sleeping Amadora, deeply concerned. After the state they found her in yesterday, he had never been so frightened in his life. He knew her scheme would lead them down a treacherous path, but he never expected it to unravel so quickly. The pain he felt at that moment. Seeing her motionless body sprawled across the lobby floor, his heart sank into despair as he feared the worst had befallen his sister.

Zanipolo sat at her bedside, running his fingers through his hair. Gratitude and relief washed over him, because they put his fears to rest, and Amadora was unharmed. He thought he lost her in that moment. He feared their tango with the devil robbed someone precious to him.

Zanipolo whisked away a strand of hair from her cheek, quietly thanking God for protecting Amadora. The touch of his skin against her cheek stirred her from her dreams. When she woke, her eyes met her brother's worry-ridden ones.

Zanipolo grabbed her in his arms and kissed her all over. "You're alright. I'm glad. I feared you'd never wake again."

Amadora hugged him back and tried to speak while smothered in his arms.

"I'm fine, Polo. Sorry for worrying you."

Zanipolo smiled lovingly. "It's fine if you are okay. Do you remember what happened? Who drugged you?"

Amadora paused, trying to recall the happenings from the day before. Every feeling and word replayed in her mind.

"Viper drugged and dragged me off into a dark, empty place. I'm remembering everything," Amadora said softly.

"You met Viper! I'm surprised you're still alive," Zanipolo exclaimed in shock.

"I felt the same, but the only reason he brought me there was to warn me."

"Warn you about what?"

"About Lana. According to him, she is obsessed with me."

"This isn't good, Dora. If the blood queen has you in her sights, she won't stop until she gets what she wants from you. You must be more cautious now more than ever before. Lana is extremely dangerous and very unpredictable."

"Don't you think I know that? I'm more cautious than ever before. Something about his warning bothers me."

"What do you mean?"

"I doubt his real reason for bringing me there was to betray his mistress. I need to find out his actual reasons."

"I don't think that's wise. You shouldn't go searching for any more trouble, because you barely escaped him with your life. Next time, you might not be so lucky. You need to focus on reducing complications," Zanipolo warned, watching Amadora rise from her bed and pace back and forth.

"I'm guessing you're no longer referring to Viper but Darian," Amadora frowned.

"Of course. Your rendezvous with Darian creates unnecessary risks. He's one of Johnnie Barbone's targets. If he uncovers who you are, there will be trouble."

"I know that, but I plan on avoiding that outcome." Amadora answered, looking at her brother with slight determination.

"You're overconfident, aren't you? How long do you think your ruse will last?" Zanipolo pressed.

"I hope it will last until I reach my goal. Then I'll figure out what to tell him."

"Are you really planning to tell him the truth? You're risking him to hate you and possibly coming after you for revenge. Are you willing to risk your life just to be with him?"

Amadora's expression softened as she turned from him. "Yes. I do. I will risk my life if I can be with him. Our precious moments are more important than anything in this crazy world. They kept me sane this whole time. I regret what I did to him, but I can't change the past. I will find another way to make it up to him."

"Are you falling for him?"

Amadora blushed. "No. I'm not falling for him. I have already fallen in love with him."

Those foreign words paralyzed Zanipolo in shock. He dropped his hands and stepped away from her. He never believed that he would see the day when Amadora would be determined and passionate about something other than her twisted goals, especially not about love.

Zanipolo was not sure if he should smile or stand, mouth agape. Darian was a blessing in disguise distracting her from this life, but his relation to Johnnie was a dreadful joke. Fate's cruel answer made everything more complicated than it already was.

Even if her romantic tryst was a cruel joke by fate, Zanipolo felt slightly pleased that this nightmarish plan might end soon. If Amadora risked her life for Darian, then maybe she will leave Johnnie Barbone and this whole dark world behind if it meant they could love with no problems. Only the future will tell.

Anticipation fueled Giacinta's anxiety and preventing her from sleeping. Finally, she had the trump card she needed to destroy Amadora in everyone's eyes. She was not sure if finding out that Amadora and Johnnie Barbone were one-and-the-same was a blessing or a test from God, but she planned to use this information to her advantage.

This revelation surprised Giacinta. She overheard Casimiro, Gunny and their father speak about Johnnie Barbone many times. They exalted him and considered him one of their most promising soldiers. From learning about his exploits, even she grew fond of him.

She could not believe Amadora was the brilliant soldier, Johnnie Barbone. Giacinta never thought Amadora was cunning enough to come up with a ruse that could fool Gunny, Casimiro and their father. How could a pathetically idiotic girl like her pull off an ingenious scheme in such a short time?

Everyone in their family knew of her father's disdain towards Amadora joining the business. To think she pulled the wool over their eyes for this long without getting caught made Giacinta's blood boil. That was one secret that would crush Amadora's perfect world.

Giacinta smiled as she looked up at the gray, cloudy sky above. Today was going to be the worst day of Amadora's life, but the best of hers.

Focused on her revenge plot, she did not notice her fiancé sneaking up behind her. He wrapped his arms around her waist, pulling her into a loving embrace.

"Are you daydreaming about our wedding day?" Casimiro asked, kissing her softly on the cheek.

Giacinta cooed at the touch of his lips against her skin. The heat of his breath aroused her longing for his intimate love; but for the sake of tradition, they made a promise to wait until their wedding night.

Normally, Giacinta would not care about tradition, but this day was as special to her parents as it was to them. If upholding silly rituals made her parents happy, then they could contain their passions a little while longer. Ever since their first kiss, she longed for his love; and now that she had him, she would wait for eternity if needed to.

"Of course, I have. My anticipation has made me restless. I can't wait until the moment I say, 'I do', and I will be yours forever," Giacinta said, turning around to face him.

Casimiro brushed away loose strands of hair from her face and traced the curve of her face. He gazed deep into her eyes. "Don't worry, my darling. Our wedding night will be here sooner than you think. Just have patience."

Giacinta nestled into his chest. "I can't wait. I wish it comes sooner."

"It will." Casimiro kissed her head. "I must get ready. There are a lot of things I must do while your father is away. Do you have any plans today?"

"I'm going to catch up with Zanipolo. He gave me the address of where he's staying, but I misplaced it. Do you know the address?"

"I might. Do you know about where he's staying?"

"I don't know where, but I know who he's staying with a friend, Anna."

"Anna? I know her. She's well known among Gunny's men."

Casimiro let go of her, walked over to the nightstand and rummaged through the drawers until producing a pen and paper. Giacinta looked over his shoulder as he jotted down the address. An expression of dark satisfaction crossed her face.

She was right. This day was going to be a busy day, one full of revenge.

Amadora did not know what Viper used to drug her, but the aftereffect was worse than the initial trip. Her head throbbed in excruciating pain. Being in the light, thinking, and even chewing hurt like hell. No matter what she did, pain coursed through her body.

Amadora mustered what little strength she could to rise from her bed and walk to the kitchen for an aspirin and a glass of water. The empty apartment was quite unsettling, but it was a godsend to her hungover body. She wanted to go visit Darian at his store, but she was too weak to travel. She cursed Viper for ailing her with his horrible drug, but a part of her was relieved she only left with a few aches. If it was not for Lana's interest in her, Viper would have killed her.

Amadora sipped the cold water and flinched as the liquid aggravated her throbbing head. She opened a vial of aspirin she found tucked away in the cabinet and hoped its pain-numbing power would take effect soon. She crossed the room towards the couch, where she hoped to rest until her miracle drug took effect; but before her body nestled into the cushion, a soft rapping on the other side of the door echoed through the room. Amadora grumbled and reluctantly walked over to answer the beckoning call. She quickly undid the locks and forced a smile to greet her guest; but once she saw their faces, her smile faded, and dread filled her heart. Because standing there with a huge sadistic smirk plastered on her face was Giacinta, Amadora's greatest nightmare.

Amadora was in such a shock it took a moment before she could respond. Her words came out in hushed, broken whispers.

"Gia... Gia... Giacinta! What are you doing here?"

"I came looking for Zanipolo since I heard he was staying here. I should ask you the same question," Giacinta said, walking past Amadora into the living room and scanning the apartment.

"Why you would prefer to hold up here instead of at home is a mystery to me. Are you punishing yourself? Or are you running away because papa won't let you have your way?"

Giacinta's presence petrified Amadora. She did not know why her sister came here, but she knew deep down that whatever her reason, it was not a good one.

"That's not any of your concern," Amadora sneered, watching Giacinta slowly stroll about the living room. "You're not here looking for Zanipolo, are you? It's not possible to find out he was staying here."

"Is that so? How can you be so sure that I wouldn't learn about this place?" Giacinta countered, piercing her sharp eyes at her intensifying Amadora's discomfort.

"Because I know Zanipolo didn't tell anyone that he would be here. How did you find out? What are you doing here?" Amadora pressed, treading carefully as not to provoke the dark intentions hidden behind Giacinta's cocky grin.

"To tell the truth, I came here to meet the notorious Johnnie Barbone. And since I'm Casimiro's fiancée, getting information about his boss's whereabouts, my brother, wouldn't be hard. I just didn't expect you to be here." Giacinta knew by the intensifying terror painted across Amadora's face that she knew the real reason she came.

"Johnnie Barbone? What makes you think he would be here?" Amadora asked nervously, trying to keep Giacinta at bay.

"Quit the act. I know you're really Johnnie Barbone." Giacinta's wicked grin grew when she noticed her words were having their desired effect. "You know, when I first found out. I was in disbelief and couldn't believe our family's promising new rookie was actually a clumsy dog like you. Who knew papa's little angel would go behind his back and betray him like this? What a shame."

Amadora was too frightened to speak. All her hard work and progress were going to be destroyed by her cold-hearted sister.

"To keep such a secret from him or Gunny, I wonder what they would do if they found out the truth. It might disappoint Gunny that you didn't confide in him, but what about papa? Do you think he'll be as forgiving?"

"Giacinta, please. Telling them would have grave consequences." Amadora pleaded, trying to reach what little bit of sympathy might lurk inside her heart.

"Do you think I would pass up on a golden opportunity like this? You're sadly mistaken. Whatever consequences befall you; I hope their impact increases tenfold." Giacinta brushed past Amadora confidently.

"Everyone will finally know their perfect Amadora is nothing but a sneaky, cunning bitch who can't be trusted. After today, you will finally understand the loneliness and pain I felt for so many years of being cast in your shadow."

Amadora did not have the strength to stop her. She collapsed to her knees, allowing the frozen tears to flow freely. Her world crumbled before her eyes. Not only was she the primary interest of Lana's twisted desire; but now she was the center of Giacinta's vengeance.

Out of all the challenges she faced so far, this one was the most troubling. She was not dealing with the slights of a stranger, but her own flesh and blood. She did not know how to combat it. How could she handle a sister determined to destroy her? How could she overcome the wrath of her sister's scorn?

Months passed and still Darian was no closer to discovering the identity of his attacker. Even Amadora's love could not hide the memory of the demon who plagued his mind. He haunted his sleep, making dreaming nothing but a hopeful fantasy. To return peace to his mind, Darian needed to uncover the identity of that villain.

Darian tightened his grip around his steering wheel as he glided down the streets on his way to Riley's apartment. His friend promised to use his father's contacts to see what he could find out, but weeks passed with no word from him at all.

There was little to no traffic, which made getting to his house a cinch. He parked his truck in the alley behind the pub, then went to Riley's apartment and rang the doorbell. Moments drifted by without an answer. Darian pressed the bell repeatedly until a grumbling, thin figure yanked open the door and glared at him with murderous intent.

"Have you lost your mind? Do you know what time it is?"

"It's nine o'clock in the morning. What are you still doing in bed?"

"I run a bar. Nine in the morning is like the crack of dawn. What are you doing here, anyway?"

"I need to know if you found anything from your contacts about my attacker."

"Didn't I tell you I would contact you when I learned something?" Riley yawned and stepped aside to let him in.

"I know, but I can't wait any longer. I need something... anything now." Darian said, watching Riley close the door.

"You're being impatient. I have no control over my contacts. I guess the Morelli girl wasn't good enough to satisfy your anxiety." Riley motioned over to a chair in his living room.

"I'm sorry. I'm being obnoxious, but I must know the truth," Darian said sitting down across from Riley.

"Fine. I will check on their progress."

Darian smiled. "Thank you. I truly appreciate it."

"Nothing to worry about. I'd do anything to get you out of here, so I can get some rest. Is there anything else you need help with? Maybe romancing your perfect little girl?" Riley smirked mischievously.

"No. I don't need help in that department, you sick-minded dog." Darian laughed.

There were many things Darian needed help with, but loving Amadora was never one of them. Being with her was simple, yet complex. She was a pleasant mystery he was in a rush to solve but just enjoyed each challenge it threw his way.

Spending the morning with Zanipolo helped Samantha forget about her insecurities towards Maxine and the horrible state her dear friend was in. Everything went well on this wonderful day. The sun's rays dispelled some of the chill from the winter air. Not a single cloud hung in the sky as she sipped on her sweet coffee, talking with Zanipolo about the various goings-on at work. As they talked, Zanipolo carefully avoided talking about Amadora's encounter with Viper to save Samantha from any further worry.

When Zanipolo brought Amadora back unconscious, Samantha almost had a nervous breakdown. She spent most of the night sleeping beside her until she woke up. He could tell her worry wore her out, so he took her to get breakfast to help restore her peace of mind.

Samantha gazed at the sky while exiting Zanipolo's car and returning to Anna's building. Spending a peaceful morning free of any concerns was a precious pleasure; but she wanted to return to the apartment to check on Amadora's condition. When they walked through the front door, they found Amadora curled up on the couch. Her face was red and puffy from crying.

"Amadora, what happened?" Samantha ran to her friend and scooped her into her arms.

"Sam," Amadora said weakly. "Leave before you're trapped under the hell that's going to fall down on me."

"What are you talking about?" Samantha asked, hiding the fear and concern building inside her.

"She knows everything. She's going to reveal everything."

"Who?"

"Giacinta," Amadora answered.

"How do you know that?" Zanipolo asked, closing the door.

"She came by earlier and threatened to do so. I begged her not to say anything; but she ignored me. She plans on telling everyone by the end of the day," Amadora explained, burying her face in her knees.

"This isn't good. We must stop her." Samantha turned to Zanipolo, worried.

"You can't do anything. She hates you and won't listen. But she might listen to me. I'll try to convince her against telling," He focused on Amadora as he continued.

"Did she say where she was going?"

Amadora shook her head. "No. But I'd bet my money she went to Gunny's house."

"Alright. I'm off. You two check out the complex in case she went there."

Amadora and Samantha nodded in response. She dried her eyes and followed Samantha to Anna's car so they could leave for Jersey. She tried to suppress her fear to focus on stopping Giacinta from creating an irreversible catastrophe.

Giacinta strolled through the dark halls of the main house searching for her illusive fiancé. He was supposed to deal with a few business matters, but he was not in his usual hangouts. She wanted to know more about Amadora's alter ego's status among the family and their men to better understand the hold he had on them. Giacinta overheard the few positive ravings of Gunny, Casimiro and Lorenzo, but those did not dive into his actual impact he had on them. She wanted to ruin Amadora in her lies, not Gugliehno.

After wandering around for a bit, she finally found Casimiro in the banquet hall meeting room buried under mountains of paperwork.

"Aren't you a busy bee today?" Giacinta teased.

"Giacinta, what are you doing here? Weren't you going to spend the day with your brother?" Casimiro placed his pen down on the desk and looked at her surprised.

"We're meeting later. First, I wanted to come here and see how you're holding up," Giacinta replied, walking over and kissing his forehead as she ran her hand along the side of his face.

"Not that it isn't a pleasure seeing you, but I'm very busy right now and don't have time to talk," Casimiro said, fighting the pulsating urge to ravage his enchanting fiancée on the desk.

"I understand. But please, my darling," Giacinta plopped on the corner of his desk and guided his lips to hers. "I promise this will only take a moment."

"Fine. If it won't take long, then I can spare some time." Casimiro replied, still dazed by her sweet lips.

"Tell me everything you know about Johnnie Barbone."

"Johnnie Barbone? Why are you interested in him?" Casimiro looked at her with a raised eyebrow in suspicion.

"I'm just curious why everyone obsesses over him," Giacinta smiled sweetly, biting back her actual reasons for her interests.

"I wouldn't say they're obsessed. But he is an impressive figure among Gunny's new recruits." Casimiro leaned back and stroked his chin.

"What do you mean?"

"I handle mostly the legal matters of our business and don't interact with the men, so I haven't met him personally, but neither has Gunny. Therefore, my opinion is based solely on Lorenzo's reports."

"Why hasn't Gunny met his own man?"

"He has thousands of men under him. He doesn't have time to have a meet-and-greet with each one."

"I guess that makes sense," Giacinta said partially to herself.

"Especially a recruit like him. Barbone only joined at the end of last September. He was the favorite of Larry Musilli and his last before his death in the warehouse attack. He quickly became the favorite of one of Gunny's top men, Brock Santana, and his right-hand man, Lorenzo, because of his various skills. His promotion to soldier only a month after joining that makes him the only recruit to achieve that feat."

"Only after a month? Impressive. How did he achieve that goal?"

"He finished a few top priority jobs for Gunny." Giacinta's growing fascination with Johnnie Barbone ignited Casimiro's suspicions. "I hope you're not planning to run off and leave me for Johnnie after learning this."

An amused grin crossed her lips when she noticed her beloved's jealousy.

"I promise, my darling. I would never leave you for another, especially not him."

Casimiro's jealousy simmered down as Giacinta gave him one last kiss before leaving. Her amusement grew darker as she turned away from him. If he knew the truth about Johnnie Barbone, how would he react? She longed to reveal the truth, but a part of her wanted to hold on to her ace just a while longer. She wanted to wait for the perfect moment to use it to bring Amadora's prestigious house of lies crumbling down.

When Samantha and Amadora reached the complex, they searched the ins-and-outs of the main house but could not find Giacinta. They found her while searching the banquet hall. She stood in front of a mirror by the second-floor bathroom, primping herself in the mirror. The sight of Giacinta roused Samantha's anger. She sprinted over to her, ready to grab her and smack the bitch out of her, but she restrained herself so she could hear what the selfish witch had to say.

Samantha glared at her through the mirror, but Giacinta did not acknowledge her. A sadistic grin crossed her mouth.

"Giacinta, you should be careful. Mirrors play tricks on people, showing them only what they want to see, not who they truly are."

"And what's that supposed to mean?" Giacinta baited.

"It can't show the heartless monster you truly are," Samantha sneered, suppressing her growing anger.

"If I'm the monster, I wonder what that makes Amadora. Between the two of us, only one has blood on their hands."

"You bitch!" Samantha flew into a rage and lunged at Giacinta but was stopped by Amadora.

"That's it. Lash out like the foul beast you are. I guess even Amadora can't control her untrained dog." Giacinta roared into laughter. "You make me sick. Helping her with this ridiculous scheme just so you can use the opportunity to get close to my brother and take advantage of him."

Samantha tried to break Amadora's hold, but she just tightened her grip and pulled her farther from Giacinta.

"Sam, don't listen to her. She lives to make others miserable," Amadora said, stepping around Samantha and glaring at Giacinta.

"I don't understand how a woman who has the love of a kind, caring man, lives a comfortable life free of poverty and flawless beauty, still isn't satisfied. Why do you enjoy causing others pain?"

"You're wrong. It's not others that I enjoy causing pain, just you. It's only you, Amadora!"

"But why? I haven't done anything to you," Amadora asked, confused by her sister's growing hatred.

"Why? You want to know why!" Giacinta grabbed Amadora's coat collar and pulled her close. "I loathe your entire existence. For years, you have haunted me. Anything I did was always measured up to your actions. It was my job to protect and guide you, but did I get any thanks in return? No! Instead, I was ridiculed for my mistakes and compared with their 'flawless angel', who could do no wrong."

Tears flowed from Amadora's eyes as Giacinta's hatred penetrated her heart. She was unaware of the torment Giacinta went through over the years. If only she was not so self-centered, maybe she could have stopped them and lessened the darkness in her sister's heart.

"I can't stand being compared to a hypocrite like you. I'm going to tell the world the truth and break the illusion that shrouded me for years."

"Giacinta, please reconsider. I understand why you hate me, but this matter won't just endanger me if it's brought to light, but many others as well." Amadora begged, breaking from Giacinta's grasp.

"I don't care about the consequences as long as I can bury you under your lies," Giacinta snarled.

"I never thought you could be so vicious." Giacinta turned pale at the familiar voice coming from the stairs.

"Polo..."

"You're so clouded by your reckless vengeance that you won't even register the possible aftermath of your actions," Zanipolo said, frowning while suppressing the disappointment in his voice.

Zanipolo understood Giacinta's pain more than anyone else. Growing up, the vast shadow Gugliehno cast over him followed him everywhere. Everyone measured anything he did to Gugliehno, although he never took out his frustrations on his brother. He could not control how others treated Zanipolo, so he would never sell out his own flesh-and-blood in revenge.

"You have every right to be mad, but not at Amadora. She didn't have anything to do with their actions. You should blame them." Zanipolo's stern voice trembled with annoyance and disappointment.

"But it does. If it wasn't for her, being the manipulative cow that she is, they wouldn't have treated me that way." Giacinta snapped. Her face glowed red as hot tears poured down her face.

"You're wrong! Look at her! Did Amadora ever once discourage you?"

Giacinta looked over at Amadora, who was also crying. Her eyes pleaded for some sense of Giacinta's hatred. She seemed afraid not because she was afraid of being exposed, but because she was trying to quell the black demon growing inside Giacinta.

Giacinta saw Amadora look like this before... Each time Giacinta lashed out at her, Amadora pressed forward with this pitiful expression.

"No. She didn't. She always tried... to help me."

Zanipolo softened his tone and wiped a tear from her cheek.

"Don't you see? No matter how you treated her, Amadora never stopped loving you. Now, tell me. Why are you hellbent in destroying someone who cares so much about you while others ridiculed you?"

"But this pain... How can I rid myself of something that's plagued me for years?" Giacinta clung to his shirt and helplessly looked into his eyes.

"Let it go, forgive, and start over. You are about to marry Casimiro. Cling to that happiness and leave your desire for vengeance behind you."

"Polo..." Giacinta paused. "You are right. I don't know if I can snap out of my darkness, but I can take it one step at a time." Giacinta turned to Amadora, and all hatred vanished from her eyes." I don't know why you're determined to put on this charade, but you won't have to worry about me blowing your cover."

Zanipolo smiled, relieved this mess was fixed. He wrapped his arms around his sisters and hugged them tight. "About time. Since you know the truth, you're now a part of the doomsday squad. I guess we should head over to Anna's and fill you in."

Giacinta smiled in agreement as Zanipolo led them towards the stairs. She never thought that the hatred raging within her for years would ever disperse from just a few words, especially with them. Who knew that just her sister's tears and her brother's wisdom could satisfy her blind vengeance?

Amadora left, bringing Giacinta up-to-speed to Zanipolo. After all the drama, Amadora wanted to unwind with the only person who brought her peace, Darian. She drove to his shop; but by the time she got there, it was closed. She peeked out her window to see if he was still stocking inventory, but there was no one there.

Amadora stepped out of her car, walked over to the door of his apartment, and opened it. A narrow stairwell stood before her, leading to a plain wooden door.

Amadora paused, ascended the stairs, and prepped herself before knocking on the door. Her nerves raced. This was the first time she came to his apartment. During the time they've known one another, they only met at her house or various places in Manhattan.

Amadora raised her knuckle to the wood, pausing for a moment. When the rhythmic sound echoed through the hall, her stomach leaped into her chest. She breathed deeper while waiting for a response.

Her anticipation grew when the tumblers of the lock clicked. She was ready to fly into Darian's arms until it opened.

A short, silver-haired man hunched over a bronze tipped cane stood before her. Even though he did not look a day over sixty, moving pained him; but he hid his discomfort behind his dim eyes that beamed with kindness. Amadora's anxiety intensified while in his presence because he was Darian's father, Domenico Mancini.

"Sorry to bother you, but is Darian home?" Amadora asked softly, concealing her discomfort behind a meek expression.

"No. He's not here. He left early this morning and hasn't returned. You must be Amadora. It is wonderful to finally meet you," Domenico said, smiling and extending his hand.

"Yes. I am. You must be his father. What a pleasure to meet you! Darian spoke highly of you," Amadora said, taking and shaking his hand.

"Likewise. Please come in," Domenico said, stepping aside and motioning for her to enter.

"I don't know if I should. I don't want to impose," Amadora said softy.

"Nonsense. You're not bothering me at all. Besides, I want to get to know the woman who captured my son's eye."

Amadora discarded her protest and agreed to Domenico's request. They talked about various things. Hearing his stories and enjoying his light-hearted disposition eased her reservations about being here without Darian. She enjoyed interacting with someone outside of her insane life.

Darian spent the day camped by Riley's phone, waiting for his contact to call back. It never rang until the wee hours of the following day. Riley jolted awake from the high-pitched ringing of the phone. He jumped from his chair and snatched up the receiver.

Darian stirred when he heard Riley speaking. He sat up, wiped his eyes, and eagerly watched Riley.

"Well, my friend, you're in luck because my contact found the name of your attacker. His name is Johnnie Barbone. He isn't some random thug; so, if you're looking to exact revenge, be careful. He is one of the most dangerous soldiers out there."

"I'm going to make him pay, no matter how dangerous he is."

Anger and vengeance radiated from Darian as he spoke. Desire to finally rid the world of the menace Johnnie Barbone pumped through his body. He would bring him down before he harmed another human being.

Lana's Desire

'To the outside world, we're heartless monsters unable to feel, dream and love. Then, what happens when someone untainted by all this blood and madness peers inside and realizes that the monster is only a mirage and sees the desires we try to hide? Can their purity dispel our darkness and wash our souls clean?' Thoughts of Lana Rosilli.

Youth... a precious rarity. Invincibility and perfection derive from its being. Cunning, pride and courage spawn from its bosom. It fuels desires of discovering the unknown and the true purpose of one's life. Is that what fuels Johnnie Barbone?

Is youth his drive? What could a boy his age want so much that would make him long for this world? Money? Independence? Love? Family?

Lana longed to know more about her new adversary. Even his picture could not quell her pulsating yearnings. She needed to know everything about him. What were his dreams, fears, secrets, weaknesses and strengths. She wanted to know if a fearless man like him even had a flaw.

Lana ran her finger over the outline of Johnnie's face. How could someone so young interest her in this way? Why did this child fascinate her?

His youthful appearance drew her to him. His innocent face was not one of a trained mercenary and now her greatest rival.

Looking at his picture sent an unfamiliar yearning through her body. She recognized this boy from somewhere before; but from where, she could not put her finger on it.

Lana covered his body with her hand and looked closer at his face. She saw those eyes before. She went over to her desk and rummaged through a pile of old tabloid papers looking carefully at each article. She stopped at one about the Morelli's Autumn Ball. Those eyes lingered among the participants of their family portrait.

So, that's how it was... The youngest daughter of Basilio Morelli was actually the source of her burning intrigue. Lana's interest in the mysterious rookie, Johnnie Barbone multiplied. It surprised her that Gugliehno's youngest sister had the cunning to conceive such an ingenious ruse. But why would she go through such lengths? Was it only to get into her family's business? No... There had to be more driving her. Lana needed to know more. She longed to know what fueled the infamous "Johnnie Barbone's" passion.

Guilt ravaged Amadora ever since meeting Domenico Mancini. His gentle nature consumed her manipulative heart. Attacking his shop was the only way she could win some favor, but the more time spent with the family she impacted, the more guilt she felt. What she did to them was not right; but was there any other way? That job solidified her position and trust helping Johnnie Barbone gain a place in Gunny's stronghold. So, why did she feel like this? This was what she wanted all along and understood the risks involved.

Talking to a sweet man like Domenico wounded her resolve. She wanted to make up for all the trouble she caused. Apologizing was a great first step, but she knew the danger of revealing herself. Domenico's kind heart could easily become corrupted by hatred, but she was prepared for that. Even if it turned his heart black, she would tell Domenico the truth.

Amadora parked her car a little ways from Darian's shop and waited until he came down to set up for the day before going to his apartment door.

The journey up the narrow stairwell leading to his apartment was longer than it felt before. Her heart pounded wildly in her ear. Sweat poured from her palms as she gently knocked on the door.

A few moments passed before Domenico's cheerful face appeared in the threshold.

"Amadora, what a pleasant surprise. If you're looking for Darian, then you'll find him in the store."

Amadora disguised her torrent of feelings behind a pleasant smile. "I actually came to speak with you."

Domenico's brows furrowed. He stepped aside to let her enter. "If that's so, please come in."

He led her to the kitchen and motioned for her to join him, pointing at one of the thin, white wooden chairs surrounding the table.

"Tell me. What's troubling you this fine morning?"

"I appreciate the kindness you showed me the other day. But a deceptive creature like me didn't deserve such kindness."

"What do you mean, my dear?"

"I hid a dark secret from you. You will probably hate me for what I've done."

"What are you talking about, child? There's nothing you could've done that would make me hate you."

"Do you remember the vandal who ransacked your store and attacked Darian?"

"Yes. What do you know about that?" Domenico asked.

"That man was me in disguise. I'm sorry," Amadora apologized, hiding her tears in the palms of her hands.

"Why would you do such a thing?" Domenico asked, shocked.

"Ever since I was young, I admired the depths of my family's secret world. However, even though I can handle its ins-and-out, my father wouldn't let me join; so, I created the persona, Johnnie Barbone, to infiltrate my brother's circuit and attacked your store to prove myself. I'm sorry for all the harm I caused."

Amadora waited for Domenico's harsh resentment and hatred, but only silence followed. He touched her arm gently, causing Amadora to drop her hands and question his unusual notion.

"No need to cry, my dear. I forgive you." Domenico said.

"But how?"

"Because you're not a bad person, Amadora. You only followed orders. I understand how hard it is to break from your orders in that business."

"You do?"

"Yes. Just like you, I was once a soldier for the cosa nostra. I worked for the Rosillis and witnessed firsthand how a child raised around that world would act. They either leave their family or joined their 'business' by choice or force. I didn't want my son tainted by that corruption, so I left."

"Corruption?"

"Save your family and the Lorenzos. The other families trick and scheme to make immediate family members do as they wish. However, the Rosillis were the worst of the lot. Did you think Lana was always ruthless and mentally unstable? No. They turned her into that, because she was an important asset. They destroyed everything she loved to keep her unwittingly devoted to them and would've done the same to Darian," Domenico explained.

"Does Darian know this?" Amadora asked.

"No. And he's better off not knowing. He would gain nothing from learning about his past. However, you must tell him about Johnnie Barbone. You wouldn't want him learning the truth some other way."

"I will once I reached my goal. I haven't told many people, so he couldn't find out any way except you."

"I won't tell him, but the truth always finds its way to the light. The longer you suppress it raises the chance of revelation in some other form. My son isn't stupid. Even though he tries hiding it, I know he's looking for his attacker. Sooner-or-later he might find a clue connecting you to the truth."

Domenico noticed her fear and placed a comforting hand on hers. "I know the decision may be difficult. But you'll have to decide what you want more than anything?"

Amadora cast her gaze to the table. "I'm not sure. A part of me just wants to be with Darian, the other wants my father to acknowledge me as an important asset. I want them both."

"You know that's not possible. You must choose. If you disclose your secret to him and give up your dangerous goal, Darian might forgive you for your part as Johnnie Barbone. Although, he won't stay if he discovers the truth from another source while you're continuing with that ruse. So, which will it be? My son's heart? Or your father's approval?"

The day of Marty Lenoir's party arrived without hesitation. Samantha barely spoke to Zanipolo about anything that was not related to Amadora. She avoided voicing her concerns about accepting this invitation from his ex-fiancée. Zanipolo wanted to go to this event. Samantha just hoped it was not for Maxine. If he wanted to get consolation from the woman who ran away with his heart, then why did he bring her.

They stepped out of the marble and iron elevator onto the ruby carpet of the 80th floor entry way. She clung to Zanipolo's arm as they passed under the large, golden threshold into Lenoir's lavish penthouse's grand foyer. Even in one of Amadora's most elegant dresses, Samantha failed compared to the dazzling beauties of New York's rich and famous. From well-known starlets to scandalous socialites, they all seemed to gather under this magnificent gold and ivory dome palace in the sky. Plump cherubs and mischievous gods danced above their heads while ethereal marble statues of angels outlined the corners of each room.

When they passed by the large golden mirrors outlining the main hall, Samantha looked herself over and compared herself to the sea of sparkling glamor surrounding her. She did not belong here with Zanipolo. She was a commoner playing dress up. How did she expect to fit into this world... his world? What could Samantha offer Zanipolo that Maxine could not? Samantha grimaced. Nothing.

"Sammy, what's wrong? You've been acting strange for a while now." Zanipolo asked, concerned, leading her to a lightly crowded corner of the main hall.

"Don't worry. I'm fine. I need to run to the bathroom. Be back," Samantha released him and dashed away to find the restroom.

Zanipolo watched after her, concerned by her peculiar behavior. She did not seem physically ill, but something else bothered her. He wondered what it was and why she tried so hard to conceal it from him. After all the hell she gave him about keeping his troubles from her, then why would she hide hers from him?

"Polo, I'm glad you came." Zanipolo's wandering thoughts shattered at the sound of Maxine's voice. Maxine's soft eyes searched the area surrounding them and frowned. "Did you come by yourself?"

"No. Sam's here. She's in the bathroom and should be out soon. Thank you for inviting us, but we might not stay for long. Sam isn't feeling well." Zanipolo responded, glancing back towards the bathroom.

"That's too bad. I must make the most of our time while you're still here. I'll show you around. The lights from the rooftop garden sparkled like stars from the third-floor veranda. It's a marvelous sight," Maxine said, pulling Zanipolo's arm.

"I should wait here for Sam. She should be back soon," Zanipolo declined.

"Don't worry about her. It will only take a moment. I'll have my companion guide her there once she's finished," Maxine motioned to a plain-dressed woman standing a few steps behind her.

"I guess," Zanipolo agreed dryly.

Twinkling white lights wove around frost-covered, leafless trees and whimsical statues.

"Doesn't it just take your breath away? Just like the last Christmas at the beach house. You knew how much I hated this holiday season, but you strung up lights throughout the entire garden and proposed to me. That was the first Christmas I ever enjoyed."

Zanipolo glanced at her, then looked away. The bewitching spell she had on him overtook him. He fought back the foolish words threatening to break free.

"Maxine, stop. This isn't going to work."

"What isn't going to work? I'm just reminiscing about some of our old memories," Maxine faced him, batting her long lashes innocently.

"You're trying to highlight some of our better moments, but you're overlooking the darker ones that followed." Zanipolo looked over the glistening earth. "The only memory I have of you is the one when I came home early from a business trip to surprise my fiancée and found you fucking another man in our bed."

"I'm sorry for betraying and hurting you so deeply. But is there not a spec of love for me left in your heart? Was one foolish moment of weakness capable of ruining years of love?" Tears formed in Maxine's eyes. She grasped his arm.

"How I feel now isn't relevant. What are your intentions? You had years where you could have tried to reconcile. Why are you trying now? What do you want?"

"Polo, I want you. It might be too late, but I beg of you give us another chance." Maxine wrapped her arms around his neck and gently pulled him close as she whispered the subtle longings of her heart. Caught in the silky embrace of Maxine's arms, Zanipolo lingered unable to resist as her lips pressed against his.

Samantha left the bathroom and searched around for any sign of where Zanipolo went. As she walked through the elegant hoards, a plain-clothed woman stopped her.

"Are you looking for Mr. Morelli? He's on the third-floor veranda with my mistress. Follow me. I'll take you to them," the woman said, bowing her head and guided Samantha through the ever-growing crowd.

Samantha was not sure who this woman was, but she followed her through the luxurious maze to the third floor. When they reached the windows overlooking the veranda, Samantha froze as her deepest fears turned into reality.

Samantha grasped her chest as a surging pain crushed her heart. She fought back some hot tears burning her eyes as agony ripped apart what little hope she possessed. She backed away from the window and dashed into the crowds, hiding the few tears she could not restrain.

Zanipolo never kissed Maxine back. He pushed her away and stepped back.

"That's enough. You must be mad if you believe I'd ever return to you after all the pain you caused me. Samantha is the only woman I want, and I would never betray her as you did me. Goodbye forever, Maxine."

Zanipolo left the veranda and went in search of Samantha. He searched through the entire penthouse, but she was nowhere to be found. Anxiety built in him because of her sudden departure. Samantha would not leave without him. Something propelled her to leave. Fear consumed him as he reached the cruel realization. The true intention of Maxine bringing him there and her kiss was to destroy Samantha's trust in him by witnessing her advancement, and her plan succeeded.

Amadora left Darian's apartment in the late evening. As she descended the stairs, Darian entered the hall. Her eyes curved as enthusiasm washed over her.

"What a pleasant surprise. Did you come here looking for me?" Darian asked.

"Yesterday, I did; but today, I came to see your father. We had such a pleasant time the other day that I wanted to express my appreciation."

"I feel torn. I'm glad you and my father met, but I'm jealous you came to see him and not me." Darian wrapped his arms around her and stole a kiss from her lips.

"Don't be. I'll be back tomorrow. Let's go for a walk in Central Park," Amadora said.

"I would love to," Darian answered.

"Until tomorrow then," Amadora kissed Darian and dashed down the stairs, leaving her lover amazed and anxious.

A brisk, white mist masked the night in its breast. Since Gunny's family returned, the grounds of his property crawled with droves of guards. Nothing could sneak past them. Nothing except the specter lurking in the mist.

Invisible to the eyes of man, it maneuvered past the guards shrouded in the mist, but it was not a figment of the imagination. It crept along the ground to reduce any chances of discovery until it reached an open window covered by purple curtains. The specter peeked inside the room of Gugliehno's eldest daughters, glided inside and kneeled by Loretta's bed.

It removed its white glove, revealing its small, pale hand as it reached down and stroked the small child's cheek. The sight of the sleeping child peacefully sleeping filled her with emotion. Even through all the painful changes in her life, she kept that joyful grin that she had ever since she was a baby.

As she rose to leave, a small hand stopped her.

"Mommy, you came," Loretta whispered sleepily, looking at the white figure standing over her bed, Lana Rosilli.

Lana embraced the child. "Of course, little one. I promised you I'd come. I would never break my word to my most favorite girls in the entire world."

"Why can't you stay with us instead of Susan?" Aniela asked, running from behind Lana, climbing into her lap and hugging her.

"Yes. You should, mommy. We miss you." Loretta's innocent eyes gazed at her mother's confused.

Lana scooped her daughters in her arms and kissed them on their heads.

She smiled. "I wish I could, my darlings. Papa is still very mad at me. For now, we must cherish these brief moments until he cools his head. Until then, give Susan a chance. She's a good mommy. Don't you enjoy living with her?"

"We love Susan, but she isn't you, Mommy. And I don't think papa is happy living with her. He still thinks of you and isn't mad at you anymore," Loretta said, nuzzling into her mother's chest.

"Why do you think that?"

"I overheard him saying your name while looking at an old picture. He sounded very sad. Doesn't that mean he misses you and is not angry anymore?"

Lana turned to the window and pressed them closer to her.

"I'm not sure, but don't worry. We'll be together soon."

Hope returned to her daughters' innocent faces. Lana picked them up, tucked them into their beds, and kissed them.

"It's getting late. I must get going."

She stood by the window and smiled once more at her girls as they nestled into their beds.

"Sweet dreams, my darling girls. I love you more than life itself."

As Lana dashed into the mist, she buried her tears into its frigid caress while moving farther from her most precious treasures. It obscured her. Its bosom allowed her to hide her heart and the powerful desire surging through it. The desire to regain what

271

she lost no matter the cost and get rid of anyone who got in her way.

Lana wanted to be with her children more than anything in this world. Their innocent love was a light that kept her from the brink of destruction frequently. She would not stop until she reclaimed the only hope left in her life. If that meant she had to overcome the inferno of the very depths to reunite with them, then she would do so gladly, without hesitation. She would tear down this entire world if it returned her daughters to her arms.

Confrontation & Realization

16

Torn Between Love and Lies

"If you want to succeed in this world, you'll have to throw away all emotion and sacrifice your heart," Words by Lana Rosilli.

When Zanipolo returned to Anna's apartment, his fear intensified. He searched every corner of the apartment, but she was nowhere to be found. Her things were gone, and he knew right away that she left for good.

Zanipolo's anxiety welled up inside him. He was certain Samantha saw him with Maxine. He paced back and forth, suppressing his anger towards his foolish weakness. How could he risk everything with Samantha just for a faded specter from the past?

Zanipolo could not afford to lose Samantha. She was the source that reigniting the light in his heart. She drove away the sadness created by Maxine. Zanipolo needed and wanted her. He could not imagine living another day without seeing her smile every morning.

Zanipolo flopped down on the couch and threw back his head, exhaling loudly. He had an idea where she ran off to, but it was too late. No matter how much he wanted to hunt her down and desperately beg for her forgiveness. He would give her a night to calm down before he threw himself at her mercy. This might give him time to prepare for any unknown dangers awaiting him.

The midday sun's rays fought through the gray clouds looming in the sky above. Amadora frowned as the fear of rain became a great possibility. The frigid winds whispered a warning to her as she waited for a carriage. Amadora did not want to ruin the wonderful day she planned with Darian. Rain or shine, she could not waste their precious time together for a bit of ominous paranoia.

They waited a few minutes at the northeast entrance of the park for their carriage to arrive. Once the open black carriage, driven by a hooded caddy, pulled in front of them, Darian took Amadora's hand and helped her inside, then entered behind her.

"Take us through the park," Darian said, wrapping his arms around Amadora shielding her from the impending winter air. "I hate the cold; but for you, my dear, I'll brave it."

Amadora snuggled into his chest and smiled. "I guess I'm very lucky that you love me enough to venture into the cold, even though you dislike it. You're a treasure. I don't deserve you."

Darian traced her chin with his finger and guided her cool lips to his. "You're wrong. I'm the lucky one to love an angel like you."

"You flatter me. I'm no angel." Amadora said, turning from him to hide her growing guilt and discomfort from his compliments.

Darian smiled and coaxed her to look at him. "Don't be modest. You are a blessing that restored balance and hope to my life. Your innocence brings light into this dark world, making each day worth living."

Darian's sweet confession shocked her and their purity worsened her guilt with each passing second. She wanted to respond, but suddenly their carriage stopped, garnering their attention.

"Driver, why are we stopping?" Darian asked, surveying the secluded area they stopped in.

"Cousin, listen to her. She is not the innocent girl you believe her to be." A woman's voice said from underneath the cloak.

"Who are you?" Darian snapped in defense.

The driver jumped from her seat, walked to the carriage's side, and removed her hood. When a pair of familiar hypnotizing sea-green eyes fell upon them, Amadora shrunk behind Darian's shoulder to hide the discomfort Lana's presence created. Lana glanced briefly at Amadora, then returned her focus to Darian with a devilish smirk pasted on her lips.

"I'm disappointed. Didn't Uncle Domenico tell you about me? I'm Lana, your older cousin," Lana said, extending her hand. Even though she wore a friendly mask, Amadora did not believe she was only there for a family reunion.

"It's nice to finally make your acquaintance."

"You are Lana, as in Lana Rosilli. You're a caporegime for the Rosilli mafia family. You must be more psychotic than rumors indicate to believe we're related," Darian said, declining her gesture.

Sadistic amusement colored Lana as she brought her hand to her hair and played with a few curly tendrils.

"Your stubbornness… It's an annoying family trait, but I shouldn't be surprised. You got that from your mother."

"My mother?"

"Yes. Your mother... Didn't your father tell you? She was a Rosilli."

"Enough of your lies!" Darian snapped, stepping out of the carriage and moving closer to Lana. "Why are you here? What do you want from me?"

Lana roared in laughter. "Oh, my dear boy. You have it all wrong. Even though I adore family reunions, you're not the one I want. Your girlfriend is."

Those words infected Amadora's body, paralyzing her in an unbreakable fear. The icy determination lingering in Lana's eyes strengthened her fear, but she fought through her discomfort to stand by Darian's side and face this demon head on.

"Amadora, stay behind me," Darian said, stepping in front of Amadora, shielding her from whatever Lana had planned. "Leave her alone. There's no business you could possibly have with her."

"How wrong you are, dear cousin? She's an interesting creature, and I would like to pick her brain." Lana grinned, looking through Darian to the object of her attention.

"What the hell are you talking about?" Darian demanded, growing furious at Lana's little game.

"I want to learn from a master. How can a seemingly innocent girl hide your ruthless nature? Doesn't your charade grow tiresome after a while?' Lana pressed, observing Amadora's reaction carefully.

Amadora's jaw tensed. Lana was goading her to reveal her identity, but she could not understand why. What could Lana gain from ruining her relationship with Darian?

"You must have me confused with someone else, because I don't know what you're getting at," Amadora said.

"Bravo. You truly are a brilliant actor." Lana applauded, stepping closer. "I could never carry on such a ruse for this long, because I don't have the patience."

"What the hell are you talking about?" Darian demanded, confused by Lana's ramblings.

"Oh, dear cousin, don't you know? I guess everyone is keeping you out-of-the-loop nowadays, aren't they?" Lana glanced back at Amadora with a sharp, satisfied grin. "Your precious little angel and your attacker are one-and-the-same."

When Lana's words left her lips, Amadora's fear ravaged her heart, and shattered it into a million pieces. The revelation of the truth pierced her body and riddled her in agony. Lana's sadistic grin grew as she watched her adversary writhing in the pain of her revelation.

Darian's frustration boiled over after hearing Lana's accusation.

"Enough! You have clearly lost your mind! Do you think I will believe such nonsense?"

"No. I never expected you to believe me, because her expression is proof enough." Lana laughed, pointing at Amadora.

Amadora could not control the terror ravaging her body. It broke her mask and made it impossible to hide her feelings. Even if she protested, the seeds of suspicion were already planted. The truth was out. She could not fool him anymore.

The world surrounding Darian faded as he focused on Amadora. She remained silent and never said a word in protest. She could not look him in the eye or move. The pure image of the woman he loved was cracking.

"Dora, please. Tell me she's lying." Darian begged, grabbing her arms and forcing her to look him in the eye.

Amadora looked into his eyes and tried to force out any words to combat Lana's allegations, but she could not. She could not speak anymore lies, not to him. Keeping this secret from him exhausted Amadora and a part of her was relieved that the truth was out. Although, the weight of her guilt could not prevent the heartache this secret caused.

When the first tear fell down her cheek, Darian realized Lana's words were true. Anger, disgust, and confusion suffocated him in a poisonous embrace. He released her and stepped away. His feelings went into a frenzy, making it difficult to make sense of what was going on around them. He did not recognize the woman standing before him and needed to get away.

This woman was not the person with whom he fell in love. He did not know this deceptive creature. She did not differ from the members of her monstrous family.

Amadora snapped out of her grief to grab Darian before he ran off, but he pushed her away, causing her to fall to the ground. He did not say another word to her as he left her sobbing on the cold earth. Amadora called after him, begging him to return, so she could explain; but her cries fell on deaf ears.

As if masking her own tears, the sky opened. The rain drops stung her face as they drowned out her cries. They drenched the earth and froze her in all her heartache and lies.

During the commotion, Lana escaped without being noticed; however, another pair of ears overheard everything that unraveled. While on his routine jog, Brock noticed Lana while on a side road and overheard the entire exchange.

"How could he?"

The cruel memory of Maxine wrapped in Zanipolo's arms as they shared a passionate kiss replayed repeatedly in Samantha's mind. It made her sick to her stomach. As if bleeding, her chest ached uncontrollably. And instead of fading away, it intensified when she realized the memories, they shared were all lies. He used her just to distract him until he got back with the woman he truly loved Maxine.

Samantha's breathing became labored as her hot tears clouded her sight. She wanted to escape the pain and forget all about Zanipolo Morelli. She was such a fool.

He never cared about her at all. It was always Maxine. She was the one who had his heart.

Samantha sat in her bed and watched the rain fall upon the earth. Its rhythmic melody as it hit her windowpane irritated the wounds on her heart. The raindrops mirrored her pain and sang her woes to anyone who listened.

Samantha wiped her face as she masked her sorrow. She needed to put the thoughts of Zanipolo's betrayal from her mind and suppress her heartache, because she did not want her parents to notice something was wrong. Her parents were asleep when she returned home, so they did not know she had returned.

Samantha rose from bed, fixed herself in the mirror before leaving for her parents' room. She did not want to spook them and end up at the mouth of her father's gun after being mistaken for an intruder. After coming back late in the night, she knew any unusual noise might startle them.

She walked to the second floor and stood outside their bedroom. Samantha took a deep breath and was going to knock when she overheard her parents arguing. She peeked through the old-fashioned keyhole on their door to see what it was about.

"Malcolm, stop being so unreasonable. It's only right to tell Samantha about Diederich." Samantha's mother yelled at her father, grabbing his arm.

"Are you mad? Don't you know what will happen if she knows the truth?" Her father snapped.

"I don't know that, and neither do you. But shouldn't we do what's best for our daughter? This could help heal the wound we both know hasn't closed in her heart. She needs this."

"He won't take Joey's place and return things to how they once were. So, how can he help?" Her father turned from her mother and tensed.

Samantha's mother wrapped her arms around him and embraced him from behind.

"Oh, my darling. Do you think that's what I want?"

A tear fell down her mother's face as she forced a smile. "No one will ever take our Joey's place. He will always be our heart, but we can't shut out Diederich. He's a precious part of you, your son, and deserves to be in our lives. Let's give him a chance. Maybe... just maybe, having him around will help mend some of our pain."

Samantha backed away from the door, clasping her hands over her mouth, preventing her revulsion of her mother's words. For a moment, her heartbeat paused, and she became pale and clammy. That stranger was actually her brother.

Samantha ran to the stairs and descended slowly, one step at a time, while caught in a trance. She swayed slightly, stepping lightly so not to alert them to her presence. That man seemed no older than Gugliehno, which meant he was almost the same age as Joey. How could he be her brother?

Her tears would not cease once they began. This was too much pain for her heart to take. How could her father keep a secret like this from her for so long? He saw the pain she suffered over the years because of Joey's death; so, why would he hide this from her?

Samantha wanted to scream. No matter where she was, someone betrayed her. She wanted to forget everything and escape her heartache. She wanted to be far from all the pain and just hide from the world.

Her tears clouded her vision, making it difficult to see as she ran out the front door and into the freezing rain. When she ran through the front yard, she bumped into someone. She apologized and turned from them to hide her tears.

"I'm sorry. I wasn't paying attention." Samantha wiped her face, hoping to clear her vision, but her despair was too great.

Someone brushed her cheek with their hand. "Sam, you're crying. What happened?"

The sound of their voice paralyzed her in anger. Once her sight cleared, she looked at her good Samaritan, then scowled. It was Zanipolo.

"That's not your concern. You don't need to worry yourself about me," Samantha snapped, pushing past him.

Zanipolo grabbed her arm. "Don't be silly, Sammy. If something is hurting you, then that concerns me."

"Let me go. Enough lies. Stop pretending like you give a damn about how I feel." Samantha cried, fighting to break his hold. She glared, challenging his unwavering grasp. "Why do you toy with my feelings by pretending you care? I know you don't, so please just leave me alone."

"Sam, you're wrong. I'm not pretending. I care about you."

"Stop! No more lies! Get away from me! Go see if your precious Maxine will have you!"

"Maxine? What does she have to do with anything?"

"Ever since she appeared, she ruined everything. I foolishly believed your sweet words, embraces and kisses meant you're mine, but how foolish I was; because it was clear the moment she intruded on our lives, that Maxine is the only woman you could ever love," Samantha said, suppressing the excruciating pain tearing her heart apart.

"You think I love her? That's ridiculous. Why would you think..." Zanipolo hesitated, releasing her when he realized the source of her anger.

"Yes. I saw you with her." Samantha cried.

"You've got it all wrong. Please let me explain." Zanipolo replied, blocking Samantha's path so she could not run away. He held her shoulders, forcing her to hear him out and face him. Samantha fought vigorously, but she could not break from him and could only look away while her tears continued to fall.

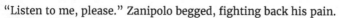

"Listen to me, please." Zanipolo begged, fighting back his pain.

"Why should I?"

"Because you've got it all wrong." Zanipolo started choking back tears. "Yes. She kissed me, but I pushed her away immediately after. You want to know why I did that?"

"Why?"

"Because it's not her I love but you, Sammy."

"You're a liar!" Samantha cried.

Zanipolo shook his head, letting his captured tears fall. He cupped her face and pressed his forehead against hers.

"I would never lie to you, because I love you, Sam... Only you."

Samantha's lips trembled as she saw the sincerity in his words. "You're a fool. You know that."

Zanipolo smiled, pulling her into his tight embrace. "I know, but I'm your fool."

Samantha wrapped her arms around his neck and kissed him passionately. Zanipolo lifted her off the ground and swung her around happily. Relieved of the pain from almost losing the sole joy in his life. He never wanted to experience that fear again because he did not plan on doing anything to jeopardize losing the heart of the woman he loved most.

Locked in his office for days mulling over old properties he frequented with Lana, sleep became an undesired luxury. He would not rest until he found her. He looked at the scattered pictures on his desk of his buried memories, and his heart weighed heavily on his chest.

Sifting through these glimpses into Gugliehno's past life stirred a mix of unfamiliar emotions. Where was the woman he loved? This ruthless woman was a stranger. Did the woman he once hold dear even still exist somewhere deep inside that empty shell? Was there a small part of his children's loving mother remaining in her heart?

Gugliehno's thoughts raced, mixing with his anxiety and increasing concern. He had many reasons to hate and crucify her for the hell she's put him through; but now, all he wanted to know was her wellbeing. He longed for the affectionate lover and mother, who hailed her family over all else...

Drifting in his feeble desires, only a gentle knock on his office door returned him to reality.

"Who is it?" Gunny mumbled, displeased by the sudden disturbance.

"Sir, it's Marta," called his children's nanny from the other side of his door.

"Come in." Gugliehno said, leaning back in his chair.

"Sorry to disturb you so late, but I was worried about Mrs. Morelli."

"What do you mean? She should be fine. At least, she was when I saw her this morning."

"I haven't seen her all day, which is unusual. She checks on the children at least once a day."

"That is strange." A cornel of fear settled in his gut, causing him to jump from his chair and go with the nanny in search of his wife.

"Are you sure she didn't check on them when you left the room?" Gugliehno asked, ascending the stairs heading towards his bedroom.

"No, sir. I've been by their side all day. The only time I left them alone was to speak with you," Marta assured, covering her nose.

As they walked down the hall, a poignant odor filled the air. Its stench made it difficult to press on. Gugliehno covered his face with his hands and walked cautiously to his bedroom.

Fear overtook him when he recognized the vile smell. Being in this organization, he immediately recognized the stench. The smell of...

Gugliehno turned the knob of his room, but it was locked. He motioned for Marta to move away so he could ram the door. The thick, wooden door held until the third hit broke the lock, and it swung open.

The foul stench burned Gugliehno's eyes and throat as he looked on in terror. Marta's screams deafened him as the horror he suspected manifested in reality... death.

The bloody scene trapped Gugliehno in a repulsive terror. His wife's killer was ruthless. Susan's body was strewn on the floor. Her face pressed against the grate of the heater disfiguring her face and leaving behind a foul stench of burning flesh in the air. Stab wounds riddled her body. What was left of her face was twisted into a horrifying mask of agonizing despair.

Gugliehno could not withhold his tears. They poured down his face as he tried to calm the hysterical woman behind him.

"Marta, where are the children?" Gugliehno demanded, blocking her gaze. Petrified in fear, she cried while uttering nonsensical words. She was unaware of his words or presence. Gugliehno grabbed her by the shoulders, shaking her lightly.

"Where are the girls?" Gugliehno yelled once more, guiding her focus to him.

"Downstairs... in their room." Marta stammered.

"Compose yourself and get them. I want you to take them to Elda's house and remain there until I arrive. Don't tell them what happened but tell my sister everything. Understand?" Gugliehno said.

"Yes, sir. I understand. But what will you do?"

"I'm going to deal with the cops," Gugliehno responded, dropping his hands. "Hurry and make sure the children are fine, then leave immediately. I don't want them to know about this yet."

Marta hurried away to follow his instructions. Gugliehno waited until they drove off before he went into the office and called the police. His voice remained calm and composed, but his tears bucketed down his face. He never believed someone would ever target Susan. She was an innocent, loving woman who did nothing deserving of death.

It did not take long for the police to arrive after Gugliehno called. They investigated their bedroom from top-to-bottom while also checking the grounds below their window for any evidence about her murderer. After hours of turning his property upside down for clues and questioning Gugliehno about the events leading up to the discovery of his wife's body, they concluded Susan's death as a murder by an unknown burglar. They covered her body and carried her off.

Entranced, Gugliehno watched as they dragged Susan away. Moments like these were why he hated this world. Because of his family's influence, they covered the true nature of her death up, so they could settle the matter on their own. Frustrated tears threatened to fall, but Gugliehno held them back. For it was not time for tears, but for revenge.

Gugliehno's man inside the police department revealed everything they found during their investigation. A gruesome murder like that where the killer brutally mutilated his wife's body was not the act of a mere thief. No. that was an act fueled by hate. There was only one person alive who bore a grudge against Gugliehno and even swore to do anything to make him suffer. The only person capable of sneaking in and carrying out this heinous act without detection, Lana Rosilli.

Once the police left, Gugliehno went to tell Casimiro about the tragic event. He sped down the slippery roads, not caring how fast he went during this late hour. He cared about nothing now except revenge.

Frigid winds whipped through the car, keeping his tears at bay. His thoughts raced against the streetlights whizzing by and became more distorted as time marched on. His wife's brutal murder tore his heart apart. All the evidence pointed to his ex-wife. But was it true?

Lana was a cynical, heartless bitch at times, but she was not stupid. The crime scene was sloppy. Bloody footprints were scattered throughout the room. Footprints that were too small for a man, but perfect for a woman her size.

However, this all seemed too obvious and deliberate. Lana would not leave incriminating evidence behind. She also was not known for getting her hands dirty. Normally, she sent a hitman, like Viper, to do her dirty work for her. Finally, why would she target her when she was close to their children? Nothing about this made sense. If there was something she would protect more than anything, it would be their girls. If she wanted to kill Susan, she would have done it when she was not with their girls. So, why? Lana was the only one with a plausible motive, but it did not add up.

While driving down a dark street, Gugliehno noticed a familiar figure walking down the sidewalk. He slowed down to get a better look at the person in case it was only his mind playing tricks on him. However, when the woman adjusted her scarf, he recognized her curly, strawberry blonde hair and pixy face anywhere. It was Lana.

Gugliehno parked, stepped out of his car, withdrew his gun and ran over to her, pressing his gun against her back.

"Lana! Don't move you, sick bitch!" Gugliehno yelled, observing her.

Lana took her hands out of her pockets raising them slowly in the air. "My... My... My... Gugliehno, what an unfortunate surprise to run into you tonight. May I ask what has you in such fine spirits this evening?" Lana asked calmly.

"You know very well, you cold-hearted whore!"

Gugliehno's rage grew at the sound of her cold, indifferent tone.

Lana turned around slowly, keeping her hands in plain view so not to startle him. The hatred emanating from him confused her.

"What's with the name calling? Okay. Yes, I ordered the attack on your warehouse, but I did not know how attached you were to it."

Gugliehno went into a blind rage and pinned her against the wall, choking her with his hand while his gun pressed against her abdomen.

"You fucking monster, stop acting dumb! I'm not here for that! I'm here to get revenge for my wife, who you slaughtered!"

Surprise overtook Lana as she gasped for air. "Slaughtered? You mean Susan is dead?"

"Yes! She is dead! You killed her!" Gunny's grip tightened on her neck.

"No! I had nothing to do with that!" Lana gasped, wriggling her hand on his to help loosen his hold before he snapped her neck. "The girls... Are my babies alright?"

Shocked by her convincing act of concern. Gugliehno loosened his grip but kept his gun trained on her.

"Enough with the act! I have proof you did it! You left your footprints all over!"

"I swear to you. I had no hand in her death. I had no reason to harm Susan," Lana reassured.

"Don't lie. You, of all people, had a motive to want her dead, since she replaced you in our daughter's lives."

"Gunny, you're wrong. I never cared about that. I'm happy she was in their lives. She gave them something I could not..."

Gugliehno cut off her words. "Do you really expect me to believe that? Am I supposed to think compassion lies somewhere in that dark abyss, where a heart should be, of yours?"

Irritated by Gugliehno's onslaught of accusations, Lana became flustered. "I don't care anymore! Believe what you want!"

Lana grabbed the mouth of his gun and moved it to her chest, over her heart. "If

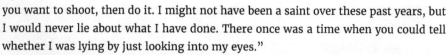
you want to shoot, then do it. I might not have been a saint over these past years, but I would never lie about what I have done. There once was a time when you could tell whether I was lying by just looking into my eyes."

Lana placed her hand over his. "Put your hatred aside and look. Tell me what you see. Is it the truth or lies?"

Stunned by her actions, Gugliehno froze. Her words and behavior reminded him of a moment long passed. He looked into her eyes' depths and saw a speck of her heart.

His rage still burned strong but could not overcome his will. He lowered his gun and stepped away from her. He lowered his hat so she could not see the few tears beginning to form.

Lana watched him as he dashed to his car and drove away. She held onto her own sadness until he pulled off. She cried not only for the heartache they both carried, but because of the light she saw buried behind his rage.

Underneath all the hatred hid a tiny light. Its size made it seem fragile, but it was far from it because a great power fueled it. One mighty enough that it could slice through the darkness and restore a bit of the hope she lost, love.

The Rules of the Game Change

'She's the reason my heart breaks, but she's also the reason it beats. She's both the cause of my sadness and happiness. If I abandon her now, I might regret it for the rest of my life,' Thoughts of Darian Mancini.

They say. 'There's always a great woman behind every great man'. Brock never thought it could be taken literally. He would have never guessed that fearless kid, Johnnie, was actually a woman and not just any woman, but the daughter of his boss, Amadora Morelli.

Brock saw her many times when guarding the family on business trips. He observed her from time-to-time, but she was nothing like Johnnie Barbone. She was a carefree and charming girl with no interest in business matters, which made him doubt Lana's accusations. If she did lie, why didn't Amadora defend herself in front of her boyfriend?

Brock normally kept out of other people's business, but this situation interested him. He needed to find out the truth.

The pain from Amadora's breaking heart kept her up all night. A void filled her chest, consuming any happiness she once had. In a few minutes, she lost everything. The one man she ever loved was gone and would never return.

This was not supposed to happen. Amadora was supposed to maneuver her way up her brother's circuit and impress her family with no complications. How could she be so careless? What possessed her to entertain a man who could ruin everything with ease? She should have never allowed herself to fall for him. Maybe if she did not, then everything would have been fine, wouldn't it have?

Amadora wondered what she would have been like today if she never agreed to see Darian at the ball. Would she have been happy?

Her mind drifted between a world of fantasy and reality. She imagined her ideal life as she initially desired, but the more she probed into that possibility, the more

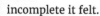

incomplete it felt.

Darian was the only thing keeping her heart alive and mind sane. His love stabilized her last tie to humanity, protecting her from corruption in this dark world. Without him, she would have never found the strength to manage all the mental and emotional wear and tear.

A high-pitch ringing shattered her thoughts and returned her to reality. Amadora wiped her face and controlled her sniffling before answering the phone.

"Hello." Amadora said in Johnnie's deep voice.

"Johnnie. It's Brock."

"Brock, isn't it too early for a social call? Do we have a job to do?"

"Yeah. I need some help to guard a small front since one of my men is home sick. Are you interested in helping me out?"

"Sure. Where's the place at?"

"Can you swing by my place? We could save some gas if we carpool."

"Sounds good. I'll be there in thirty minutes." Amadora hung up the phone and went to get ready.

However, she could not shake the nagging suspicions in her gut. During the time she knew Brock, he never invited him over to his house before doing a job. Something felt amiss, but whether it was paranoia leftover from her encounter with Lana or her sixth sense for trouble, she was not sure.

When Johnnie arrived at Brock's place, his quaint quarters surprised him. Larry made less than him but had a nice house in a quiet neighborhood. He expected Brock to live somewhere similar, especially since he was married, but this place was no bigger than Anna's living room and kitchen combined. The small studio had a kitchen, bedroom area and living room all-in-one. The only other room was a small bathroom in the living room's far corner.

Johnnie contained his confusion as he followed Brock into the living room.

"Nice place you have here. It's a safe house, right?"

"Yes. It's my private island, away from the chaos of my old lady and rugrats. You must have a place like this too, don't you?"

Johnnie shook his head. "No. I don't. When I need to escape, I just go for a walk outside."

Johnnie could tell by his tone and the way Brock looked at him that Brock had another reason for inviting him here.

"You invited me here for another reason. What is it?"

Brock sighed, then smirked. "You're very clever, kid. I invited you here to speak with you in private."

"About what?"

"I wanted to let you know out of respect that I know the truth, Johnnie."

Johnnie's blood ran cold, and fear took control. "The truth about what?"

"I know you aren't actually Johnnie Barbone, but actually Don Morelli's daughter, Amadora." Brock answered. "Don't worry. I won't tell your secret to anyone. I'm impressed by your courage to put on a dangerous ruse. No matter what, you have an ally in me. I will help you in any way possible."

Amadora's expression eased, and she extended her hand to shake his.

"Thank you. I'm glad to have you as an ally and friend."

Guarding the front seemed like a waste of time and manpower, because it was just an import firm by the docks. It dealt with importing and transporting exotic goods to small Italian markets throughout the city, but there were barely any deliveries since there were some delays on the supply boats. Johnnie wondered why Lorenzo would waste fifteen men to guard a low-key place like this.

Johnnie leaned against a stack of crates and yawned. He was not sure how long he would last, because his lack of sleep mixed with the cool fog and this mundane routine made him drowsy. Even though it was boring, he had to do his job. He promised Brock.

A little past two in the afternoon, things heated up. A loud explosion came from the west warehouse. Johnnie ran over to Brock, who signaled for him to go with him to check it out. They readied their guns while stealthily checking every crevice for the attackers, but there was no one.

When a second explosion sounded, they ran over to the warehouse. They stopped a few feet short of the towering inferno in shock. Brock tapped Johnnie's shoulder after noticing the culprits at the gate by some cars. He signaled for Johnnie, but he was still mesmerized by the flames ahead. Johnnie looked away only when he heard Brock's voice and the first roar of gunfire echo through the air. Johnnie ducked for cover before returning fire.

The thick fog made it difficult to distinguish between foe and comrade. Only the debris from the enemies' bullets scraping the metal containers behind him was visible to him. Agonizing cries from faraway as enemies were struck down cut through the air.

Johnnie backed away as a bullet scraped a crate he stood behind. He tried to see past the white fog to find his next target; but before he could fire a shot, he was grabbed from behind. He tried to fight free, but his body grew weak and became drowsy once they pressed a cloth over his mouth. In only moments, he fell unconscious, not seeing who attacked him.

Once the shooting ceased, Brock ordered some men to check for any survivors. It took them a few moments to assess the area and report back. There were not many survivors or signs that anyone escaped. The situation seemed odd.

There was nothing important stored in the warehouse. Only a bunch of crap brought over from Europe. Then why destroy it? What did they accomplish? What was the point of it all?

Brock searched the surrounding men before noticing Johnnie was nowhere to be seen.

"Have you seen Johnnie?" Brock asked Ronny, looking around the yard in case he was injured.

"No, Boss. I haven't seen him. In this fog, I can barely see you," Ronny answered, squinting.

Ronny was right. The fog was so thick now that even Brock found it difficult to see who stood in front of him.

"Find him! He may be hurt!"

They searched the entire area but found nothing except for his gun behind a container. Brock understood immediately why they attacked. They wanted Johnnie.

Brock stood in terror while taking in the truth. They captured Johnnie Barbone. He prayed their enemies did not know how precious their captive was. They did not just take Gugliehno's best man, but his younger sister, too.

Amadora Morelli was about to be a modern-day Helen of Troy and start another never-ending war drenched in innocent blood.

Anna leaned against her kitchen cabinet, taking a few pulls from her cigarette, watching Brock pace back and forth in the middle of her living room. In the years she knew him, he never acted like this before. His peculiar behavior worried her, but her expression rejected her true feelings.

"If you're not going to say what's wrong, then do you want something to calm your nerves? Tea? Cigarettes? Or a sedative, maybe?" Anna said.

"No. Thank you. I'll just wait until the boss gets back." Brock glanced at his watch. "Do you know how long he'll be out? This is an urgent matter."

Anna shrugged. "Not sure. He left to smooth things over with his gal. Who knows how long matters of the heart can take?"

"Tsk. This is a horrible time to be fraternizing." Brock sneered.

"Why is that?" Zanipolo asked, closing the front door behind him and Samantha.

Brock turned around suddenly and ran over to his boss with terror imprinted all over his face. "Boss, I have some terrible news. Johnnie was taken."

The room went silent while fear seized their hearts. Samantha dropped to the couch, petrified by his revelation. Anna's mouth fell open, causing her cigarette to fall on the floor. She stamped out the ashes, but the force of her movement caused her to reel over the counter. Zanipolo restrained his body's initial reaction until he got a better understanding of the situation.

"When? And how did this happen?" Zanipolo demanded.

"When we were guarding the exotic market docks, an explosion went off in the warehouse. In all the confusion, they snatched him up, leaving only his gun behind." Brock explained, reaching into his pocket and placing it in Zanipolo's hand.

"I know the kid very well. He wouldn't go anywhere without that."

"Have you reported this to Lorenzo?" Zanipolo asked.

"No. I came straight here," Brock answered.

"Why?" Zanipolo asked, confused.

"Because I know this hits home for you, and you would want to hear it first. He is your sister, Amadora, after all." Brock said.

He noticed the silent warning emanating from Zanipolo's eyes, so he softened his tone. "Don't worry. I'm not going to tell anyone. I like the kid. She has spunk. Also, I understand the danger involved if her identity gets out. My lips are sealed."

Zanipolo's eyes softened. At that point, revelation was the last thing on his mind. He had to figure out a way to get her out of a deadly mess. It was about time all this madness ended once and for all. If they were going to get her back, they would need everyone's help.

He took the gun, contemplating the flood of emotions racing through his head at that moment.

"Thank you for your loyalty. For now, I only care about rescuing my sister," Zanipolo said, pocketing the gun. "Don't worry about telling Lorenzo. Since I have to tell my siblings anyway, I might as well let him know what's going on."

Brock nodded, then left. Zanipolo walked over to Samantha, who was paralyzed on the couch. He touched her shoulder, smashing his own concern with a calm smile.

"Don't worry. We'll get her back."

Samantha looked into his eyes and noticed the effort he put in reassuring her despite his own pain. She placed her hand over his and smiled.

"Polo, I know we will. We must."

Anger, hate, and confusion were a dangerous concoction. Darian's psyche was at war with itself while his heart hemorrhaged slowly all the feelings that he once had for Amadora. He thought he saw his share of monsters in his life, but never had he encountered one like her. She was not like the monsters driven by greed, bloodlust, or power. Amadora was a manipulative seductress who could break down the barriers around a man's heart just to stab it once they were vulnerable. She was a siren lurking in innocent prey with her beautiful mask and enchanting song. She was driven by deceit and blood, using ignorant fools only to fulfill her own selfish, twisted desires.

He was an idiot. How could he fall into her trap? How could he fall under her spell? Why did he let his guard down around the seed of that demon, Basilio Morelli? Nothing related to that man was ever good.

Darian never wanted to see Amadora or hear her name again. He wanted to forget all about her betrayal and remove every memory of her. Every memory of her smile, laugh, voice, the warmth of her skin, lips and the foolish entity he believed to be love he would banish from his mind and heart. However, fate had different plans for him regarding Amadora.

Ferocious pounding on his door rattled Darian and ripped him from his thoughts. The hour was too late for visitors, and they rarely received any packages at the front door. There was only one person it could be, Amadora. Darian ignored the incessant noise, hoping she would give up and go away. However, after twenty long minutes, the knocking persisted, growing harder with each passing minute.

"I'm coming!" Darian yelled, undoing the locks as fast as he could.

He yanked it open, coming face-to-face with Amadora's brother, Zanipolo.

"Not the Morelli I expected at my door. If you're here on her behalf, my answer won't change. She can send God himself, but that won't change my mind. I don't want to see her ever again."

Zanipolo looked at him, confused, then brushed off his words. "I don't know what you're talking about. I'm not here to resolve any spat you had with my sister. There is something more important I need to discuss with you. Can we talk inside?"

"I have no business with you or your deceitful sister," Darian answered, dryly blocking the way.

"Fine. Tell me what she's done to make you a stubborn asshole this evening. You're nothing like the lovesick pup, shoving his tongue down her throat, that you were a few days ago."

"She didn't tell you what happened. I thought you gangster children were supposed to be close." Darian snickered. "Maybe she's keeping it a secret from you too."

"Keeping what a secret? Amadora tells me everything. If something happened between you two recently, then she wouldn't have time to tell me since I haven't been home, and someone kidnapped her earlier today." Zanipolo replied, maintaining his composure towards Darian's slights.

"Kidnapped?" All color drained from his body. "Please. Tell me what happened."

"I'd rather talk inside. This is a very sensitive matter." Zanipolo said.

Darian nodded and stepped aside to let him in. Once the door was shut, Zanipolo explained the situation.

"Before I begin, there's something you must know about my sister..."

"That she's Johnnie Barbone. Save your breath. I already know about that."

"She told you?" Zanipolo asked, surprised.

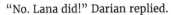

"No. Lana did!" Darian replied.

"Lana? Do you mean Lana Rosilli?"

"Yes," Darian said shortly.

"Do you know her?" Zanipolo growled, struggling to withhold his anger.

"No. I don't. She ambushed our carriage at the park and spilled the beans on her little secret. Amadora never denied it, so that's when I realized it must be true." Darian answered, suppressing the hurt resurfacing from the memory of Amadora's betrayal.

"I see. So, that's why you now hate her?"

"Yes. How am I supposed to feel after learning the woman I loved and the man I hate are the same?"

Zanipolo glanced at his watch and frowned. "I know this may be hard to believe, but my sister had her reasons for doing what she did. Whether or not her actions were good, I don't have time to debate that now. She's in danger. Can you put your feelings aside and help me rescue her?"

Darian paused. "I'm sorry. I can't. I hope you bring her home safe, but I want nothing more to do with your sister." Darian tried to hide his concerns, but Zanipolo saw right through his charade.

Zanipolo was going to press further but saw clearly that Darian was at war with himself. Darian's worry and fear for Amadora's life battled her betrayal that was fresh in his heart. Zanipolo recognized this state-of-mind from a time not so long ago. Words would not ease his conflicting emotions only time could. Unfortunately for her, time was not one of their allies.

Zanipolo brushed past him, pausing at the threshold briefly.

"You know... Even if my sister kept her identity a secret, it wasn't to play mind games. You're special to her. That's why she entertained your relationship. She risked everything just to witness a glimpse of genuine joy. She lied because she was afraid of losing you. However, the only things she never lied about were her feelings for you."

"Gugliehno, what do you plan to do? How can you get revenge when the culprit is a woman hidden from the world?" Elda pressed, sitting on the arm of a chair in the living room.

"I'm not going to focus on Lana. I only want to find my wife's murderer." Gugliehno said, staring into the embers of the fireplace.

"Why don't you think Lana is her killer?" Elda pressed.

"The crime scene doesn't match her M.O. It was sloppy with evidence purposely planted to frame her."

"Don't be naïve, Gunny. You know she's cunning enough to stage the scene that way to fool investigators." Lorenzo pointed out, sitting in the chair next to Elda.

"He's right. Why are you defending her?" Elda interjected, annoyed.

"I'm not defending her! I just know she's not responsible!" Gugliehno snapped.

"Responsible for what? Did something happen?" Zanipolo's voice trailed into the room from the entryway.

"Someone murdered Susan last night. Everyone here, except Gunny, believes Lana did it," Casimiro said.

Zanipolo went over to his brother, placing a hand on his shoulder.

"I'm sorry, Gunny, but it wouldn't surprise me if she did it. Lana has been more active lately and is why I'm here," Zanipolo started, walking to the other side of the fireplace.

"Why? What has she done now?" Gugliehno asked.

"She revealed herself before, and I believe she sent her men to kidnap Amadora earlier today."

"Amadora kidnapped! Where? How?" Gugliehno exclaimed.

The news shocked everyone in the room. They were terrified of the unknown circumstances that led to this recent development and the state Amadora was in at that very moment.

"She was guarding one of your fronts as Johnnie Barbone," Zanipolo answered simply.

"Interesting. You're saying your little sister is our best man," Lorenzo grinned.

"You met him. Didn't you think he looked familiar?" Elda asked.

"No. I couldn't. Donny's place was filled with smoke, and she was heavily disguised. I couldn't make out her features in all of that." Lorenzo shrugged.

"That's impossible! Someone would've noticed she wasn't really a man." Casimiro rubbed his temples while trying to digest the news. Saying Amadora was Johnnie Barbone was like saying the sun was actually the moon. It was preposterous to even entertain that light-hearted Dora was the ruthless rookie.

Gugliehno plopped into a chair and stared at the floor by his feet. He blocked out most of the back-and-forth to sort through the information Zanipolo relayed.

"Don't underestimate her. She's brilliant and crafty. Something like this isn't out of her realm of capability. However, I'm curious how she pulled off this scheme," Elda said, masking her grin behind her hand.

"I wondered that as well. A ruse like this can't be pulled off without a decent amount of people helping. Also, I'm curious how you found out it was her who was taken if she was disguised when it happened." Lorenzo added.

While their attention focused on Zanipolo, he masked his concerns and explained everything from start to finish. He told them about Lana's fascination with Johnnie Barbone, that drove her to confront Amadora recently. Gugliehno tried to mask his fury while Casimiro tried to mull over this new information. It was clear by the way he mumbled and pace that he was role playing how to break the news to their parents.

Lorenzo remained indifferent and just waited to see what Gugliehno wanted to do while Elda seemed amused.

Gugliehno's jaw clenched while he balled his hand into a fist. He took a deep breath before regaining his composure and speaking again.

"I have nothing to say regarding all you've told us. Everything else will have to wait. Because for now, our only priority is bringing Amadora home safe."

After Zanipolo left, the war between Darian's heart and mind raged on. His heart pressed for him to put aside his hurt and save Amadora, but his mind held him back to spare him anymore pain. He did not know which to listen to sinking him in greater confusion.

He cradled his head in his hands and closed his eyes, hoping to ease his torment, but nothing could calm the storm raging inside him.

Domenico hobbled down the corridor of his apartment. When he saw Darian curled up on the couch in the living room, he went over to check. For a few days, his son acted strangely. He became quiet and distant, but Domenico did not understand why.

"Are you alright?" Domenico placed a gentle hand on Darian's shoulder.

"No. I'm not. I feel like my heart has been ripped right from my chest, and my life has been nothing but lies," Darian grumbled, refusing to turn and face him.

"Why? What happened?" Domenico was confused.

Darian faced him with eyes bloodshot red embedded with dark bags. "I know about everything. Why didn't you tell me my mother was one of them?"

Domenico sighed while he sat beside his son.

"I wanted you to live a normal life away from the world that destroyed your mother." He paused, meeting his son's intense gaze with one of understanding.

"Your mother and I met when I was a Rosilli associate. She was a headstrong beauty brimming with ambitions. We fell in love, married and conceived you. When you were only two years old, the Rosilli don pressured me to have you follow in his footsteps as soon as you turned 18, but I refused. I already saw this business corrupt too many souls, including your mother's. I wasn't going to let that happen to you, too; so, I took you and ran to Don Morelli, who agreed to protect us. That's why I paid them protection money, not because I was being forced, but because Don Morelli took care of us for all these years."

Darian looked at his father wide-eyed in shock at his father's words. The world he hated was more a part of him then he realized. If his father did not protect him years ago, maybe he would have ended up like Amadora.

Darian sat up and shook his head. "I can't believe I share blood with them. What does it mean? Am I no different from the power-hungry fiends I detest?"

"Ridiculous. You're nothing like them. You may share blood, but that doesn't make you the same. That also goes for Amadora as well." Domenico smiled, putting his hand up to prevent Darian from interrupting.

"I may be old, but I notice things. Yes. I can tell when my once starry-eyed son comes home looking all doom-and-gloom. You must have uncovered Amadora's secret. However, before you let your mind go wild, let me tell you. That girl isn't the monster she pretends to be."

"How do you know?" Darian asked, surprised

"She visited me the other day to confess the entire business and beg for forgiveness. The poor girl is just as confused about all of this as you; so, I forgave her."

"Ha! Confused!" Darian scoffed. "She wants to be a monster like the rest of them! She'd rather be a cold, heartless killer! That's what she really desires... not me."

"Are you blind?" Domenico snapped, annoyed. "The dark world is all she ever knew. Of course, she'd find it appealing. But after immersing in it, she realized there was something she desired more... You, my stubborn boy."

"You're wrong. If she really wanted me, why would she continue that ruse?"

"Do you really think it's that easy to break away from that business? Do you think Johnnie Barbone, Gugliehno's most decorated man, could just vanish from the world?"

Domenico calmed and patted his shoulder. "It will take time to overcome your pain. As the moments turn to hours and hours to days, your heart will long for the woman who immersed you in hope of a pure, carefree love. Hopefully, by then, you can put your pain aside and help her make this difficult escape. Otherwise, you may live the rest of your life bitter and alone, wondering what could have been."

Darian turned away from his father, letting his tears fall. His father was right, but Amadora's deception still plagued his heart, which was unmoved by his words. Darian was not sure if he could ever forgive her; but if he did not help save her, and she died, he would live the rest of his life buried in regret.

18

Beware the Viper's Lair

'The greatest pleasure in this world is knowing you have the power to mold other's fates without fear of it impacting yours,' Thoughts of Viper.

Finding Zanipolo's whereabouts was easy. Since Amadora was taken, her family's complex bustled with their men. He flashed his ID at a guard in front of the main house and followed them inside to where everyone gathered. When he entered the room, questioning glares bombarded him.

"Who are you?" Gugliehno demanded.

"I am Darian. I want to help get Amadora back," Darian replied.

"How do you know about this matter? What's your relationship?" Gugliehno pressed.

"I told him." Zanipolo said, entering behind Darian with Elda. "He's Amadora's lover."

"Since when does she have a boyfriend?" Gugliehno asked, surprised, while looking over this strange man.

"Does that really matter? He's cute." Elda smiled, walking over to him and taking a closer look.

"They met at the ball and have been seeing each other ever since," Zanipolo said.

"Amadora has been a busy girl. Vicious soldier by day and gentle lover by night." Elda jeered. "There truly is nothing she could do now that could surprise me."

"Sorry to interrupt this interrogation, but shouldn't we be looking for her instead of sitting around?" Darian asked, annoyed by her siblings' relaxed manners.

"Patience, rookie. We're not just twiddling our thumbs doing nothing." Elda started. "We're waiting to hear from our men about a potential lead. Once we get that information, we'll act."

"While you're out, I'll hang back in case there are any fresh developments." Casimiro added.

"Sounds like a plan. Let's get ready. Once Lorenzo calls, we can roll out." Gugliehno guided everyone into an adjacent room filled with weapons and ammunition.

Zanipolo tapped Darian's shoulder and handed him a gun. "Thanks for reconsidering. Take this. You'll need it."

"Thank you. But why this one?"

"It belongs to Dora. I think it's best if you're the one who gets to use it."

Darian grabbed a holster off a crate, tucked the gun inside, and concealed it underneath his coat. "Thank you."

After an hour, Brock pulled up with his men to report Lorenzo's findings. Lorenzo was looking into several probable locations but one he was most suspicious of was an abandoned dock yard in South Jersey that was crawling with Rosilli men, but it was far from their known territories.

Everyone went outside to meet the others at the cars when they saw Elda and Brock arguing with Anna and Samantha.

"This isn't a field trip. It's too dangerous to bring you along," Elda stated.

"Don't treat us like children. We understand the danger and will risk our lives to bring Dora home." Anna snapped.

"That's noble. But are you willing to jeopardize our lives and the efficacy of this plan as well?" Elda pressed.

"What do you mean?" Samantha asked.

"What she means is that neither of you have the proper training to hold your own out there? If we bring you along, you could slow us down or jeopardize ours or Amadora's lives. That would do more harm than good." Brock explained.

"We're not as useless as you think. My father taught me how to handle a gun." Samantha said.

"And I've learned more than a few party tricks from fraternizing with your men, Elda." Anna smirked.

"A strange thing to take pride in. Fine. Do as you wish. If you hinder our efforts to rescue our sister, I won't hesitate to get rid of you myself." Elda shrugged and entered her car.

With everything said and packed away, they set out in their cars. These people, with different lives, set out for one cause; to save the one person who linked them together, Amadora.

Flat square buildings scattered the dockyard. The area seemed vacant, with its boarded windows and weathered bricks; but the new gate surrounding the property and guards pacing around the yard told a different story. Something hid behind this vacant mirage.

They parked far from the site to hide their arrival, prepped their weapons, and put on their body armor to assure they were dealt as few casualties as possible. Zanipolo watched as Samantha checked her gun. Her knowledge of guns was a new discovery that fascinated him, but a part of him worried about her ability to use it on actual targets. It was something shooting at a gun range could not prepare you for.

When she struggled to fasten her armor, Zanipolo went over and offered his help.

"You're nervous, aren't you?"

Samantha did not reply, but sheepishly looked away.

"Stubborn as always. Calm your nerves. I'll make sure nothing happens to you." Zanipolo reassured, buttoning her shirt.

She picked up her gun from the hood of the car beside her and tucked it in her holster.

"Don't treat me like some helpless damsel-in-distress. We're here to save Amadora. She should be your only concern. I can handle myself."

Zanipolo fastened the last button, smiling without protest. "Fine, Sam."

Zanipolo's amusement shone through his soft eyes. He saw right through her stubbornness to her true feelings and refrained from arguing with her anymore, because she was right. At the moment, Amadora was their primary concern.

Anna walked over to them, breaking up their moment.

"We're taking out the guards in the yard first and then enter the center building cautiously. Gunny's men will check on the others. We're going to use the thick fog to mask our presence and numbers. Let's go. We're heading out."

Using the fog as a shield, they swiftly enclosed on the gate's perimeter without notice. Gugliehno led the way, guiding them behind the trucks parked nearby until they reached a safe distance. He signaled the leaders of his teams, along with Brock and Elda. Once his hand fell, they lit Molotov grenades and hurled them over the fence. As soon as they released them, they ducked back behind the truck.

Breaking glass and explosions of roaring fire alerted the guards, drawing them to the front. They waited until enough of them gathered before tossing another round. This time blood-curdling screams mixed with a chorus of the blazing flames.

The guards flew into shock as confusion spread through their ranks. Demands for the cause of the disturbance echoed through the crowd while others frantically helped put out the flames of their comrades. The commanding officer ordered his men to prepare themselves and leave the dying men alone.

The darkness and thick fog made seeing their attackers difficult. Their whereabouts and numbers were a mystery; and they were losing men left and right to waves of Molotov grenades crashing down upon them.

Cesar Moncelli, a Rosilli soldier, stepped back as bottles of flames shattered nearby. He tried navigating the chaos while the flames engulfed his comrades. He readied himself, drawing his gun and preparing for the assailants' next move as the front gates came crashing down.

Smoke from the blazing inferno further complicated their vision. Cesar could not tell how many men were lost or how many remained. He called out to the silhouettes he could make out.

"They're coming from the front gate! Take cover and fire!"

Distorted by the confusion, his men took some time to respond. By the time they did, many fell to their attackers' bullets. Cesar took cover and shot back; but their conditions made defending impossible. The fog played tricks on their senses, transforming mere men into phantoms they could not faze.

Cesar rushed into the main building to warn his boss and the rest of their men. The noise from outside caused panic inside. The men clamored to the windows for a glimpse of what was happening. Some surrounded Cesar, pressing him for answers.

"We're under attack! I don't know the numbers, but we need to prepare to fight back! Call the other warehouses to get ready!"

Death surrounded them on all sides. This scene sparked hidden memories of Darian's service years. His focus wavered as those dark memories resurfaced; but he held firm, pressing forward. His determination to find Amadora and save her from her fate restored his composure. He followed behind Gugliehno and his men as they cleared a route to the main building.

"Since they already know we're here, let's blow open the front door." Elda said, holding a large bundle of dynamite and glancing at Gugliehno.

Gugliehno nodded and signaled for everyone to find cover while Elda placed it at the entrance. She lit the fuse and ran for cover.

A few minutes passed, the booming blast, and a cascade of debris rang through the air. Agonizing screams joined the deadly chorus of the explosion shortly after. They waited until everything settled before charging inside.

Cesar entered the depths of the building until he reached a dark, fog-filled cavern. He walked along the dank walls, calling out to the surrounding darkness.

"Boss, we need to get you out of here now! The yard is under attack!"

Only the echo of Cesar's voice bellowed through the shadows. He waited for a response, but the darkness and the current circumstances filled him with fear.

"Are you there? We must get out of here before they find you." Cesar called out.

"I know they're here. I expected their arrival." Viper's dark voice reverberated off the rocks, startling Cesar.

"I have orders from the don to get you to safety if things go array. We should use this chance to escape." Cesar replied, calming his nerves as Viper drew near.

"I don't plan on running away. That's a foolish trait of the weak-minded, and I despise the weak." Viper snapped. "Are you afraid? Is that the real reason you're here?"

Cesar froze at Viper's touch on his shoulder. "No. Of course not. I'm here purely to follow the strict orders of our don."

Viper's hand slid down his arm, stopping over his elbow. "You're lying. No matter how hard you try, you can't hide your fear. It shows clearly, and I... don't need a coward defending me."

Before Viper finished speaking, he drove his blade deep into Cesar's back. Cesar twitched, trying to reach the blade, but it was too late. Viper twisted his blade, causing Cesar to fall to the ground, paralyzed in his own blood. He desperately grasped onto the fleeting moments of his life; but as he took another breath, he knew his time had come. Soon, the pain and fear would be no more, and death would soon free him from all his ailments.

Zanipolo searched the scattered remains of the fallen Rosilli men for any survivors. However, while he progressed through the bloody sea of mangled corpses, hope grew scarce. No one seemed to escape death's clutches. It was only when Brock left his side to investigate a strange gurgling sound from behind a mountain of crates on the far end of the main floor that their luck changed.

A man, bleeding heavily from his abdomen and shoulder, struggled to prop himself against the wall. The agony from his wounds clouded his awareness of his surroundings. His skin was almost pasty-white as his life force drained along with his blood.

Zanipolo looked over at his wounds. They were deep, but could be treated if they rushed him to the hospital soon. Otherwise, this man would die within the hour. He crouched by his side, grabbed a scarf from a corpse and pressed it against the wound on the man's abdomen.

The man resisted at first; but when he grew weaker from his blood loss, he stopped. Disdain settled in his eyes from being too helpless to prevent his friends' killers from helping him.

"Why don' you just lemme die?" The man snarled.

"I don't want you to die. None of us wants that. We're just here to get our comrade back. Your bosses kidnapped him, and we're here to take him back."

"My bosses? If yer afta them, then why did you come here?" The man asked.

"Don't act dumb. We know you're hiding Lana or Viper here, because there's no way old man Rosilli would have an army of men here just to guard an empty dockyard." Zanipolo grinned.

"I don't know why you're keeping your lips shut. You're about to die, anyway.

Whether we help you or not, your fate is sealed. You don't have to worry about the consequences, if you tell us what we want to know." Brock sneered.

"Yer right. Imma die. That's even more reason not to tell you a damn thing." The man smirked. "There's nothing more you can do to me."

"You're wrong, my friend. You still have lots of time before you meet your maker. Whether those moments are peaceful or an agonizing hell, all depends on the choice you make now."

The man flinched when Zanipolo's dark gaze fell upon him. He could tell by his rising bloodlust that his threats were not hollow. Now, he feared something more than death, Zanipolo Morelli.

"Fine. You'll find a door on the far-left corner of this level next to an office. That door will lead you to the stairwell to the underground dockyard. If they haven't escaped, they should be hiding there."

Zanipolo could tell by the fearful look in the man's eyes that his words were true. He thanked the man, motioned to some of their men to tend to him, then headed back with Brock to inform the others of what they learned.

The cold kiss of a stray draft brushed against Johnnie's cheek, rousing him from his unconscious state. Dazed and distorted, he tried to make sense of his whereabouts. The darkness concealed the features of his prison. Only a stray glint of moonlight illuminated small spots throughout her cell.

Johnnie could not move his hands or legs because they were bound around a metal pipe above him. He tried to break his restraints, but they were too strong to break without shattering every bone in his body.

Johnnie searched the moonlit ground for any sharp instrument to help free himself, but he was helpless, with no way to free or defend himself. He did not even know who captured him.

For the first time since entering in this world, Johnnie could not come up with any ingenious ideas to escape his problem. He had no other choice but to wait and see what fate had in store for him.

They descended into the depths of the warehouse and ended up in a secret cavern. The smell of the ocean filled the room as they descended on its rocky ground. Tiny oil lamps hung around the dock cast will-o-wisps onto the black sea. A distant cloud of fog crossed the black horizon outside, nearing the cave with the ebb and flow of the waves. A small boat floated in the center of the water, seemingly as dead as the rest of this building.

Gugliehno motioned for them to stay close as they pressed on. Dread of the unknown, masked by the shadows, spread like an infection. They did not know what lurked in the darkness, but they felt an evil presence drawing near.

"It's too dark. How are we supposed to see anything?" Zanipolo whispered.

"We have some flashlights. But using them would make us easy to spot. We light some Molotovs and throw them around. At least that way, if they are waiting to ambush, we can take some of those bastards with us." Gugliehno answered, gazing into the unknown.

"Now... Now... Gugliehno. If you need light, then you can just ask." An eerie, deep voice bounced off the shadows.

When the lights flickered on, a tall, thin hooded figure stood on a cliff in the distance before them. They stood in awe, but kept their weapons trained on the creepy figure. There stood the very essence of evil. The devil's assassin, Viper.

"Welcome to my humble abode. What an honor to have not one but three of the Morelli caporegimes in one room. What could I have done to deserve such an honor?" Viper announced.

"Cut the crap. You know exactly why we're here." Zanipolo snapped, aggravated by Viper's theatrical manner.

"For Barbone? But why would capos risk their lives for a mere soldier? I didn't realize your men matter so much to you." Viper pressed, feigning ignorance of their true reason.

Tense silence permeated the air as they concealed their true motives. Viper grinned in dark amusement. "But that can't be the case because you're with Darian Mancini. It's well-known that he despises Johnnie Barbone. Which means there's another reason you're here."

Darian clenched his teeth, suppressing his rage. The sick way Viper treated threatening someone's life as a game made his inside churn. Scum, like him, was the reason he hated this world. His hand trembled while it tightened around his gun. His hatred festered, taking control of his common sense.

Viper's devious grin widened. "So, I was right... The notorious Johnnie Barbone is actually Basilio Morelli's youngest daughter, Amadora. Very intriguing." His voice cooed with excitement.

"Damn, you sick bastard! Where is she!" Darian demanded, aiming his gun at Viper's shadow.

Viper roared with laughter. "I see you're not the brains of this operation."

Darian rested his finger on the trigger. Samantha noticed he was going for a kill shot and pushed his hand towards the ground.

"Darian don't do it. He's the only lead we have." Samantha begged.

Darian took his hand off the trigger. Ashamed that he almost let Viper bait him into killing their only link to finding Amadora in time.

"You should listen to her, boy. She seems to be the only one not letting her emotions cloud their judgment."

Viper looked over at the others, who still had their guns trained on him.

"Go ahead and kill me. However, know that once you do, you seal your sister's fate."

Viper extended his arms wide, giving them a clear shot. It was clear he was baiting them into a foolish trap that could jeopardize their entire mission. Although his trick failed and they lowered their weapons, they never dropped their guard.

"Enough games! Tell us where you're keeping Amadora!" Gugliehno demanded, dropping his gun to his side.

Viper dropped his arms and grinned. "I don't have her or even know where she is. Maybe you should check with your precious Lana. She is Johnnie's number one fan."

Viper slowly stepped from the ledge. "Too bad though. No matter where she is, you won't make it out here alive to see her again."

Gugliehno yelled for everyone to take cover; and within seconds, Viper disappeared into a dark crevice before returning with a group of men, who immediately fired at them.

The booming thunder of gunfire echoed throughout the cavern. The invasive noise rang through Samantha's ears as she returned fire. She hesitated to move and fire back until she felt a hand touch her shoulder.

"Don't be afraid. Remember why we're doing this." Zanipolo said.

Samantha looked at Zanipolo wide-eyed and nodded. She took a deep breath and followed his instruction. All the moments she shared with Amadora flashed in her mind, filling her with an unwavering courage. She no longer cared about anything other than seeing her friend again.

Amadora was the sole drive for everyone as they fought through Viper's men. Victory was a genuine reality. Viper's men quickly fell, leaving only a small fraction behind.

Once the last fell, Viper reloaded his gun and continued shooting back at Johnnie's calvary. His efforts seemed useless when the rest of his men fell, leaving him alone to fight on his own.

Viper fended them off for a while without alerting them to his circumstance. However, even his long solo stand could not last forever. With ammunition running low and them realizing his true numbers, he needed to slow them down. He needed to take one of them out.

Viper surveyed the area for his enemy, searching for the easiest target. His soulless eyes landed on Anna, who hid behind some tin drums. She was busy loading her gun and not paying attention to her surroundings. For a moment, she moved away from her hiding spot and into his line of sight.

He raised his gun and took aim. Viper placed his finger on the trigger, looking for the perfect angle to take his shot.

Elda scoured the cliff for their enemy's whereabouts. When she noticed a gleam coming from behind a stack of barrels, she followed the direction it pointed and noticed it aimed for Anna.

Elda could not warn Anna, because she was reloading her gun. So Elda aimed and shot at the small piece of metal. Her gun roared through the cavern, alerting the others. Anna ducked back behind the drums and an agonizing scream followed.

After the echo of Elda's shot faded, the cave fell in silence. They waited before investigating the noise.

"I think you nicked someone." Anna said after hearing the scream.

"Sounds like it. Since the shooting stopped, I might've hit Viper." Elda said, gazing at where she shot. There was nothing. She turned to Gugliehno, who kneeled near her. "Should we check or wait in case it's a trap?"

Gugliehno scanned where Viper and his men once were. "Let's move in and check for survivors. We don't want Viper to escape. Be on your guard. There's no telling what traps he's set up there."

Gugliehno led them to the top of the cliff. A vast field of motionless bodies greeted them. Samantha winced at the sight of the slain men soaking in pools of blood. She wanted to hide behind Zanipolo, who walked in front of her, but she knew she could not. She needed to stay strong and press forward for Amadora.

Staying strong was difficult when confronted with so much gore and death. Just the sight made her stomach churn, making her feel nauseous. Even though these were her enemies, Samantha could not help but feel guilty. However, that feeling soon faded when her eyes fell upon the cause of this massacre, Viper.

Zanipolo was second to notice Viper, hunched over in pain. His pent-up rage boiled over as he ran over to him, grabbed his collar, and slammed him against the wall, making Viper grunt in pain.

"You think that hurts? Just wait until you feel the hell that I have planned for you if you don't start talking," Zanipolo warned, tightening his grip.

Zanipolo's hatred pulsated at the sight of Viper's mocking fear. He pinned him to the wall with his arm pressed against his throat. "Tell us where Lana is hiding."

"You want me to trust that you'll spare my life if I snitch. I've been in this business too long to know things like that never happen," Viper sneered, grinning.

Zanipolo jabbed Viper in his ribs, causing him to collapse in pain. His patience was growing thin.

"Cut the crap. You don't have to trust everything I say, but trust if you don't tell us

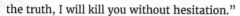

the truth, I will kill you without hesitation."

Viper gasped for air as Zanipolo increased the pressure against his neck. He tried to speak but could not. Zanipolo eased his grip, allowing him to speak.

"She's hiding in a safe house near Wildwood." Viper gasped. Once he caught his breath, he told them exactly where it was.

Zanipolo released Viper and turned to leave. When he turned his back, Viper gave one last warning.

"Zanipolo, good luck. You will need as much luck as you can get. Because I doubt that, you'll reach her in time. If she isn't dead already, she will be soon."

His words ignited Zanipolo's rage and hatred until they consumed him, blinding his actions. Seconds felt like minutes as the world faded. Frozen in that moment, he turned to Viper.

Once time continued, he noticed his gun in his hand, finger still on the trigger, the barrel still smoked, and Viper laid dead before him. He was shot dead by Zanipolo's hand.

Samantha looked shocked. Never had she seen Zanipolo react rashly in this world. She did not recognize this person. This person, full of hatred and rage, scared her. He was nothing like the man she cared for. This stranger almost consumed that man completely.

Samantha knew she insisted on helping them find Amadora, but she could not bear watching this darkness consume Zanipolo. It broke her heart. She feared if they did not save Amadora soon, this monster of hatred would consume the man she loved.

19

The Rose's Thorns

'If I fight back, I will sacrifice what's left of my heart. So, I will wait and do nothing. I will take this moment as redemption for my sins and accept my fate, whatever it may be.' Thoughts of Lana Rosilli.

The invasion of Viper's hideout took a physical and mental toll on everyone. Concern spread throughout the group, infected each with doubt, which drained them more than their fatigue. Noticing their mood, Elda had them rest at her home before pursuing Lana.

They rode in silence on the way to her house. They only spoke when assigned their rooms for the night. Darian retired to his room first.

Darian's mind raced with thoughts of Amadora. He no longer cared about her lies, but worried about her whereabouts and well-being. Viper's last words concerned him. He hoped wherever she was that she could hang on just a little longer. Darian would not stop until she returned safely to his arms.

Darian walked into the shadowy bedroom, tossed his coat aside on a chair while crossing the burgundy carpet to the opposite side of the room. As if entranced by the mystical allure of the fog, he went to the window and gazed into the mysterious, white clouds.

The gentle, white billows concealed the stars, moon and earth as if trying to wipe away the bloody massacre from earlier. The horrific event became a distant memory as the fog returned when he gazed at the snow-covered garden with Amadora.

Every word exchanged, every feeling felt and every passing moment they shared replayed in his mind. Her charming smile, so radiant and inviting, became an ornament of pleasure in his mind. Her voice, so soothing and gentle, wrapped him in an intoxicating melody that filled him with hope. The warmth of her touch transformed his lingering resentment into a profound, decadent love he craved for more and more with each passing second. Every moment with her conjured her presence from his memory.

Then, just as his memories brought peace to his heart, Viper's words destroyed it. "If she isn't dead, she will be soon."

Anger rampaged through his mind, seizing control of Darian's senses. Thinking about the horrors she could be enduring filled him with a vicious bloodlust for any who laid a hand on her. His desire to save her burned hot with anticipation. He was not sure how reliable this lead would be, but he prayed that God would guide them closer to her before she fell under the greedy clutches of those bloodthirsty monsters.

Zanipolo drifted into his room, numb to the world around him. He tossed off his hat and coat, then went over to the mini-bar and poured him a glass of Bourbon. He chugged down the warm, bitter liquid, not even wincing as it burned his throat. Zanipolo poured more into his glass, slowly sipped its contents, and leaned over the bar.

Amadora really got herself into a mess this time. He knew something like this could happen, but he never wanted it to. No matter how much he tried to suppress his feelings, he could not help but worry. Maybe being in this world so long made him a pessimist by default; but he needed to fight for a little hope. Viper could not be right. Amadora... No... Johnnie Barbone was too stubborn and savvy to die. He still had to reach his goal.

A loud click coming from the direction of his bedroom door startled Zanipolo, causing him to drop his glass on the chair by the bar, spilling what was left of his drink. When he looked up, Samantha stood in the doorway.

"Sam, you scared me. Why are you sneaking around like that?" Zanipolo asked cleaning up the mess.

"Sorry, Polo. I didn't mean to startle you. I just wanted to check on you." Samantha answered.

"Check on me? Why?" Zanipolo asked, confused.

"You've been acting strange ever since we left Viper's hideout. I was concerned the pressure was getting to you."

"Thank you for worrying, but I can handle it. We expect stress in this business, especially in these uncertain situations. I don't know if there's a person in this house who isn't stressed about all of this. So, don't worry about me and go to your room to rest."

"You're not getting rid of me that easy. Something is bothering you. What is it?" Samantha demanded, moving closer to him.

Zanipolo withdrew from her and sat on a couch nearby. "You're a persistent one." Zanipolo kicked his feet up on the coffee table, leaned back, and looked up at the chandelier hanging above him. "Do you think killing Viper was a mistake?"

"No. You did the necessary thing. Who knows what he would've done if you spared him?" Samantha reassured.

"If that's true, then why do I feel like killing him might have jeopardized our one chance to save my sister? What if he lied? Then we've lost our only link because of my lack of self-control?"

"Don't think like that. I'm sure he was telling the truth."

"Why are you so confident?"

"His behavior... When he revealed the location, his cocky demeanor faded. I'm sure you did the right thing."

Samantha sat next to him and placed her hands on his arm. "There's no need for you to worry about that any longer."

"How can you have so much faith in me?" Zanipolo asked.

Samantha nuzzled against him, wrapping her arms around his body.

"Because I trust you. I trust you will do whatever in your power to bring Amadora back alive and safe. We will find her together." Samantha smiled looking at him. Zanipolo did not respond immediately. He just wrapped his arms around her tight and kissed her gently on the forehead.

"Yes. We will."

'Why? ... Why do I ruin everything I love?' Gugliehno thought, staring into the flames before him.

First, his cowardice prevented him from standing up against his father, sacrificing his family for the sake of propriety and ego. Maybe if he stood his ground and denied his father's proposal, then Susan would still be alive. She could have lived a peaceful life with a man who could love her whole-heartedly, one who had no ties to any evil so not to jeopardize her safety.

Second, doubting his gut feeling prevented him from saving his sister from the world. Maybe if he acted on his suspicions when his father announced Amadora's plans to visit California, he could have stopped her from going through with this charade. If he did that, he would not live every passing moment in fear that she was lying dead somewhere in a Rosilli stronghold.

Third, his unforgiving heart prevented him from saving the first woman he ever loved. Maybe, if he supported Lana in the beginning when he started seeing the signs of corruption forming in her mind, he could have saved her from this destructive path she took.

Golden embers flickered in the hearth. Their whimsical dance mystified Gugliehno, leading him deeper into the depths of his mind. What was he supposed to do now? Susan dead... Amadora taken... Even if he believed Lana had nothing to do with all of this, the train was in motion, and he could not stop it now, because all roads lead to her.

"Are you conjuring a premonition from the flames? Or is there another reason you're hunched over my fireplace?"

Gugliehno jolted from his thoughts and turned around. Elda stood behind him with two mugs in hand. She extended her hand, giving him one.

"I wish that was possible. Knowing what will happen in my future would ease my anxiety."

"Anxiety seems like a common symptom around here lately. Our little Dora has really gotten herself in quite the pickle." Elda responded, while sipping her drink.

"If I didn't know better, I'd think you're enjoying this." Gugliehno said, sipping his drink while cocking up his eyebrow.

"Not at all. This is very inconvenient. I dislike having to put my life on hold to clean up her mess. That's one reason I was against her joining." Elda's eyes trailed to the flames dancing before them. "However, seeing all she accomplished and how quickly she gained your men's respect and trust, my reservations are nearly gone. Dora may be a little reckless, but she'll grow out of that like I did."

"I'm surprised you, of all people, changed your mind. Sometimes, you can be as stubborn as pops," Gugliehno grinned.

"Maybe. However, in this circumstance, I can relate to her."

Gugliehno did not answer her. He just sat back in the chair, sipping his drink while trying to control his conflicting thoughts.

"Tell me what's bothering you. I know you and Dora are close, but a situation like this wouldn't put you in this type of stink." Elda said, leaning on the arm of her chair.

"What makes you think there's anything bothering me right now other than Dora's safety?" Gunny asked.

"Because I know you. You may be still grieving over Susan; but even something like that wouldn't hinder your mindset at a time like this." Elda took another sip then continued. "Are you worried about what's going to happen to Lana?"

"Why would I care about that?" Gugliehno asked, surprised.

"No need to play dumb. I know you still have feelings for her."

"How do you know that?"

"I can see your feelings engraved all over your face," Elda answered.

"You can?" Gugliehno asked, confused.

"Yes. You've never been good at concealing your feelings about things that matter deeply to you. And with Lana, you're less in control of your feelings than normal. Do you want to lie back, and I bring another soldier with us tomorrow? If you can't think rationally and keep your feelings in check, you'll be of more use to us here."

"I'm fine. No matter what you think, I'm perfectly capable of putting my feelings on the back burner to save Amadora."

"You say that now. But what if it comes down to taking Lana's life for Dora's?

Could you still do it? Could you kill the mother of your children to save your sister's life?"

Gugliehno returned his focus to the flames while he pondered about Elda's questions. His heart and mind battled over her words. For one, saving his sister should be their only priority; but for the other, hesitation about losing the woman who taught him the beauty and troubles of love ran rampant. It still believed in her innocence and wanted to save her this time around at all costs.

"Regardless of our past, I will do whatever I need to do to save my sister, even if that means sacrificing my ex-wife."

On the morning of the attack, Elda brought everyone to her private weapons' vault buried underneath a large, raggedy barn's basement in the woods behind her house. Weapons of every size, shape and function lined every inch of the vault. Primitive weapons hung on the wall behind thick plexiglass. The main area held rows of shelves holding different guns while several pantries branched from the room containing different ammunition and explosives.

While the others gawked in awe, Samantha fell to the rear of the crowd. She slipped back upstairs and out to the back porch, hoping the brisk air could settle her nerves. She closed her eyes, basking in the rays peering through the clouds, and took a few deep breaths, embracing the icy winds whipping around her. The cool gale swept away all her troubles into the sky above.

Samantha had to stay strong. No matter how much she wanted to revile at the countless number of human lives she aided in ending, she could not back down until they saved her friend. She promised Amadora that she would stick by her side and help her see this ruse until the end. Samantha would not let her die before reaching her goal. She will never let this world consume the life of a person who she loved again. She will risk everything for her dearest friend. Besides, Amadora was too stubborn to die before achieving her goal.

"Miss Samantha, what are you doing out here?" The creaking floor planks alerted Samantha, yanking her back into reality.

"Darian... It's you." Samantha sighed in relief.

"I didn't mean to startle you. I'm sorry." Darian said, smiling sheepishly.

"Don't worry about it. It's my fault for not being more aware of my surroundings." Samantha replied.

"You're not on the battlefield. It's alright to space out here. You're probably worrying about Amadora, aren't you?" Darian walked over to the railing and looked out at the frost covered ground.

Samantha looked at him, surprised. "How did you know?"

"With everything that's going on, it's a reasonable guess." Darian leaned against the rails.

"I think she's on everyone's mind at the moment."

"I guess you're right," Samantha smiled, turning her attention back to the clouds above. "Thank you for helping us. I can't even imagine the heartache you felt after learning her secret. You could've left everything up to us, but you didn't. I'm grateful for your help and don't think we would've gotten this far without you."

"I don't deserve your kind words. I'm still at a loss about how I feel about her betrayal, but I wouldn't let my feelings jeopardize her safety." Darian's face became unreadable as he spoke. However, Samantha had a good idea of his present state of mind.

"I don't think there's anything I could say to help you understand her reason for her little charade. However, I can help you better understand her feelings for you." Samantha adjusted the scarf around her neck to shield her from the incoming wind. "Falling for you was not a part of the plan. It just happened. But ever since you met at the ball, she wrestled with her desires and what mattered more to her, you or her goal."

"How can you be certain of her feelings?" Darian smirked.

"If you spent any time with Dora, then you know she doesn't share how she truly feels. However, being her oldest friend, I've learned to read her like a book, because even though she doesn't talk about her feelings, she's terrible at controlling her reactions. I've noticed the restored innocence and warmth growing inside her after meeting you that she lost at the beginning of this ruse. Being with you helped maintain her sanity in her darkest moments."

Darian remained silent. His mind became riddled with confusion, weighing down his reason. Samantha patted his shoulder and smiled.

"I don't need a response. My goal was to help you better understand my friend. You're the first guy to ever catch her interest. You bring out a side of her that even I have never seen. When this is all said and done, I hope you find it in your heart to forgive her."

Samantha's words made Darian's mind swarm with various conflicting thoughts. Some of her betrayal and the pain it created remained, but they were miniscule compared to the new ones growing inside him now. Thoughts of reason and understanding settled in his broken heart, slowly tending to its hemorrhaging cracks. He might not have understood her reasoning, but he understood her heart a little better.

Susan... She was Lana's dearest and oldest friend, only confidant and the only woman in this world she trusted to raise her daughters. She was dead. Murdered in her home by a mysterious assailant. It took everything in her to bottle up her rage just to think clearly. Lana needed to uncover the identity of her killer and discover why they targeted Susan.

Was her death a warning for Gugliehno? Lana paced back-and-forth racking her brain for answers. Overseeing the gathering of intelligence about the rival families, Lana was familiar with their known and unknown vendettas. Other than herself, no one in the other families had any grudges against Gugliehno. His sister, Elda, rubbed more people the wrong way than him. There must be another motive behind Susan's murder.

Lana could not let her friend's death go unavenged. It was obvious from the evidence left behind that they were implicating her in the crime, but luckily for her, they paid off most of the cops on the case or were too dense to piece the clues together. She now understood the rage behind Gugliehno's eyes when he confronted her. He must have reached the same conclusion, but what was the assassin's purpose?

Lana sat at her desk and peered up at the ceiling. Who was behind Susan's death? They were fanning the flames of their war, giving the Morellis even more reason to take her head. Their plan almost worked if she did not convince Gugliehno that she was not the culprit.

Gugliehno's eyes, burning with rage, pain, hatred and vengeance, flashed in her mind. He wanted to avenge his wife, but in the depths of his eyes lurked a sliver of hope that believed in her innocence.

The memory of his face and that bit of precious hope brought tears to her eyes, blurring her sight. After everything they went through and all the dark deeds she committed in her past, he still cared for her. A pale shadow of the love they once shared lived on in those depths.

Lana chuckled at her foolish assumptions, for she knew it was not possible for him to still love her. The damage was done. Even if he believed she had no hand in Susan's murder, the trust they once had was gone. To the world, she was a heartless monster clinging to a privilege not afforded to the wicked. How could she truly believe that he would let someone like her back into his life... let alone his heart?

Lana pulled her thick fur coat tightly around her body as she stepped onto the roof. She embraced the harsh sting of the winter winds as they colored her cheeks. Silence fell upon the earth. Not even a nightly critter stirred. Normally, a serene atmosphere as this one would calm her heart, but tonight Lana could not find solace in these simple pleasures. Her heart remained cautious, disallowing any rest. Soon she found out why when a booming roar of thunder broke the tranquility.

Looking at the sky, Lana scanned for any sign of a storm, but only a sea of sparkling stars shone. No cloud obstructed her view or crawled across the horizon. Lana's blood ran cold when she realized the true nature of the "thunder". It was gunfire.

Lana stood paralyzed in shock. She was wrong about Gugliehno's feelings. His vengeance was too great for the mere shadows of his feelings for her to overcome... if any feeling remained. What could she do, run or stay?

Two of Lana's soldiers burst through the roof doors and ran over to her, panting heavily.

"Mistress, the Morellis found us and are attacking. We must get you somewhere safe." The burliest one said, ushering her towards the door.

Lana heard their words, but her mind drifted elsewhere. She could not believe after everything the night before, Gugliehno would continue to pursue her. Didn't he know she had nothing to do with Susan's death? Was his vengeance so great that it swallowed his judgment, preventing him from seeing the truth? Couldn't he see past his hatred to the depths of her heart? The very depths filled with a gaping hole because one of the most precious people in her life was taken from her forever.

"Mistress... Mistress..." the second guard urged, pulling her lightly towards the door. "We must go now while they're distracted by trying to get past the front gate."

Lana snatched her arm out of his grasp.

"No. I won't run anymore. I want to put an end to this and see what fate has in store for me."

Breaching the front gate was easier than expected. Bullets flew, nicking a few men on both sides, but Gugliehno's group remained virtually unscathed. Catching them by surprise in the dead of night hurt Lana's men's reaction time, leading to a few casualties.

Lana's men scattered the grounds and ducked behind the vehicles parked there, taking cover from the incoming barrage of bullets. Gugliehno's team pressed forward, clearing their path to the gate. Maneuvering past the sea of corpses, Zanipolo and Brock made their way over to the gate and broke the lock. The rest shot at the men on the other side, eliminating as many as they could before crossing into the yard.

Lana's guards fell as quickly as Viper's men had. Their raging desire to save Amadora drove them forward while Gugliehno's guidance helped them break through her defenses and into the heart of her hideout. Time became nonexistent. Deafening explosions and the roaring blasts of their weapons echoed through the vast halls while they fought their way towards the east tower.

Gugliehno led the charge as they cleared Lana's remaining men at the base of the tower. They ran up the winding staircase, shooting any stragglers.

With a shattered heart and wild rage, Gugliehno led his army of vengeance to the tower's peak. Once his foot stepped on the last step, entering a narrow corridor, all worry faded along with his memories and troublesome emotions. He had only one goal to find his sister.

At the corridor's end, a tall, gray wooden door blocked their path. Darian cut in front of Gugliehno, turned the knob, and pushed it open. Gugliehno charged in first, swiftly scanning the interior for any enemies, but the enormous chamber was empty.

The eerie silence unsettled Darian as he followed Gugliehno's lead. The absence of anyone when they heavily guarded the tower riled his suspicions. Gugliehno was not fooled either. He signaled for them to split up and search the cluttered maze.

Darian and Anna searched the westside of the grand hall. Boxes stacked high close to the ceiling shielded a small, black door with an ornate porcelain knob. Anna checked behind some of the box towers before opening the door for Darian. He scanned the dimly lit corridor on the other side, then walked to the archway on the other end.

Darian dropped his guard while crossing the threshold. Shelves packed with volumes of books circled around a large stone hearth on the far side of the room. In the center of the circular room, a massive armchair stood facing the massive fireplace. The flames dancing in the hearth cast a great shadow across the room. Darian moved closer to the chair but froze when a familiar voice echoed through the air.

"I thought we settled this matter during our last encounter. I really thought you believed me when I said I didn't kill your precious wife. I guess I was mistaken."

A black silhouette rose from the chair and turned to Darian and Anna. Darian did not need to see her face to recognize the owner of that cold, heartless voice, for the memory was still freshly imprinted in his mind.

"Lana." Darian sneered.

"Darian? What are you doing here? Why is a self-righteous pup like you helping Gugliehno exact his revenge?" Lana rose from the chair and stepped into a stream of light from one of the dangling ceiling lamps. Surprise painted her face as she looked over at the two intruders opposite her.

"I do not know what you're talking about. I'm here for Amadora. Where is she?" Darian demanded.

"Amadora? How should I know where she is?" Lana asked.

"Quit the games. Your man, Viper, told us everything." Anna said, training her gun on Lana.

"We know you took her. Now, tell me where she is." Darian pressed, trying to control his growing rage.

"Viper? Why would he say that?" Lana grew pale while she searched for answers she did not know. She did not know why Viper, who was always loyal, would betray her.

"I'm sorry. You're mistaken. I don't know anything about her whereabouts and didn't know someone kidnapped her."

Anna observed Lana's behavior carefully and noticed she was genuinely confused and how scared she was. However, Darian was so blinded by anger that he was not paying attention to anything around him. Before Anna could block his path, Darian wrenched Lana into his grasp, forcing her to her tiptoes.

"Enough lies! Tell me where she is now, you heartless bitch!"

Fear emanated from her face as she stared down his bloodthirsty glare riddled with vengeance and anger. Lana opened her mouth to respond, but a loud pop sound echoed through the air, followed by an excruciating pain thwarted any action.

The sound resonated through the chamber, alerting the others and striking them with fear. That sound... It can't be. Gugliehno ran toward the nerve-wrecking sound.

When they gathered at the entrance, they noticed Anna standing over Darian, who held something in his arms. Gugliehno's legs willed him forward as his heart raced. Darian held a limp body bleeding from their abdomen. Gugliehno collapsed next to them, fighting the heartache breaking him apart. It was Lana. They shot Lana.

Darian glanced down at his pocket, shocked. A small hole burned through his coat pocket. He shot Lana. Darian dropped her on the floor. His rage subsided as he let the bloody scene before him sink in. Lana covered the wound on her side with her hand and struggled to look at Darian. She saw his fear and grinned.

"What's wrong? Are you going to let a minor incident like this discourage you?" Lana laughed. "Silly boy, you won't accomplish anything with that flimsy resolve. I might not have had a hand in your girl's kidnapping, but I have a good idea who took her."

Lana's smile grew as she tried masking her pain. She took a deep breath, then continued.

"If you truly love Amadora, then there is only one person who has the power and motive to take her from you and make Viper betray me."

"Who is it?" Darian pressed, fighting to regain his composure.

Lana shook her head while she tightened her grip on her wound. "I can't say that. You'll learn the truth soon enough. However, I will tell you where you can find them."

Lana grunted as her pain worsened before continuing. "Gladiolus Compound in Brooklyn. If my hunch is correct, Amadora should be there. There's a small black notebook in the top drawer of my desk in the other room. The address should be in there."

Darian turned away to retrieve the notebook; but before he left, Lana called after him. "I hope you find her in time. She's a rare find. If you lose her, you will never find the likes of her again."

Darian did not respond. He left with the others in search of the notebook. Only one person remained, the one Lana least expected, Gugliehno.

Gugliehno scooped her into his arms, examining her wound frantically. He removed his scarf and wrapped it around her waist, then applied pressure to the wound. Lana watched while he tried his best to help her. In those brief moments, she realized all those years he denied their past or pushed her away were all a front.

When the first tear crept down his cheek, the last crack in his mask formed, shattering it and revealing the true colors of his broken heart. They shone vividly. Their beauty creating a chain reaction in the shriveled mass in her chest. This time it was not her wound causing pain, but her heart.

Lana placed her hand on Gugliehno's arm. His tear-stained eyes looked at her, surprised.

"It's alright, my darling. You've done enough. I think it's time you finally let me go." Tears streamed down her face as she tried to smile.

Gugliehno pulled her closer to him, refusing to let her go. "I can't... I won't let you go ever again."

"You must. You need to find Amadora before it's too late."

"I know, but I won't abandon you like this..." Gugliehno gently brushed her cheek, fighting his aching heart as he watched Lana struggle to stay strong through her pain.

Lana's hand drifted to his chin. She gently caressed his face and smiled.

"You're still my stubborn boy. How I've missed being in your arms. Although, I never expected it would be in a circumstance like this." Lana giggled.

"Lana... please." Gugliehno said, fighting back his overwhelming grief.

"You need to find your sense of humor in times like these, my dear. Otherwise, you'll end up an emotional wreck," Lana teased, wiping the few tears from his cheek. "Your heart is so big. I adore that part of you. Don't ever let hatred consume it again. Even when I hated you, I don't think I ever truly stopped loving you."

"Lana, please stop talking like that. You're going to be fine. I promise." Gugliehno said.

Lana paused and stared at him wide-eyed in shock before a huge grin crossed her face.

"You're still as optimistic as ever. Promise me you'll take care of our girls. Remind them of all the happy times we shared. Guard their hearts from any pain and shield them from the darkness of this world. Don't let them follow in their mother's footsteps."

Gugliehno held her hand, closing his eyes while taking in her gentle warmth. "For far too long, I ignored my feelings and was complacent in doing whatever others thought was best for our family, even at the risk of losing you. I was foolish. I can't expect you to go along with my wishes after all I've done to you, but please forgive me. I cannot honor your wishes, because I want you to fulfill them yourself. I won't allow you to leave me now."

Gugliehno kissed her hand as she pressed it against his cheek. "I love you, Lana. I will never forsake my heart again."

Those sweet words jumpstarted Lana's fragile heart. As darkness swirled around her, she could do nothing but smile and let her few remaining tears flow down her face. As her body turned cold and the surrounding world faded, Lana basked in this final gift life granted her. Finally, after so much despair, she received the only thing she ever wanted: the heart of her one true love.

20

The Rosilli's Heir

"You call me a monster. Then you're one too, because my blood runs through your veins," Unknown.

Their search was nearing an end. Darian could tell Lana's last words were true. Unlike Viper, Lana seemed genuinely concerned about the situation with Amadora. He wondered if the motive behind everything had to do with her and Gugliehno's connection. Darian noticed Gugliehno's distraught when he saw Lana bleeding on the floor; and he also stayed behind and did not return until early the next morning. This whole mess was ruining many lives. Who concocted this scheme?

According to Lana, the mastermind took Amadora because of him. He did not know who would use Amadora to get to him. He had a few enemies from the other families, but he never ruffled the feathers of anyone with the rank or power to pull this off. Also, few knew of his ties to Amadora.

For a moment, Darian smirked. All this time he cursed Amadora's dark life for her predicament but come to find out all of this was actually his fault. Amadora was only a pawn to get at him. But who harbored so much hatred towards him to target someone he held dear?

Amadora swayed as the drug they used on her weakened its hold on her consciousness. Her mind was still in disarray and her body felt weaker than before, but she could sit up if she wanted to get a better view of her prison and she was no longer attached to that pipe. She did not remember her attack or how she got here. While peering through the darkness, she could not make sense of where she was. The concrete floor did not seem like any that might have been used at the properties along the docks. With hazy sight and distorted senses, everything seemed like a foreign world. Amadora could only lay there and await her fate.

Amadora heard someone coming towards her prison. She closed her eyes and laid completely still while pretending that she was still unconscious. They paused outside her cell's door.

"That is Darian Mancini's lover?" one voice scoffed.

The drug muddled the pitch of their voices, making it difficult to distinguish their gender. "I guess it's true what they say: love is blind...To think he'd mingle with one of Basilio Morelli's whore daughters. Disgusting."

"What should we do with her?" another voice asked.

"Nothing for now. We'll wait until he comes for her, then we'll dispose of her." The other voice answered.

While their steps echoed away from her cell, Amadora trembled at their words. Darian? They used her to reach him, but why? Who were they and what did they want with him?

All hope faded once she realized her fate. If she was bait for him, then they would be very disappointed. Darian hated her and would not trade his life for hers. She would die here alone and abandoned because of her sins.

With the exceptions of Anna, Brock, and Gugliehno, everyone gathered in Elda's office.

"Gladiolus Compound is the heart of the Rosillis territory. It's where their don lives. I've gone there a few times with my father, so I know it well." Elda started pulling out a few large scrolls from under her desk.

"There's no way we'll know for sure where they're hiding her. That's an enormous property." Zanipolo said, watching her open the large cannisters and unraveling the scrolls flat on her desk.

"That's true." Elda nodded in agreement. "Knowing the layout should help narrow down the most likely areas."

Elda weighed down the paper with random objects on her desk so they could look it over while she explained.

"These are the layouts for the compound. How did you get them so fast?" Darian asked.

"Don't underestimate me. I've never trusted that family. I got Lorenzo to pinch these just in case they betrayed us." Elda scanned the plans. "I'm just surprised we'd use it for something like this."

Her answer satisfied Darian, so she continued.

"Unlike our complex, their main house is at the back of the estate. The other buildings are quarters for servants, their men, and some capos. Luckily for us, Lorenzo reports that the other four caporegimes are out of state, which means the compound's guard structure is weakened. But we'll still have to fight through a good number; but with Gugliehno's men and mine combined, we should be fine. Regarding Amadora's location, I'd bet they're keeping her somewhere in the main house."

"What makes you so sure?" Zanipolo interrupted.

"It has many rooms where they could stash her. Also, from the surveillance reports, security is unusually tight there. Even if the don is the only one there, there shouldn't be close to a hundred men stationed there. I will split up our men to search the rest of the grounds, so we will cut it close while searching the main house. We'll have only a few men to help us search through the main building. I want us to split in teams of two to lead those search parties. Except for one group will only have one leader. I'll volunteer to head that group."

"No. I'll do it." Darian said.

"You? Are you sure? You'll have a few men with you, but Lana said this mastermind is after you. Do you think it's wise for you to be leading it on your own?" Elda questioned.

"Like you said, I won't be completely alone. Also, it's safer if I'm on my own if they come after me. Then I won't have to risk your lives since Anna won't be there," Darian refuted.

Elda did not press the matter further, instead, she silently agreed and continued reviewing their plans for the attack. Elda admired his bravery but questioned his true allegiance. Learning about his connection to the higher ranks of the Rosilli family, she was not sure if he could be trusted. Depending on their relations, he could jeopardize their entire mission. She wondered if they could trust him to save their sister. Or would his bond with that tainted bloodline lead him to betray her?

Dark clouds billowed above, shrouding the moon's luminous kiss from the dark, cold earth. Subtle sparks momentarily lit a small alley as they flickered on and off. Two men leaned against a car, gazing at both ends of the alley. One smoked while the other placed a hand on his holster.

"I'm surprised to see you here after everything." Lorenzo said, puffing on his cigarette.

"I can't just abandon my job when Amadora's life is on the line." Gugliehno said.

"That might be true, but are you mentally prepared? With Susan gone and now Lana, I don't think anyone will hold it against you if you sit this one out. I think we can manage without you." Lorenzo took one last pull, threw his cigarette on the ground, and stamped it out.

"I can't just sit at home wallowing in my sorrow while my sister is still in danger. Also, you don't need to worry about me holding you back. Elda's taking the lead, and I'm mentally sound enough to watch your back when we enter the fray." Gugliehno responded.

Lorenzo grabbed the door handle, yanked open the door, and grabbed his rifle and handgun.

"If you say so, my friend. Luckily for you, I'm an expert in babysitting you, mentally challenged Morelli boys. Thanks to your cousin." Lorenzo grabbed another rifle and handed it to Gugliehno. "We're lucky your witty sister planned for every probable outcome. Elda wants to minimize our losses as much as possible. That's why we're going to take out as many guards at the front gate once they get into place." Lorenzo looked at his watch. "They should be here soon. Let's get in position."

The beginning of the raid went smoothly. Their men mopped up most of the guards stationed in front, making a path for Elda's group to move on to the main building. Her men stormed in first, taking out any in their way. Once they cleared the entrance, they split into their groups and began their search.

Zanipolo and Samantha took their team to scour the uppermost floors. Samantha listened as Elda and Brock's team's pursuit thundered through the stone halls of the first floor. A few moments later, Gugliehno and Lorenzo's men pressed on, clearing out the middle floor. She walked behind Zanipolo, following his lead as they crouched behind some large plants lining the entrance of the hallway near the stairs. He motioned for his men to search the other side. Then they ducked into a crevice until the sound of their attack lured them away. As they waited, Samantha's heart pounded wildly, causing her blood to race and her hands to tremble.

"Stay calm, Sammy. Everything will be fine. I won't let anything happen to you. Just follow my lead." Zanipolo whispered.

Samantha nodded in understanding. She closed her eyes, trying to calm down, but her nerves would not settle.

"Don't lose it now. Just remember why we're here."

Zanipolo's hushed words and genuine concern stabilized her nerves. They were too close for her to lose her mind now. Amadora's life was on the line. She needed to press forward and save Amadora, no matter what.

After hearing the commotion, it did not take long for some Rosilli men to come rushing down the hall. Samantha waited for Zanipolo's signal before ambushing them. A cascade of gunfire echoed through the hall, and then the enemy fell, one after another.

Zanipolo checked around before signaling Samantha to follow. She remained close by his side while they searched every room, taking out anyone in their way. They pressed on, fueled by their determination.

Their search took less than twenty minutes to almost nearly complete. Silence drenched the last corner of the floor. Samantha's hope faltered when they found no signs of Amadora or her whereabouts. Consumed by concern, tears formed on the brim of her eyes. She turned back to Zanipolo, hoping he had some answers to their current situation.

"Polo, where is she?" Samantha cried.

Zanipolo scanned their surroundings, then answered, touching her shoulder and smiling.

"Calm down. We knew this wasn't going to be easy. We might have not found her, but we've narrowed down the potential hiding places. We did our job. Now, let's go find the others and help them."

Samantha wiped away her tears and smiled back. Looking into his caring eyes restored her faith. Her heart swelled with unfamiliar emotions. Just being in his presence banished all fear. His powerful love emanated from his eyes. Its warmth consumed her, reassuring her that everything would be fine and ignited the feelings in her heart. There was no place she would rather be than by his side.

She touched his hand, signaling that she was ready to continue. However, instead of moving on, a terrifying expression painted his face as he looked past her. The fear consuming him grew while he violently grabbed and pushed her to the floor.

Samantha's side ached after the impact of the fall, but she ignored it, because her only concern was the source of Zanipolo's horror. A booming thunder echoed through the air after Zanipolo pushed her. Terror seized her as she scurried to figure out what was going on.

Samantha took her gun and turned to face the source of the noise. They were entering the room when she trained her gun on them and pulled the trigger, striking them right through the heart. She rolled away from the direct sight of the door, checking for any others. When she was sure the threat was gone, she scanned the room for Zanipolo. Her heart sank when she found him. He laid motionless on the floor near where she fell.

Samantha ran to his side, stumbling slightly from her pain. She grabbed his shoulders and shook him vigorously, trying to wake him.

"Oh god! Polo, please wake up!" Samantha cried desperately, trying to get any response from him.

Samantha pulled him close, examining his body. Blood poured from his right leg. Samantha ripped her shirt and wrapped his leg, desperately trying to stop the bleeding. However, no matter what she did, the bleeding did not stop.

Samantha cradled him in her arms and kissed his hand while applying pressure on his wound. This could not be happening. She was not going to lose him... not now. They still had so much they needed to experience together. There was a lot she wanted to tell him. He could not leave her. He would not. Zanipolo promised.

Samantha's voice grew hoarse from all the crying that she could barely speak.

"Polo, please wake up! You can't leave me now! Didn't you promise me we'd always be together? Please don't leave me all alone... I need you." Samantha's voice broke as she forced through the mounting agony tearing through her chest.

"I can't go on with you. Please... stay with me..."

Tears fell down Samantha's cheeks as she scoured the area for something to stop the bleeding. She refused to let death rob her of someone else. She could not prevent it before because she was too weak. But she was stronger now and would do anything to save the man she loved.

Samantha kissed Zanipolo's lips as she hid him from the view of the door.

"Wait for me, Polo. I'll get help. This time, it's my turn to protect you. I love you with my entire being. I will save you, no matter the cost. Just wait for me."

Darian descended into the depths of the cellar, hiding in its shadows. A cold draft whipped past his face as he walked down the spiraling, dark stone stairwell. He slipped to the final landing, hiding his presence from any dangers lurking in the shadows.

Dark stone tunnels made up the bottom floor. Only the soft glow from small spherical wall sconces made the path somewhat manageable. A cold draft whistled along the towering stone walls and rushed past him towards the stairwell. Darian ran one hand along the other while it clasped his gun. Where there was a draft, there had to be another entrance. He had to find it just in case they needed it.

Darian instructed his men to search the uppermost cellar floors while he descended below. If he encountered the mastermind while searching for Amadora, they would focus on him and might take out any tag-a-long. Going by himself reduced the chance of that happening.

Darian followed the winding path, checking every room he passed, but each one was empty. Darian felt sick when he looked at the dark rooms with their medieval iron chains and cuffs. He could not imagine the brutal things these monsters got away with down here. He sped up his search, determined to rescue Amadora from whatever gruesome torture these monsters put her through. Nearing the end of the tunnel, one of the prison doors would not budge.

Darian peered through the small, barred window on the door. Darkness bathed the room in shadows, with only a few streams of light pouring in from a small window on the other side of the cell. A person's silhouette was shackled on the floor underneath the window. He did not need light to see who it was.

"Amadora!" Darian called, ramming the door several times until he forced it open.

Darian ran to Amadora's side and checked her pulse. He sighed, relieved once he felt her faint heartbeats. Amadora was in awful shape. She had bruises on her face, along with a shiner and a fat lip. Darian burned with rage and began undoing her restraints. He wanted to pummel the assholes who did this to her, but he needed to get her to safety first.

"Darian, leave her there to die. She isn't worth saving." A woman's soft voice echoed from behind him.

Darian turned towards the voice, blocking Amadora from the person hidden in the shadows.

"What did you do to her?" Darian demanded.

His body trembled whenever she spoke, but he did not understand why. Her voice was not intimidating, yet he shivered at the sound.

"She's a little roughed up, but she'll be fine. She's only sleeping," the woman chuckled.

"Who are you? Why have you done this?" He asked, trying to conceal his trembling nerves and maintaining his composure.

"My dear, I did this all for you... to save you." Her gentle voice laced the dark bitterness beneath it.

"Save me? From what?" Darian asked, confused.

"Isn't it obvious? From her, of course."

"Why would you want to do that?" Darian asked.

"I know it's been a while, but don't you remember my voice?" The woman said. "I thought children always remembered their mother's voice no matter how young they were when they parted."

"My mother? You can't be my mother. She's been dead for years."

The woman roared in laughter while a powerful light brightened the room, revealing the features of the terrorizing voice. A middle-aged woman, slightly shorter than him and with a slender frame, stood before him. She wore a long black dress with a brown fur collar, black leather fur-lined gloves, and black boots. Her short, peppered hair was neatly styled into a wavy bob, which made her wrinkled light eyes stand out more. Her intense stare contradicted the calm tone of her voice.

"That must be the story Domenico told you." The woman shook her head in disappointment.

"You would think a creative liar like him would think of a better tale than that. How cliché." She twirled around with her arms spread wide. "As you can see, I'm very much alive."

"You're wrong. Why would he lie to me?" Darian asked.

"He's always been a devious snake. He probably fed you that lie, so you wouldn't learn about your lineage and destiny."

"What nonsense are you spewing?" Darian stood, moving forward blocking her path to Amadora. "I know who I am."

The woman smirked again. "No. You don't. You're ignorant of the great legacy entitled to you."

She closed the distance between them and touch his arm. Darian pulled his arm out of her grasp.

"I longed to gaze upon the face of my precious son ever since your father took you from me." She withdrew her hand and strolled away. "When we first met, I was just the frail younger sister of the great business mogul, Don Lucio Rosilli, Hilara Rosilli. Your father was a mere associate. Back then, I was naïve and impressionable; so, I easily fell for your father's charms. We married and not long after had you. Our first few years were joyful; but that changed once my brother grew ill and needed me by his side."

Hilara took the end of her fur shawl and twirled it around.

"Your father didn't mind at first; but when my brother demanded I not only care for him but become his invisible hand in our business, that's when things turned south."

Hilara walked over to the wall covered in chains. She ran her fingers along the faded iron and grinned. "He hated my ambition. I knew as my brother's voice that I could make a world suitable for you. Because once he croaked, I could leave his entire empire to you, and no one would be the wiser. My only obstacles were my niece, Lana, and, of course, your father."

Hilara paused and stared at the metal in her hands. Darian watched her carefully, searching for any remorse, but found nothing. Her words seemed sincere, but something deep inside prevented him from trusting her.

"Your father hated the idea of bringing you up in this world. I disagree. Because isn't giving your child all the advantages in the world our job as parents?" Hilara tensed, squeezing the chains for a moment before letting them drop to the ground. "He abandoned me, stole my only child, changed your name and ran off behind the shadow of those bottom feeding Morellis for protection. I didn't find out until much later that he stayed in New York, but because you were deep in the Morellis' territory I couldn't come after you. I watched from afar, planning for the day I could see you again."

Her voice trembled in anger for a moment before another ruthless grin crossed her lips.

"Everything I've done has been for you. Being my brother's word and voice, I convinced the world that there was nothing wrong with the head of our family. I've kept his presence alive and strengthened our family more than ever before. I also convinced my brother, while on his deathbed, to relinquish full control to me, passing over his heir, Lana."

"That girl was the most unpredictable piece in my plan. Unlike the other capos, she did whatever she pleased, and Viper shielded her, my brother's most deadly assassin. I needed to rein her in to make sure she did what I desired. When she married that Morelli trash, Gugliehno, I used her love for her little family as leverage to make her do what I wanted and solidify her loyalty.

However, Lana was not stupid. She knew about my ruse and the lengths I went through to maintain it. I needed to get rid of her; but with that annoying assassin on her side, it was near impossible. If she received anything close to a scratch by my hand, I would have to deal with him as an enemy, which was too high a risk to take. So, I used her bull-headed ex to pull the trigger."

"Was all this destruction worth it? You destroyed so many lives. You could've just let Lana live a normal life. Why destroy her whole life?" Darian asked, trying to wrap his mind around the madness Hilara spewed.

"She was too much of a risk alive. She commanded the most men and garnered the most loyalty from our men as the don's heir. I used her foolish tryst with Gugliehno to tighten the noose around her neck. First, I spread vicious rumors, painting her as a demon out of hell. Then I played on her distorted view of loyalty, sending Jack to destroy one of their holdings, knowing she'd retaliate. Finally, I shattered her heart by killing Susan and putting the blame on her."

Hilara focused on her dumbfounded audience and grinned while fixing her gloves. "However, I was foolish to think killing Gugliehno's fake wife would rile him into action. That's when I took Amadora. You see, kidnapping her served two purposes. One was to spite Gugliehno and frame Lana. The other was to protect you."

Darian stood stunned by Hilara's confession. He could not make sense of it.

"I don't need your protection. Amadora isn't a threat to me."

"She is Basilio Morelli's daughter. That alone is a threat. Your love would get in the way when you take over as my successor of this powerful empire."

Hilara raised her arms out to her side. "You are the one and only heir of the Rosilli empire. I want you by my side to embrace your birthright. You can no longer run away. This is your destiny."

21

The Tears of True Love

'No matter how much I try, I cannot find her. How can I separate the woman I love from the man I hate?' Thoughts of Darian Mancini.

Ever since Darian was a child, he fantasized about the glorious moment of meeting his mother, but then he expected to meet her in heaven, not here. The stories his father told of his warm, caring mother with a heart of gold were the only things keeping his hope alive. She was his angel, who he prayed to during his darkest moments. Even though he never knew her, he loved her with all his heart. She was his mother. His first vision of love.

Looking at this woman in black with ice-cold eyes standing before him, his pure image of his mother shattered. She was far from the warm-hearted woman from her father's stories. She was not the angel that he once prayed to. She was a tainted demon, destroying many lies just to bring her dark ambitions to fruition.

Darian noticed as Hilara spoke, her words lacked the warm compassion of a mother. The only thing she desired from this meeting was to convince him to do her bidding.

"Whether you're my mother, I will never join you or help with your twisted ambitions. I always wanted you to be a part of my life, but not if it means I must sacrifice all my morals."

"That's funny. You would distance yourself from your own mother because of the life I lead, but you will get involved with a mafia don's daughter? How is that fair?" Hilara said, questioning the contradictions.

"That wasn't the same. I didn't know she was involved." Darian answered shortly.

"Now that you know she is. Have your feelings changed?" Hilara questioned, studying his reactions.

Darian paused for a moment before responding. "That doesn't matter. My answer remains the same."

The lights and commotion between Hilara and Darian roused Amadora from her unconscious state. She fought, adjusting to the brightness and regaining control of her senses. A splitting headache rushed over her as she tried making sense of her surroundings.

A moment passed before her eyesight restored. Darian stood in front of her, talking to a woman in black. Her lip was still swollen, and her body was too weak to speak from her earlier escape attempt, but she had enough strength to free herself from her binds. Unlike before, her binds were loose, making it easy for her to slide out of them.

Amadora moved carefully so not to alert the woman. She also kept a vigil ear on what was going on.

Darian turned away to help Amadora. "I won't join you. I'm only here to get Amadora and leave."

"Oh, my dear boy. I'm sorry to hear that. If you're not going to join me, then you won't leave here alive. Goodbye, son."

Time slowed as Amadora reacted to the woman's words. A gleam flashed from the woman's hand in her purview. Amadora picked up a gun laying on the floor nearby, aimed and fired. Darian moved out of the way when a popping sound echoed through the room. He looked back at his mother, shocked. She laid on the ground, dead, clutching a pistol.

Hilara was dead. The fallen angel, who he once called lover, shot the demon, who called herself his mother. Amadora saved him. She saved his life.

Amadora stood and trained her gun on the woman while checking her motionless body. When she was sure that the woman was no longer a threat, she took her gun, lowered her weapon and then ran to Darian's side.

"Are you alright?" Amadora asked, looking him over for any wounds.

Darian looked at Amadora, surprised, then nodded.

"Yes. I am. Thanks to you."

"I'm glad." Amadora sighed in relief, then smiled. Her casual behavior caught Darian off guard, causing him to shrink away from her.

"You're the one who was kidnapped and roughed up. You didn't know whether you'd live or die. And now you killed someone." Darian looked over at Hilara's body. "How are you calm? Weren't you scared?"

Amadora's smile fell. Memory of her torment and the distorted recollection of his exchange with that woman. Her dreams were true. Darian was Hilara Rosilli's son.

"Of course, I was... I still am. This was a nightmare but fretting about it wouldn't solve a thing. Thanks to you, it's all over. I'm grateful, but also slightly surprised because I didn't think you'd come."

"I wouldn't be here if it wasn't for Zanipolo rallying everyone together." Darian said, rising to his feet.

"Everyone's here?" Amadora's eyes rounded in shock.

"Yes. They're probably searching in other parts of the building. This place is pretty huge." Darian replied.

"If that's so, let's go." Amadora said, standing up and handing him his gun. "I'm sorry for shooting her. I overheard everything." Amadora looked at Hilara's body.

"She was your mother and tried to kill you. I couldn't let that happen. Regardless of our issues, I would never forgive myself if you got hurt," Amadora started. "I was more afraid in that moment than I've ever been in my life."

Darian scooped her in his arms and held her tight. "I'm glad that you're alright. I feared the worst."

Amadora nestled in his embrace but could not conceal her shock. "You don't have to worry anymore. I'm fine but am a little surprised by your affection after everything I did to you."

"I still have problems with that, but we can deal with that later. I bet all this trouble has made you come to your senses and throw away this deadly world." Darian smiled.

Amadora pushed him away, stepped back, and looked away. "This life is all I've ever known. I have a goal and can't quit until I reach it." Amadora responded.

"And once you do, will you quit pursuing this dangerous life? Even for me?"

Darian's words surprised Amadora. They triggered some unanswered questions still lingering in her heart. Her desires went into a frenzy, paralyzing her. It was time to choose. Would she continue as Johnnie Barbone or give up everything for Darian?

"I guess that's your answer." Her prolonged silence was enough for him. He walked past her to the exit. "I guess our love isn't enough to break your twisted desires' hold."

Amadora followed him, frozen for words. She adjusted her hat to hide her tears, threatening to fall.

Amadora said nothing. When asked which her heart preferred, she froze. Why didn't she say anything?

Amadora loved Darian. But why was that so difficult to decide? The answer should be simple. Did she not know what she wanted? Or was she too afraid to acknowledge it?

The Ultimate Goal

'After all the rejections, I've reached my end goal. But why don't I feel elated? Why is my heart filled with worry and doubt? Wasn't this what I fought for and wanted all along?' Thoughts of Amadora Morelli.

Thick blankets of snow covered the grounds of the Morelli Complex. Not even the golden rays of the sun piercing through the clouds could melt the frozen earth and break its crippling hold on its barren frame. The snow sparkled, giving the passing mourners a bit of hope as they walked in and out of the main house. The snow, so innocent in its being, played a powerful role in Basilio's heart while he looked at it from the comfort of his office. A stale frown stained his face while he absorbed the news of what happened in his absence from Casimiro.

"I never thought when I pulled up to my house this morning that I would be greeted by so much sadness, especially when we should rejoice in the union between you and Giacinta. I went to Italia to fix my sister's house, only to return to find my own crumbled down." Basilio said, turning from the window and faced Casimiro.

"I cannot look at the snow anymore. It mocks me with its beauty, yet it's not very different from my heart. Its sparkling crystals bring joy to some who behold it, but to others, its icy embrace brings only sadness and despair. Even though my heart rejoices at you officially becoming my son, it also breaks, for I have lost a daughter."

"We're all torn about Susan's death." Casimiro said.

"How's Gugliehno and the girls holding up?" Basilio leaned back and rubbing his temples.

"They're fine and taking it well. While they renovate his place, they're staying at Cyclamen Manor. The girls inherited it from Lana."

"This will be a heartache that won't ever heal. My poor children. We should give him space to grieve, but please check on him from time-to-time. He trusts you the most." Basilio said, taking in all the news.

"I will. I know the coming days will be hard on them, but they will overcome it and find peace." Casimiro replied, then looked at the folder on his desk. "How was your trip? Did you resolve Nero's problem?"

Basilio looked at the folder and waved. "Look at it for yourself."

Casimiro picked up the folder and flipped through Gio's notes. Then Basilio went on, visibly exasperated.

"I think we've reached an agreement. The only problem is my stubborn nephew. Nero is a short-tempered little halfwit who would rather die than apologize. I don't think he'll comply. I'm also worried about whether Bruzzano will keep his word if we can convince Nero to play along."

"If you feel uneasy about Bruzzano's intentions, then we should bring your sister and family here until we sort everything out." Casimiro said, replacing the folder on the desk.

"That's a good idea. Let's arrange it now. Susan's funeral is an excellent cover, so Gaetano doesn't see the action as an act of betrayal."

People buzzed around the halls of the main house; but it was not to get ready for a joyous occasion. It was to get ready to lay Susan to rest. Amadora stayed far removed from the main house. She wanted to avoid her family and give them time to grieve.

Amadora knew her family was itching to talk to her, but this time could not be consumed with her problems but with Susan. She avoided attending the funeral and the wake as a courtesy to her dear sister-in-law. Amadora wondered if her death was in any way her fault. If she never fell in love with Darian. Hilara might have left her alone... Darian.

Amadora's heart ached at the mere mention of his name. His words stung her very core, leaving her paralyzed in confusion. Her love for him was true, and that would never change. And buried deep underneath his pain, Amadora believed Darian still loved her. She saw a glimpse of it when he held her. So what now?

Would Darian ever return to her? Or would he find another to ease his hurt? Amadora could not bear the pain of losing his love to someone else. She wanted him all for herself. He was the only man she ever dreamed of sharing a life together, having kids, and growing old with. Darian Mancini was the only man she ever loved. So, what was she to do?

Weeks passed without a word from him. Time was supposed to help reveal his answer. However, how much longer was she to wait? Days? Weeks? Months? Years?

How many moments must her heart suffer until it felt whole again?

Smoke billowed from an iron teapot's curved stout perched on a porcelain stand before Darian. He poured its flowery fragrant contents in his cup, then replaced it on its stand. He cradled the warm cup in his palms, watching its steam dance in the air.

Several weeks have passed since they rescued Amadora. Darian uncovered a lot of mind-boggling information at Gladiolus Compound. He was not sure what to make of it. He lived his whole life idolizing the image of what he believed to be his mother, only to have it ruined in a few moments. Hilara was gone now, but the seeds of doubt she sowed remained in his heart.

Darian was not sure if knowing about her sooner would have affected the person he became. Maybe he would have become someone more understanding of Amadora's lofty goals and dangerous lifestyle. Whether this was something to ponder about and long for, Darian was not sure but hated not having the choice.

"You look as chipper as ever." Riley said, leaning against the doorway's arch and watching Darian stare helplessly into the tea. Darian looked at Riley for a moment before returning to his tea.

"Are you heading down to the bar?" Darian asked.

"Yes. It won't run itself." Riley crossed his arms and scowled. "Do you plan on moping about all day again? Come now. It's been weeks since you've been home. Don't you think it's about time you try to smooth things over with your old man?"

"I don't think I'm ready to talk to him yet." Darian frowned.

"I know you're confused about everything you learned about your mother, but the longer you run from and avoid him, the worse off you'll be. Talking to your father is the only way you'll find some clarity and peace of mind."

"I know it will, but I can't face him just yet. He lied to me my whole life. How can I trust anything he says again?"

"Good grief. You've known your dad your entire life. He's a decent man and wouldn't lie to you unless he had a good reason. He didn't want to hurt you, but give you a little hope and preserve an ideal image of a mother. He wanted to protect your heart, because he knew finding out your mother was a murderous whack job would've done more damage."

"You might be right." Darian said.

"Of course, I am. Now, fix yourself up and go have a heart-to-heart with your old man, so he can shed some light on this sticky situation." Riley smiled.

Amadora strolled through the garden, hoping to find solace in a familiar place. She scanned the barren land freckled with small piles of snow. The icy air cradled the earth in its possessive embrace. Amadora did not wince when the chilling wind brushed against her face. The cold air was nothing compared to ice enveloping her heart.

Amadora was as barren as the earth of all joy and beauty. The only difference between her and the earth was that it would regain its beauty in the spring, while Amadora may never recover.

No matter how hard she tried, Amadora could not hold back her tears. They fell as her heart fell deeper into an impenetrable darkness. All their memories were too painful to endure as they replayed in her mind and then resonated in her frozen heart. She desperately wanted to end the agony these precious moments caused, but she feared the only cure was far from her grasp.

Amadora ran down the winding path and into the greenhouse. She cried amongst the shadows, releasing her pain along with her tears. Nausea washed over her, making her light-headed. She sat on the bench, bent over her hands and sobbed into her palms. This pain was like none she ever encountered before and wanted it to end. If Darian never returned, then she wanted to regain control of her heart and finally rid herself of the never-ending torment.

"So, this is where you've been hiding," Gugliehno said, fighting through the dry vines to get to Amadora.

Amadora quickly wiped away her tears and regained her composure after hearing her brother's voice. She faced in his direction and saw he was not alone. Elda trailed behind him, covering her mouth from the dust-filled air.

"I wasn't hiding." Amadora snapped. "I just needed some time alone to grieve for Susan. I miss her."

"I'm sure she misses you too." Gugliehno replied gently, scanning her for the truth.

"Good thing Darian found you before you wound up sleeping next to her. What the hell possessed you to concoct this dangerous scheme?" Elda scolded, swatting away some cobwebs hanging by her face.

"Sorry for all the trouble I put you through. That last stunt wasn't a part of my original plan." Amadora responded.

"Even if it wasn't, you should have known there was a possibility something like that could happen, especially when you become romantically entangled with someone who is connected to our most dangerous rival. It was a foolish game you played, brat." Elda said.

Amadora cast her gaze to the ground and mumbled.

"You're right. Sorry."

"Look, Dora. We know you did all of this to prove yourself, but don't you see why we're worried?"

Gugliehno's gentle voice could not conceal his breaking heart or the concerned look he wore. His words cut like razors. Both of her eldest siblings tried to put on a brave front; but at that moment, she saw their weakness. For the first time in her life, she discovered their vulnerability was her..

Amadora was their weakness. She was the only thing on the planet that could crack the impenetrable shells of her family's leading caporegimes. She saw their exhaustion and worry. Her capture put stress on not only them, but their hearts as well.

"I can't imagine what you must have felt through this entire ordeal. I'm truly sorry for everything and am grateful for all you've done for me." Amadora said softly, releasing her trapped tears.

Elda's expression softened after seeing Amadora's tears. She walked over to her sister and scooped her in her arms.

"You don't need to say sorry. We'd do it all again, because you're our little sister. We love you, Dora, and will do anything to keep you safe. You have no idea what would happen to this family if we had lost you too?" Amadora rested against Elda's shoulder as Elda kissed Amadora softly on her head. "You're our light. Without you, we would never survive the darkness that would follow."

"To tell you the truth, we aren't angry about your charade as Johnnie Barbone at all. It's impressive how much you pulled off in such a short amount of time," Gugliehno smiled. "You won over Lorenzo, which isn't a simple task. If your charade continued, you might have made it into my inner circle."

"Whether father allows you to join, we will support whatever path you decide to take." Elda said, tightening her embrace.

Hearing her siblings' words of support was something she always wanted. Their words gave her strength to overcome whatever comes next in her future. She finally fulfilled something she always longed for. After overcoming many obstacles, she finally accomplished one of her heart's desires.

Amadora dipped her hands under the facet and caught some water in her palms, then she doused her face in the cool liquid. She repeated this ritual a few times, washing away the salty tears staining her face. The touch of the water refreshed her mind and soothed the flurry of emotions racing through her head.

Amadora spent weeks avoiding her family under the guise of giving them time to grieve for Susan. However, that was just a convenient excuse. She was avoiding them because she was afraid of the outcomes of these confrontations. Gaining her family's approval was initially her end goal, but the longer she remained alone with her thoughts, the more she doubted her true desire.

Speaking with her father was her last task. That confrontation was most important. It determined if she would accomplish her initial goal. Fear stopped her from rushing out to find him. She knew their meeting would not be as welcoming and heartfelt as the one with her siblings.

Amadora settled her nerves while drying her hands and face, then set her towel aside and looked at her reflection. There was something different. The person looking back at her changed. She looked older and wiser. The innocent veil over her eyes vanished. She was now a woman, weighed down by heartache, failures, and a ton of sins she would spend the rest of her life atoning for. This woman longed for the truth behind her heart's desires; and even in her weary state, she will fight on until she uncovered what it really wanted.

Amadora walked into her bedroom to rest but was interrupted by a surprise visitor, her mother. Fiorella sat in a chair across from the bathroom door.

"Amadora, I haven't seen you since we've returned home. Where have you been hiding all this time?" Fiorella said, standing up, walking over to her, and embracing her lovingly.

"I needed some time to mourn on my own." Amadora explained.

"This is a tough time for all of us, but you don't have to shut yourself out and grieve on your own. We're family. It's our duty to help one another out in times like these." Fiorella smiled, then motioned to the couch. "Let's sit down."

Once they were seated, Fiorella held Amadora's hand gently.

"I'm not as oblivious as I seem. I know about everything that goes on in my house. I know you're avoiding me and your father, but there's no need to do that. Yes. I know what you did and don't blame you."

Fiorella's smile softened. "You're no different from Elda. Once you set your mind on something, you won't stop until you get it no matter what obstacles get thrown in your way. I never thought you would come up with such an elaborate ruse just to get what you want. You really are your father's daughter."

Amadora looked at her mother, unable to hide the flurry of tangled emotions and thoughts clouding her mind.

"Your father joined this business to protect those he loved. He had no other choice, but you do. You seem confused. Tell me. Is this really what you want?"

Amadora looked away from her mother and stared at the ground. Fiorella gently touched Amadora's shoulder.

"I don't know what you've been through, but you are struggling with what you really want. If there is something in your life that can give you true happiness, then that should be what you chase after. Don't throw it away for a life that can only bring you sorrow. Because if you do, you may never get another chance."

Darian returned home a little after five in the evening. When he reached the door to his apartment, he noticed the lights in the store were still on and walked over to the front door, peering inside through the large glass window. Behind the counter, his father hobbled from one side of the store to the other, carrying a large box. Darian knocked on the glass with the back of his hand.

Domenico placed the box down on the counter and looked towards the door. His face lit up when he saw Darian. He hurried over, unlocked the door, and let him inside.

"My son, welcome back. Come in and take a load off." Domenico stepped aside and gestured to a stool by the counter. He waited until Darian sat down before hobbling over to the counter and sitting across from him.

"Sorry. I didn't call. I had a lot on my mind." Darian said.

"That's not a problem at all. I'm just glad that you're safe. I thought I had lost you for good."

"I just needed some time to think things over. It was difficult because you, of all people, lied to me for most of my life." Darian responded. His hurt displayed clearly on his sullen face.

Domenico's smile faded as he started. "I kept the truth about your mother from you, not to hurt you, but to protect you."

Domenico sighed, then continued. "I know my son. If you knew that your mother was still alive, then you would never stop searching for her. Even if I explained the circumstances, your good heart would still reach out for her, hoping to save her, and then Hilara would've gotten just where she wanted."

"Do you believe I would be that foolish?" Darian snapped.

"Not intentionally. But Hilara would easily manipulate your hopeful heart. She would take on the mantle of your mother only to use you to do her bidding. She's done it many times before. I couldn't let her corrupt my son, too."

Domenico watched as his son scowled in response to his words. He reached out and touched his hand.

"I understand your frustration, but please. Try to understand my position. If we stayed with her, you would've turned into a twisted, depraved monster like your mother. I wanted to preserve your innocence for as long as I could and give you a happy, normal life, distant from the darkness of her distorted world. Isn't that something worth cherishing?"

Darian's expression softened. "I guess it is."

Domenico smiled. "My son, you have a strong heart driven by your unwavering morals and resilient sense of duty. However, the world is not as black and white as you may think. Sometimes, you must open your heart to see the brilliant colors lurking in the blurred lines mixed in between the two. Only then will you see that sometimes there are no simple answers when it comes to protecting those you love."

With all the chaos surrounding Amadora's capture and Susan's death, Samantha almost forgot about the secret her parents kept from her for years. The thought of their lies made her boil over in rage; but as the weeks passed, she gained the strength to call them and set up a meeting to finally address the matter. No matter how angry Samantha was, avoiding them would solve nothing and create more heartache than reduce it.

When she arrived at her home, Samantha slowed her pace while walking down the path nearing the front door. She took these last few moments to gather herself and muster up what little courage she had to address her parents. The door was unlocked, so she entered without having to rummage through her bag for her keys. The light in the hall was off and the only light trickled in from the arch leading into the living room.

Samantha peered inside and saw her parents on different sides of the room. Her father leaned against the wall next to the fireplace and stared at the photos on the mantle. Her mother stirred the contents of her cup while staring miserably into the distance. Both were unaware of her presence when she entered.

"You two seem preoccupied. Are you thinking of more lies to tell me?"

"Samantha?" Her mother said, setting her cup down on the table.

"Then you know the truth," Malcolm said, emotionlessly interrupting her mother.

"Yes. I do. Why would you keep something as important as that from me?" Samantha snapped, fighting back the tears trying to escape her eyes.

"We did it for your own good." Her father answered indifferently, turning to face her.

His words wrapped her heart in more confusion. She searched her parents for any sensible hint, but they were unreadable. Her mother buried her head in her palms, frozen by her own shame and regret, while her father displayed no emotion or reaction.

"For my own good? What could make you think keeping the existence of another brother would benefit me in any way? Having him around could have helped more than your lies did."

"I just wanted to pro..." her father started before Samantha cut him off.

"Don't you dare say that word!" Samantha yelled in anger. "Do not use protection as a guise for your own selfish cowardice! You saw how much I suffered for all these years! Why would you lie about this?"

Samantha's pain pouring into her words softened the hard shell surrounding her father's heart. It shattered his pride and finally made him listen to what his heart was telling him.

"Samantha... You're right. I didn't tell you the truth because of my selfishness." His tone softened as he continued explaining.

"Diederich is the product of a life I wanted to keep buried and far removed from my family. I was afraid if anyone discovered our relation then it would bring you all more pain and ridicule. Then, after Joey died, I became even more determined to shield you from such horrors."

"That's ridiculous. Diederich isn't someone you should or want to be ashamed of. He is your flesh and blood, your son, just like Joey. You shouldn't avoid him as if he doesn't exist." Malcolm stared at his daughter as tears poured down her cheeks and shook in rage. "He is family and deserves every bit of your love like any of us."

"Aren't you afraid you're just using him to fill the void Joey left behind?" Malcolm asked, looking away briefly to hide his own breaking heart.

"No. Of course not. No one could ever replace Joey in my heart. However, having him around could help put the pieces of my shattered heart back together again. He could've eased the years of emptiness, guilt and loneliness that followed my grief."

Malcolm's heart faltered. For the first time, his quiet Samantha, who kept to herself, gave them a small glimpse into her heart. He felt her pain and could see how truly broken she was during these years. He wondered how much pain his sweet little girl buried behind her smiles each day. How much responsibility did she endure after her brother's death? And when did his heart grow so cold that he became blind to his own daughter's pain?

"I didn't know how much hurt you held inside of you because of Joey's death. As your father, I should've noticed, but didn't. For years, I thought by stepping away and letting you deal with your grief that things would just get better, but I was wrong." Malcolm walked over to his crying daughter and wrapped her in his arms. "Once again, my selfish decisions have hurt you more than helped. I thought keeping Diederich's existence would save you from more disappointment and heartache, but I was wrong. Can you ever forgive your stubborn father for being a senseless fool?"

Samantha nodded, accepting her father's apology. Her words drowned in her tears while she melted in her father's embrace. For years, she prayed to feel the warmth of her father's heart. Something that disappeared shortly after her brother died. Someone, up above, must have heard her tearful pleas and finally responded. She held on tight to her father, treasuring the moment as long as she could.

There were many things she regretted on her journey with Amadora, but their little adventure changed Samantha for the better. It taught her how to love. It gave her the courage to trust again and open her heart. She found a bravery she never knew before that helped her fight for her loved ones; and found a powerful voice to finally let the world know her true feelings; and, most importantly, she found an unwavering patience that tamed her fury and finally learn how to forgive and move on.

Basilio shut himself from the rest of the cold world in the observatory on the first floor of the main house. He sat in front of the gigantic fireplace, letting its gentle embers warm his body. He slouched in the soft cushions, staring deep into the fire's orange glow as its dancing flames trapped him in his thoughts.

A lot happened during his absence and some things still occurred, both good and bad. Giacinta and Casimiro's engagement, which brought joy to his heart, was overshadowed by so much misfortune and tragedy. First, Susan's death, which nearly crippled the senses of his first-born son; then, Amadora's secret masquerade, capture, and rescue. Finally, the fall of the Rosilli don. His family endured a lot without him. He admired their strength and resilience, but he could not help worrying about what was going to happen next. Without Lana or their don, the other Rosilli caporegimes might seek revenge; and in their current state, they might not make it without more casualties. In addition, they were not sure who other than Lana and the don knew of Johnnie Barbone's identity. Did Amadora's charade bring a new target on her back?

"Papa, can we talk?"

Basilio froze as the person's, the one at the center of all his worries, voice echoed from behind him. He turned around coming face-to-face with his youngest daughter, Amadora. Basilio did not speak. He composed himself and returned his attention to the flames.

"You don't have to say a word, papa. I know you probably hate me after all the trouble I've caused you and the family. I want to apologize for that, but I don't regret what I've done. Everything I've done was to prove to you of my capability." Amadora explained.

"Amadora, I don't hate you. I could never do that, but I am disappointed by all your lies and trickery," Basilio said, watching her as she sat on the ottoman in front of him. "I didn't stop you because you couldn't handle it. You are MY daughter. Of course, I knew you could handle it. I wanted to protect you from it."

"Protect me... from what?" Amadora asked, confused.

"I've been in this world for years. I know the dangers it harbors and have seen it corrupt the purest of hearts while staining their hands crimson. I've seen people lose their very souls just for greed." Basilio sighed. "I wanted to protect you from all of that. I wanted to make sure your heart remained untainted, and your light never went out, but that doesn't matter now, does it? Your hands are stained; no matter what I say, you will do whatever you please. Won't you?"

Amadora turned away and gazed into the hypnotizing glow of the flames, grinning.

"I can't answer that, but now understand your reasons. I have seen a lot of darkness on this path I've chosen. Still, I don't regret a thing. Without venturing down this road, I may have never found something I treasure more than finally gaining your approval."

Amadora met her father's gaze with a caring smile. "Through all the pain, I found something that restored my hope, innocence, and light. At this moment, I can't tell you what it is or my decision for my future until I know for sure I can reclaim my heart's true desire. However, I hope you can forgive me, papa, because I couldn't bear losing your love as well."

When the first tear fell down Amadora's cheek, Basilio wrapped her in his arms and held her tight.

"Amadora, you will never lose my love. You are my hope, the light of my heart. No matter the path you choose, I will always love you. And don't you worry. You will get what you desire. I've always known and believed that."

Caught in her father's loving embrace, Amadora could not stop her tears from falling. Finally, she knew what her heart truly wanted. Her heart no longer desired a goal filled with loneliness, darkness, or blood. Instead, it longed for a destiny filled with joy, hope, and love.

23

The Heart's True Desire

'My heart is torn between two men, Johnnie and Darian. One is the incarnation of my dark desires shrouded in despair and deception, while the other is the manifestation of my heart emanating warmth and hope.' Thoughts of Amadora Morelli.

Giacinta's wedding day came with the blooming blossoms, welcoming the warmth of spring. Joy infected the Morellis' home while the hustle and bustle of last-minute preparations filled the complex.

Samantha ran through the crowded corridors balancing a large plastic bag on top of her head while clutching onto a pair of men's shoes. She swiftly moved around the congested traffic in the halls, taking care not to trip over her dress's flowing skirts. She panted and fought a few beads of sweat while climbing the main stairway and racing down the halls. Samantha stopped in front of a large wooden door at the end of the hall of the east wing.

Samantha pushed opened the door, ran inside, and placed the heavy bag on the bed while putting the shoes on the floor next to it before standing straight to regain her composure.

"Sammy, you didn't have to get those for me. I could have sent a servant to get my clothes."

Samantha looked on the opposite side of the room, surprised. There, dressed in a white robe and hunched over a pair of wooden crutches, smiling at her lovingly, was Zanipolo.

"I told you I didn't mind doing it myself. Besides, I promised to take care of you, and that's what I'm going to do. Why are you out of bed?" Samantha replied, walking to his side, and helping him back to his bed. "You're not supposed to walk around without someone with you. Doctor's orders."

"I had a strange dream and could not stay put in bed," Zanipolo said, watching Samantha support him with all her strength.

"What dream?" Samantha grunted, moving her arm when he finally sat on the bed.

"It was a dream that I had when we were back at the Rosilli Compound. In it, you told me you loved me. But lately, I've been wondering, was it really just a dream?" Zanipolo explained, observing Samantha's reaction.

Samantha's cheeks flushed red. "It wasn't a dream. I said I love you while you were unconscious."

"Did you mean it?" Zanipolo asked. His eyes looked at her with more warmth than ever before.

"Of course, I did. I love you, Polo." Samantha nodded. "I meant it then and mean it now."

Zanipolo grabbed Samantha and scooped her into his embrace, then claimed the sweet lips that spoke those gentle words. Never did he believe in guardian angels; but as he held Samantha, enveloped in the purity of her love, he doubted his skepticism.

This woman never stopped fighting. She guarded and saved his life. No matter how exhausting he could be, she always stayed by his side, loving him without fault or thought of abandonment. Unlike any women from his past, she wanted and waited for only him. She was no ordinary woman. She was a gift sent from up above, one with a beautiful, kind heart. She was his alone, his guardian angel.

Amadora wandered around the church, following the orders of the wedding planner. She was the maid of honor; so, instead of watching the procession from the pews, she watched from the sidelines. She tried to command her face, mimicking a resemblance of joy as she followed her instructions. However, no matter how much her body wanted to, her mind could not pay attention.

Lost in the events over the months, Amadora could not focus or even socialize. Save Gugliehno, who still mourned his wife, most of them found love and happiness during all this madness, yet she was denied it. Darian had not spoken to her since he rescued her from the Rosillis' don.

Amadora tried reaching him, but he was not there or never answered. Every moment she spent apart from him made what little hope she had crumble. Her heart, though broken, struggled to beat. She grew indifferent to others when they talked and eventually grew numb to all goings-on surrounding her. Amadora fought to put on a mask for Giacinta's sake. Ever since they buried Susan, every word spoken and event she attended focused on her sister's upcoming nuptials. It made her sick listening to the never-ending back and forth about her sister's joyous union.

Amadora wondered if this loneliness consuming her was punishment for all her sins. Was this justice for her crimes? Was her fate to live the rest of her life without knowing an inkling of the precious love she once possessed?

As the procession began, Amadora hid her pain behind a well-rehearsed smile fooling the on-lookers. She regained her composure, walking with her grace and dignity intact. She tucked away her heart's tears and played her role with ease.

After all they went through, Giacinta chose her for the honor of being by her side on this special day. Amadora could not let her foolish emotions ruin this moment for her sister as well.

The exchange of words about love, trust, loyalty, and dedication overwhelmed the audience with heartwarming joy, but they did not affect Amadora one bit. These words stung her heart. They drove a wedge through it, splitting its fragmented pieces, then slowly peeled it layer by bloody layer.

Amadora saw the beauty in those words and was truly happy for her sister for finally finding love. However, she also loathed them. They were a brutal reminder of the love she would no longer possess.

Hypnotized by the sound of her shattered heart and the cries of the last bit of hope that remained, she stood hidden by a false mask, pretending to be one of the happy entranced members of the pew. Her smile concealed her true feelings from anyone watching, but her eyes struggled to hide the truth.

Emptiness lurked behind them, tainting her very soul and ridding her of any emotion. They stared blankly at the merriment, unable to register it for herself.

'From now-on, this is my fate. Every glimpse of happiness, love, or the life I once desired will drag me deeper into despair. A tainted soul, like mine, will never know blessings like them. I will live the rest of my life longing for the hope of one day mending my broken heart but will die without seeing that day come to pass.'

Gugliehno drifted to the balcony of the grand ballroom. He looked down at the guests dancing in the garden celebrating the union of his best friend and sister. A smile painted his face as he watched his girls playfully dance with their cousins. He was relieved to see that after so much heartbreak, they could find joy on this day.

Gugliehno surveyed the crowds, wondering if this celebration of love could lighten the hearts of more broken souls.

"Mr. Morelli?" Gugliehno turned around to the balcony door and smiled.

"Oh, Mr. Diederich. I'm glad to see you here."

Baldemar Diederich stepped onto the balcony and walked to Gugliehno's side.

"Thank you for inviting me to this splendid celebration. But I must ask why I'm here?" Diederich said, partially confused.

"I promised a dear friend that I would look after Samantha. Uniting you with your sister will help heal Samantha's broken heart. However, before I bring you over to her,

there are two people I want you to meet first."

Melodious music, roaring laughter, and conversation, along with joyous dancing, filled the air. The refreshing scenes warmed Samantha's heart. She danced with a few of Zanipolo's cousins while he laughed and clapped along with the music.

After a few rounds along the green, Samantha grew weary and thirsty. She pardoned herself from Zanipolo's persistent relatives so she could get some punch from the fountain.

After downing her third glass of punch, someone tapped Samantha's shoulder. She placed her glass on the table and turned to face the person. Her face froze in shock after their eyes met.

"Mr. Diederich, what are you doing here?" Samantha asked.

"Gugliehno invited me," answered Diederich. He smiled; and for the briefest moment, the warm, infectious smile of her late brother flashed in Samantha's mind. "I'm glad he did. I wanted to thank you."

"Thank me for what?" Samantha asked, confused.

"For whatever you said to our father. Shockingly, I received a call from him a few days ago." Diederich started. His smile softened as he looked down at her, his eyes brimming with warmth and gratitude. "He apologized about the horrible way he treated me over these years and asked for a chance to make amends and start over. After many painful years of feeling like an unwanted outcast, finally, I felt more like his son during that brief telephone call than I ever have in my entire life."

Samantha's heart swelled. She gently touched his hand and smiled.

"There's no need for thanks. You are my family, my brother. You deserve to be treated as such and deserve all the love you were denied for so long."

"Thank you." Diederich smiled, then placed a hand on her shoulder. "We've lost many years to bond properly as siblings. Where do we begin to make up for all that time?"

"We forget about the time we lost and focus on the here and now. We dapple briefly in our yesterdays to learn about who we are now; but we will focus on forgiveness and love; and how to use those to help us move forward and embrace our futures together."

Relatives and friends bombarding Amadora with greetings and cordial conversations almost drove Amadora to madness. She slipped away from the reception to gather herself. Amadora escaped to the garden entrance, hiding in the gazebo's shadow and behind the lush blossom trees.

Amadora watched while the sun danced across the red-orange sky. Entranced by the birds' sweet song while basking in the majestic twilight. Amadora's mind drifted far from the joyous noise to the unknown future. It was blocked from her vision. Now that she knew what she desired, all was quiet. She had no plan or scheme to win him back. Amadora only threw herself at the mercy of fate. Only it knew if she would ever feel her heart beat again.

"Are you hiding from the evils of the reception?"

Amadora's heart sank after hearing that sweet voice. She did not face him in fear that he would see her dried tears, overwhelming despair and all the scars carved into her heart.

"I do not need to seek protection from this reception. It's my sister's wedding, a joyous occasion." Amadora answered briefly.

"Is that so? Then why did you seem distant during the wedding?" Darian pressed, moving closer to where she stood.

Tears flowed down her cheeks while she wrestled with her emotions.

"Why are you here? Just to torment me? Please don't make me say it." Amadora begged, half-heartedly.

"Dora, why not? What do you have to lose by just telling me how you feel?" Darian said, closing the distant.

"Everything... My heart, pride, and whatever bit of hope remains inside me."

"Then risk it. Tell me what's bothering you." Darian demanded.

"I'm numb. My heart was shattered after our meeting with Lana, then partially restored when you rescued me just to be broken again. Ever since I've waited, hoping that one day I would see you again. But when days turned into weeks and weeks into months, I realized my only chance for happiness had passed. I took pleasure in the emptiness you left behind, but these kinds of lovey-dovey events can be overwhelming. Why are you here?"

Amadora's sadness and pain was written all over her tear-stained face. It ate away at her very heart and soul, a torment he was far too familiar with.

"Gugliehno invited me." Darian said, leaning against the railing beside her. "Your feelings sound too much like my own. For some time, I wanted to see you, but I let my fear get the best of me. However, when he delivered the invitation, your brother helped me overcome the worries plaguing my mind."

Darian looked down at Amadora and wiped a tear from her cheek. "I no longer fear whether this love will bring more pain, because I have the courage to face it head-on with you and the determination to keep fighting until I guide you away from the dark path your heart desires."

Amadora smiled and sighed. "I'm afraid there's nothing you or anyone else can do to turn me away from what my heart truly wants."

Darian's expression became unreadable, but she ignored it and softly brushed his cheek with her hand.

"There is no power great enough in this entire world that can keep me from what I have and will always desire above all things, you, my angel. You are all I will ever want in my entire life."

Amadora flung her arms around Darian's neck and kissed him. In that moment, she surrendered her heart to him fully, letting all the pain that once plagued them fall with her tears. Finally, the pleas of their broken hearts were heard. Their destiny was linked by the beating in their chests and the passion of their kiss. All darkness dispersed as their hearts united as one. They would walk down this new path together without a worry in the world, just their love to guide their way.

Author's Thoughts

Thank you for reading *Eyes*. I hope you enjoyed it. This book took me fourteen years to publish, and I'm beyond relieved to finally get it out there. This is a bitter-sweet moment. I'm over-the-moon that I've finally finished the book that literally sparked my dream to become a published author, and now, I can move onto other projects, but I feel sad that this part in Amadora's journey is over. Don't get me wrong. This doesn't mean I have finished with Amadora or these characters. I have put my blood, sweat and tears into this book and have grown fond of each of these characters. I know after reading this, you, my reader, will have a lot of questions about events in this book. Don't worry they will be answered in subsequent books.

As stated in my letter in the beginning of this book, *Eyes*, was the first novel I finished. It was inspired by my love for The Godfather: Don Edition (PS3) game (inspired by the novel of the same name by Mario Puzo). I wrote this book to see if I could write and finish a romance novel. It was my first test as a writer to see if I could make something readers could enjoy and grow closer to my goal to create memorable and/or inspiring works.

If you liked this book or any of my others, don't forget to review them on all their pages and spread the word to other readers. Also, don't forget to follow our pages and join our exclusive groups, http://linktr.ee/eyesthebook & http://linktr.ee/imaniamar-gria for more updates on upcoming projects for this series. Doing these things help introduce Eyes and my other books to readers around the world.

Also, if you're itching to know more about the Eyes cast or just love exclusive content, please join my patreon, patreon.com/imaniamargria. I post bonus content like short stories, character letters, character art, early access content/news, and much more. I will also start monthly one on one Q&As to answer some of the questions you may have.

However, for now, I am going to focus on my next books. I hope you continue to read and support my future projects. Until next time.

About the Author

Imania Margria is a New Jersey native author and poet, whose words have inspired readers worldwide. Currently, she is working on her upcoming books. For more updates on Margria and her future projects, follow her on her sites: https://linktr.ee/imaniamargria.

CPSIA information can be obtained
at www.ICGtesting.com
Printed in the USA
BVHW071237170223
658733BV00006B/208